REVELATION

THE JOURNEY TO FREEDOM

D0931960

Gary Mollica

ISBN 978-1-64416-909-4 (paperback)
ISBN 978-1-64515-313-9 (hardcover)
ISBN 978-1-64416-910-0 (digital)

Christian Faith Publishing, Inc.
832 Park Avenue
Meadville, PA 16335
www.christianfaithpublishing.com

Printed in the United States of America

To my beautiful wife Joyce, our family, and especially to our Creator-God and Savior, Jesus Christ, with thanksgiving for all who helped throughout the years.

To my six children, given to us by Jesus Christ to raise and demonstrate to them His love for them and all mankind. I'm proud to say they have been a true blessing to us, showing us the love they have for each other by spending time together, encouraging each other, and working together to secure our family's welfare and traditions. We show them how they can have a personal relationship with their Lord and Savior, who suffered and died to give them eternal life, not because of anything they did or can do, but to receive the gift of eternal life by accepting Jesus Christ as their Lord and Savior. He gave us the ultimate gift, to die for His people so they can conquer death. I say to them: "Since the children have flesh and blood, He (Jesus) too shared in their humanity so that by his death He might destroy him who holds the power of death—that is, the devil—and free those who all their lives were held in slavery by their fear of death" (Hebrews 2:14).

Also I say, "Tell it to your children and let your children tell it to their children, and their children to the next generation" (Joel 1:3).

CONTENTS

ACKNOWLEDGMENTS

My deep gratitude to Jim Sligar, a gifted and loyal friend, for being the catalyst in the development of this project. Without him, it would have been truly impossible. To him, I say, "Mizpah, for he said Jehovah watch between me and thee, when we are absent one from another" (Genesis 31:48).

I also want to thank Michael Richardson who worked on this project fulfilling a calling to bring to life this manuscript through the strength of Jesus Christ despite his personal hardships. I am truly grateful for his professionalism in editing, history, and explanation of love, and to him I say, "And may the peace of God, which passes all understanding guard your heart and thoughts in Christ Jesus" (Philippians 4:6).

And a very special thanks to my best friend and soul mate, my wife, Joyce, for all her love, devotion, and encouragement even when I felt discouraged. It was her inspiration that kept me going, changing, and rearranging during this long and arduous process. She is the love of my life. To her I say, "It is not good for the man to be alone. I will make a helper suitable for him" (Genesis 2:18). And again I say, "A wife of noble character is her husband's crown" (Proverbs 12:4).

CHAPTER 1

The Friendship

A light foggy mist hovered beneath Balem tonight as the sky turned from a bright yellow to a burnt orange, then to a renaissance red. The night was clear, but in the near distance, a small cloud formation started to develop. As the blue, darkening sky turned to black, another Star City similar to the one I live in was seen through my telescope, even though the mist was entirely engulfing it now.

My name is Joe. I love astronomy, serving in the Air Force, and beautiful nights like this. Rays of sunlight fanned out from beneath the floating city, giving it a celestial appearance. The city stood as a reminder of some ancient castle perched high on a cliff overlooking a vast ocean. Its array of tall and short buildings glistened through the brilliant light of this midsummer night. I hurried over to my telescope and focus in on the enormous entity.

There I saw the border patrol guarding, protecting, and surrounding the whole structure. Human-like forms could be seen along the border and near the buildings, moving briskly throughout the city. Its existence seemed like another world, and each day when weather permitted, I looked and wondered what it was all about. Soon, dusk settled in, and the city could no longer be seen, so I focused the telescope up to the heavens. The sky was clear except for patches of clouds intermingled between the star constellations. The full moon was brilliant, and its aura seemed to block out most of the constellations to the west.

The night was so magnificent, even though the entire moon shadowed the full beauty of the constellation near it; to see it always fascinated me. To the east and north, thousands upon thousands of constellations filled the sky with a sparkle and glitter that exploded the mind with memories of great celebrations of our culture, Triumph Day and Harvest Day.

I like to look for shooting stars, as I have done hundreds of times before. As I focused my telescope, an object rose from the west. It's much brighter than a shooting star, and it left a stream of brilliant particles along its trajectory. The size of the radiantly displayed object across my modified telescope appeared five times that of a star, and after traveling halfway across the sky, it had slowed down to emerge nearly motionless. Another light showed up directly behind this first object. It moved much slower but with the same array of spectacular particles trailing it. As the two objects approached each other, there were flashes of red, orange, and white all over the night sky. Within a few minutes, the sky glimmered like celebrations of Nuclear Day, which clearly was the most compelling festival of the year. Fireworks filled the sky all night long, and everyone stayed up late to celebrate.

Suddenly, amid all the grandeur, a huge flash, then only one star-like figure appeared in the sky. The colors were gone, and the first object—ship, meteor, or whatever it was—started moving slowly across the sky once again.

Knock, knock, knock.

"Yes, who is it?" I said as I peered through my telescope. "Who is it?" I demand.

"Who do you think it is?" Derek said.

I looked up for a moment to see him as he walked through the door, and I quickly returned to the eyepiece.

"You just will not believe what you see through this telescope. It's really spectac—it's gone! Where did you go, you... you little rascal."

Oh no, I completely forgot about dinner.

"What's gone? Joe, what are you talking about?"

"Oh, uh, nothing! I was just gazing. What a breakthrough this evening."

"What? You invited me over for dinner. Don't you remember?" Derek blatantly bellowed out.

"Oh right, now I remember! But don't fret, I can whip up something real fast. Have a seat! Some spirits, maybe?"

"Yes, I'll have a glass," Derek said, as he lay down on the sofa, kicked off his shoes, and opened up a magazine called *Computers of the Century.*

"What are you reading, Derek? *Computers of the*—Oh, I should have known you always have your head in that magazine."

The room became very quiet, so I proceeded to go into the kitchen to start dinner. Derek was my best friend. We were also neighbors. Right across the hall from my apartment was his living quarters, and his Protector was a good friend of mine. Derek and I were inseparable. We would go everywhere together, and we participated in almost every competitive event available. It was commonplace and natural, and some even thought we were roommates, but we had earned enough credits to warrant our own separate living quarters. My Protector had passed into eternity a few years ago, but Derek's was still alive and living a couple of units away from us. Protectors were the elderly men of our culture who were chosen to raise the new entities given to our society. Our association consists strictly of men. No one really knows how we got here. At least, no one has ever told us. The subject was simply not discussed.

We were told the other Star City that was located just north but a great distance from here was a society exactly like ours.

Anyway, Derek and I went to school together. He studied computer technology and specialized warfare, and I studied aerospace design and became a fighter pilot in the Air Force sworn to protect our beloved Star City of Altaur. We were numbered among those called the Guardians of our society. We were told that we have the same job as our personal Protector and united we defend our society by having the best and most explicit training. The expert teachers, our protectorates, not only taught true doctrine but what was not written in any book or given in any lecture. They also provided us with practical knowledge found only with experience.

They provided us with the ability to put common sense, insight, and physical strength together so that we could excel in an ultra high level of performance given any situation. This unique endowment was gained by first-hand experience and many, many years of intense investigation. Both of us graduated from the University of Selected Intelligence and have been loyal subjects for more than twenty years. We studied at the university for seventeen years, and both of us received special honors awarded only to students showing excellence in our fields.

Our food was assigned to us, quality based on our worth to society just like our living quarters and other benefits including the opportunity to participate in the special events of Altaur. The food has to be processed or conditioned before we can purchase it. The supply sector is open all the time, and we can pick up the food we are accustomed to eating just by giving our class number and a purchase order. Our association is not well informed about the conditioning process, but it has been understood that after the Macrocaust, the food has to be processed before distribution is possible.

"You're really going to enjoy this dinner, Derek. It's my best recipe."

"I hope so," Derek grunted, "because I could eat this sofa that I'm laying on, in a heartbeat. I couldn't be hungrier than I am right now."

Derek is a tall, fair, blond-haired fellow, probably from the Norse sector on the old settlement called Earth. He stood erect, tall like a giant monument and was well-tempered among friends, but do him or his companions wrong and he explodes with the fury of the fires of hell. I sometimes want to run the other way, but knowing he is on my side gives me comfort. I remember when we were just of that age, and legally our association limits a citizen to two spirits every hour per half day. We had just finished an Old World game of rapper ball and decided to stop in and see the rest of the team. We walked up to the long thin table, which seated about fifteen guys around it. You sit down, and a spirit comes up through a small hole in front of you on the table. To receive your next spirit, a button was located in the upper right hand corner of your square.

The seats were sectioned off into squares too, with one seat per square, and a computer oversees your limit. The long thin table resembled an Old World board game called a checkerboard. We were consuming our final spirit, and the conversation ranged from the building of the new warships, to computers, to the discussion of new tractor-beam ships that are supposedly invincible. Then we focused our conversation to the rapper ball playoffs and the highest placed teams. Suddenly, a tall dark-haired man with a long scar running the length of his forearm walked into the club. He was fairly muscular and looked as mean as the Old World grizzly bear they used to kill for sport. He walked up to us with two friends and looked Derek right in the eye and said, "Yes, sir, he looks like the one. Let's take him in for questioning."

"Questioning?" Derek said. "For what?"

"You and another man stole a warship and raided the gunnery over in Sector 8. You beat up two guardian patrolmen there, stole fifty laser guns and blew the outpost all to hell. You will be arrested and tried for your crimes then spend the rest of your lives in the Detention Sector."

Without blinking an eye, Derek responded, "These chaps must be joking, and besides that, I think they are absolutely crazy."

The three of them walked around the table, and the big one, who was doing all the talking, grabbed Derek by the collar and threw him across the room. As he got up off the floor, another man threw a blow to the head, and once again he flew over the table. The other man broad-sided me from behind knocking me unconscious. The next thing I remember was cold water and some bad-smelling pow-der under my nose. I was helped back to the table, and before I knew it, two more spirits were sitting in front of me.

Everyone in the club was cheering and yelling congratulations to Derek. I had asked the fellow next to me what had happened, and he told me that Derek was back across the table as fast as he was thrown over. Then the big fellow—after a blow to the abdomen, an upper cut to the jaw, and a ferocious left hook—looked dazed and weak. It all took about seven seconds. He, then, explained to me how Derek threw the fastest combination of a right hook, backhanded facial blow and, a 360-degree spin kick he had ever seen.

Next, Derek took the other two guys and struck one guy's head onto the table, never spilling the three spirits that were there, lifted him off of his feet, and threw him across two tables, crashing him into the wall. He just slid down the wall and passed out into a pool of unconsciousness. The third fellow, who couldn't have been of sound mind, grabbed Derek from behind.

Instantaneously, Derek backed up, running him through the bathroom door, grabbed him by the neck, flipped him over his head, and took two steps, just enough to clear the doorway, and proceeded to throw him in the air across the room and onto the bar. By the way, the distance was about ten to fifteen feet! Incredible! The story was getting so good that I couldn't wait to hear the rest. My eyewitness teammate said that one by one, Derek threw them out into the street. The last words he heard were, "Don't talk to me without a warrant."

Shortly, after they were gone, Derek decided to straighten up the club and pay for the damages, but the Tender refused, thanked him for standing up to them, and added, "That was one helluva show." He said the trio had been in before looking for trouble. He also identified them as Guardian patrolmen from Sector 6 and said he wouldn't be surprised if they were the men stealing the weapons.

"They sure needed someone to put them in their place," the bartender said.

Needless to say, they were never seen at the club or in the area again.

Dinner consisted of my three favorite recipes, black Corso stew, flaming vegetables, and trendsetter pie, and we both enjoyed it very much. In fact, Derek ate three helpings, and I'm sure glad it filled him up because there wasn't a drop left in the three pans. I did assure him that there was more if he desired and that it would only take a short time to prepare it, but he politely refused. After dinner, we sat in the living quarter and chatted for a while. I asked Derek what he thought of the other Star City, Balem.

"I don't know," he said. "Probably the same type of society we have here on Altaur."

"Then why is it so far away and no communication allowed? I wonder who really resides there. The Committee meets twice a year, usually in the Committee luxury ship. They say the talk is about the quote unquote, 'preservation of human life.' Whatever that means, and then why is Gamnon called Star of Creation? Where is it? What does creation mean? I can't find it in any textbooks, and no one seems to know."

"I don't know, Joe. Maybe it's a food farm."

"Ha-ha! Right, a star of food… You have to be kidding me."

"I think the Committee picks several hundred members from each Star City to meet on a place called Gamnon, which is probably another city beyond Balem."

"What for? Maybe you'll get to find out some day," Derek said, as he flipped through his new computer magazine. "Maybe they discuss the latest and greatest technology involving our defense systems, you know preserving human life!"

"Yeah, it could be, but why doesn't anyone remember anything or talk about it?"

"Well, that material doesn't seem to interest many fellow companions."

"So you never talk about the fighters or handheld lasers in everyday conversation?"

"No, I guess not, but I am curious."

"Well, maybe we'll get picked someday. Who knows!"

"Hey, let's ask Tarcon!"

"Maybe we can get some information, or maybe that brain of yours can extract more data than he is programmed to tell us."

"Sounds like a challenge to me, but if we get caught, it's life in Sector 5 or death by ejection from an aircraft."

"Live fast, die young. What do you think?"

"Sure, life has been getting a little boring lately anyway."

"So you're with me, Derek?"

"Well, why not… Sure, I'm with you."

"Let's do it!"

"Now? You really don't waste any time, do you?"

"No, sir. 'Until death do we part.' It's weird. I must have read that somewhere or something."

"Tarcon, warm up your circuits. It's time to burn up some solid state hardware."

There was a standard computer in every living quarter and ours were both named Tarcon. My Protector told me it reminded him of a common item like a refrigerator or the stereo console he had read about in the Old World. Every apartment was equipped with a computer, but each was programmed only to provide the occupent with a certain amount of data. It was your personal library and a close friend, especially when times were lonely. Your computer could talk to you, hold a very intelligent conversation, or just ramble on like an old friend with information dated back to the earliest civilization. Derek always wanted to take Tarcon apart and reprogram it to give us any information we wanted to know. He said it could be done with a voice code, and that would eliminate anyone from extracting the same information. But death by ejection! How cruel and probably the worst way to die, floating into a black endless universe until you can't breathe or choke on your own vomit… or just free falling and being scattered to pieces on earth. Both were considered "an enforcement tool."

"Tarcon, how are you tonight?"

"Fine, sir, and you?"

"Oh fine, how about some conversation? Are you up to it?"

"Affirmative,"

"The Star City across the way. Can you tell us about it?"

"Affirmative, it's the second Star City, Balem, built in 2255, approximately the same time Altaur was constructed, and the two cities are a mirror image of each other. Every improvement or new development made on this city is made in the second Star City, Balem. The dimensions of each building are exactly the same as on Altaur, and fifteen million members reside in each."

"We understand all of that, Tarcon. That's common knowledge. Now tell us something we don't know! Tell us who lives on Balem. Are they men like us maybe fellow companions or are they aliens?"

"I'm not programmed to disclose that information to the given voice code."

"Then, tell us why the two cities meet periodically?"

"I'm not programmed to give that—"

"Okay, Tarcon, then let's have a history lesson."

"Affirmative. The Star Cities began—"

"No, no. Go back to the Old World, around the time of the Macrocaust, and forget the regular information. We want specifics."

"I'm not programmed to give that information to the given voice code."

"Joe, you better stop prying. I think after fifteen minutes of 'I'm not programmed to give that information to,' the computer sounds an alarm at central."

"Just one more question. Derek, we have to make sure he has the information before we start, or you know you will be doing a lot of work for nothing."

"Okay, Joe. Just hurry!"

"Tarcon, do you have more information stored in your memory banks than you are programmed to give us."

"Affirmative. My pride is to boast that I have the capacity and knowledge to store and deliver every bit of information known to man."

"Derek, can you do it? I mean program it to give us that information."

"With some time, I can get all the information you want. Why? You are really curious, aren't you, Joe?"

"Well, why don't they tell us? That is what bothers me the most. I just have to know what is going on."

"Now remember, we are dealing with death or life in Sector 5 if we get caught!"

"I would rather be put to death," Derek said. "You know that they can scan our brain to find out how much we know. Once we receive the information, there is no turning back."

"I understand, Derek. I'm willing to take the risk. Are you with me?"

"Of course, we are partners to death!"

"You and your drama."

"Let me go and get my tools. I've collected every computer tool you could think of, and they are all in my apartment. Actually, let's do it at my place?"

"No, Derek. If we get caught, I'll tell them that it was all my idea, and no one else was involved."

"Come on, Joe. They aren't stupid. They'll know you don't have the knowledge for this extensive undertaking, and your best friend has a doctorate in computer design. I'm involved, no matter how you look at it or where we do it. At least, they won't see me take my tools out of my apartment which should give us a little more security."

"You're finally making some sense, dude. On second thought, if we get caught, why don't you say it was all your fault? Yes, I like that better."

"Get real. If we go down, we go together. Do you think I'm crazy or something?"

"Do you really want me to answer that question?"

The conversation ended as we walked out the door of the module because, as usual, the scanning monitor engulfed us. The halls were brightly lit with very high ceilings. They were also very narrow and contained six doors, but no windows. At the end of the hall was a single elevator. Derek lived in the same module as me but one door closer to the elevator. Frequently, we came and parted together, so there wouldn't be any suspicion and to show them we were close friends. Today, we walked down to the local club, had a quick spirit, then proceeded to Derek's apartment. This was several days after our decision.

We talked about work and the coming future festivals as we walked down the hallway. As soon as we closed the door and locked it tight, Derek, without hesitation, went to his office to get his tools.

"I've been working on Tarcon for about seven days now. I think I'm really getting close."

"That's great. I'm really starting to get excited, Derek."

"I was going to surprise you with the news, but I just couldn't wait. I can get fueled up on this stuff. Just imagine what we might learn."

"I didn't know you were interested in the heavens, Derek. That is a superb telescope you've acquired. By the way, when did you purchase it?"

"The day after we started on Tarcon, I figured that if I purchased a telescope, security wouldn't get suspicious of our meetings every night."

"Great idea, Derek. See, you're even starting to think like me. I like it."

"Oh, don't flatter yourself, Joe... You snake, you—ouch!"

"Now, don't hurt those delicate little fingers, Derek. Hey, they sure have left us alone. Not even an inquiry or visit by a Committee member."

"Yes, we have had some real privacy but only because I first had to bypass a small computer inside Tarcon to check for tampering."

"It's a good thing I never tampered with mine."

"You probably would be in Sector 5 by now associating with all the other hardened criminals."

The job took longer than Derek had anticipated. We were together every other night, and many times we waited two or three nights just to keep suspicious scanners unaware of our work. We didn't want to take any chances. After three weeks of programming and reprogramming, changing circuits and replacing chips, Derek finally finished the job. The challenge became so obsessive, Derek even called in sick from work a couple days just to finish a certain sequence of circuitry. It was just three days before the Committee on the Preservation of Humanity was to meet. The COPH gathered once every five years, and certain men were chosen to represent us on Gamnon. That is really about all we know about it. Everyone who goes there comes back with no memory of what happened. Derek and I always wondered what that place was all about but knew we couldn't ask anyone for fear of displacement to Sector 5.

We were at the chosen age, so our names were considered as applicants for this year's representation on Gamnon.

"Well, well, did you do it? Does it work? Derek, come on! Let's try it!"

"Soon, Joe. Probably tomorrow after work."

I woke up so excited that Friday morning that I could hardly concentrate on anything. I got up an hour early around sunrise, trying to rush the day's work through, and you know it was one of the longest days of my career. I was in the simulator all morning, and I was eliminated three times. Eliminated all three times! Can you imagine? That simulator was tearing me up consistantly all morning. My concentration was shot; I couldn't focus enough to compete, and all I kept thinking about was Derek's work on Tarcon.

"Just one more chip and this wire over there, check the bypass system, and turn Tarcon on! Maybe... Yes! Joe, I think I have done it!"

"Think, think. Don't you think you better be quite certain? We'll be in a lot of trouble."

"Sector 5."

"Turn it on, Joe. Turn it on!"

"Wait! Wait! Plug in the earphones. You never know who might be listening. Someone might be loitering in the hallway."

"Good idea. Let's put on the regular headgear and connect it to Tarcon so that we can softly initate our voice communication too."

"Right."

"Tarcon, do you recognize my voice pattern?"

"Affirmative. Derek Johan, this is the voice pattern recorded in my memory banks?"

Tarcon gave a positive identification of both voice patterns and was prepared to give information asked by those patterns.

"Tarcon, what is your response when someone asks you about the Old World. Let's use the time of the great Macrocaust."

"My response is that I am programmed to give that information to the proper voice pattern."

"The proper voice pattern? Are those of the Supreme Committee?"

"Affirmative."

"See, Joe, I have a habit of doing professional work, don't I?"

"You sure do, and let me say you are the best."

"Now, Tarcon, let's bring up those old dusty chips from the past. Tarcon, tell us what is in your memory banks, providing that it is not information known to our society and start with the Old World and the events leading up to the great Macrocaust."

A huge map flashed on the screen.

"This is the Old World," said Tarcon. "A very progressive state it was."

Tarcon continued with his lesson, which was very detailed, and revealed to us a society that traveled from horse and buggy to space exploration and nuclear war in a matter of 250 years.

Tarcon continued, "This society consisted of male and female human beings that lived in peace and harmony together in the same world. They lived as families mating and producing beings in their own image. The free or democratic world was headed by a young but very strong nation called America. It featured free enterprise, capitalism, and the desire to make progressive changes by giving freedoms to all their citizens providing them with the right to choose their destiny. Their freedom was secured by the God who created the universe, and by following his commands and covenants, He secured freedom and liberty. Those beliefs were two of the basic building blocks of this nation. The rest of the world consisted of many violent, disorganized anarchies, several dictatorships, and two very powerful communistic states: The Republic of China and the country of Russia.

"The sole purpose of the dictatorships and communistic states were to dominate the world, controlling it by any means possible. They achieved this goal by suppressing their people and infiltrating other societies by terrorism and deceit. They would infiltrate and control them by setting up strong government regimes and then proceed to destroy the country from within through economic turmoil. A state of nuclear war existed for a period of about one month. The communistic states, now a conglomerate consisting of two-thirds of the earth, launched major offensives around the globe, destroying most of the earth. The powers of the communist states were too great for the free world, and soon the world collapsed. The communist states, although victors, were virtually decimated, and the surface of the planet was unlivable. They won the war and conquered a world where now no one could survive. One percent of the population survived, leaving a band of people living underground, a select portion who chose to live and colonize the universe, plus the society that planned and constructed the Star Cities."

"Incredible, Joe. This is fantastic!"

"Yes, Derek, fantastic or should we say more like unbelievable. What did he say about female and male living together, as fami… families and eventually mate and produce offspring in their… ah… own image? Do they have some kind of bond that holds them together? Do they produce other beings to promote and enhance their own little society?"

"Tarcon, what happened to all the females? Only men live here on Altaur." Derek raised a question baffling both of our minds.

"Derek, good question. Wait, wait. Derek, the other Star City, Balem. It must be… It has to be female!"

"Affirmative," Tarcon interrupted.

"Tarcon, explain this process of promoting our society. This mating process, I think is how you referred to it."

"Slow down, Derek. We have plenty of time."

"Historically, when the two Star Cities were constructed, one was colonized with men and the other with women, then a process called mating occured. This process is learned by a group of young citizens and carried out on the third Star City called Gamnon. Through the mating process, descendants are created in the image and likeness of the men and women involved in the mating process. After the act of creation is completed, the healthy offspring are taken to their respective Star Cities of Altaur and Balem and raised by an elder who cares for and educates them. The elders are called their Protectors."

"So that was Balem that I saw through my telescope—my modified telescope, that is."

"Tarcon, how do we mate? I don't understand," said Derek.

"Not now, Derek," Joe interrupted once again. "We need more important information. There will be plenty of time to talk about that later."

"Tarcon, why were the two groups of people separated?"

"The two societies exist as separate entities and were constructed solely for that purpose. Each society has its own government, justice system, industry, food supply, entertainment, and security system. They were—"

"Tarcon! Tarcon! The real reason for their separation—the real reason."

"Yes! Cut the garbage, Tarcon. It's starting to appear like we have been in the dark about our true society all these years."

"Affirmative."

There was a short pause where you could hear Tarcon scan his memory banks, and it took several seconds, but soon Tarcon was back in action. He stopped and paused for another moment and then spoke.

"To suppress emotion, eliminate crimes of passion and greed, to increase the survival of the two sexes, to discipline the masses, and to uniquely provide the human race with the perfect society. The best reference for the explanation can be found in a best-selling novel in the year 1999 called the *Perfect Society* written by John Slezovich."

"Where can we obtain a copy of this book, Tarcon?"

"All copies were destroyed shortly after the Macrocaust."

"That sure doesn't surprise me," replied Derek.

"Tarcon, you mentioned the word *emotion*. Define this term."

"Emotion is a feeling or sensation felt within the human body during times of excitement, sadness, or depression, a kind of moving of the mind or soul. Examples are fear, anger, love, hatred, compassion, sadness, jealousy, excitement, and frustration. There are many more, and they all are an expression of human feelings."

"Tarcon, define each of these emotions."

"I am not programmed to give you that information."

"Derek, what happened? He was doing so well. What happened? What do we do now?"

"Oh, just some minor adjustments, old man. Patience, patience. No one is perfect."

"Sorry, Derek, I just can't control myself sometimes. Sounds like an emotion, doesn't it."

"Sure does. This is amazing! I guess we never thought about it in that way."

"Besides, no one has ever told us about them before. Let me get my tools. I'm sure it won't take too long, probably just some circuit adjustments."

Derek worked on Tarcon for about one hour, and during that time, the wheels never stopped turning. I had one thousand questions for Tarcon and none of them could wait. Just as I was really starting to get impatient...

"That does it!" Derek shouted. "Ask the next question, Joe."

"Great! Tarcon, you stated that these emotions are feelings. Exactly, what are feelings?"

"A feeling is a conscious awareness that takes place in the human body. It could be hormonal or environmentally induced. It can be anger, excitement, joy or sorrow, and a mind-boggling array of thinking processes that produce explicit gamma and delta wave-thought patterns."

"Joe, let's go on. There is so much more information we need to find out, and that scientific and medical jargon is way above me."

Just then, the door signal went off, startling both of us. Then once again, the buzzer sounded.

"Derek, shut Tarcon off and hide your tools! I'll get the door—no, maybe you better get the door! It's your apartment! Yes, you answer the door. That should lower the suspicion," I whispered.

"What?" he whispered as he came running from the utility closet."

"The door! The door! You better answer the door!" I whispered.

I motioned for him to open the door.

"Now don't panic," I said. "Remember it's only programmed for our voice pattern. Relax, Derek. Relax."

Derek appeared so calm and collected after I spoke, but my heart was beating frantically. It made me think of Tarcon's explanation of emotions. It was different to know what I was experiencing, rather than being in the dark about my feelings. It really gave me a new state of composure.

"Tarcon, off for now," Derek said. "I'll put on some music."

"Think calm and collected," I said to myself.

"Coming, coming!" shouted Derek. He walked over to the door and put his scanner on the approaching visitor. The man was dressed in a white gown with a white hood covering his head and hair. He promptly flashed a Supreme Committee identification card after noticing the scanner.

"Joe, it's a Committee member."

"Well, open the door before he gets real suspicious. I hope they don't know what we were doing! What went wrong?"

"Maybe it's for something unrelated to our interest in the computer," said Derek.

"Unrelated! Come on, Derek. I can't think of anything the Committee would want to see us for—except Tarcon. Maybe, Tarcon has a fail-safe system that checks on citizens tampering with the equipment."

"Well, anyway, put your card into the slot and let the man into the module."

"Okay, okay!"

As the door opened, there appeared a very old man, portrayed by his long white beard, wrinkled skin, and hunched posture. His head was now covered by a wide-rimmed white hood and attached to it was a long white robe. These members didn't come out very often and only for something very important.

"Yes, sir, can I help you?" said Derek.

"Derek Johan?"

"Yes, sir."

"And you… Joe Capuzzi?"

"Yes, sir."

"The Committee would like to see both of you directly. You will meet them now in Sector 737 and be prompt! I will close the door. Come on now, hurry!"

The old man proceeded to close the door and move consecutively door to door down the hall selecting certain modules along the way as Derek and I made our way slowly to the elevator.

"Derek, they found out about Tarcon, and we have had it. You know what they will do. I can see it now. The both of us being dropped off the end of Altaur to be scattered into pieces on the Earth below. What a way to go."

"Come on, Joe. They couldn't have found out. It takes at least a day to locate a fault in the computer system. You should have more faith in me, friend. Just calm down."

"Just testing you, good buddy. Besides, I think our reception would have been a Guardian patrol."

"They wouldn't have buzzed either. You can count on that," said Derek.

"Hey, that reminds me, it's time for Gamnon. Maybe we were chosen."

"We are of the chosen age," Derek added.

"I hope so, Derek. A couple more years, and I would have missed my chance to promote our illustrious society."

Buzz. Buzz. Buzz.

We were ordered to ring and wait for instructions.

"Speak, loud and clear," demanded a voice from within.

"Master Derek Johan and Captain Joe Capuzzi reporting as ordered, sir."

"Enter, please."

We walked in, and there were two chairs that stood in front of a long table. At the long table, there were twelve men dressed as the man who approached us at Derek's module. As we took our places, the members shuffled through many papers, then looked up at us, stared, and once again started shuffling through the parchments. Then, every member wrote something on a small piece of paper and passed it to the center of the table. There, an elderly man who wore old-fashioned spectacles and retained a short, well-groomed white beard, read all the pieces of paper, paused, and then looked up at us. He spoke softly but with a voice that demanded attention and filled the room with reverent authority.

"Very impressive. Both of you are very close friends. Would you give your life for your friend?" he asked, motioning with an out-stretched arm.

"Who?" asked Derek.

"That's a question, boy. I want an answer!"

"Yes, sir. Most definitely, sir."

"And you comrade?"

I looked at Derek, then to the man in the center of the table. "It depends, sir."

The old man's eyes lit up. He took his wire spectacles off and rubbed his eyes. Then he put them back on his tired looking face and asked, "Depends, young man? Depends on what, Captain Capuzzi?"

"Well, sir, it depends on the circumstances and the situation I was put into at the time. It would depend on his state of mind and whether giving my life would benefit the promotion of our society."

"Very good. Excellent. A soldier's response. Your training will begin along with 498 others. They are exceptional young men who are to represent Altaur on Gamnon, the Star City. This training will be for several weeks and will consist of six-hour sessions per day. Your assignment will be announced during your training period. Represent us well, citizens. Dismissed."

"May I ask a question, sir?"

Derek whispered, "What are you doing, Joe?"

"You may proceed."

All looked attentive as if no one ever had asked a question before. Probably no one ever did, but I have always been the inquisitive type.

"Sir, by what means of selection are we chosen for this task?"

"Listen here, boy, the Committee has certain parameters it uses to make their selections, some of which are performance, your interview, work ethic, chromosomes, intelligence, personality, and a good recommendation from individual Protectors. These and many more qualifications are taken into consideration. Your life history is right here in front of me. It is our right to choose the specimen that will promote the society's well-being. It is best for the society that you have been chosen. Dismissed, and report immediately to Sector 382."

"Thank you, sir." Then Joe muttered. "Well, I guess I really couldn't ask any questions. I don't think he appreciated my inquiry."

We closed the door behind us as we left the room, and as the door shut, we could hear the Committee talking rather loudly, acting as if alarmed by the question.

"Joe, you sure have a lot of guts. I can't believe you asked the Committee a question!"

"'Boy'? What does that mean? I want an answer, Derek. What does that mean? *Boy*."

"How am I supposed to know? I still can't believe you asked them a question. You are unbelievable."

"Derek, we have to get back to Tarcon. There are a lot of unanswered questions. Let's go!"

"Are you crazy? Joe, we're supposed to—"

It took us fifteen minutes to reach our sector, only to find our doors locked and a notice posted on the door from the Committee. It read as follows:

**You will be provided with everything
needed for your assignment.
Proceed to Sector 382. Gamnon Classes will start immediately.
—By ORDER of the COMMITTEE**

"Great! Just great! I can't even get my tools, Joe."

"Just give me a couple minutes, Derek. I'll be inside in a flash."

"Wait, Joe! Wait! There is a Guardian coming down the hall. He is headed right for us! Let's go, now! Joe!"

"All right, Derek, listen. I've got to get some more information."

"It will have to wait until another time," replied Derek. "The Guardian patrols are everywhere tonight, and the Committee members are all over the place rounding up the chosen ones."

The walk to Sector 382 seemed very long. I wanted to talk to Tarcon just one more time to find out what we were really getting into, being included among the chosen ones. As we entered the Sector, a Committee member met us at the door and said, "You are of the chosen ones. It is good to be chosen. It is very good."

"What does that mean, Joe?"

"I don't know, Derek, but Tarcon knows. If we only had a little more time… just a little more time."

CHAPTER 2

The Hall of Creation

We found the classes for Gamnon held in Sector 382, Building 505 of the Altaur Structures. It contained the Guardian headquarters plus the offices for the Committee. In total, the edifice spanned fifty stories. We were told that the offices and department governing the city legislature occupied the first thirty stories, and the remaining twenty stories housed and trained the students preparing for Gamnon. The lecture hall was the largest room in the development, and it was located on the top floor. It also had the best view of the surrounding city in the whole municipality. The composition of the walls in the lecture hall were unique. They were made of a material as clear as glass, but stronger and much lighter than any other substance made in our society.

We walked over to the elevator and entered along with ten other men. I looked upward as the elevator started its ascent, only to notice that the first floor was numbered 31. My curiosity grew as we passed consecutive floors, my mind demanding to know what really lies ahead on level 31. As we continued to the top, my curiosity was directed elsewhere. The elevator opened into a rather large hallway, extending fifteen meters long by seven meters wide masked in brilliant ceiling tiles of blue and yellow. The carpet was plush, and the ceiling was extended high above the floor, not common in the usual construction of Star City buildings. The walls were all transparent just as in the lecture hall, which made the view of the city spectacular. The hallway was filled with men from all professions, each built so differently that it made me wonder how the selection process actually worked. At the end of the hallway was a line of men that moved slowly toward the entrance of the lecture hall.

"Hey, Joe, I didn't realize that there were so many different men involved in this event."

"It only comes around every five years. It must be a pretty big deal," I said.

"I still don't understand why no one ever talks about it," commented Derek. "I don't know, but I'm sure we are going to find out."

We made our way to the outside wall where we could see over the city's empire and out into the heavens. The city looked immeasureable and the men below, going about their daily routine, reminded me of little beetles scurrying around their nests, looking for food. That really brought me back to my school day science experiments.

Everyone was running in and out of sector buildings, catching metro transits and dodging in and out of shops and offices all over the city. As I looked off into the distance, the Old World could be seen clearly. It looked lifeless and desolate, depicting the photographs we were shown in school. It is hard to believe that men once lived and prospered on earth. I thought to myself how lucky I was not to have lived in that time period.

I felt horrified to think of the Great Macrocaust as being part of my lifetime. I couldn't imagine the pain, death, and destruction that went along with nuclear war. I looked across the surface again and felt so alone. It was so barren and appeared as a huge mass suspended in space. There was no movement or life, except for an occasional Guardian patrol ship as it skimmed over the surface of the earth. Life there was nonexistent, time stood still, and reality had no meaning. Rock, dirt, and devastation were all that remained. There were some remnants of a very large city off into the distance. It must have been a beautiful metropolis in its time, I thought. A sad feeling came over me to look upon our history. I wondered what made the earth's civilization destroy itself. What was so important? Was it power? Was it tokens, or was it just a big mistake? No one really knows.

As I gazed around, I noticed that the Balem Star City off to the west didn't appear to be the same as I pictured it through my telescope. It lost its majesty from this viewpoint, especially as the sun fell below the level of the city. The sun's rays peered up through the buildings, cutting them like a knife, disturbing the structures and masking the true beauty of the silhouette. Over to the east of Balem and quite a distance from us was a third luminary. It looked like another Star City, although it was brilliantly lit with more colors, taller buildings, and unique architecture.

"Hey, Derek, look over there!"

"What is it, Joe?"

"I think that's where we'll be going. At least that's what I heard the guy next to me say."

"That's it, Joe, that must be Gamnon. It's so beautiful. No, it's spectacular. It's too bad Gamnon can't be seen more clearly from our apartment. It's looks luxurious. The distance makes it appear smaller than our Star City, but that brilliant glow gives it a heavenly appearance.

"Yeah, Derek, it looks so majestic and exciting."

"Well, it will be an adventure. That's for sure."

"I agree. I'm kind of looking forward to this project. How about you?"

"Well, a change can be good, and with change comes excitement, growth, and usually abundant knowledge."

"I'm sort of getting a funny feeling, Derek, like some force is pulling me over there."

"What are you crazy?" asked Derek.

"I feel an attraction of some kind. I really can't place it. Do you feel that way?"

"No, I don't think so. Let's move on. These guys are waiting for us to get in line, and some of them don't look very friendly."

"Let them go, Derek. I just want to look outside for a while, okay?"

"Go ahead fellows, we'll see you inside. Now, move along, move along."

I kept feeling more of a magnetic impulse drawing me to that Star. I couldn't explain what was happening. It was as if some force was calling me, giving me the desire to just rush to my fighter and go to that no fly zone this instant. It was a very strange desire, one of many new changes that I would soon encounter. I seemed to be in a trance for what seemed like a long period of time when I felt Derek pulling me toward the lecture hall.

"Joe, everyone is in the lecture hall. We have to go. Come on."

The dome had the ability to change its appearance from clear to opaque, preventing citizens from looking out into the city. The hall was filled with men, and the room started to change as flood-lights illuminated the hall. We moved closer to the door, and sure enough, we were the last ones in line. There were seventeen men in front of us. The hallway walls were still clear, and our view really was a spectacular sight. Then out of nowhere, an object flew across the window. As I turned, I saw two Guardian patrol ships streak across the sky after it.

We often heard of other civilizations but were told that they were vitally inferior. The Guardians had always done a very good job of keeping unidentified flying objects from flying to close to the city, preventing us from total recognition.

Most of our inner-city commuting was done by a local transit system that was located beneath the city, and the streets were usually pretty clear of citizens after work began except for Guardian patrols. The unidentified aircraft appeared to be a fighter well equipped for battle. It was heavily armed with lasers on the nose, two torpedo tanks mounted below each wing, and a center harness bearing a different type of bomb I had never seen before today.

The deflector shields seemed extraordinarily strong withstanding continual attacks by the Guardian ships. The blitz put on by the Guardian ships looked sort of silly. Their blasts just bounced off the shields of the intruder ship like pebbles off a building. It nearly looked as if he wanted them to attack, like the invader was playing a game with them, as the Guardian ship tried desperately to defeat the alien threat. Then, he retaliated, but not against the Guardian fighters, just against their offensive weapons. Every Guardian rocket, torpedo, and laser blast was met and destroyed with an opposite but much more forceful countermeasure. The alien airship proved to have great maneuvering ability. Whether it was a computer or a pilot, I'll never know.

The Guardians were now out in full force with about ten fighters converging on the alien. Chills came over me knowing that the alien fighter was now so outnumbered. It didn't seem fair, and being a fighter pilot with the Royal Air Force, I sympathized with him, putting myself in his position. But soon, it was very noticeable that he was in full control of the situation. He flew all over the city, in and out of Altaur proper, around the building and through the streets. His elevation as compared to our city varied anywhere from twenty to two hundred feet from the street and out to the protected city limits. It reminded me of the challenge game we competed in every year. I had won the competition for the past seven years, every year that I had entered. I obtained fourteen medals to go along with the contest rewards. The medals that were bestowed on the winner were the highest commendations awarded during peacetime. To compete, you had to race through and around the city.

There is a certain course that has to be flown, and no computers were allowed. The competition demanded complete pilot skill. Two pilots have lost their lives trying to beat me in the past four years. The game is the biggest event during our festival celebration.

Then, I saw the alien taking the offensive. He flew the ship brilliantly, fading, 360s, start and stalls and destroying Guardian ships at will. He ran ships into buildings and ran them into each other. It was the first battle I had seen within the city limits. News reports often told of the wars and battles in the atmosphere and beyond, but always portrayed Altaur as being fortified. Now, I wondered about the validity of our news reports. It claimed that no alien ship had ever entered our airspace. There were similar explosions of buildings in the past, but the media always explained the event as either Guardian ships or Royal Air Force aircraft. Even all of the destruction the city experienced was blamed on faulty equipment in our defense system. I had engaged in many dogfights, but they were outside the city limits, and the aircraft were not of this caliber.

Suddenly, the alien ship disappeared, deliberately flying between a cafe and the administration building, leading toward the new housing development and the business district. The Guardian securing the entrance to the lecture hall started to move down the hallway toward us. The hall seemed empty except for Derek, me, and a few men at the entrance. As the Guardian grew closer, we could hear a conversation coming from his radio. He picked up the frequency coming from the Guardian ships in pursuit of the alien. The communication was quick but very understandable.

"Where did he come from? Does anyone know?"

"Come from? Where did he go, Captain?"

"I don't know, but this guy is good. I've never seen anyone maneuver like him, and look at the ship it's incredible."

"Dan, is that you?"

"I lost him too. What a ship. My lasers bounced off his shields like I was throwing stones at him."

"Yeah, we had four torpedoes simultaneously locked in on him. Within seconds, he destroyed two torpedoes and outmaneuvered the other two directing them into the Silver Pub and Gin Sing Restaurant. Looks like no Chinese food tonight."

"That's amazing, and look what happened to Steve and Phil. He forced them right into the Beltin high rise. He just got Patrick! He went up like a Roman candle. The explosion was only second to the fireworks ignited at the last Harvest Festival."

"Captain, we're no match for this alien ship. Should we call in the Air Force?"

"Dan, look out! He's on your tail. Go hard to port. I'm coming in. I'll try to disrupt his balance with my jet-stream. Now hard to port! Hard to port!"

"Thanks, Captain, he's gone. I can't even see him on my radar. Wow! Look out, Captain. He just flew by my cockpit heading your way."

"Captain, I can't hold her. His jet stream really messed up my gyro. I'm heading out of the city. Maybe I can regain control up in the atmosphere."

"Affirmative. Head out!"

"Captain, I lost him again. Do you have a fix on him?"

Then out of nowhere, the alien ship made a pass along side the Guardian command post and headed straight for our building.

"Okay, move along. The fun is over. Move along, men," said the Guardian sounding uncomfortably as he moved closer. "Excitement's over, move along."

All of a sudden, the four Guardian ships converged on the alien ship as it made a pass alongside our building and headed straight for the ammunition depot. As he drew closer, I noticed a marking on the wing which was clearly identifiable. Everyone in the hallway scattered for cover as he roared past the building. I just stood at the window peering out at him, knowing he wouldn't fire at us. Then within milliseconds, he was history.

He simply disappeared. The ship must have been designed with an engine that provided him with light speed instantaneously. It was spectacular! One minute he was flying over our city, and the next through a brilliant array of colored lights and a glimmer of bright particles—yes, in an instant, he was gone. His exiting path lit up the sky like the celebration of Competition Day.

I was hoping for a news summons to be aired directly inside the dome, but I knew better since the alien made fools of the Guardian patrol ships. I will always remember the incident that day and that identification mark on the vertical stabilizer and wing will forever be locked into my mind. There were letters and numbers. It looked like "America 77." I wondered what they could mean. I hoped that someday I would find out.

"Okay, move along," said the Guardian who was restlessly standing next to us. "The disturbance is over. Move along, men."

"Come on, let's go," Derek said.

The lecture was very brief, providing us with our routine assignments for the training and a detailed schedule for our daily lessons. Soon, we were shuffled off to our rooms. We took the elevator down three floors and entered another hallway where there seemed to be alot of commotion.

"Two to a room. Two to a room," bellowed a hall supervisor. "You've had enough excitement for one day. Move along."

We proceeded to walk down the hallway. Derek and I ran into a crowd before seeing the man bellowing out the orders. He was a large man with a bushy black beard, dressed in a long white Committee gown, which also bore a large hood. His sash was bright red, different from the Committee members we encountered earlier. His head was covered with a small opening showing his face from his forehead to his chin. It was rumored that they can never cut their hair and that it must be wrapped up inside that cover until they become full-fledged Committee members. He handed us some colored cards, Derek a blue one and me a red one. Then they shuffled us off down the hallway. As we approached our rooms, he separated Derek and me assigning a roomate to each of us.

"Sir, sir, can I room with my good comrade, here?"

The man didn't take time to listen and kept about his business assigning rooms. "Two to a room, move along now, move along."

"Sir, sir," I raised my voice so that everyone in the hallway could hear me.

The hallway became very quiet and heads started popping out of the rooms already assigned. He slowly turned around to look at me and as he focused in on me the whole hallway turned and looked. I felt like I was on exhibition with the Committee again. He turned away and once again went about his business.

"I said move along. Can't you hear?" he replied. "Move along now!"

"But, sir," I protested, "I would like to be with my good companion, sir."

He slowly walked back toward me and, with deep concern, looked at us for a minute in silence, demonstrating the power and authority he blantly flaunted.

"Give me that blue card, son. Who has the red card?"

"I do, sir," said the man behind him.

"Give it to me now! Come on, we don't have all night."

"You! Yes, you!" he said, pointing to the comrade who had the red card. "Switch with this chap and make it fast! Move along now. Move, move along."

"Good work, Joe! I thought we would never see each other again."

"We've got to stick together, right? Do the numbers match on these cards?" asked Joe.

"My number is 1460-L?"

"Yes, that's it! Let's get inside before he changes his mind! Close the door, Derek."

"Well, I'm glad you said something, Joe. I don't think I could have—"

"You didn't have to, now, did you?"

"No, I guess not. You are always so vocal, and you seem to always get what you want. It just amazes me."

"Yes, that's one of my good qualities," remarked Joe.

We went back to the lecture hall shortly after admiring our newly assigned rooms. They gave us a briefing, once again, on our assignments and duties for the days to come and proceeded to give us our first allocution. We were then told to return to our rooms and relax for rest of the evening. We decided to use the stairs, hoping to stay in some kind of shape since an exercise program was not on the agenda. We went down to the end of the hall and through a large door. We entered a very bright stairwell and proceeded down to our floor. Once again, through a large door and about seven rooms to the left, and we were home.

"I didn't think we would ever get here," said Derek.

"Out of shape, comrade. I'll take care of that, The stairs will do nicely."

We put our card into the door lock, and it opened immediately.

"I'm going to bed. I'm beat."

"It's been a long day. I'm ready for the sack too. Hey, Derek, do you smell something?"

"Yes, but what is it?"

"I don't know, but it sure smells sweet. It's unfamiliar to me."

"Me too. Oh, over here, lighted candles. They sure smell nice."

"Hey, this room is a heck of a lot bigger than our own apartment."

The room was not just bigger but more luxurious than our usual dwelling place too. It was very clean and everything was in its proper place. There were two refrigerators, a built-in stereo system and a ninety five-inch monitor screen for our entertainment. There was a component underneath the monitor and a library of projections to be viewed. The refrigerators were gorged with every type of food known in our society. Derek was the first to notice the extremely large refrigerators and his tired body gave way to his appetite.

"Joe, look at all this food! I haven't seen this much food in years. I wish we had this variety at our commissary. I don't even recognize some of this stuff. It all looks delicious though, and I'm in the mood for an early evening snack. Let's try some of this stuff, you know. I'll try anything once."

"You go ahead. I'm going to check out the accommodations."

As Derek devoured his snack, I went into the living area to look around. What could be wrong with two baths and two relaxing bed-rooms in the rear of the apartment? The time spent here was going to be very pleasant. And yes, over on the other side of the living quarters was another computer, probably more elaborate than the old model in our own apartments. Now, I'm not putting Tarcon down, he was very good to us, but this one looked more sophisticated. I looked at Derek, now with only a portion of his food remaining, then at the computer. I produced this large grin, and he knew the wheels were turning.

"No, no, Joe, not this time. I'm not fooling around with another one of those machines. Tarcon was a challenge, and I proved that I could do it. That's as far as it goes. Besides, I've never seen a computer like this one, and we have no idea of the security system in this building."

"Oh, come on, Derek," I began to whisper. "You can do it. It will be a breeze. They are probably all the same on the inside, and it should be easy after all the knowledge you gained manipulating Tarcon's components."

"But the time limit… We only have a few weeks."

"Don't give me that line, Derek. You will have it all worked out. It will be easy and just think we will be the only ones with the knowledge of what lies ahead of us. We will know all about Gamnon, our past, and the earth's civilization… and… and females. Come on, Derek. It's definitely worth it."

"Oh no, you are doing it to me again. No, no, I'm not going to let you persuade me this time."

"Good, good. This time, we will wait a couple of days and work out the security system before we start."

"Well, I'll need tools, Joe. Wait, what am I saying?"

"Let's look around here. I'll look in the back sleep rooms. You look in the kitchen. Hey, Derek, look at these sleep rooms. The sleeper is big enough for two people."

"Where, let me see. Joe, I can't find anything that looks like a tool anywhere. There has got to be some tools somewhere. How are you suppose to fix things?"

"Do you have one of these beds?" asked Joe.

"Of course. What do you think is in this other room? I'm going to the kitchen. There has to be some tools somewhere."

"Well, these are fit for the Creator himself. I wouldn't mind staying here for a long time. These quarters really are quite comfortable. Have you found any tools yet?" Derek asked.

"No, not even a screwdriver in here and no ohmmeter either. I thought every apartment had its own set of tools. I don't believe it. There has to be some tools somewhere."

"I guess we just call room service if something breaks."

"How convenient. This is like heaven. I'm not used to 'not working.' I guess we should enjoy it while we can," Joe said.

"Hey! Here's a knife!"

"Oh big deal. I already found that. That's about the clumsiest instrument man has ever made. I need fine instruments to work on this computer. I need my tools, and they are just not available."

"Well, Derek, we'll just have to go get your tools."

"What! Get my tools? Are you sure you're not going a little crazy?"

"No, I'm not. Where there's a will, there's a way. Give me some time. I'll think of a plan. I always do, you know. In the meantime, let's see what this computer has to say."

"I'll turn it on, okay, Joe? There we go. It's fired up! After you."

"Hello. What is your name computer?"

"My name is Parrot. I am here to educate you in the matters of survival of the species."

"Do your memory banks contain material of the old Star City computer?"

"Affirmative. Every computer on Altaur has the same capabilities, but I'm only programmed to give you information concerning the preparation for Gamnon."

"Great! Did you hear that, Derek? We are in business."

"Your assignments were given earlier," Parrot spoke in an excited voice, "and your scheduled routine will be as follows: 7:00 a.m. breakfast; class from 8:oo a.m. until 12:00 p.m.; lunch from 12:00 p.m. to 1:30 p.m.; classes again from 3:00 to 5:00 p.m. in lecture hall 3. Dinner begins at 5:00 p.m.; doors will be closed and locked by the central computer at 1:30 and 6:30 p.m. and lights will be extinguished at 8:oo p.m. sharp. The time is now 4:30 p.m., so prepare yourself for dinner."

"Hey, Joe, I thought we had the rest of the evening off. They sure don't waste any time!"

"You can say that again. There goes our nap right out the window."

"Joe, there are no windows. I guess that takes care of our scenic view."

"Well, we might as well get use to lack of sleep and lets count on having some long nights. They sure don't give us much time during the day around here."

"I'm going to take a shower. Hopefully, that will wake me up."

The structured schedule we were put on was pretty brutal. It took me about thirty minutes to get ready, and by that time, I was really hungry. Derek was also hungry, although he just finished a snack that would equal a dinner to me. That man can put away the groceries. He had also eaten lunch, which I had completely forgotten about with all the excitement today. Derek, he would never miss a meal. We walked down the hallway, up some flights of stairs, through the lecture hall and then down another hallway, which eventually led to the dining area. Parrot's directions were accurate and straight to the point. He even spit out a couple maps for us. The dining area was set up in somewhat of an unusual manner. There was one long table that was set in the middle of the room. In fact, it was the entire length of the hall. It was filled with every kind of food known to our society.

There was an array of fruits and vegetables in every color imaginable. On the table were six different types of meat, two of which I had never seen or heard about. Rice, potatoes, and salads all lined the huge buffet table, and for dessert, there were cakes, pies, cookies, and parfaits. Every five feet stood a beautiful flower arrangement, and the tablecloth was a brilliant red with white lace around its edges. It was a beautiful sight, nearly too beautiful to destroy which is what happens when hundreds of men converge and eat as much as they want. Every ten feet there was a server, once again the men with the white gowns with red sashes. He would attend to your plate until it was full, and if you wanted more, you just had to bring back an empty plate. At the end of the table lay forty-eight sides of beef, seventy-five turkeys, a hundred chickens and two hundred plates of lamb chops, and four hundred platters of ogzor. I never did find out what those last two items were. The meats were all glazed with a sauce well-known to Altaur but very hard to acquire. At the other end of the table lay a huge crystal bowl filled with a variety of fruits and nuts. Vegetables and casseroles were spread out all over the table. It was the most magnificent feast I had ever seen.

The dining area was to each side of that beautiful table, and there were hundreds of tables set up in a line and very close together. They were very small and could only fit two people. The layout was in stark contrast to our dining areas in Altaur, which had only long community tables. My guess is that they wanted everyone to get familiar with their roommate, but the thought passed quickly as we took our plates up to the servers and filled them up as if there were no tomorrow. You couldn't even see Derek's plate; it was so full. We sat down at the closest table and began eating everything in sight. The food was delicious, but for some reason, it wasn't like the food we ate normally. We both went back for second helpings, and as we finished our main course, the desserts seemed to slip our minds. We both satisfied our appetites and decided to leave the desserts for another time.

"I haven't eaten this well in years," said Derek with a grin.

"I think the last meal that impressed me so much was the party for my graduation."

"Yes, I remember that quite well," Joe said.

"We ate so much our Protectors couldn't get us to move off that couch for the rest of the afternoon. But, Derek, what is going on with all this special treatment? Different food, fancy place settings, all you can eat. Just look at these tables, they're only big enough for two people. What's going on?"

"I don't know, but I'm sure glad we were picked to go on this mission 'cause it looks like we are going to be very comfortable."

"Derek, does this food taste different to you?"

"Yes, I noticed a subtle difference, but it quickly passed as that savory food covered these delicate taste buds."

"It's sure looks like the same food we buy at our commissary, but something is different about it, and I can't pinpoint it. It had a better taste than our food, a little richer maybe. It sure is prepared differently."

"Yeah, maybe we can get the recipes. I sure would like to try this at home."

We felt so satisfied after that delicious meal we quietly got up and walked back to our room barely making it to our couches. Derek quickly passed out, and I proceeded to figure out a plan to acquire—that is, retrieve Derek's tools to reprogram Parrot's computer banks. I couldn't concentrate though, because I kept thinking how strange it was that Derek and I couldn't resist the second plate of food, and I couldn't figure out the reason why the food was so tasty. I especially noticed the difference among several of the meat groups. It looked and smelled the same as our food, just as I prepare it, but the taste was different.

As soon as Derek reclined on the couch, he fell into a deep sleep.

"Derek! Derek, are you awake?"

"What, what… No! Yes! What did you say?"

"The meat, it definitely was the meat! It was different. I mean it looked and smelled the same, but it tasted different."

"Yes, I know. It was a subtle change, but you are right. The taste was original, and even the fruits and vegetables were slightly altered."

"Well, I guess we shouldn't complain. It sure was good eating, and don't forget, it was free. You can't beat that, now, can you?"

"No, for me, free food means heaven," Derek remarked with a smile.

There was silence for a while, then Derek proceeded to explain something about Parrot to me, but I fell fast asleep in the middle of his dissertation. I remember nothing of the last conversation, and I think Derek fell asleep in the middle of a sentence. So satisfied and tired, we both slept soundly until the next morning.

CHAPTER 3

The Chase

The night seemed to slip away very fast, and soon it was morning. Parrot decided to wake us up bright and early in order to get us prepared for breakfast. Parrot's alarm was so abrupt that I nearly fell off the couch that had comfortably swallowed my unconscious body. I jumped up as if I was on Sigma Red Alert. Derek was sleeping so soundly that the horrible alarm startled him also, but he quickly realized where he was and laid back down on the couch, burying his head into the soft feather pillow. He had hoped to get another ten minutes, but Parrot sounded off again this time playing some heavy metal Old World music that was impossible to fall asleep too.

"Derek, Derek, shut that crazy thing up. It's too early to be getting up."

"What? What? Oh, okay, crazy alarms."

Derek looked frantically for a Shut Off button but could not find one. "Man, you've got to be kidding!"

"What's the matter?"

"Either there is no Shut Off button, or I'm too stupid to find it. They sure make a point of getting us up early around here."

"You are right, Master Derek," Parrott exclaimed. "There is no turn off switch. So there is no way to get around this awful alarm. Get up! This music will continue playing until both of you are out of your reclining positions and into the showers. I have very sensitive scanning sensors. You cannot hide from me."

"Oh great," Derek said softly. "Where are we going to sleep tonight?"

"I'm going to try and fool this alarm and sleep on the floor in the bathroom."

"I don't think we can trick this computer. I think I'll just sleep in the bed tonight."

"Sir, it does not matter where you sleep. My sensors show me your state of mind, where you are, and when wakefulness occurs. Then and only then will I refrain from playing this ghastly music."

"These computers are getting out of hand. The next thing you know they will be tracking us everywhere we go. Right, Derek?"

"Give us time, sir. Give us time," said Parrot. "Master Joe, arise, it's time to rouse."

"Rouse? Oh come on, Parrot. You had to go deep into your memory banks for that word. All right, all right! I'm getting up. I'm rousing or whatever you call it."

"Move along now. Move along, Master Joe. No one is to be late. Never late. Move along."

"I can tell you are going to be a pain in the…"

"Now, now, I am just doing my job."

"Oh, blow it out your tubules, Parrot!" Derek bellowed from the bathroom.

"Nasty, Master Derek. Nasty you are in the morning. Oh well, you will change. You will change. Everyone does. I'll see to that. You will change."

We made it to breakfast ten minutes earlier than required just to get away from that noisy computer. The meal was not as elaborate as dinner the night before, but the long table, servers, and five hudred hungry men appeared right on time.

"We sure don't get to meet any of the other men. This two-to-a-table is for the birds. I can't figure out the importance of it, two to a room and two to a table. I'll bet we do everything in twos."

"I don't care, Joe. This food is terrific. I'm sure going to put on some weight if these meals stay the way they are."

"You better slow down now, Derek. I don't want you to pass out during our learning sessions."

We finished a bit early and went straight back to the room hoping to catch a few quick winks before our classes started, but sure enough, as soon as our minds started to rest, Parrot started running at the mouth again.

"It's time for class now. Let's get moving," said Parrot.

It was a much more of a monotone voice than before. It sounded like a eulogy at the military funerals I've attended in the past, short and sweet.

"Oh, that's great! Did you hear that voice, Derek?"

"Yes, it sounded like a dead man's last words," Derek whispered.

Parrot announced, "No conversation is tolerated. Questions can be asked at the proper time and only if addressed in the proper coded sequence. For example, Parrot code A-27 question, then slowly ask the question. It will be answered promptly. Now attention. here is your first lesson.

"Throughout man's history there has been a means to survive and replenish the society with new beings such as you. This event takes place on Gamnon, and it enters the time zone of our ages every five years as the moon passes seven times around the Star of Casper. The second Star City, Balem, has within its boundaries the proprietors who directly participate in the act of preservation of human society. These beings are called females or women, and they serve as the receptacle for the seed produced by men to further the survival of both societies. One woman is selected to mate with a man of equal or greater abilities who can perform the duties required by their own respective Star Cities. These selections and pairing of mates are made through extensive research on physical capabilities, mutual classification, worth to society, need within society, and class of operation. Members of each age group will mate when they become of the age when hormonal levels peek and the desire to mate overrides any other desire.

Each mate must excel in his or her class to qualify for the process of mating to further the survival of their respective societies.

Each mate is chosen within their class, and each shall produce a being to promote a prechosen society, either Altaur or Balem."

"Code A-27, Question Parrot," I said.

"Affirmative. This question will be recorded. A-27 acknowledge."

"Define *class*, Parrot?"

"Class is defined as the specialty one was trained for to qualify as a respectable member of one's society. Example, one person from Altaur with a professional ability to be a defense planner will mate with a person of the same professional ability from Balem. The partner is chosen by certain parameters, which include age, recreational habits, desires, and professional abilities. The match is perfect so together the unit can produce an offspring equal to or better than the two producers."

"Code A-27 Question."

"Affirmative."

"Define the word *produce*," Derek asked.

"Produce. This means bring forth another being in resemblance to yourself and your mate. It will be explained in detail later. May I proceed?"

"You didn't precede your question with Code A-27. Come on, Parrot, the rules are for everyone."

"Coded questions are for your benefit only. They will be recorded and processed on today's transcript. Now may I proceed?"

"Affirmative, Parrot." Derek said.

"Cut out the jokes, Derek. I don't think they programmed a sense of humor into this one."

Parrot, without further responding to the insult, proceeded, "Together you and your mate will be a family unit for a period of several months after conception and will give birth to a new human being."

"Give birth! Who? Us? Ask him, Joe! Do we give birth, or do they produce these new beings? Code A-27," responded Derek rather quickly.

"Just hold on, Derek. He will explain. Just give him a chance."

"Affirmative. Thank you, Master Joe. I will continue as soon as my audience calms down and is ready to listen."

Parrot finally continued, "Your mate, that is, the female has the responsibility of giving birth. It's called a son for male and daughter for female. Afterwards, they will be given to the selected Protectors in the respective Star Cities. During the time of the birthing process, you will be living on Gamnon, and you and your mate will live together supporting, encouraging, and helping each other prepare for this trying occasion we will call labor and birth. You and your mate will coexist as one unit. Entertainment, given duties, recreation, meals, relaxation, and sleep will be done as this unit. Work, as you perceive it, will be terminated for this time period. Pilots will be the only profession required to practice on the simulators provided for them. This work session will last approximately five hours per day at any given time, and the simulators are available twenty-four hours a day. Other professions are not required to work but will have the option to do so."

"Code A-27 Question, Parrot."

"Affirmative."

"Can we take a short break?" asked Derek. "I have to let all this information settle into my brain. There is way too much data that has to be absorbed!"

"Affirmative," remarked Parrot. "I will shut down for fifteen minutes."

"Joe, did you hear that? No work! It's going to be great. I haven't been off a day from work in three years."

"That's for you, Derek. I still have to work with the simulators, but I'm glad. They should keep my reflexes sharp, and I wouldn't want to get bored."

"You know I won't. You can count on that, Joe." The session resumed shortly afterward.

"Code A-27 Question Parrot," asked Joe. "How long will our stay be on Gamnon?"

"Approximately nine to ten months."

"That's a long time, Derek."

"Long time, that's a year of no work, and I am going to enjoy every minute of it. Extended vacation, what a deal!"

Soon, it was midday, and our introduction to Gamnon along with the training program was complete. Parrot continued by describing our schedule. First, our lessons consisted of anatomy and physiology. Second, we learned about some unique characteristics of our mates. Third, the structures, design, and the layout of Gamnon were given to us so we could get familiar with the location and proximity of all the facilities.

Lastly, he explained how to prepare physically so our bodies will be ready for the act. This last part of Parrot's explanation was vague, and it didn't seem to fit into the scheme of things. It was hard to understand, but Parrot summarized the explanation, for the time being, by saying there would be an act to perform and our physical condition was relatively important. Parrot continued for a while longer, and we kept the questions to a minimum so he would finish well before dinner and give us some free time before we scurried off to the dining room. Eventually, we realized how important our free time was, and the only way to maintain a fair amount of it was by limiting our questions.

Parrot, once the lesson was over, disengaged sensing circuits giving us some private time to ourselves. This would give us plenty of time to figure out how we were going to recover Derek's tools. It went like this:

Several sensors would make sure that we were attentive and receiving our day's lesson. But once the lesson was over the sensors would disengage just like Parrot. Then, stating that the lesson was completely over, Parrot shut down. Concurrently, we detached the security probes located all over the room, as we proceeded to open up Parrot's computer panels.

Derek prepared himself with as many crude tools he could find around the apartment. Soon, he was engulfed in trying to figure out if Parrot's circuits were capable of displaying any information we wanted. Derek looked around for a long time, studying Parrot thoroughly trying to figure out if it was possible to accomplish our goals.

"Yes, yes," said Derek. "It can be done with the right tools, enough time, and a reorganization of the internal components. I can do it."

"How, Derek? Are you sure?"

"Yes, positive. I'll bypass the sensors, realign circuits and cross switches, link zones, divide splicers, disengage flaps, and dismantle physical beta and electron reservoirs. Then, I just add sets of alpha, theta, and sigma waves, which would give us access to the memory banks only when the system was turned off… Oh and enter the voice codes. That's very important, and don't let me forget it, Joe, or we'll be in a lot of trouble. After bypassing the power sensors and signaling the specter device, we can control the historical time period, then hone in on just the information we want. I hope that will expedite some of our time. Actually, earphones and brain wave sensors would be ideal, and then we wouldn't have to talk. It can be done and relatively easy too. The computer would have to be modified, and all the work would be done under this panel. I hope it's been serviced recently because they would find our work just by opening the panel. Well, ask Parrot when it gets serviced and when the next appointment is. We might have to tear the work down before we leave."

"Don't worry. I'll find out the next service date, Derek. Leave that to me."

"Okay, that's your job. We're in this together, right, buddy?"

"Right, Derek, all the way!"

The security system was very sound. After every meal, we had fifteen minutes to get back to our rooms. Exactly fifteen minutes, no sooner, no later after the designated meal ended, and the doors would close and lock automatically. A central computer at the security booth on each floor controlled every door. The halls were monitored by security, but they rarely paid attention to the monitors since it was highly unlikely for anyone not to be in their correct place at the correct time. The time was very precious to us. Getting into the hallway wasn't hard to figure out at all. The locking sensor controlled by central was located inside the recessed portion of the lock contained in the wall.

As the door closed and the lock filled up the space, the sensor perceived the door as being locked. It was similar to the old one, what they used to call bolt lock. Previously a turn of the latch engaged the lock. Here the latch filled the hole automatically and the sensor, a very primitive one at that, would sense the space being filled. Keeping the door from locking was relatively simple. The doors in our living quarters back in Altaur opened electronically with a plastic-coated metallic card inserted into a power driven electronic locking mechanism. Luckily, I kept my card when we were shuffled off to the Committee meeting. First, with a piece of chewy bubble gum, inconspicuously acquired at dinner and vigorously chewed for five minutes to reach the texture needed to block the sensor. We would force the bubble gum inside the hole where the bolt normally meets the sensor.

This would fool the sensors into thinking the lock was in place. Subsequently, as the door closed we would slip the plastic card between the bolt and the bubble gum. As the sensors were fooled, no alarm would sound and the bolt would hit the plastic card keeping the locking mechanism from engaging. The door could then be opened and closed leaving the card in place for easy access back into the room. Subsequently, the door would appear to be normal.

After three days of deliberation and building up the courage needed to perform our task, we decided the best time to go would be in the afternoon. The servers and Committee members were always running around in the mornings and early evenings, but during the afternoons, their job was running their Star City. This included management, defense, and many other duties and obligation set forth by the ones called the Educators. The place was basically deserted except for the guardians responsible for the entire building security. There were two probable trouble spots involved in our plan: We might be recognized by the Guardian Patrols defending the city, or by someone who knew we were supposed to be at the Hall of Creation.

Also, we had to break into Derek's apartment for his tools. The locks had been changed when we left for the Committee meeting. Last, but not least, we would have to think of a good alibi just in case we were caught and questioned. We both decided on a story, something about our desire for a spirit, and we felt sneaking out for one would do no harm. We knew we would be questioned separately, and we both had the alibi down pat, making no mistakes about every detail. But that wasn't a major problem until we were caught, so we put it in the back of our mind for the time being.

We got up earlier than usual the next morning, probably because of our queasy stomachs. It seemed like the perfect day. The sun was shining through a partially cloudy sky or that's what they told us on the communicator and the temperature was a cool 65 degrees. This day wasn't very different from the day before and probably wouldn't vary much to the next day. I guess that's what made it seem so perfect. At least we had acquired enough courage needed for the attempt to execute our plan.

The session with Parrot gave us insight on the physical and mental differences which included the interests aspired to by our mates. It was very informative and held our interest tremendously. He pointed out characteristics and personality traits, trying to make it easier for us to hold an intelligent conversation with them, which I hoped would lead to a well-established relationship. Parrot gave us insight on how to develop that relationship by showing respect and kindness to our mate.

He also reassured us that we would developed a close bond with our partner. He went on about pregnancy, labor, and the birth of a new being. We were so amazed; we felt it would be such a special occasion that together it would be a great time to celebrate because that beautiful union would give us such joy.

As we secured this binding relationship, Parrot stated we would enjoy fully this wonderful gift given to us by our Creator. We would become comfortable in time, and it would come naturally once we developed such intimacy. He also stated as we established a relationship that we would feel more comfortable being more affectionate with them, another feeling that was new to us. This material was extremely sensitive, and Parrot told us that we would have to trust our Creator to give us a natural ability and propensity to enjoy and foster this friendship; a gift that He bestowed on His creation. All this information, the desires we would have, the act we would perform, seemed to make us somewhat uneasy. We had to trust an invisible Creator, have faith that he would help us to feel adequate, comfortable and able to enjoy this wonderful gift given to us.

Derek and I decided that this was the best and only time we had to make an attempt for his tools since this lesson period was only about thirty minutes long and the rest of the time was to be spent in studies. After the relatively short lesson was over, we had precisely an hour and a half to complete our plan before the sensors were initiated. Our plan would take only one hour, which gave us approximately a half-hour leeway, which I hoped wouldn't be needed. Parrot shut down promptly after our session, and we moved quietly toward the door.

We hadn't tried our door yet, but we're positive that our plan would work. Everything started out beautifully. The droid sensors turned off after the act of creation was explained and reviewed; the bubble gum and entry card worked perfectly. I slowly opened the door and nonchalantly looked over at Derek. He displayed one of those awful little smirks of victory he was well known for. He always displayed that same expression when one of our plans came together. But little did we know what was in store for us now:

I took one glance down the hallway and noticed the guard was still in the entryway. I quickly pulled my head inside and promptly closed the door. We waited for a few minutes, and then opened the door once again. It was clear this time, and the security booth was empty. We entered the hallway and made our way over to the fire exit. As we reached the door, we noticed the security guard looking out the window. We were extra careful not to make any noise to alarm him. We started to make our way down the steps. There were forty-seven flights, 470 steps.

"That's a long way down, Joe," Derek whispered.

"Oh come on, Derek. You're in good shape, aren't you? Hey, what's that?"

"What?"

"That smell."

"Smells good, something like our lunch."

"It sure does."

I walked a little farther and entered the next stairwell, motioning Derek to be quiet. After a couple steps, I could see down the stairwell. There were two servers, and it looked as if he had two or three plates of food lined up on the stairs. One other plate was empty, and they were attacking the food like yesterday was the great Macrocaust. I was glad one plate was already gone for our time was very precious. After the second plate was empty, they left the stairwell. You could tell it wasn't their first time because together they cleaned up the mess rather quickly and moved back toward the dining hall. As we passed the doorway, Derek commented that they were stealing our food, and we should tell the Committee. They would give them a lesson in discipline. I thwarted the idea by mentioning the fact that we would have to explain our reasons for being in the stairwell at what was now thirty minutes past the lunch time session. I didn't think the Committee would appreciate our spying techniques. Derek quickly forgot the whole ordeal, and by the time we reached the first floor, we both felt that the plan was coming together rather nicely. The first floor was mainly a file room. It contained a file on everyone entering the Hall of Creation. This was the best access to the outside because human workers weren't there. The file room was organized and operated by droids that were highly sophisticated, but their ability to designate human from machine was nonexistent.

It was funny because I thought it was vacant until I saw a droid returning from across the room. I dove behind some shelves and file boxes, but Derek kept on walking. He had recognized them instantly only because he had designed them. He started laughing hysterically, and as I picked myself up off the floor, I asked him a very trivial question.

"Derek, why weren't humanoid-detecting sensors put into these Droids?"

"Well, the main reason was cost. We get down to that bold stuff again."

"Right," I said.

Derek explained, "The sensors are imported, and the cost is extremely high. The sensors were one of seven items made by Balem to trade between the Star Cities. We exported mainly defense weaponry, building materials and integral circuit boards to them."

"How do you know this, Derek?"

"It's simple. Remember, I made them and I had to know where to buy parts or where not to buy them. Actually, we aren't supposed to be able to get that information but my Protector told me."

"He told you about Balem?"

"No, no, just that Balem existed and that all our sensors were made there, exclusively. Their technology in sensors was far ahead of ours, but their defense system, believe me, stunk. Our superior aircraft and technology of defense simulator arms and tracking devices were exchanged for their highly sophisticated sensors."

Navigating the droids was simple since their only alarm was based on touch. Soon, we were out of the Hall of Creation and on our way to Derek's apartment.

"Now, that was easy, wasn't it?" Derek asked.

"Yes, but we've only just begun. Don't forget we have to get back inside the Hall of Creation and undetected too."

"With a reliable plan, it can be done. We just have to be determined."

Most of the citizens were at their positions so the streets were pretty barren. Just a few late patrons were scattered about. It would take about thirty minutes to get to Derek's apartment, acquire the tools, lock up and leave, that in turn would give us plenty of time to reach the Hall of Creation. The plan was foolproof.

"See, Derek, it can't get any better than this. What do you think?"

"I think it's a little too perfect, and that means trouble."

During our training every pilot and navigator was given a special wrist bracelet, which had some special instruments on it. It had a sophisticated navigation device, which would direct you home from anywhere in the universe. It was supplied with an active distress signal, which lasted three years, and a small laser implement for cutting even the hardest material made, namely, tritactium (strong but very light.) That substance was used in the making of nearly everything on the Star Cities, from weapons to war planes and buildings. It was even found in the Central Aviating Elevator and in the Otis solar anti-gravitational generator, which provides the star with its levitation power. The bracelet device was also equipped with a 337-2

B-ray, Alpha Ray, and X-ray scanner on it. In the warship, it was connected to the main computer when flying, and it stored and provided all the information needed for maintenance, flying, combat, and navigation. So for instance, it could scan and decode locks, a simple task, or diagnose damage or malfunctions on aircraft, a more complicated duty. Also it was compatible with every computer.

In this instance, it would decode the new lock on Derek's door and give us access to its combination. By law, this device was never to be removed but was only permitted to be used on official work-related business, which was in accordance with promoting life, energy, defense, and stability on Altaur. The penalty if caught using it out of context was death by ejection. That is ejection from a warplane into space, what a horrible death! It took about two minutes to get into Derek's apartment and nearly ten minutes for Derek to gather his belongings. Everything was on schedule, and it seemed to go like clockwork. Plus, we still had plenty of time to get back since most of the society was still consumed by their work schedule.

The Guardian patrols were our only concern. Coming over we hadn't even seen one patrol but our chances of not seeing any on the return trip were slim to none. Their main function was the defense of Altaur, but they also patrolled for delinquent citizens and kept peace and tranquility in the city streets. We gathered all the instruments that we needed to work on Parrot and left promptly.

"This isn't so bad, now is it, Derek?"

"Easy for you to say. I'm the one sweating my behind off. I'll tell you for sure once we are back in our room at the Hall of Creation."

No sooner were the words out of Derek's mouth, than a Guardian patrol came unexpectedly from around the comer.

"Oh no, Joe. I think I spoke too soon!"

"Did they see us?" Joe quickly asked?

"They sure did. Here they come! Let's go!"

"No, did they recognize us, Derek? Thats's more important to know."

"No, no, they were a good fifty yards away from us but our New Hall of Creation emblem sticks out like a sore thumb."

They followed us through an alley up a stairwell and into the city streets. I heard laser blasts behind us but took no time to turn around and find out what they hit or how close they were to us. The alley was filled with boxes and containers and as we reached the streets I heard a loud noise, then a couple more laser blasts and a huge explosion. I turned briefly to see red and yellow flames following our path. It was a break we sure needed."

"Hey! Up these stairs!" a voice shouted from behind us.

"Fire, fire!" another one exclaimed. "Hey! There they go! This way!"

Then, we heard sirens and the alarm that rang out individually from each patrolman. They were going off all over the place.

"Derek! Derek, wait! Over here."

We ducked into an alley; my wrist device got us in the back door to a hobby shop. "Hey, Derek, I think it just hit the fan."

"You can say that again. What's next?"

"Let's rest here a second until things cool down a little, and we can go to plan B."

"Wow, am I glad you have that wrist device. It sure comes in handy and just let me say it has worked perfectly so far?"

"Yes, but if I get caught, I'll have to see you in our next life."

The scurry of footsteps and men running everywhere was heard from inside the shop. We both tucked in neatly behind a table. The shop was small and was overcrowded with many different types of hobbies and crafts. One of the items included a scaled-down model electronic fighter that actually shot a small harmless laser powerful enough to wreck another plane of its kind, but that was about it. There were roller balls, tower nets, stargate holes, and quarter racks. The store was utterly amazing in that it seemed very small but contained every popular hobby known our society. All of a sudden, we heard some voices from the back of the store. Derek and I moved closer to them so we could hear what they were saying. They were unaware of our presence.

"Okay, we'll sell those Cretins some lasers, but I don't like it. It seems too risky, especially at this time. Guardian patrols have been doubled and the heat is on right now."

"Seriously, I have a good business here, and I don't want to jeopardize my trade. I especially don't want to spend the next eighty years in confinement or worse, ejection."

We slid behind some boxes toward the middle of the store, and now, we could hear the conversation extremely well.

"Who are they talking about, Joe?" Derek whispered.

"You got me."

"Hey, isn't that? That voice sounds really familiar."

"What's going on out there?" said the familiar voice.

"See what I mean? The Guardian patrols are all over the place again. The third time this week."

"Don't worry," the voice said. "There is no problem. I can go wherever I please. I retain an all-day pass. It's probably a poor fool shipping corbets so he can trade for an afternoon spirit. It happens all the time. They will never learn, will they? It just doesn't pay to be dishonest, right? Ha ha ha." The men began to laugh together as the crowd outside began to increase.

The man walked over to the door and slowly opened it, looked back with a smile, then quickly exited. The storeowner shook his fist at him then returned to the storeroom in the back of the shop.

"Can you believe that, Derek? That guy was a security investigator and chief of the Guardian forces. I finally put a face to that voice."

"Yes, and he's in with this guy selling lasers to… lasers to whom?"

"Derek, we just acquired some real damaging evidence that may help us later."

"I know. Let's get out of here. Our time is running out," Derek whispered. "We should be happy that this guy is crooked. If he wasn't so busy setting up a delivery of laser guns, instead doing his work like catching delinquent citizens, we probably would be in Section 5 right now."

"You're right. Let's go! It looks clear. We have fifteen minutes to make it."

As we left the hobby shop, I couldn't stop wondering about the laser guns. I kept saying to whom? To whom? It wouldn't be Balem. There were strict commerce laws, and they probably are already equipped with laser guns. We ran through the city now, using every alley we could find. It was much longer, and it felt like eternity, but the main streets were crawling with Guardians. We ran the whole way, and finally we were within fifty yards of the entrance to the hall. Those fifty yards included crossing a walkway, a street, then another walkway. It would be miraculous if we could make it undetected. We waited patiently for each patrol to fan out and head in opposite directions.

"Joe, this is going to be tough. If we make this crossing, I'll follow you to the ends of the galaxy."

"Well, if we don't make it, this will be the end of the galaxy—that is, for us." Joe looked at his wristlet and noted the time dwindling away.

"Derek, it's now or never. Let's go!"

"But Joe, they are not far enough."

Just then, we both moved toward the door. I went across the walkway ahead of Derek. We made it across the first walkway, mainly with slow and easy steps. Our pace picked up as we entered the street. Then halfway across the street, we heard a Guardian yell.

"Over there in the street!"

We took off running.

"Derek, the window!"

Laser blasts flew all around us. I knew we weren't close enough and would never be able to unlock the door, so about a meter and a half from the window, I shot it with my wrist device. It shattered, and I jumped right through it. Derek followed behind me. We hit the floor and rolled three times before we stood up.

"We did it now, Joe! There is no way out of this one!"

"Are you cut? Are you cut?" I want to know fast.

"No, why?"

"I've got a plan. Just follow me and hurry."

We practically flew through the file room and ran up the stairwell skipping steps on the way. Inside we heard whistles and alarms and men yelling orders.

"Three men move to the other side of the building. You two around this corner, four of you into the file room, and get those characters."

Meanwhile in the stairwell…

"Joe, why did you want to know if I was cut?"

"Don't talk. Just follow me and run. Derek, run!"

We ascended to our floor.

"Wait, I hope with all this commotion the guard will be at the window." Sure enough, the security guard was looking out the window trying to figure out what was happening out there.

"Great! Just great! That sure was a beautiful diversion, Derek. I'm glad you thought of that. Give me your tools, stay here and just trust me, Derek."

"Thought of what? Joe! Stay here? Are you crazy?"

I knew we were in deep trouble, especially with the Guardians closing in fast, so I quickly walked down the hall, jamming the monitor with my hightech radio device on my wristlet. I pushed the door open and set the tools down inside the room. Back at the door, I picked up my keycard and proceeded to move down the hallway to the fire alarm. Meanwhile, the Guardians only had three floors to reach Derek.

"Come on, Joe. Come on! They are getting closer," Derek mumbled to himself.

I pulled the fire alarm, and soon a very loud annoying siren rang all over the building. The doors to the rooms automatically flew opened, and before the security guard knew what was happening, the once quiet and dark hallway was bright and filled with men leaving their rooms and moving toward the fire escape. I made my way back to the room and removed the bubble gum from the sensor, put it in my mouth, and started chewing. Then, I moved with my fellow classmates down the hall to the fire escape.

Back in the stairwell…

"Wow! Great plan, Joe," Derek stated under his breadth.

More and more men were moving out of their doors, down the hallway and into the stairs. Derek waited until I reached the door and then joined me. The Guardians were one flight down from us, and soon we were face-to-face.

"Let's get out of here," said a Guardian.

"Yeah, we will never find them in this confusion," yelled another.

There was so much noise and confusion in the stairwell that if there were a real fire, not many of us would have survived. Men were putting on clothes and shoes, tripping down the stairs, shoving, yelling, and carrying on.

"Joe, that was brilliant," whispered Derek. "I just can't believe it."

"Well, Derek, if they wanted to use the fire escape, I felt it my duty to honor and welcome their request."

We finally made it to the first floor somewhat fatigued, and we proceeded to go down the hall and out into the street. By now, stories about a fire had spread throughout the crowd. Everyone had been formulating their own opinion. Firefighters were there instantly, and the place was covered with Guardians looking for two delinquent and missing citizens. No one really knew what happed except Derek and me. Soon, more fire ships were shooting up their ladders and hurrying into the building. Some of the firefighters carried axes and others were spraying sorbisol around the area. Oxygen tanks and smoke-spewing machines filled the streets. Then, the scanner ship flew by and hovered above the building searching for the fire. It was pure chaos, and I loved every minute of it. Guardian patrols were walking all around us without a clue as to whom they were looking for.

"I want those two delinquents, Sergeant, and I want them now!" called a patrol leader.

"Hey, Derek, I just feel great when a plan comes together, don't you?"

"It's like music to my ears, Joe. But answer me one question? Why'd you want to know if I was cut?"

"Simple, this plan couldn't have worked if we were cut. Those Guardians will surely inspect us before we reenter the building. If we were bleeding or had some fresh cuts, they would put two and two together. The broken window, fresh cuts. We would have been caught for sure."

"Now you tell me. What would you have done if one of us was cut?"

'Well, Derek, that was plan C, and let me just say that I'm overjoyed we didn't have to use it."

"Joe, I thought my heart was going to jump right out of my chest. That's the most excitement I have had in a long time."

After twenty minutes of scanning the building, the firefighters along with some help from the Guardians decided that it was a false alarm and let everyone return to their rooms. They did scan and search our bodies, but as I had figured, no positive proof could be found to identify the two marauders.

As we entered the room, Derek looked over at me and said, "Joe if we did get caught, what was your famous plan C? You know the one that was going to save our lives? I am sure it was just some dazzling stragedy."

"Well, it goes something like this. Mr. Committee man, this roommate of mine was so obsessed with his tools that he just positively had to have them or he'd go crazy. He would scream and yell every night, waking up constantly with horrifying nightmares. He just couldn't go anywhere without them. It was like leaving his toothbrush. Mr. Committee man, he was driving me just plum crazy."

"Are you kidding, Joe? That's terrible. We would have been either flown to Section 5 immediately or executed right on the spot. If you would have told me that before we left I would have never gone."

"I know. Ha ha ha, a great plan C, wouldn't you say?"

"You know, it's a good thing we didn't get caught."

"Well, I wasn't counting on getting caught, Derek!"

There was silence for a moment. Then we both burst into hysterical laughter that lasted nearly fifteen seconds. Slowly, we regained our composure, but the ordeal could have been fatal, Derek reminded me. I think the outburst was due to the stress we both built up during the chase, but we definitely felt better afterwards. We again became silent realizing that we were blessed to be alive.

"Joe, I still can't believe we caused all that commotion. I'll tell you that I have never been that frightened in my entire life.

"It's good for you, Derek. It builds character. I deal with fright nearly every week in my fighter. Maybe, not to that extent but close to it."

"Have you ever been more frightened than you were today, Joe?"

"Oh, yes, I have but just once. I was flying in competition throughout the city. I think it was the third year I participated in the event."

"Oh, yes, the race. Haven't you won that race every year that you entered the competition?"

"Well, not every year, but four years ago, I was in first place most of the race and was thirteen miles from the finish. I had to bank right, increase speed past the Omega building, then past the Sentoid Complex. Finally, I descended briefly under the Bridgeport walkway and up over the beautifully constructed Towers. Everything would have been perfect except as I banked right my landing gear malfunctioned and engaged. I couldn't get them up with the computer and didn't have time to diagnose a solution. It follows that once I flew under the Bridgeport walkway the only way to cross over the Towers would be to perform a 180-degree maneuver and fly over upside down. If I didn't, my landing gear would catch the building exhaust vents, and I would crash, and as you know crashing inside the city limits is about 99 percent fatal."

"Man, Joe! I never heard or read anything about that incident. Was there a write-up in the Chronicle?"

"No, I never told anyone. I will tell you something, though, coming out from under that Bridgeport walkway my heart was down in my boots. My mouth was so dry I could hardly swallow and my heart was doing triple time. I haven't been that frightened ever in a race. You know I only cleared that building by three meters, and I was on my head when I did it. It all happened so fast that for several minutes after the race I could hardly breathe. I really started hyperventilating from the Omega building and continued until I reached the finish line. I nearly passed out."

"That's an amazing story, Joe," Derek said in a soft, consoling voice. "Yes, I believe it is old buddy, I believe it is."

For the next three days, we worked on Parrot diligently every opportunity that was available. Derek worked day and night, and I was right beside him handing him tools, chips, condensers, relay sensors, and other tiny little parts I had never heard of before our adventure. Derek knew exactly what to do with them. He was undoubtedly the best with computers in the galaxy. At least, it sure seemed that way to me. My curiosity about the events to come was tremendous, and my body was going through changes I never experienced before the Hall of Creation. Even my curiosity about the Macrocaust and the laser gun-runners seemed to diminish, but I never let Derek know about it. I knew this change was transient, and I would be back to my own self very soon. It was strange, though these desires were really uncommon, because my only interests were flying, swimming, and competitive sports on Altaur.

The interest in my work never seemed to end. My work was my life. Now, I felt that I had to know more about Balem, women, and Gamnon. I started wondering why we never had any communication with Balem or Gamnon, and why our societies were totally independent except for the tracking devices. How did our defense systems match up? Was there another society that needed our laser technology or did they just lack the material or machines to produce them. I had many unanswered questions. My desire to be with a woman was so intense at times I felt as if I were going to mentally explode. I didn't have these cravings before my schooling in the Hall of Creation. It really frightened me. Derek had similar drives, and we were both unaware of what was producing these types of urges. To say the least, tension was extremely high and our actions really showed it.

"Well, Derek? How is the work coming along? Do you think Parrot is ready to, let's say, educate us?"

"No! No, Joe, not yet!"

"Wow! Jump all over me. I was just asking a simple little question."

"I'm sorry, Joe. I don't know what's happened to me lately. I've never felt or acted this way, before this Hall of Creation. My nerves are all shot. Maybe it's these four walls that bother me. I can't wait until we get out of here."

"Yeah, I've been pretty edgy myself, Derek. I've noticed a lot of changes, not just physically but mentally too."

"Right, Joe. I wonder what they are doing to us. These past three weeks my mind has been playing tricks on me. I daydream, my mood has changed, and all I want to do is meet my mate and produce offspring. I can't even concentrate on this stupid Droid much anymore. I was sure I could do this in two days and look, four days later, I'm still working. I just can't concentrate."

"Yes, it only took you about seventy-two hours in total to reprogram the Tarcon in your apartment. Derek, let's try to figure out what has happened to us. What has changed in the past twenty-one days? There has been several changes. The first one being our environment."

"Yes, and two, our lack of exercise," Derek said. "Three, confinement. Man, that's killing me."

"Four, don't forget the food, Joe. It tastes somewhat different."

"Now let's try to analyze all of the changes."

"Okay, first, Joe I don't think our living quarters could have changed us. This place is three times better than our apartments and we are best friends. You can't be more compatible than that, right, Joe?"

"Right, maybe the confinement is the culprit. No, we've been confined before, especially in school. That was worse than this environment."

"And besides, we have always done projects together. Just you and me for weeks, all day and sometimes late into the night."

"What about the lack of exercise?" asked Derek.

"If it were lack of exercise, we would have noticed a change after the first week, and I haven't even thought about exercising consistently since before the meeting with the committee panel, and that has been for over three weeks."

"Well, I'm not one for alot of physical exercise, but I love to exercise my brain."

"Yes, and it looks like this act of mating involves some real exercise. Well, cardiovascular exercise anyway. Can you believe your heart rate increases well over one hundred beats per minute when you mate? Unbelievable!"

"Well, it can only be one thing," Derek said.

"Yes, the food." replied Joe. "That's got to be it!"

"Food, well, it does taste different than our normal nutrition. It tastes a lot better. Do you think it has been drugged?"

"It is either drugged now, or we have been drugged for twenty-six years."

"For twenty-six years. Come on, Joe. Could we have been drugged for that long? Well, I guess it wouldn't really surprise me with all we are learning."

"Sure, just think. Why is this training period so long? We could learn this material in one week."

"You're right about that, Joe. Hey, do you think that drug suppresses all these normal, you know, emotions or changes or whatever they are called. Could they have that much control over us? That definitely would make a man pretty angry."

"It sure would, but how are we supposed to know. If it wasn't for the Hall of Creation, we would have never known about these feelings, these emotions, these very unusual sensations."

"That's really scary, Joe."

"Scary? More like *unbelievable.* I guess they could have that much control over us if we are being drugged."

"I guess so. I'm sure it's possible," said Derek.

"Derek, you are just going to have to program this droid to give us some useful information, and it has to be soon."

"Why is that?"

"Well, we feel different, don't we?"

"Yes, I don't know what has come over me."

"That means the drugging or purification process could end any time, and I'm sure we will be shuffled out of here as quickly as we were shuffled in from our apartments. No warning. Just transported."

We agreed to work on Parrot every opportunity that was available, and needless to say, we acquired very little sleep during the next few days.

"Well, Derek, how are we coming?"

"I am nearly through with the circuit transfer, then establishing a direct alpha relocating switch to realign the beta cross-sectional resistor, plus the rewiring of the memory banks locator. Yes, that should do it."

"Oh great, that will take hours," I thought to myself.

"There we go!"

"There we go what?" replied Joe.

"That's it! I'm done."

"Well, what happened to the relocating switch and alpha rewiring of the—"

"I just did! Come on, let's see if we can get some answers."

"You're crazy, Derek! Are you sure it will work?"

"Sure. I can't believe you asked me a question like that. I am positive it will work, trust me."

"Okay, let's give it a whirl."

"Is your name Parrot?"

"Affirmative."

"Are you programmed to give Derek Johan and Joe Capuzzi special information that no one else is to receive?"

"Affirmative."

"Oh great! What if someone else asks that question?"

"Come on, Joe, do you think I am that stupid? You're working with the best, I'll have you know."

"Parrot, are you programmed to answer only to our voice pattern?"

"Affirmative."

"If this question was asked by someone else, what would be your answer?"

"I am not programmed to give information to that voice code."

"See, Joe, he'll only answer questions asked by us."

"Oh, he better or you know what will happen."

"Parrot, what time is it?"

"It is the tenth hour, and fiftieth minute standard of time."

"Oh no, Derek, the computers shut down in ten minutes. We'll have to wait until tomorrow morning."

"I hope that's not too late, Joe, but I'll tell you this. I'm so tired by the time I wake up, it will be tomorrow morning."

"True, I'm pretty tired too."

"Man, I could hardly wait that long. I hope we don't get shipped out tonight. You know it could happen."

"We could get up early before breakfast and try to get some information, and tomorrow before the afternoon classes, we can get the rest of the pertinent data," said Derek.

"Just think, we will know all about the past, the future, the other Star City, Gamnon, and much, much more. I can't wait until tomorrow."

"We better get to bed, Joe. Tomorrow is a big day."

I went to the bathroom and took out my toothbrush. I looked into the mirror and could hardly believe the events and changes that engulfed my life. I stood there for a while and just stared into the mirror, hoping that it would tell me what lay ahead. My face had changed somewhat, and my beard appeared dirty reminding me of the wire brush photos I found in the history library. My eyes were itching, all red, and they burned slightly from the lack of sleep. I also seemed to be losing more hair, but that could have been my imagination. I definitely appeared older than I actually was. My intense trance finally ended when the computer signed off, and the lights went out. It really felt good to brush my teeth. I wondered how long have men been brushing their teeth. Then, I paused, and with a small grin on my face, I thought maybe tomorrow I would find out.

"What are you doing in there, grooming?" Derek yelled from the other room. "Come on, let's get some sleep."

"I'm coming, Derek. Give me a break."

As I lay down on my bed completely exhausted, Derek exclaimed from the other bedroom, "I am really beat!"

"Me too. This bed feels great!" I bellowed from my quiet bedroom.

"I think our stay here is soon coming to an end. They sure have been cramming this information in lately," said Derek.

"Well, let's review this material so we know whats going on when we reach Gamnon. I don't want to look like a fool."

"Yes, we haven't studied or reviewed our lessons for days."

"I would hate to get there and act like we don't know which end is up."

"I'll review the information, and you correct me if I am wrong or if I miss something important, okay?"

"Yes, sounds like a good idea. It's all yours, Joe."

"The sole purpose of Gamnon is to promote the existence of our wonderfully perfect society."

"Yep, we have been told that forever."

"How long between mating periods? How many years, comrade?"

"Oh, four or five, I can't remember."

"It's five. A select group of very qualified men and women are chosen by the Committee and are to have…"

"Relations, Joe, relations."

"Oh yes, relations with women from Balem and produce a being. The gestation period is nine months, right Derek?"

"Right. Well, forty weeks is a little more than nine months"

"We are to live, work, eat, and sleep with our chosen mate. I hope I like her. That would be bad news if we didn't hit it off, kind of uncomfortable, you know, Derek."

"You can say that again. It would be awful!"

"Okay, there will be time for recreation, entertainment, relaxation, and fellowship, but will we be able to see each other or just our mate?"

"I don't know for sure. That part of Gamnon has been really unclear."

"Roger that, but there has to be some way we can find each other?"

"You know, Derek, it's starting to makes sense. Look, we have been doing everything together—eating, living, learning everything. They have been conditioning us to live with our mate by making us do everything in twos."

"Well, it makes sense to me."

"First, they choose our mate who has the same profession, intelligence, and qualifications. We probably even like the same food, entertainment—"

"That means that my mate will be a qualified, well educated, an extremely smart computer and design engineer?"

"It sure does, and my mate will be a pilot."

"At least we will be able to communicate since our professions will be similar."

"Yes, that's a good start, right, Derek."

"Yes, but what about this mating business. Do we really have to undress in front of them?"

"First of all, it's just one woman, Derek, and they have to take off their clothes too. Besides, the books say we will want to take our clothes off."

"Not me, old man," said Derek.

"Oh yes, you will. Anyway, then we come to the unification of our bodies."

"Yes, they declare that it's a natural state on Gamnon, and that we should partake in the pleasure whenever both of us agree to it."

"Unification! Wonder what our great-great-grandfathers called it?"

"Then, once unification occurs after an egg is fertilized, the fetus takes hold in the women's uterus."

"Uterus, that's an unusual name. Then another being, whether male or female, will grow from a fertilized seed into a baby."

"You know, Joe, that is pretty amazing! Listen, that mating stuff is kind of personal. Do you know what I mean? I don't know if I want to do it."

"Derek, you have to do it. Why do you think they chose you and gave you all this free food and trained you, and don't forget: no work for a whole year. Remember, you get all this free food and a great vacation."

"Yeah, you're right. I have to do something to pay for all these benefits."

"That's basically it, Derek. As soon as this being is born we pack up and go home. It sure seems like we are not going to want to just leave everyone?"

"What about our mate? Our little being?"

"Moving on, as this being grows inside the woman, it gets stronger and stronger until it is developed enough to be on its own. We have to make sure our mates eat right and exercise, and we have to take care of them if they get sick. We kind of oversee the whole process. Our job continues even after she has… What's that word, Derek?"

"Concide… concive… No, *conceives*, that's it."

"Right, then as her abdomen swells, the being grows, and they say we can feel it moving inside our mate. After nine months, the being decides to come out and live in our world. We are obliged to help it come out."

"That seems like the tricky part."

"Yes, first there are irregular abdominal pains caused by that organ called the uterus. Eventually, the pains come at regular intervals, and they are extremely intense. That means the being is progressing down the birth canal. That process sometimes involves a great deal of time."

"What if it comes early or upside down or the wrong way?"

"There are a certain number of women who specialize in those births. If there is a problem, they will assist."

"What if the being has some type of deformity or what if it's not strong enough to stay alive?"

"Then the being is eliminated. There is no room for imperfection in our society, at least that's what the book stated."

"Is it possible for the women to expire during the birth process?"

"Yes, they sure can if the birthing process gets complicated, or they have that syndrome… What's it called? Embo-something."

"Embolis… amniotic, I think."

"Yes, that's right. The birthing process may get complicated, and the baby and or the mother may die."

"There were other reasons too, Joe."

"I'm not real sure. No wait, the causes of death from the birthing process are extreme bleeding, infection, and toxic reaction."

"Toxic reaction?"

"Yes, if the symptoms are extreme, it involves a dramatic rise in blood pressure, an increase in pulse rate, swelling, and sometimes convulsions. The syndrome is called eclampsia."

"I hope they don't test us on this stuff. There is a lot to remember. Where does it come out, Joe?"

"Oh come on, Derek. You should know that."

"Just keeping you on your toes. How big is it when it comes out?"

"Small, I hope, for her sake. Right, Derek?"

"Right. I would think small would be good."

"Let me see. They say it usually weighs between six and eight pounds and is as long as a rollerball stick."

"Gee, you wouldn't think those muscles could stretch to let the little being out. I am glad it's not me having that being."

"That's an assignment I'm glad we don't get."

"What happens after the being comes out?"

"Now this is important, let me see. I know! First, we catch the little bugger, then we clamp the umbilical cord, in two places that is, and then cut in between the clamps. Then we put the being into a towel and rub its back until it starts to cry. Afterward, we give it to our mate."

"Cry? What's that?"

"It's some kind of noise the being makes to let you know he is well and alive and probably hungry."

"Now, we are nearly finished. After the being comes out, the woman expels the placenta which is the inside of the uterus that gives nourishment to the being while it's inside her."

"Did you see the picture of the placenta?"

"Yes, and I don't think I want to see it again."

"We are supposed to discard the placenta. Now remember, Derek, all this is done with her legs up in those things called, uh, stirrups?"

"Good, Joe, good. Great explanation."

"I wonder where they got the name of those leg things?"

"I don't know, but I will tell you this process of birth and all sure seems like a lot of trouble just to promote the society. You think in this day and age, they would have thought of another way to promote our society."

"They did try to find other ways, Derek. At least, that is what they told us. Remember, they gave up after years of experiments. It was called artificial artificial something."

"What went wrong, Joe?"

"I don't know, in fact, all it says is that the process was abandoned."

"Abandoned? I wonder why."

"I'm not sure, but something must have gone wrong. Let me get the book. Oh, yes, here it is. There were too many multiple conception along with other problems. I think we have had enough for now. I can't wait until tomorrow to see what Parrot has to say. I hope I remember all these questions I have.

"Yeah, I know. Me too! It won't be long now. Good night."

"See you in the morning bright and early!"

"Don't forget to set your wrist alarm. We want to be dressed and ready to go before the computer turns on at 0700 hours."

It took both of us a long time to fall asleep. For me, my mind kept bombarding me with what seemed like a hundred questions. I wondered why I was never allowed to meet the people who mated to produce me and what was the mark or sign placed on my ankle? It didn't seem fair for me to create this being and never be permitted to see it again. Shuffling these offspring, a being that has part of me inside itself, to Protectors, who were picked by someone else to teach them; it just didn't seem right. I also wondered about my mate, her thoughts, her personality, and her desires. I wondered if Gamnon was so simple as to put it all in black and white. It just seemed more complicated than that.

My mind became very uneasy, but finally, exhausted, I fell fast asleep.

CHAPTER 4

Historic Download

The cool, undisturbed night passed quickly, and soon it was time for Parrot to brighten up our morning. We had been awake for at least an hour, taking showers, getting dressed and trying to find something to snack on before breakfast. As we sat down to await Parrot's good morning cheer, Derek looked over at me and through somber eyes stated that he needed more beauty rest than I was allowing. Before I could speak, the power surged through Parrot's resisters lighting up the colorful display panel.

"Good morning! Wake up, you sleepyheads, wake up!"

"Parrot, we're right in front of you! What happened to your sensors?"

"Oh, you're not the only ones who gets a slow start in the morning. Give me a break. It's early you know!"

"It's pretty unusual for both of you to be up and ready to go before the alarm. Usually I have to yell and scream to get you out of bed. I can't remember any being getting out of bed and being ready to go to breakfast before the ten-minute cut off time," Parrot stated.

"Well, you sure will remember us! Good morning, Parrot," Derek said.

"Cheerful too, I see," said Parrot. "Are you fellows sick or something?"

"No Parrot, we're fine. We would like you to answer some questions if you're up to it."

"Affirmative. I have not been refreshingly stimulated so early in the morning for a long time. In fact, it was twenty-seven classes ago. Yes, yes, it was with storeowner Craig Jones. Carry on, fellows, I always have information for your inquisitive minds."

"Parrot, give us a brief, somewhat detailed account of man's early history."

"That is a very general question, sir. To cover each year, even ten-year time periods, would take a very long time. Highlighting the important ten years could bring us to this period considerably faster. Any ten-years chosen could then be reexamined in detail at any given time. Some of the categories to be selected could be religion, progressive politics, important people, wars, societies, countries, cities, states, races, geography—"

"Wait, wait. Parrot, you sure are loading us up with a lot of information."

"Joe, where do we start?"

"How about starting with some questions."

"Sounds good to me."

"Parrot, we will ask generalized but simple questions related to what we are concerned about, and we would like to have brief, direct answers. If more detail is needed, we will inquire for more assistance."

"Affirmative."

"Now you know why it took me so long to program this contraption. You are reviewing many—no, thousands upon thousands of memory banks. They all have to be explored, correlated, weeded out, and simplified to answer our questions."

"I know, Derek, and don't think for one moment that I don't appreciate everything you have done here."

"Let's continue, Joe. I'm just teasing you!"

"Okay, Parrot, here is your first question. We want you to give us a sequence of events, progressively in chronological order which led to the formation of the Star Cities."

"Affirmative. Man's quest for perfection and comfort started with a great influx of progress and technology beginning in the early years of the nineteenth chronicle, then called the nineteenth century. It lasted through to the nuclear Macrocaust approximately 150 years later. Man progressed through an age of telephone communications and horse and buggies to landing on the moon and developing satellite communication within one hundred years. This period was so fast and so traumatic to the human societies existing all over the earth that eventually it led to their nearly total destruction.

"There were seven major wars on earth during this period. The first six were fought with what was called conventional weapons. These included bombs, airplanes, tanks, gases, rifles, rockets and artillery."

"Parrot, can you give us some pictures of such weaponry?"

Many pictures of old weaponry began flashing on the screen.

"Derek, take a look at that arsenal. That stuff is downright dangerous. I wouldn't be caught dead holding on to that garbage."

"Yes, really. Continue, Parrot. This is getting real interesting."

"Affirmative. The final war was brief but the most devastating. It was brought about by a military computer malfunction unrecognized by both the world's super powers. Offensive nuclear missiles launched within seconds of each other utterly destroying the earth. It ended up as we see it today. Only a select group of scientists was prepared for such a catastrophe. All other societies were destroyed or mutilated to such a degree that the promotion of their existing societies were virtually unwanted by the scientists."

"What do you mean by that, Parrot?"

"Meaning that there exist societies isolated in many of the countries on earth, mainly underground. The radiation effects left by these nuclear devices were devastating, producing mutant forms of the human race. These few scientists eluded the destruction and retained normal genetic makeup giving the human race one more chance to survive as it existed for centuries."

"Parrot, does this mean that there are mutant societies of human beings living on earth today?"

"Affirmative, that is, only mutant societies."

"Are there any more survivors, and how genetically unstable are they?"

"Affirmative, there is one other society, living on a Spaceship colonizing the universe, that survived the Macrocaust. They are genetically undamaged."

"Derek, can you believe this information? All these years the Committee kept telling us that our perfect society was the only society that survived the Macrocaust."

"Parrot, who governs this other untarnished genetic society?"

"Commander Joseph Cavelli, a former pilot and defender of the existing Star City named Altaur."

"Parrot, how does this society survive?" Derek questioned.

"This rebel colony broke from our society approximately two hundred years ago and designed a self-surviving Star Planet that grows and produces every item needed to maintain and sustain life. It travels throughout the galaxy supplying the early Earth colonies created by the Starship with needed food, weaponry, clothing, and any item needed to survive in their environment. They also provide needed articles for the mutants on the Earth colony. They remain very close friends. Without this Starship, the earth and many of the Starships colonies would have perished."

"Parrot, what does this Starship call itself."

"It is called *Station America.*"

"America… America… Where did I hear that name? Derek, yes! Derek, that sounds familiar. Parrot, spell America, as it exists on the *Station America.* Show us a picture of this emblem."

"Affirmative. A-M-E-R-I-C-A. View it now below."

"That's it! Derek, look!"

"What? What do you mean?"

"Derek, do you remember that day we entered the Hall of Creation. We were all in the hallway, and the alien ship that streaked across the window. Remember, that ship just toyed with the Guardian ship. Then, quite suddenly, it vanished?"

"Yes, so what?"

"Well, I got a glimpse of the marks on that ship. I'll never forget it. It was America 77, and it was written just as Parrot displays it now. It was written on the underside of the wing. I remember it distinctly. It must have been from the *Station America.* I remember thinking about it for a long time. Do you remember you couldn't get me away from the transparent wall? The insignia had me puzzled and confused. I couldn't get those letters out of my mind."

"But, Joe, why America? What does America mean?"

"I don't know, but I am about to find out. Parrot, why was the name America chosen?"

"America was the name referred to a large group of states called the United States. This was a country, a very powerful country that existed before the Great Macrocaust. It was a nation made up of fifty separate states, each having equal representation throughout their government. The people who existed there were of many colors, races and religions. Both men and women lived together in peace and harmony. They coexisted within the most progressive and highest standard of living on earth. They were free to speak out and voice their opinion. They lived and were ruled by the laws of their Constitution, assembled early in their days of independence. Their symbol was the eagle, the sign of strength, power, and freedom. Their policy stood for life, liberty, and the pursuit of happiness. Their technology was the most enterprising, and they were the first country to use the might and power of the atomic bomb. The use of this bomb saved hundreds upon thousands of lives of their military personnel in the second of the World Wars. This country made history by forgiving its enemies and actually spent millions rebuilding the devastated countries. This country was also the first country to land men on the moon and run excursions into space. They were the first to develop a shuttlecraft and design and build early primitive satellite societies. The nation was destroyed with the nuclear war, the last war on earth.

"The *Station America* bases its operations more on being governed by the people rather than being governed by an all-powerful governmental entity. They proclaim that men and women should live in peace and harmony and govern themselves by electing officials based on their moral values and their political views to represent them.

"On earth and on *Station America*, men and women live, work, and are entertained together. They live in a group called a family. Each family consists of a man, a woman, and all the offspring created by this pair of human beings. As the beings grow and mature, they leave their original family unit to start their own family, never losing sight of their past heritage. Families grow larger and larger and many times throughout their lives they meet together, which is called a family reunion. The family is the backbone of their society."

"Parrot, are you telling us that is how *Station America* exists today as men and women did on earth before the Macrocaust?"

"Affirmative."

"Is the *Station America* at war with Altaur?"

"Gee, Joe, should we really ask that? What if—"

"Please, Master Derek, don't interrupt me. That is very rude."

"Sorry, Parrot."

"Forgiven. To answer the question, Master Joe asked before I was rudely interrupted. We declare that Star Cities are not at war with the people of the *Station America*—that is, officially we are not."

"Hey, Joe, maybe the *Station America* is where those laser smugglers were going to sell their goods. What do you think?"

"Could be, but with the technology of the *Station America* and their supplying of arms to their colonies, it doesn't seem likely. Those lasers were probably going to an earth colony."

"Yes, that makes more sense. They probably don't have the technology or maybe they don't have the materials to make the lasers."

"I would guess it's the lack of materials, Derek."

"Parrot, how far is the nearest earth colony from Altaur."

"The largest colony called the Omega colony exists within fifty kilometers of Altaur. The colony was established approximately at the same time as the Star Cities. After the Great Macrocaust, there was a split among the survivors. The mutant population that exists in the Omega community were band from the perfect society with its rules and regulations, so they organized on earth to start their own society. The other survivors who were not mutants developed and created the *Station America*. The mutant society helped develop and build the *Station America* but decided to stay on earth. They're very good friends. The last existing genetically normal survivors looked to the new frontier of unexplored space for their survival."

"Parrot, do the earth colonies live as we do here on Altaur and Balem or do they have the family unit?"

"They exist, like America, as a family unit."

"How do they survive?" asked Derek.

Parrot answered, "Survival... The mutant colony is a very intelectual society having extraordinary technical capabilities and research facilities. They designed the defense system of the *Station America* and supplied them with many electronic devices, computers, sensors, intricate propulsion units, and many other commodities. They exchange them for food, resisters, and expanded technology in agriculture. Also they receive supplies for their water purification facilities. A list of all exchange commodities is available upon request."

"Oh, by all means, Parrot, I'll take a printout, directly, that is," Derek said.

After a few minutes, the list started to appear at the base of Parrot's brightly lit computer panel.

"Joe, take a look at this list, lasers, fighter plane parts, communication and scanner devices, computers, high-tech alpha triaxle compositors. The list goes on and on. This society is brilliant. I sure would like to meet someone from these earth colonies. We could learn a lot from them."

"Parrot, tell us about the Star City, Balem."

"Balem is a replica of Altaur. They were built at the same time by the same scientists. At their completion, the scientist decided that in order to have a perfect society the males and females of their society should be separated. This idea they thought would eliminate crimes of passion, guilt, jealousy, greed, murder, rape, and according to the Committee, many more crimes."

"Parrot, does this mean that every building and every street number is exactly the same as they are on Altaur? That is a genuine, complete replica?"

"Affirmative, except for some minor differences."

"Wow, Derek, we sure are learning a lot this morning."

"You can say that again. How much time is left before we go to breakfast?"

"About thirty minutes."

"Great, I still have some unanswered questions, and the more information I receive, the more questions I seem to need answered."

"Parrot, elaborate on the destruction of earth and who was involved in the building and developing of our Star Cities?"

"Affirmative. There was a time in man's history where countries coexisted in peace. At this period of time, unknown to the populace, the major countries of the world—seven in all—were stockpiling nuclear arms proclaiming publicly that it was in the name of electricity and domestic development. The arms race went on for years, and two of the seven major countries were deeply involved in nuclear experimentation. The two countries were the former Soviet Union now called Russia and the United States of America."

"We have somewhat of an idea of this nation called America. Tell us about the country of Russia."

"Affirmative. The sovereign state of Russia is a vast country, most of which is barren tundra. The populace congregated mainly in the west and lived under a strong totalitarian-type socialist government. This government suppressed many ideals that were practiced in America and put strict controls over their people. Among some of these ideals were freedom of press, the right to vote, equality, and the design of a capitalist government. Commodities were rationed and the government proclaimed to the people the idea of working for the good of society. They survived to expand their territorial borders and spread their governmental beliefs of communism to the people of the world. They lived, worked, and died to promote their society which promised a socialistic empire that would provide security to its people at the expense of individual liberties."

"That explanation sure hits close to home, doesn't it, Derek? I guess we know who won the war, that no one really won, don't we?"

"We sure do and let me tell you I don't like the way things turned out."

"Affirmative," said Parrot. "Many of the ideals and principles that support the design of the Star City societies were those that existed within the great nation of Russia."

"Continue with the events leading up to the Macrocaust, Parrot."

"Affirmative. As the two countries were stock piling nuclear arms to secure their strength, the world grew concerned about the possibility of a nuclear accident or war, which would end all wars on the planet Earth. Inevitably, total destruction followed. Preceding the destruction of earth, were many demonstrations around the world in an effort to reduce arms and eliminate the possibility of a nuclear threat. Obviously, these demonstrations were futile, and the building up of nuclear warheads escalated. These governments assured their citizens that the probability of a nuclear war was very small.

"It apparently was all about energy-sharing. Hydrocarbon-heavy oil was the propellant in most engines. Many nations, most of them poor, China, Iran, Syria, Pakistan and North Korea, joined what was called 'the nuclear union.'

"But these weapons were seized by a radical organization in the name of Allah of Islam. The president, actually dictator of Iran, which along with Iraq was Persia, announced he wanted to help bring in a new earth government led by a mystical Mahdi. He said he wanted to 'wipe all Jews and the nation of Israel off the face of the earth.' Both the United States and a reconfigured England tried to stop the Persian leader, but he was hell-bent on killing Jews and anyone who came to their defense. (especially the nations of England and the United States.) That was the 'lay of the land' when the Macrocaust began, and sadly to say, the world order prevailed, and the earth was destroyed.

"A computer in Iran malfunctioned sending stragecally placed cruise missiles against Israel who then retaliated. Iran then used nuclear weapons followed by Israel's use of nukes. Subsequently, Iran's allies of North Korea and China joined in, at which time America and Great Britain fought back with nuclear missiles fired from submarines. The time period was early in the twenty-second century when several wars broke out all at once and several eager high ranking military officials expanded a war that no one could stop. There were thousands of nuclear missiles launched worldwide with Russia leading the pact.

"Seven hundred long-range missiles were launched from Russia, which previously pledged itself to Iran and the Arabs against Israel, many aimed at cities in the United States of America. The American defense system failed first and only 170 long-range nuclear missiles entered Russia. All major cities in the United States of America were destroyed. These included Washington DC, Chicago, New York, Houston, San Diego, Seattle, Atlanta, Sacramento, Los Angeles, Denver—"

"Move on, Parrot. That's too detailed. Go on, please."

"Affirmative. In the retaliatory effort of the United Sates 87 percent of Russia's major cities were destroyed. Missiles were being launched on every country in the world. After a brief period of time, the defense missiles were destroyed and missiles were exploding and being launched everywhere by every nuclear country. The countries of Japan, China, Australia, France, England, Italy, and Spain all joined in the fight. In a matter of weeks, the world was either destroyed by missiles or devoured by radiation fallout. Men and women who survived went underground giving birth to a new society of human beings."

"Parrot, how did the *Station America* evolve into a new society?" asked Derek.

Parrot continued, "Just prior to the great Macrocaust America sent a very large group of scientists and professionals into space to develop the first major Space Station. After news of the war reached them from the new earth society, they decided to stay in space to create a new society based on the principles of their own acclaimed government. Soon, the *Station America*, which already was in service began restructing the Starship on a principle known as the Intricate Core Principle. The *Station America* constructed an inner core of high technology and communication, and manufactured it to accommodate the expansion of their society. Piece by piece, the *Station America* added to its core as the society grew until it expanded to what is now one thousandth the size of the original United States. Its population as it stands now, with its colonies, is equal to the population of the combined Star Cities. It provides everything needed for its own population and contributes twenty persent of the needed commodities to the mutant societies on earth, including the Omega society."

"Parrot, describe the *Station America* giving us a detailed account of it's defensive capabilities."

"Affirmative. The *Station America* is a spherical spaceship made up of approximately 900,000 units. Each unit varies in size from 500 square feet up to 7,500 square feet. The agricultural section lies deep within the sphere and almost all of the important functions, such as the defense computers, communication capabilities, ventilation, direction and propulsion mechanism, and engine synchronization are located exactly in the center of the core. As the sphere grows outward, the less important sectors such as housing and entertainment among the few are moved toward the perimeter. The existing internal compartments are expanded to accommodate the growing population.

"The sphere contains three layers all covered by a protective layer of simatox, the hardest and most durable substance known to man, acquired on planet Mars. The inside layer on last report houses 150,000 sections. The middle layer houses 250,000 sections, and the outer layer houses 500,000 sections. Each layer can survive on its own and if any of the layers are penetrated, all can eject and travel in any direction desired. Each section contains fuel, engine power, supplies, technology, and leadership to start a new society. Although each layer has a specific function for the whole planet, they are basically all core societies breaking off and reattaching as spheres.

"The second layer is mainly manufacturing and accentuates the internal core. Only one-third of the population is in the housing sector at one time. The third layer which consist of the housing also holds the most important responsibility of the station, defense. A multitude of panels that also are made from simatox surround the sphere and can rotate 180 degrees to expose a complex droid-operated defense system with the weapons being controlled within the core of the sphere. The modules can be easily added on to in space for expansion. As you can see, it is highly impregnable."

"Parrot, does this mean that all important functions except for entertainment, housing, and defense are at the center core and only during an emergency do the other core layers separate to form their own sphere?"

"Affirmative. Nearly all of the defense sectors could be destroyed without the society within its core being destroyed. If the outer layer is destroyed, it is ejected, and the second layer becomes its defense, not as extensive but very effective, and can well defend the society."

"Parrot, what is the speed of the Star Planet and its layers?" Derek asked.

"The sphere can reach a top speed of 0.1875 the speed of light. That speed is considered slow, but progress in this field is under investigation within the research facility of the Starship. They have been experimenting with a new propulsion system, which is supposed to increase its speed by seven times. The smaller layers have a top speed of 0.5192 the speed of light."

"That's not to bad for their size!"

"Yeah, that's the speed of those cargo barges we fly for our precious society."

"Yes, the *Station America* sounds a little sluggish, but we have to consider the size and its mass-to-velocity ratio. I'll tell you what, though, the defense system must be phenomenal for it to travel that slowly."

"Affirmative. The defense system is technologically precise."

"Explain, Parrot," I said.

"Affirmative. The sphere is covered with approximately 140,000 anti aircraft, laser missiles launchers. It also contains 170,000 manned protector gun emplacements with 15,000 nuclear plutonic torpedo hangers. It is covered by a cylindrical force field and contains 3,000 landing bays, harboring approximately 45,000 aircraft. Of the 45,000 aircraft, 15,000 are transports, cargo and maintainance ships, the rest are military. The cargo ships move arms and supplies to different parts of the sphere and to the colonies. The transportation of commodities and arms can be done efficiently, and during a time of war, it's quicker to use the military ships. The maintenance ships also bring supplies, but their main function is to conduct repairs especially on the defense installations. The cargo and transports also supply the Omega facility and all the *Station America* colonies. Once the *Station*

America is within close proximity of the colonies, cargo, transports and maintenance ships under close protection of the fighter ships are sent to the satellite communities. The 30,000 aircraft, fighter, bombers, transports, and refueling vehicles are housed 15 ships per bay. These bays can release waves of five aircraft every three minutes. The whole task force could be launched in approximately 10 minutes. The *Station America* is quite infallible. It also has a radar system that can detect and identify artifacts as small as a waste container 300,000 kilometers away."

"Derek, this *Station America* is just unbelievable. I wonder how long it took them to put this Star Planet into operation."

"Approximately ninety years, not including the three years it took to design and blueprint the ship."

"You really did a great job on Parrot, Derek. I never expected him to be that precise or give us all that information."

"I never expected him to have all this information in his memory banks. His knowledge must be nearly unlimited."

"Unfortunately not," Parrot proclaimed.

"I only know what man has known before me, written down and placed in my memory banks. It feels good to get some of this rusty material out of my dusty circuit boards."

"Oh come on, Parrot. You nearly sound human. Derek?"

"Okay, okay, I thought I would throw that phrase in just to give us a break from all these facts."

"Well, Parrot, you nearly had me worried there for a minute. Derek, you're crazy."

"Back to business, Parrot. Let me see… Tell me about the *Station America*'s fighter plane."

"Affirmative. The fighter plane is very sophisticated. It maneuvers extremely well at very high speeds and can use ultralight speed if necessary. The ultralight speed can be sustained for approximately seven minutes before fuel consumption becomes critical for reentry. Each ship is equipped with a computer that analyzes the battle situation and gives several alternatives to achieve a certain task. There is an extensive navigation system and fuel efficiency is extremely high.

One gallon of fuel can last up to two hours under normal conditions and this is separate from the ultra-light speed fuel reserve."

"Can you believe that, Derek? What kind of fuel does it run on? I've never heard of a vehicle running for two hours on one gallon of fuel. That's hard to believe considering present technology but amazing that it can be done."

"What is the fuel, Parrot?" Derek said nearly instantaneously. "Unknown to the Star City Society."

"Wouldn't you know it. I guess I'd keep that a secret too," Parrot continued. "The fighters radar is very powerful and can identify any size object up to 100,000 miles away. Also, once the object is detected it automatically relays the information back to the *Station America*, this increases the range of the *Station America* to nearly infinity depending on how many fighters are released and how far they are spread out."

"Parrot, how long can the fighter ship run at the speed of light?"

"The Starships' fighter can run for approximately seven minutes on one gallon of fuel at the speed of light and they store three gallons on each fighter."

"Derek, that is unbelievable."

"Joe, don't sidetrack Parrot now. We need a lot more information."

"But, Derek, we can only run our fighter for three minutes on one gallon of fuel at light speed and we can only carry one gallon! That range is phenomenal!"

"Three minutes, seven seconds!" exclaimed Parrot.

"What... What are you talking about, Parrot."

"The time before running out of fuel, Master Derek."

"See, Joe, there's always someone sarcastic in the crowd. Don't you just hate these computers sometimes?"

"Yeah, yeah, let's get back on track. Parrot, what about fire power? How is this fighter equipped for battle?"

"Affirmative. Each fighter is equipped with four proton rocket feeders containing forty proton rockets each, plus twenty-five torpedo bombs and six laser guns—two in the nose and one on each side, plus two in the rear. Each laser gun contains enough power to fire constantly for twenty minutes."

"That's incredible, Derek. I sure would like to have one of those ships in my control. How about power and maneuverability?"

"The ship has three engines, enough power to fly rings around any Guardian ship and enough nuclear jump to reach light speed in fifteen seconds. It is the most efficient and maneuverable fighter ship known to man."

"No wonder the Guardian couldn't catch that ship."

"What ship, Joe?"

"Remember, the day we entered into the Hall of Creation."

"Oh yes, you keep referring to that incident."

"He was just playing games with that Guardian ship. Maybe that's why they don't bother our society. They are so technologically advanced that destroying us wouldn't be worth their time."

"Affirmative, Master Joe, and that is not their motivation. They are caring and loving people determined to live in peace."

"They sound like wonderful people don't you think, Derek?"

"They sure do!"

"Let's find out a little more about our own society, Joe. We can come back to *Station America* later."

"Oh, sorry, Derek. I seem to be hogging the computer. Go ahead, she is all yours."

"Okay, Parrot, once again why were men and women separated and why were the Star Cities created?"

"The Star Cities were designed to produce the perfect society. Every person in society has a designated function. Those who do not or cannot function for the good of society are exterminated. All citizens exist within the society to promote the well-being of that society. These men and women were separated to decrease or eliminate the importance and emphasis on greed, curiosity, emotion, passion, stealing, jealousy, hate, murder, rape. There are many more reasons, and all can be obtained in a printout upon request."

"Continue, Parrot. We will get that data later," I said.

"The society was to retain companionship, friendships, cooperative working atmospheres and healthy occupants. The separation was promoted to ensure an effort to be selective of specific professional growth and control the buildup of any one sector. The population is increased in a direct response to the number of positions available within the society, obviously upon a projected sliding scale. Each position has a set of extremely qualified veteran workers plus a number of students or apprentices, who are in the process of acquiring skills, growing of age and developing experience for the job. Since the birth rate has to be controlled, the death rate has to be controlled also. Beings who fail to meet the standards set forth by society are eliminated. Age has no boundaries. If the citizen does not perform their duties or are old and senile to a degree where they cannot support the society, they are eliminated accordingly. All comrades are well aware of the Hall of Sleep, Sector 666."

"We sure are. When I was small, my Protector always threatened me with the Hall of Sleep whenever I didn't study or do my homework. I always thought it was a place of detention. I never guessed they eliminated you there. It still puts the scare of Jacob in me."

"Well, I didn't know they sacrificed young and old alike. Did you, Derek? I thought it was for the very old who couldn't function properly and were a burden to our society, but old and young? Continue Parrot. This is getting to be very disturbing information."

"Affirmative. The Hall of Sleep is a sector used to eliminate citizens no longer useful for the good of the society. They are brought into a dining room and fed an elaborate meal. Then afterward, a colorless and odorless gas is piped into the room. The citizen gently falls asleep. It is painless, and life ceases to exist within seconds of the entrance of the gas. Their bodies are then cremated and discharged into the atmosphere."

"That's terrible, Derek, and they never know what's happening to them."

"Yes, poor old fellows... and young too. Who gives them the right to play God. They control the birth and death of their people. How diabolical."

"So, Derek, have you ever known anyone who went to the Hall of Sleep?"

"Yes, I never saw him again. Never really thought about it. Life just goes on."

"Parrot, enough about the Hall of Sleep. Continue with the description of the birth of the Star Cities."

"Yes, Parrot, finish your briefing."

"Affirmative. The Star Cities were designed to eliminate crimes of jealousy, greed and power. Cheating, stealing, murder and conspiracy were to be banished from the society. Anyone caught committing these crimes was sent to the Hall of Sleep. In fact, any crime committed will have the sentence of elimination by ejection or the Hall of Sleep, respectively, depending on the kind of the crime. Laws are enforced by the border patrols called the Guardians who number approximately one million. The so-called detention sector does not exist. It's just a scare tactic used to control the society. The Committee of elders governs the Star Cities. They make the laws, oversee the governments law enforcement agency, and perform duties such as judge, jury and prosecutor. The Committee is the only group of people that communicate between the two Star Cities and certain civilizations on earth and have no communication with *Station America. Station America*'s ships are eliminated if caught in Star City airspace or they attempt to. They have a hard time eliminating their aircraft.

They decide the times and pick the personnel for mating. The celebration given to the breeding of new beings occurs every five years. The law reads only the offspring of a given occupation can become a professional in that occupation. Subsequently, only a Committee member may breed at their own discretion and the only group who are permitted to raise their own offspring."

"Come on, Parrot. Your information is jumping between different subjects and the law? We know the law. Derek, is this a defect in the circuitry?"

"Sorry, Joe. It looks like some of the circuitry is overheating."

"Okay, let's wait a second." Joe paused.

The waiting becomes unbearable. "Parrot, what about Sector 5, the Detention Center?"

"Nonexistent. It is used to frighten citizens into submission."

"Submission. What do they do, just terminate you?"

"Affirmative."

"Oh, Great. What a bunch of lies. Continue, Parrot."

"Affirmative. Both Star Cities were created to be self-sufficient. They provide their citizens with protection, minor health care, recreation, food, clothing, work and entertainment. Nearly all debilitating diseases such as cancer, muscular dystrophy and heart disease were removed from society. Tobacco was banished, and alcohol has been subject to restrictions. These diseases existed only on the planet Earth many years ago, and their society tried to destroy and entirely eliminate these diseases. They also cared for people afflicted with the disease. After the Macrocaust, most all diseases were eliminated by its virtual destruction, and the forefathers of the Star Cities eliminated any human being not up to their standards of intelligence, strength, and physical appearance. All humans born with or developing malformations were and still are eliminated in the Hall of Sleep.

"Tobacco was an addicting form of plant material that was chewed or smoked. Smoking is the inhaling of smoke produced from the ignition of this substance. Alcohol was a liquid substance similar to what you know as spirits, except much stronger and it affected certain centers in the brain, dulling the senses and reflexes. It was used as a pastime for entertainment in the Old World. It was sold in stores all over the earth and has been in use, nearly, since the beginning of time."

"Sounds like Lysino."

"Affirmative. Lysino is the controlled spirit used in the Star Cities for mind relaxation and stress control. The only difference is Lysino is metabolized very rapidly and, within an hour, is totally eliminated from the body by the kidneys. It is therefore noncumulative, eliminating the detrimental side effects shown with alcohol, such as slowed reflexes, nausea, vomiting, and amnesia. Our spirits enlighten the mind and make it more attentive, sharp, and clear. Alcohol, a drug, clouded the mind and made some people violent and capable of committing acts of crime they would not do in a normal state of mind. Memory loss and retrograde amnesia were produced when large quantities were consumed. It was fermented from nearly any type of plant or vegetable and in high concentrations could be very combustible.

"Tobacco was a plant that after drying could be lit, producing an addictive but enticing smoke that was inhaled into the lungs of the human species. Its addictive nicotine factor led to many deaths from its abuse. The result of long-term smoking was respiratory insufficiency and cardiac disease. It also stimulated a cancer type cell that replaced and destroyed normal cells."

"I can't understand why the society wanted their members to destroy themselves, can you, Joe?"

"Master, the economic gains in society based on a monetary system were far more important than the lives who lived in it. May I continue?"

"Sure, Parrot, of course! I didn't think we were interrupting so much."

"Me either, Derek."

"Sir, these interuptions must stop!"

"Yes, Parrot, forgive me. Continue."

"The Star City concept was constituted to eliminate the classes—for example the rich, middle, and lower class of people. The wealthy designed a certain class of handpicked individuals for the Committee and the initial plebeians, consequently retaining their power and notoriety. This segregated communial system was implemented after the great Macrocaust completely eliminating all divisions of people. Previously, on earth the whole society was centered around money power and religion. Land, money, and power brought much success to many individuals, while almost all of the society lived basic, stress fill lives, and merely struggled to survive. The positions held in your society are controlled, and everyone works to promote the society's private welfare, with all positions made equally important. The Star Cities were developed to make the perfect society."

"Perfect, perfect! Derek, did you hear that? I wonder in whose eyes were we supposed to be made perfect."

Parrot continued, "And in order to replenish the citizens, the working body of society, every five years, hundreds of qualified men and women would join to produce offspring, which are subsequently taken by the respective Committee members to be redistributed to hundreds of qualified Protectors. These Protectors raise and teach these new beings to become perfect citizens. No contact is ever made with the mates who produced and birthed the beings."

"You know, Joe, it sounds nearly barbaric when he explains it."

"I know."

"You are being very rude now!" exclaimed Parrot.

"What did you do to this computer, Derek? He's pretty abusive. Proceed."

"The Star Cities are protected by their police force called the Guardians, and the most important function carried out by the Committe is to survive, grow, and maintain their basic philosophy of total control. The Guardians' main concern is to defend against outside intervention of any kind. The Guardian troops are trained and monitored constantly to uphold these basic principles to the very end—that is, with their lives if need be. Anyone defying its principles is sent to the Hall of Sleep."

"Parrot, how many—"

"Whoa, Joe, I programmed him. Aren't I entitled to some time here too? I have a couple question that I would like to ask."

"Sure, Derek, of course. I just got carried away. He's all yours. Just fire away."

"Thank you, Parrot. Tell us what to expect at Gamnon. Explain more about women and their personalities. How are we supposed to act in front of them?"

"Affirmative on all accounts. First Gamnon was built five years after the creation of the first Star—"

Buzz, buzz, buzz, buzz. Suddenly the door opened.

"Derek, what's going on? Man, I'm really getting tired of all these interuptions!"

"Relax, Joe. Let's see what's going on out there."

Over the loudspeaker and room intercom, a voice said, "Please leave your rooms now. It is time for you to meet your mates and strive to promote our society. Prepare yourself to meet your mate by entering the space shuttles available to you. Leave by Sectors. Take nothing but your personal bag containing your books, and be prompt."

"I thought we might have had several days left. We didn't even get breakfast."

"Breakfast, Derek? Is that all you can think about? Food? Come on, we have to find somewhere to hide your tools. We may need them again sometime."

"Oh no, not again. I'm really getting tired of doing this, Joe!"

"Look, I can put some in my side pocket, and I'll just leave some books behind. We can put some in your bag."

"Here, Joe. I have room, but I've got to be crazy to keep on doing this. It's not even challenging anymore."

"Hey, put the rest in here."

"Okay, let's go," remarked Derek as he started to walk toward the door.

As Derek left, I followed, and within minutes, we entered the shuttle. I felt a strange feeling come over me as I left the room. I felt somewhat wiser and more knowledgeable but wasn't quite sure what to do with all the new information. I felt starved for more material and somewhat cheated because Parrot didn't have time to relay all the important data we needed. I felt curious about the person I was about to meet and anxious to experience the act we had been given to learn. My mind was confused about my mate, *Station America*, Earth, and the Star Cities. I felt lost and afraid for a brief moment, something I had never felt in my life. What were these feelings? Why was I feeling them? Could there actually be a place where Derek and I could live free of tyranny, of complete control by a small group of individuals who thrive on power and suppressing the minds of their loyal citizens? Is there a possibility that we can contact them and see if we would be accepted and eventually allowed to be a part of their community? All these questions I needed to be answered, and I wanted them answered right now.

CHAPTER 5

Journey To Gamnon

Crisp, cool air moved in this morning as the sun slowly rose over a quiet, somber eastern sky. The sky furnished a colorful array of orange, red and yellow colors streaking across the vast heavens, streaming with serous cumulus clouds. The shadowed gray tint of night soon became day. Some puffy white clouds appeared from the south, scurrying quickly across the sky. Engulfed, I was delighted that there were some beautiful events that even man could not destroy. I felt blessed to be alive and able to take in this beautifully painted masterpiece.

The time in the shuttle went by quickly, and soon we had our first glimpse of Gamnon. It was somewhat larger than it appeared to be from Altaur, but sure enough, it was also a mirror image of our Altaur. I always thought Gamnon would be something different for a change, but it was nice to be somewhere with somewhat familiar surroundings. I sat there fairly relaxed for a while, and then a thought entered my mind that wasn't very pleasant. I knew that Derek and I would be separated, but for how long was hard to calculate. I thought they may just isolate my mate and me from everyone, as a matter in fact, isolate everyone from everyone. It sounded so cruel, but keeping us separated would be difficult especially with our desire to see each other.

"Derek?"

"Yes. What's up?"

"Now listen, we have to find each other after we meet our mates. Somehow, someway, okay?"

"Hey, I am sticking to you like a power vacuum seconic magnet. They will need *Station America*s to tear us apart."

Suddenly a deep voice spoke over the intercom. "We will now assign you to the following sections so please write down your block number. This will facilitate entrance into the proper cylinder."

"Cylinder? What is that?" Derek asked.

"I'm sure we will find out soon!"

To assign everyone aboard to a cylinder took about ten minutes. Derek and I had cylinders 340 and 520 respectively. Both of us were very determined to see each other at some point on Gamnon.

We made a pact to try and communicate as often as possible. We hoped there would be communicators in every block, and if we were really lucky, they would correspond to the cylinder numbers.

That was about the most we could ask for right now. The shuttle dropped us off one by one, and it seemed like hours from the time Derek was dropped off until they called my cylinder, but recording the time proved it only to be thirty minutes. I hoped we were fairly close. The time was about 8:30 in the morning, and I finally reached my port. The cylinder port was about seven feet high but was somewhat tight as it closed in around me. As it closed tight, I could feel the pressure building up on my shoulders. As the door clicked, I dropped my bag to the floor. Then the cylinder seemed to ease around me compensating for my larger features. I began to feel lightheaded, and after a moment, I could feel a high-energy field fill the cylinder. I became sleepy for a moment. Then as I opened my eyes, I could feel a cool breeze flow over my body. The energy field had stripped me of my belongings, and I stood naked, cool, and curious to what was going to happen next.

The cylinder started to get darker and darker until just a small soft light shown from above me. I could smell a sweet inviting type of odor that was hard to relate to anything I had ever smelled before. It put me into a kind of hypnotic trance, but I was still aware of everything occurring inside and outside of the cylinder. Then, the cylinder started to turn very slowly, and within minutes, it started to rise, taking me into another larger but inviting room. I heard the cylinder lock into place, and I sensed it was time to join my mate. I tried to move, but I was unable to do so. It was a very strange feeling, not having control of my movements.

The light from above brightened, and the room lights dimmed. It took a few minutes before I could virtually see anything ahead of me. My eyes adjusted to the dimmed light outside. I could see another cylinder rising about twenty feet across the room. As it rose to the level of the floor, the light from the top of that cylinder began to fade into darkness. As it snapped into place, the light began to get brighter and brighter. The silhouette of her body became clearer and brighter every second. I tried to move once again but was unable to stir.

My senses were keen, and my vision was finally restored, but I was unable to move a muscle. The cylinder suddenly and without warning started turning, and soon I would no longer be able to see her. As I turned now with my back toward her, I started to wonder what was going through her mind. Soon, I was once again face-to-face, and her cylinder started to rotate. It also made one complete turn, and my eyes were filled with the most remarkable creature I had ever seen. As her cylinder locked into place, a voice sounded. The voice was not deep like mine but higher pitched and very gentle and soft. I wondered if it were her own voice or just a computer generated one.

"Hello. My name is Dawn. I am of the species that lives on Balem. I'm your chosen mate. My age is…"

As the voice continued, the light inside her cylinder illuminated at the same time mine faded. Very distinctly, it shimmered over every feature of her gentle appearance. She stood in full splendor, glowing, sparkling. I'd never seen anyone so beautiful as her. She explicitly surpassed the physical appearance explained to us by our good friend Parrot. She was much more beautiful. Her features, highlighted by the now brilliant glow of light above her, reminded me of an ancient flower called a rose, which was the most beautiful flower found on earth.

She stood about five feet six inches tall with petite features and exhibited long, flowing, sunny blond hair. Her eyes were dark, but they sparkled vibrantly from the glowing cylinder light. Her skin was flawless and delicate. I knew it must have been smooth and soft. She displayed an array of freckles down her neck, leading to a superbly developed body. Wow! The briefing had referred to several parts of her anatomy, but seeing her body, well, it wondrously topped the briefing. Her muscles were in perfect tone, and she looked strong and confident, but her face showed signs of gentleness and compassion. A brilliant circle of gold hung around her neck, and her golden hair flickered off the shining light. Her smile was inviting, and the dimples on her cheeks made me think she might have a warm and tender heart. Her body seemed firm, and her eyes glowed with a longing to be held. Once again, the other cylinder started to slowly turn. Her profile was one of exquisite beauty, and her figure was petite and hour glass in appearance.

My heart started palpitating, and my body was filled with the passion of being next to her. Then, distracted for a brief moment, my mind started to wander trying to figure out how I changed and what was happening to me. I felt somewhat strange and insecure. This feeling had never been a part of me before this time. I also wondered about the thoughts she was having of me. Would she like me? Want me to be her one and only mate? Would she talk to me? Was her desire as strong as mine? I just want to know so much more about her… her life… her world… her mind. I wanted to touch her, be close to her—become part of her. I felt confused, withdrawn, and weak. My mind was clouded with thoughts that had never entered my mind before this unforgettable moment. I wasn't sure if this was reality, or if it was even proper to feel this way. What if she is not attracted to me? But that doesn't matter because we were sent here to mate—promote our society and no matter how she feels this act will happen no matter what she thinks. We have been chosen. But I feel more than that for her. I want her to like me, understand my ways, desire me, and communicate with me so I can understand both her and myself more clearly.

This gas is really strong, and it sure seems to be playing a wild trick on my mind, or is it? I hope she feels the same desire as I feel for her. I want both of us to feel the same desire to care for each other and help one another. This act of mating would be so much more meaningful if we have the same strong sensation together.

Where are these strange thoughts originating? Do I think these thoughts in my mind, or do I feel them in my heart? If this sensation comes from my heart, has it been with me since the beginning of my life? Did our Creator feel the same way? So much has happened to me in these few moments it nearly frightened me. And believe me, it's the only time that I can remember ever being really, really frightened. Then again, I'm not sure what I'm afraid of now. I'm the best pilot in our fleet, and I was taught never to fear anything. Competition, battle, flying, life and even death, none of these situations possessed the fear I was discovering this very minute and so fast, so very fast these strange thoughts entered my mind. What is going to happen next? Will we mate? Will we talk?

Soon, my cylinder started to turn, and within a few seconds, I knew it was her turn to discover me. I felt my mind at ease, and soon, I was once again in control of my senses. As my back faced her, I realized that I hadn't heard a word that was said about her. I started to wonder how I was going to find out what had slipped by me so fast.

"My name is Joe. I am a pilot for protection of Altaur. I am twenty-six years old and have many hobbies, but my main interest is…"

Dawn's thoughts began to race. *Oh, he looks so strong and valiant. He reminds me of the old gladiators who use to do battle in the coliseums of the Ancient cities. Yes, yes, a much better specimen than that projected on my scanner. Wonder if he flies as good as he looks. His eyes look so kind and gentle. His body exquisitely structured. This gas is really getting to me. He looks like a powerful man. His clean appearance, clean-shaven face, neatly cut hair profiled his image as an outstanding well-educated gentleman. His arms and legs look so firm, so muscular. I hope he likes me, and we can understand each other's needs. My desire grows stronger as the cylinder turns, and I pray his desire is as strong for me as mine is for him. I have never felt a need to have someone care about me this way. I am puzzled about this impulse to need and want someone only for myself. How self-centered. Why am I thinking this way? Has my mind lost control and have the desires of my body overcome the discipline of my mind? I don't understand what is happening to me. I feel faint, lightheaded—No, Dawn, you can't. Be strong and don't let him see weakness. Oh, it smells so sweet and pleasing. I want to touch him. Hold him!*

Like Joe, Dawn struggled to stay in control. She was feeling different and capricious.

This gas produced in the cylinders filled the mind with physical pleasures unknown to us. It was developed early after the Macrocaust and perfected long ago to assist in the act of mating. It produced a state of mind that obscured the unwanted emotions of shyness. It clouded the mind's power of reasoning and produced an undying desire to mate at any cost. There was no time for waiting or getting acquainted because their skills were needed as soon as possible back in their own societies, and their most important function was to produce a healthy normal being—to promote the society. As the cylinders came to a halt and slowly descended into the floor, they together had one and only one innermost thought—for her to become a part of this tall strong sensual man and for him to produce an image inside her that will one day live, breathe, and carry on the duties given to him by his Protector, just as he did these past twenty-six years.

The gas now started to fill the huge living quarters where they stood staring at each other with an unusual desire that neither of them understood. Still mesmerized by the gas, we watched the once very large empty room turn into a very comfortable living area. Out of the walls, ceiling, and floor emerged every piece of furniture, appliance, and modern convenience needed to live a very comfortable life. They stood in the area designated as the mating room. A bed appeared out of the floor, and the walls turned into brilliant mosaics of ancient artwork. A fan slowly turning appeared above the bed scattering the gas particles all over the room. The cool breeze surrounded their sensuously torrid bodies. A sitting chair appeared next to the bed, and a vanity emerged from the wall opposite the chair. Two end tables appeared on each side of the sleeper and a soft yellow lamp evenly lit up the room. I felt the blood come back into my hands and feet again, and I finally could move my body.

Dawn moved closer to me, and soon we embraced. She felt so wonderful. Her skin was soft and smooth, so much better than I could imagine from the cylinder. Our lips met, and our bodies were now filled with more desire than ever. We lay down on the bed and held and cuddled each other for such a long time, while not saying a word. It felt like an eternity, but soon, sooner than we imagined, we were both locked in a very close endearment—feeling, cuddling, kissing, caressing, embracing the time we waited so long for, to be together.

After mating, we both lay close to each other, massaged by the gentle breeze produced by the fan. I felt her hand slowly and firmly grasp mine as we quietly relaxed close to each other. A feeling of relief and satisfaction that I had never experienced before lay within me. The gas slowly dissipated, and I started to regain my senses and feel more like myself.

"Hello, Dawn."

"Hello, Joe. What an experience! Oh my was that beautiful."

"You can say that again. I sure felt awful strange. I felt mesmerized. That sweet gas sure gave me a scare. I felt so out of control. That's something I make sure I never feel." Joe was laying on his back looking up toward the fan. Dawn came closer and rested her golden blond hair on his chest.

"I didn't hear a word that was said about you in that cylinder, Dawn. Now it nearly seems like a dream."

"I thought I was the only one not paying attention!"

We both laughed for a while, and then fell fast asleep. I can't recall how long we slept, but it felt like a very long time. I woke up before her, and as I moved toward her, she opened her eyes. The same sparkle filled her eyes, and it reminded me of that beautiful evening when the sky was saturated with the flickering of a billion stars. I reached over and brushed away the hair that gently flowed over her cheek. Her skin felt so silky and soft. It was so pleasant to touch and embrace.

Then, just as refreshing as a cool breeze of air on a midsummer's night, she smiled and moved closer to me. A soothing feeling rushed through my body. Her hand reached up to my shoulder and slowly moved down toward my fingers, caressing each muscle along the way. Her lips touched mine, and our hands met in a firm embrace. This gesture reassured us both of the strong feelings we started to have for each other and strengthened the thought of establishing a long and meaningful relationship together.

After our embrace, I went to the bathroom intending to shower trying to take this sleep from my eyes. "I'm going to take a shower, Dawn. I hope that will wake me up a little."

"I've got to brush my teeth. I know that will make me feel better."

"What did you say?"

"Oh nothing. Are you hungry, Joe?"

"Yes, a little. In fact, I am real hungry."

"Good. I'll see what I can whip up for lunch."

"That sounds great. I'll give you a hand as soon as I finish my shower."

"Oh, don't bother! I want to see if you can tolerate my cooking. Hey, I'll make you a deal."

"Okay, Dawn. What's the deal? It reminds me of Derek, and all the deals he try to make with me."

"What?"

"Oh nothing. What kind of deal?" Joe asked again.

"I'll make dinner, if you clean up the mess."

I turned on the shower and could barely hear what she was saying, but it sounded like a great deal to me.

"What? Clean up the mess? I'm having a little trouble hearing you with this shower making so much noise. Oh yes, that sound great. I don't mind cleaning up at all. In fact, I'd be honored to do that for you."

I took quite a long shower. The warm water felt so good massaging my body. This shower was larger than the one in my living quarters, but then there was no reason for mine to be any bigger. I daydreamed for a while thinking how nice it would be to hold her close to me and let the water caress and massage our bodies together. I thought about it for a long time and decided that I would suggest it in the near future. Then I started to laugh.

This thought would have never occurred to me if I was never picked to come to Gamnon. I must be a lucky guy.

"What is so funny?"

"Oh, I was just thinking of how nice it would be if both of us could enjoy this shower at the same time."

"That's funny!"

"No, no. It's just that I would have never had that thought if I wasn't chosen and hadn't ever met you. I wonder where all these ideas come from anyway."

"Now that you mention it. That would be kind of exciting."

"We both laughed for a moment, and then there was complete silence except for the gentle sound of running water."

"Are you still there, Dawn?"

"Oh yes. I was just thinking about us."

"What? I can't hear you. What did you say?"

"Oh nothing important. Hey, dinner is ready. Hope you like it!"

"I'm sure I will. I'm starving. I'll eat practically anything."

"Now, if it is not to your pleasing, I want to know. I want you to be perfectly honest with me."

"Was that included in the deal?"

"You betcha it is!"

"You what?"

"What did you say?"

"I never heard that expression before. You betcha."

I shut off the shower and proceeded to dry off wondering if I felt merely more curious or genuinely interested in her. She was quite different from the company I associated with most of the time. Then, I thought of Derek and how he was getting along with his mate. For a good bit of time I had completely forgotten him.

"Dawn, is there any way we can communicate with the other residents who came to Gamnon?"

"I don't know. Let's check out these living quarters."

"I'll check the kitchen and living room. You check the bedroom and hallway."

"Dawn, over here. This is exactly like our communicator on Altaur. In fact, it is in the same place, right here in the hall next to the door."

"Ours is on the other side of the door. In fact, this hallway goes to the right instead of the left, except we have a comfortable little sitting area where our communicator is located."

"You must spend a lot of time on it."

"Oh, I'm on the com most of the time I'm at home. It's a great pastime and a great way to exchange news and information."

"Exchange news and information?"

"Yes, most of the time we hear it before the Chronicle can get it into print so we can spread the news faster. Besides, it's more fun to hear it from your friends."

"Let's see if I can find my friend. You are going to like Derek. He's my best friend. We grew up together and have spent nearly all of our adult lives together—that is, except for our professions. He's a genius at computers."

"That's a coincidence because my best friend is in computers too and talk about a whiz at computers. She works on all the defense scanners for Balem."

"Matching them up could be a real treat. I hope we can all get together. Do you think that they were? No, that's nearly impossible."

"What, Joe, what's impossible?"

"Oh, that they were selected as mates just like us. The chance of that happening is really remote. Oh well, I'm going to try to reach Derek. Communicator, I would like to get in touch with the living quarters 340, please."

"Joe, what did you say?"

"Hold, please. It's 340, why?"

"That's Pam's number. We made sure to remember the cylinder number in case we were able to correspond with each other."

"I can't believe it! Really? They are sure going to be surprised. Let's play a little joke on them."

"Sure, but how?"

"We won't use visual. They won't know who it is! Maybe, they'll think it's a Committee member checking up on them."

"How are you going to use the communicator without visual?"

"Oh, I'll just disconnect this wire here until we have had our fun. Just a little technique Derek showed me. We play tricks on citizens all the time at home… There, it's done. Okay, relay my message communicator, living quarters 340, please and make it quick."

"Make it quick! First, my name is Zithron, sir, and I'd appreciate a little respect from you if you are going to use my services."

"Well, excuse me. It's amazing what these things can do. It just amazes me." Joe's voice turned to a whisper. "He's even got a name."

"Thank you, sir."

"Okay, let's get on with it, Zithron."

Buzz. Buzz. Buzz.

"Yes, this is Derek speaking. Apartment 340."

"May I speak to Pam, please."

There was a pause, and I repeated my command. "Please. Is Pam there?" I turned to Dawn. "Look, Dawn, I think I finally got Derek. I think it's the first time ever."

"Oh, ah yes, she is right here. Can you hold?"

"Yes, thank you." There was a moment of silence. Then our visual popped on, and Derek was sitting right there, looking at me straight in the eye.

"That's not fair, Derek! I had you, and by the way, you never showed me how to return visual from the other end."

"Well, I can't show you everything. Then you won't need me, right, Joe?"

"I'll always need you, one way or another. Hey, how you doing?"

"Fine, fine, but how did you know Pam's name. You nearly threw me for a second."

"You are not going to believe this, but—"

Just then, in a loud voice from the kitchen spoke, "Pamela! Pamela! How are you doing?"

"Dawn, Dawn," came bellowing through the communicator.

"Yes, I just can't believe it! Two best friends mating with two best friends! The odds must be a million to one. It will probably never happen again, not in a thousand years."

"What are you doing later? They can't keep us cooped up here forever."

"Nothing. Maybe we can meet somewhere. By the way, what are the laws here, Joe?"

"Laws, Derek! Come on! Since when do you abide by rules and laws?"

"You're right. I never thought I'd ever say that. Oh, Joe, there's a booklet at the bottom of the door. Go get it, and we will see what this place has to offer. Maybe we can meet up for a couple spirits, later."

Dawn came in from the kitchen and went over to the door to retrieve the booklet.

"Dawn, check the door and see if we are prisoners."

"Hey, it's open, Joe."

"That's great news, Dawn. We can meet up with Derek and Pam anytime."

She hurried back to Zithron and sat next to me just as curious to know what was going to happen later as I was.

"It says here that there are no restrictions. We can get food and clothes at the commissary, swim, bike, participate in our normal sporting activities, and practically do anything we want to during the day. The only requirement for us is to work out at the simulators hopefully keeping up with our skills and reflexes. There is a fifteen-hour-per-week time requirement, but there is no specific time for our sessions. We just have to show up."

"Not for us, although we are encouraged to work an eighteen-hour week accruing our time in a workshop building some kind of portable security system. Must be something new. Oh, and we can take as much as four hours per week for research."

"This is like a vacation. There has to be a catch, but I tell you if there isn't, I think I'm going to enjoy our time here."

"Oh good, we can meet for dinner three times per week. Let's use our first one tonight."

"Sounds good."

"Dawn, let's see the map. Let's try Kognites. Do you see it on the map between Section 63/D and Section 52/F?"

"Oh yes, there it is. Sounds like a winner."

"Good about seven?"

"Perfect. See you then. Signing off."

"Sign off, Zithron."

"That's wonderful. For a moment, I thought I might not see Derek during our extended stay, but that's taken care of so let's see what you prepared for lunch."

We sat down to a beautifully decorated table. There were two tall thin candles spread about six inches apart, sparkling in the middle of the tablecloth. Two beautifully laced placemats colorfully brightened up the ends of the table. Utensils glistened and a beautiful flower arrangement was placed in the middle of the candles. Crystal goblets with a gold-flaked rims sat adjacent to the tastefully designed clay made china.

"This dinner table is set for the Committee Chairman," I said.

"I meant it to be… The decorator helped somewhat I surely didn't bring all this from home."

As the words left her delicate lips, she looked at me with those tender, caring eyes and stated, "To me, you are a Committee Chairman."

That gesture of respect made me feel very strong, a man who could not be defeated.

It reminded me of a statement Parrot made during our period of learning. "'She'll make you feel like a man with strength and power beyond your imagination."

"This is very special to me, and you are an exquisitely beautiful woman."

She smiled, not saying a word, which just filled me with distinctive feeling of warmth and happiness.

"Thank you very much, Joe," she said.

I proceeded to uncover my dish, and to my surprise, the meal was a sight to see. It didn't look like anything that my Protector or I ever prepared. The colors were distinctive. There were long, skinny vegetables proclaiming a bright purple and yellow color. Some small round bead-like substances were shiny red and blue with two distinctly different white sauces covering the mixture.

There were some orange leafy type vegetables that were covered with chunks of a certain type of meat. I wasn't real sure of what any of it was exactly, but it was very colorful.

"It… It looks great! Uh, never have seen anything like it."

"I hope you like it, Joe. It's one of my own specialties. I was surprised they had all the ingredients here on this Star of Creation."

"I'm sure I will, Dawn. I'm sure."

I took my fork, which actually looked more appealing than my food, and scooped up some red and blue nourishment. To my astonishment, it was rather tasty.

"This is exceptionally good," Joe remarked.

I kept eating, not stopping to say a word, and before I knew it, my plate was empty. "That was very flavorful. I really enjoyed that meal although I do have to admit I was skeptical at first."

She started to smile and quietly broke out into a subtle laugh.

"May I have just a little more, please?"

"Sure, I'll get it for you, Joe."

She brought back some more, and I ate with even more vigor. "I guess I was kind of hungry."

"I'm glad you like it."

"In fact, that was excellent, Dawn. I can't remember the last time I was served such a delicious meal."

"I was hoping to impress you."

"Well, you sure did."

I got up from the table and politely gathered up the dishes and utensils taking them into the kitchen.

"Please, Joe, I'll do that. You don't have to bother. Go relax in the living quarters."

"No, no, that was a very delightful meal, and I feel it's my duty to clean up the mess. Why don't you go put some music on and see if you can find out how we get to the simulator?"

She moved to the living room, and soon I joined her. As I approached the living quarters, I could see Dawn stretched out on the couch reading the latest flying magazine. The music she put on was as different as the meal we had just finished, but I was pleased to have some soft music after dinner. I went over and sat next to her, raising her head and putting it into my lap.

"Your music is as strange to me as your food, but just as with your food, I sort of enjoy it."

"Oh, I didn't really think about it much. I keep forgetting our lives are so different. We will listen to your music right after this piece."

"Sounds great. By the way, do you think we can catch up on our personel history lesson since we both missed it earlier?"

"Yes, Joe. You go first."

"Well, my Protector was, at one time in his life, one of the best pilots on Altaur. He was given to me just after he retired, and I was his first and only pupil. He was a veteran of fifty years in the field of aviation and had been fighting in the intergalactic wars for twenty-five years. It was amazing to me that he had survived all that time. He achieved 175 distinguished awards, the highest ever achieved. He was a great man so great. He taught me everything he knew, including his secret for staying alive."

"How interesting. What was his secret, Joe?"

"Well, his philosophy was to be the best pilot anywhere in the universe, and to achieve this feat, you needed dedication, knowledge, ambition, skill, determination and of course being blessed by the Creator. Also, one of the most important pieces of knowledge you can have is a good profile of your opponent. He studied over the plans to every mission and calculated the risk factor. If the risk outweighed the survival factor, it was aborted or changed to increase the survival factor. The lowest risk to survival factor was 1:1. He always told me there are always two sides to a coin. If one side doesn't work, the other one will."

"Did he ever turn down a mission, Joe?"

"Yes, one mission to the Cintron galaxy, and the man who took the mission never returned. He believed that there was always a means to achieve your goal, but the key was finding the right avenue. This was the only mission in his sixty years of service that he felt was impossible."

"The Cintron Galaxy?"

"Yes, but there weren't many missions that were deemed impossible, and through careful planning and calculations, he felt the human mind and body were capable of achieving any goal, literally any goal, and he believed it faithfully. It was truly like a religion, a creed. He never quit and never failed. Now, that doesn't mean he never had a failure. There were failures along the way, but the distinction was that correcting those failures through regrouping and alternate planning always achieved his goal. His mission would ultimately end in success. He was a very unique man, the best in his business, but there was one skill that he couldn't master, and you won't believe what it was."

"Well, tell me, Joe, tell me!"

"No, I can't. It wouldn't be fair."

"Oh come on! Please, I'm just dying to know."

"Well, okay. It was cooking. He sent me to school at a very early age to learn how to cook. He couldn't stand his own cooking. In fact, he was so excited when I graduated that he made me cook for 250 of his peers. Not all at once, mind you. It was every day for about eight weeks. Man, he knew a lot of people. But that wasn't the funny part. The funny part was that I couldn't even reach the oven or the stove. I was only nine years old. He made me a bench that went completely around the kitchen, so I could reach everything. I cooked for him for twenty years, and can you guess what he said when he passed away."

"No. What Joe? What did he say?"

"He said, 'Joe, now you are perfect. I could do nearly anything, and I lived to an age that many would have liked to live, but there was one—yes, one skill—I couldn't master and Joe, you did, so you are perfect.' Then he laughed and passed away with a warm smile that I will never forget. I'll always remember him and probably will respect no other man as much as I did him. I miss him very much."

"How old was he when he passed away?"

"He was 107 years old, and as bright and clear-minded as I am today. He did say something else when he was close to death, and to this day, I don't understand what he meant by it.

"What was that?" said Dawn. "Maybe together we can figure it out."

"He said, 'Remember this, son, strive to be free.'"

"*Son*. What's that word mean?" asked Dawn.

"Son is the offspring we have from mating, a boy, but 'strive to be free,' I'm hoping to find out the meaning of that phrase, soon. He was very wise."

"Oh back to me, anyway. I kind of got sidetracked."

"Yes, where was I? Oh, I started flying when I was ten years old, mostly in the simulator, and since that time, my life has been dedicated totally to flying and military tactics. My first flying experience was on tankers and transports, and I have been flying fighters now for nearly ten years. I play a lot of physical sports on my off time and feel flying and a good healthy, active body go hand in hand."

"What sports do you play?"

"Well, most of them center on reflex ability. Rapper ball is my favorite and for progressive eye-hand coordination, sophisticated video is important and fun too. I play electronic war games to heighten my intergalactic strategy. My favorite is Blister Sack and Tactical War Stragedy. For relaxation, I play sports games and listen to different types of music. Some of my hobbies are plant genetics, writing, of course cooking, and recently astrology and star gazing. I'm also very inquisitive about the past, which is forbidden on Altaur. I spent most of my time in school when I was younger going every day, never missing, for the first thirty-five sessions. Looking back, it sure was a pretty rough schedule, but I didn't know any better. Then after graduation, I started working. It seemed like a dream, three days flying and four days off. I really like that schedule. I go to the simulator on my days off. Three sessions are required, but I usually get in between eight and ten. The time passes quickly, though. It seems like I was just in school, and I have been out for a long time. The rest of the time I spend with Derek. We're really close."

"Tell me about your inner being," asked Dawn.

"I really never thought about it much, but I guess I can try to give you a fairly good analysis. First, I'm a very sensitive person."

"Yes, I realized that pretty quickly," replied Dawn.

"Oh you did… How Dawn?"

"Oh, the way you spoke of your Protector."

"You're really perceptive."

"Wait. Don't evaluate me yet. It's still your turn. We'll talk about that in my analysis."

We both laughed and smiled at each other, and then for a brief moment, just stared, feeling something I had never felt before in my entire life.

"It takes me a long time to trust someone. Derek is the only person I could say that I totally trust, and it took me a long time to really trust him. I like being around friends, and keeping busy is pretty important to me."

"Sometimes it's pretty hard for me to relax," Joe said. "Although I think being with you is very relaxing. I'm very confident in my work, and sometimes, I feel like I have no limitations to what I can accomplish. I try to think before I say or do anything, to avoid mistakes, and I'm very competitive when it comes to sports and games. I'm a pretty good loser although I'd prefer to win every time. I like to barter frequently, and most of my tokens are spent on food, friends, and some simple things in life, like music. By the way, how is your barter system set up?"

"We trade tokens also," Dawn said, "and we can acquire as much as seventy-five a week." They can be spent on the purchase of the items you spoke of previously, but I like to exchange them for clothes."

"Does everyone receive the same amount of tokens no matter what their profession?" Dawn asked.

"Yes, everyone's job is important. That's the way Altaur is operated, but there are ways to achieve extra tokens," I remarked.

"There appear to be many similarities between the two cities."

I thought for a brief second of Parrot and all the information he had given us and wanted to tell Dawn how both cities were exactly alike, but I knew I couldn't do that. My secret would stay my secret, at least for the time being.

"I'm really getting off track here, Dawn. I think I've talked enough. Now it's your turn."

"Well, I'm basically pretty much what you see, nothing fake. I say what I feel. Not many things bother me, and I can hardly wait for a new exciting challenge to come along, and you were right, I'm very perceptive. I'm gentle and caring. I also really like my work but can spend a fair amount of time reading, playing sports, and spending time alone. Plants and flowers are my favorite hobby, and I enjoy working with my hands. It's called needlework. I especially like making clothes, dresses, and complete outfits."

"Really! I like working with my hands too. I spent many hours in metal and architectural design. I even worked on some drawings for a new fighter aircraft. The Committee has the plans now and is considering a prototype. I'd like to show you sometime."

"If the plans are on Altaur, how can I ever see them," she curiously asked. "That would be very interesting, though. I would enjoy seeing the blueprints. I also like to work with cosmetics."

"Cosmetics? What's that?"

"Oh, I forgot. You don't know about this sort of woman thing. It consists of colors, pastes, lotions, and powders. You put it on your face like this."

She showed me as she pointed to her face. I leaned over and touched her face and felt a fine powder on my fingertips. "We have a contest every year to see who can come up with the most intriguing design. You put your design on a certain woman appointed by the judges. There are usually about three hundred contestants, and they are judged on beauty, showmanship by the designer, artistic imagination, and color scheme. You'll never guess who won the contest the past three years."

"Now how would I know? You're the only woman I know, so far, that is!"

"Oh silly, it was me... Oh, you're just joking with me."

We laughed together for a brief moment, and soon we were smiling, kissing, and embracing. Then she continued with her story. I was really becoming extremely fascinated by her life and found out a lot of it was similar to mine. The afternoon went by fast, and soon it was time to meet Derek and Pam. We took a shower together, still fascinated by the differences in our bodies, and I have to admit, I did a great job of getting both of us into what seemed to be a small shower stall, now, with two people in it. Soon, both of us became extremely passionate, and it wasn't long before contentment and relaxation covered us like a warm blanket. I was dressed and ready to go in about ten minutes, but Dawn was cosmetically rearranging her face, and that took just over forty minutes. She had emerged with her prize-winning face from the previous contest. This was the first time since the contest that she painted her face. She emphatically determined that the extreme wizardry of her early years had passed, but since this was a very special occasion in her life, she proceeded with the ritual.

When she came out of the bedroom, she looked magnificent. Her prints, as I called them, were of five distinct colors—yellow, red, blue, green, and pink. Her eyes were highlighted from the top of her eyelashes to an area just below her temple and down to her cheek line. The virtual half-circles from eyelash to her cheek, started from the bridge of her nose, and consisted of all five colors. Under her eyes from her nose in half circles to her lower lip and chin was a brilliant pink and red color. Her lips were soft pink, and her nose and the middle of her forehead were painted yellow with blue stripes. Her cheeks were highlighted with a circle of green, and a red line followed each jaw line.

"You look beautiful, Dawn. I've never seen anything like it. Now I can see how you won the contest. You are so beautiful."

"Oh, thank you very much. I'm so glad that you like it. Shall we go? I feel so special being with you, Joe."

"Dawn, I would go anywhere with you. You look as special as you feel."

She moved closer to me and our eyes met. We were filled with so much emotion.

As I gazed into them, I felt a special feeling come over me, for she was my mate and my mate alone. Her lips sparkled like those stars I saw looking through my telescope. Her eyes were so caring and kind. I pulled her close to me and held her tightly in my arms. Her arms surrounded me, and I felt the same gentle pressure of her body. Just then, I heard a quiet sob, and I released my embrace.

"Dawn, Dawn, please don't. Why, you'll ruin your face. I mean the paint. Won't it smear or something?"

She started to giggle, and I pulled out my handkerchief and patted her cheeks. "Joe, I'm so happy. I just want it to last forever... Forever."

"I know, Dawn. It will, it will. I feel the same way."

We held each other once again, and soon I felt some tiny droplets of water on my cheek, the first time I've ever felt like this.

CHAPTER 6

The Relationship

"Did it run, Joe?" Dawn asked about her makeup. "Run? Run what?"

"My face. Is it all right, or are the colors running together?"

"Run, no, it looks great. Do you have our entry card? I left mine on the end table by the bed."

"Yes. Here it is. You can have it."

"Okay, let's go."

We walked over to the space monitor transit system. The molecular transfer system would put you anywhere on the Star, but there was always an option to walk.

"Joe, let's walk to the restaurant. It shouldn't be far, according to this map."

"Sounds like fun to me. Can I hold your hand?"

"Sure, I'd like that very much."

There were many other couples walking. I wondered where they were going and how they felt about their mates. I imagined my very thoughts were probably in the minds of every one of them.

As we proceeded, I took her hand in mine and gently caressed it with my thumb. She looked at me and smiled, encouraging my affection. I gazed out at the evening sky and couldn't see the other Star Cities or the sparkling stars. It felt like we were all alone. I noticed the fluffy white clouds with patches of dark blue toward the west. The sun was just about to set low on the horizon and intensely brilliant colors dynamically pierced through the cloud formation. It was an amazing site. One I didn't ever want to forget.

"Look at that sunset. It's beautiful."

"It sure is!"

"I enjoy gazing out at the sky at this time of the evening. It's a breathtaking view. It really was the most beautiful sight I had ever seen."

"Was?" Dawn questioned.

"Yes, until now, that is. Until I saw you… Here's the restaurant. Let's see if we can find Derek and Pam."

"Thanks, Joe. You say the nicest things."

"Oh, look at the time. We're about fifteen minutes late."

"I hope they didn't leave," Dawn softly whispered in my ear.

"Don't worry. I know Derek very well, and he knows me. He would stay here until tomorrow morning and then come looking for me. He knows I would have contacted him if something went wrong."

"He must be a great friend,"

"The best, Dawn, the best."

There were three couples waiting in line for a table. The restaurant was very nicely decorated, and I was hoping the food matched its appearance. Tables were spread out along an open patio, and the view of the inner city was spectacular.

A large umbrella protected the dinner table from outside interference from the weather. Inside each umbrella perched a soft yellow light, now starting to glow as the romantic sunset came to an end and darkness settled in. The center of the table was masked with a beautiful fresh-smelling flower arrangement. The light was bright enough to see each other, and the surrounding darkness gave you a certain needed privacy. I couldn't understand at that moment why the lighting was engineered in that manner. I must have missed that part of my training. I promised myself to ask Derek once we were alone. We walked through the door, and as we approached the dining area, an older man dressed in a white suit met us.

"Two for dinner?"

"Yes, sir, but we are supposed to—"

"Oh, you must be Joe and Dawn."

"Yes, we are," said Joe, puzzled at this man's intuition.

"Derek and Pamela are on the patio at table number 31. I'll take you there straight away."

"Now that's service, right, Dawn?"

"Yes, it sure is. This is so pretty. I hope the food is as good as the decor."

"Yes, I am starving."

The night air was cool, and the sunset turned into a dark black night. The chairs and table that we were brought to were made of silver, and the utensils were gold once again. I heard of these metals before we arrived and studied them in school but thought they were all forgotten after the Macrocaust. The value of heavy metals, tremendous before the Macrocaust, declined after the war. Even though they were very beautiful and scarce, there was no need for such heavy metals in the new Star Cities. There was rumor that the Committee had a very large storeroom of old antiques made from these metals—gold, silver, and iron. They recovered them just before the Great War, but no one knows where the storeroom was or if it even existed.

Plants and flowers covered the dining area, and many of the articles seen in the restaurant were made from a very scarce substance called wood. It disappeared shortly after the great nuclear war. The wood so nicely preserved on this Star was the first I had seen anywhere except in books.

All the tables were private and secluded in their own little way, which was different, very different to what we were used to seeing.

As we approached our table, which was closest to the old silver railing, we could see a fantastic view of the whole city. The city now was all lit up, and the beauty of the night sky burst through the glittering of the multicolored city lights.

"Hey, Derek! How have you been?"

"Oh just great! And you?"

"Happier than ever. Derek, this is Dawn."

"Pamela, this is Joe."

"Nice to meet you!"

"Pamela has told me all about you, Dawn."

"And Joe has told me all about you, Derek."

"I guess we're even. Have a seat!"

We sat down, and Pam and Dawn talked almost nonstop, while Derek and I recollected the time that had passed between us. The man came over and took our order, and it wasn't long before our food arrived. He also brought over a refreshment drink that was new to all of us.

"Derek, how did the man at the door know our names?"

"I don't know, but he said I was the man behind the computers and that everyone knew about me. He mentioned your name before I told him that we were expecting you. I guess our names just precede us. Right, old boy!"

"Right, or they have our rooms bugged!"

We both laughed as our appetite made us dive into the meal set before us. "What's this drink, Dawn? Have you had it before this evening?"

"No, I haven't. I thought it was from your Star."

"Let's try it," said Derek.

And that we did. The drink was pretty good, and the food was very tasty, somewhat like the food in the Hall of Creation.

"Pamela, did your food change during the training period for our service here on Gamnon? Did it taste different to you?" asked Joe.

"Now that you mention it, the food did seem to change, and I noticed it almost immediately. The food had much more flavor, and the change was pretty dramatic to me."

"I noticed the change too," replied Dawn.

"We noticed a significant change too, right, Derek?"

"We sure did!"

The four of us sat around after dinner and drank more of that new savory refreshment. It was quite good, and I started to feel somewhat lightheaded. My desire to once again be alone with Dawn increased tremendously, and I found myself glancing at her more frequently than before dinner.

"I wonder what's in this drink?" said Derek. "It sure is making me feel really relaxed."

"I think it has affected all of us. Dawn, are you ready to go back to the apartment?"

"Yes, that's fine with me, Joe."

"Great idea, Derek. I'm getting pretty tired," whispered Pamela.

"Why don't you give us a call tomorrow, Derek? Maybe we can play some Rapper Ball, that is, if I can remember all the rules."

"Oh, it's like flying or working on those computers, no matter how long it has been since you have played, you'll remember."

"That reminds me, I need to go down to the simulator and brush up on my flight skills."

"I need to check out the computers on this Star also. I think I'll go in early in the morning," said Derek.

"Early? That won't happen. That reminds me, dude."

"Oh no you don't, not again. You're not going to talk me into a third challenge, Joe."

"What are you talking about? Let's go, Dawn. See you tomorrow, dude!"

"I hate it when he calls me dude."

We left the table and started to the exit, and Dawn had somewhat of a very puzzled look on her face. Pamela followed curiously, and Derek and I snickered as we passed through the exit.

"I'll talk to you tomorrow about the computers," I whispered and then loudly added, "Now be thorough with these computers, Derek. Okay?"

"Yeah, yeah, I don't know why I let you talk me into these wild schemes of yours."

"By the way, did you ever hear about Pythias and Tergas?"

"No, who are they?"

"Well, since you asked, Tergas and Pythias were two young men, Greek I suppose, who were the best of friends."

"Oh, here we go!" said Derek.

"No, they were inseparable friends. Well, one day Pythias committed an act for which the king sentenced him to death. His last request was to see another close friend. The king forbade him, saying that he would never return, but Tergas told the king he would stay in Pythias's place until he returned. If he failed to return within a certain amount of time, Tergas would die in his place. The king was astounded by this faith in his friendship, so he let him go, and when Pythias returned, the king pardoned him. That's the kind of friends we are, Derek. Would you agree?"

"Yes, you're right. I guess I'd die for you if came down to it." Then Derek whispered, "I hope I don't regret saying that."

"I heard that, pal, old buddy, you. See you tomorrow." I caught up with Dawn just outside the restaurant.

"I sure like this restaurant, Dawn. It has some great atmosphere. It kind of puts you in the mood to be... to be... What's the word I am looking for? *Intimate*! That's it. Did you notice how mate is a part of that word?"

"Yes, Joe, I like both the atmosphere and your word intimate."

Dawn looked at me with an irresistible smile, and I felt a wonderful feeling deep in my chest. We were hurrying back to the apartment, almost unaware of the beautifully moonlit sky. We seemed to share only one thought, and that was to be intimate once again.

"Well, we sure are walking fast."

"Yes, I realized that too. I'm starting to get winded. I wonder if that beverage had anything to do with our actions."

"I don't know, Dawn, but sometimes I find myself so out of character and concentrating purposely on one single thought. Like I've been drugged. How about you?"

"Yes, lately. I've felt that way too."

"Dawn, wait a second. I never even noticed how beautiful the night turned out to be. The breeze is so cool and refreshing. The sky is lit up like the fireworks on Harvest Day. It reminds me of those long nights on patrol. Let's slow down and enjoy every minute together. We have plenty of time to be intimate."

"You're right, Joe. We have plenty of time to be together."

"Look, there is Pisces and Majestic Lady and look! Look! I can see the Riding Horseman. It's one of the oldest constellations!"

"How do you know all those constellations?"

"Astronomy is one of my hobbies, remember? I've been fascinated with the heavens since I bought my telescope. They have always made me feel so small and unimportant. I would like so much to be able to just snatch one of those stars right out of the sky and hold it close to my chest."

"Yes, I get the same feeling, but mine comes when I'm holding you close to me, Joe."

"That's the nicest thing anyone has ever said to me, Dawn. Thank you very much, and you know that you are very special to me too. I never want you to leave me. I wish we could be together forever."

"Yes. Me too, Joe!"

There was silence for a long while, and then we held hands tightly and proceeded to work our way home. Not much was said during that time. I think we both were engulfed in deep thought, hoping, wishing, trying to figure out a way to be together always, knowing that the dream seemed almost impossible.

"Here we are! Home sweet home."

"That's a nice expression. I never heard of it before, Joe. Where did you hear that phrase?"

"Oh, it was one of the many expressions my Protector gave me. Whenever we were away from the apartment and getting closer and closer to our building, of course, this is when I was quite a bit younger, he would say, 'Your home is your castle.' Don't let anyone enter unless you want them to because it is your right. It's your dwelling, a place you can do what ever you want to do, where you can dream and plan. Yes, never let anyone destroy it or take it from you, Joey, you have that right, the right to choose, the right to stay and the right to abandon. Yes, that's home sweet home, doing what you want to do and deciding how you want to do it.'"

"He was a great old man. Sometimes I just wish I understood him a little better. Maybe, someday I will. Hopefully, that day will be soon."

"You miss him very much don't you, Joe."

"Yes, I sure do."

We entered the apartment and being unfamiliar with the arrangement I stumbled over some furniture trying to find the light.

"I've got it, Dawn. Well, I thought that was the light."

"Here, here is the switch, Joe."

She then proceeded to turn the lights on and move closer to me as I was now halfway across the room.

"I almost killed myself looking for that blasted light. I'm definitely not used to the arrangement. I wonder who did the decorating?"

"I'll do some revamping tomorrow, Joe, hopefully make things a little more efficient and less obstructive."

"That's a good idea, Dawn."

I went over to the couch and lay down to relax for a while. Dawn went into the bathroom to dismantle her prize-winning face.

"Hey, babe, come in here," I beckoned.

"Hey, what? *Babe?* What does that mean?"

"Gee, no one has ever asked me that before. I don't actually know, but my protector used to call me that sometimes. Affectionately, of course, when I was young. He would never tell me what it meant. He probably wasn't allowed to tell me but he would say. It's just a nice way to show you that I care for you more than anyone else in this world."

"That's so heartfelt," said Dawn.

She came out of the bathroom and sat next to me.

"You know, I don't say that to everyone," replied Joe.

I felt the warmth of her touch, and we began to kiss affectionately. As I put my arm around her to hold her close and feel the great passion of this unique moment, I accidentally touched the light. This motion shut off the light, but neither of us noticed what had happened since we were deeply involved in such a romantic kiss. It was a very exaggerated action compared to how we were taught by Parrot. Soon, after this long and refreshing kiss, I opened my eyes to a darkened room.

"Oh no, is the power off? Gee, that's all I need. I can't find my way around here in the light let alone in the dark. We might as well go to bed."

"Yes, I agree, Joe. Here, take my hand."

She led me into the bedroom, and surprisingly enough, I only tripped two or three times, and wouldn't you know it, she never did trip. As we approached the bed, I let her hand go, and she started to undress. She then turned her head and said, "Could you give me a hand?"

"Why sure, Dawn. What do you want me to do?"

"Unzip me, please!"

"I'll have to find you first." I walked over to the other side of the bed, trying to feel my way around. My eyes still hadn't adjusted to the total darkness yet. I reached for her with both hands extended, thinking she was facing the other direction. "Oh, sorry about that. I really can't see a thing."

"I know." She giggled. "You're excused."

"You turned on purpose, didn't you? Come on, didn't you? You little rascal, you!"

"Yes, I admit it. I planned to catch you off guard."

We both started laughing, and finally she turned around to be unzipped. Then I announced, "I'm going to brush my teeth, I love garlic, but tonight, it was a little too strong."

I walked into the bathroom and instinctively reached for the light switch. The light came on so bright I had to close my eyes for a couple of seconds so they could adjust to the brightness.

"Hey, the power is back on," I said.

From the bedroom, Dawn shouted, "Oh shoot! It was just starting to get fun."

"I'll bet the electricity never went off," I said. "I must have hit the lamp by mistake when we kissed each other on the couch."

I brushed my teeth laughing at myself realizing what a fool I had been. As I finished and entered the bedroom, I once again turned the light off, and soon total darkness appeared. After tripping one more time on my way to the bed, I said, "You know, it was just as exciting when the lights were off, I think we'll just leave them off for now. What do you think?"

"It sounds great to me! You better get in bed now before you kill yourself."

"Okay."

Our intimacy that evening was even more fulfilling. Our imaginations were free to enjoy the ultimate gift of mating that could ever be perceived. Her touch, her smell, her actions were enhaned tenfold.

Her words blanketed me in total concentration. It was enlightening, gratifying, and a complete mental and physical consummation. This time spent together was absolutely wonderful.

The night went amazingly fast, and soon it was 8:00 a.m. I really wanted to get down to the simulator before the crowd. Dawn was already up and about moving the furniture like she promised the night before. I took a quick shower and was out the door almost immediately. As I closed the door, I realized I had forgotten to say anything to Dawn. I quickly opened the door and apologized, "Oh, Dawn, I'm sorry. I'm not used to having anyone around when I get up in the morning. Let me start over. Good morning, Dawn. How do you feel this morning?"

She quietly chuckled and said, "Oh fine, in fact, fabulous. I feel kind of special. Do you want some breakfast?"

"Oh, not really. I want to get down to the simulator. Maybe I can get in a good four hours this morning.

After lunch, I have a rapperball game scheduled with Derek. "Could you do something for me when you get some time this morning?"

"Sure, what's that?"

"Call over to Derek's and tell him to meet me at the courts about 1400 hours. He usually never gets out of bed before noon. What a life!" I walked over to her and kissed her gently on the lips.

"Oh, that was nice. I sure would like to have more of that behavior."

"Sounds great to me."

I kissed her one more time and hurried to the door, for I was surely going to be late now.

"Bye, see you later."

It was a beautiful morning. The sun was shining bright, and the sky was a brilliant blue with not a cloud anywhere. I managed to make it to the simulator on time. I misjudged the travel time, and to my surprise, it was fairly empty. As I approached, a man at the door greeted me.

"Good morning, and how are you this fine morning, sir?"

"Fine, sir. It looks pretty empty. Do you have a flight simulator ready for some tactical and battlefield scenarios?"

"Sir, on this star, there is availability twenty-four hours a day, a simulator. In fact, a personal simulator that will be yours for as long as you're with us. If I am not mistaken, yours, sir, has been upgraded to the ultimate challenge. It's number 55 down the corridor, to the left, and it's the seventh machine on your right. It's all yours, Captain Capuzzi, and I'm honored to meet you, sir."

"Do you know everyone who comes here?"

"We have heard a lot about you. Your skills, awards, and your reputation precede you, sir."

"Well, thank you, and what is your name?"

"Just call me Cappy, and if you need anything while you are here on Gamnon, do let me know!"

"I sure will. Thanks again."

I went to my simulator, and once inside was amazed at the new technology. These simulators were so close to reality, it was frightening. We received 35 at home on Altaur, but you had to sign up on them, and the Committee felt the less skilled should get priority. I had only used them once before. The older machines on Altaur were used so much that 30 percent of the time they simply malfunctioned. The full benefit could be achieved only when the weekly maintenance crew showed up to repair them. It was going to be a real pleasure having my own personnel simulator. After about fifteen minutes, I felt real comfortable flying again and really believed that I hadn't lost any of my agility or reflex skills. In fact, I was pleased with my performance.

These simulators were expertly programmed, and they were extremely tight, handling beautifully. My best score was achieved on the strategical chase.

During this simulator test, you, the pilot are chased by seven to ten aircraft. You can add up to twenty aircraft, which is about eight more than most pilots can take, with attack patterns changing every time you destroy a plane, and the attack patterns were almost unlimited. I'd been using the simulator for fourteen years now and have seen the same attack pattern only two or three times. The best score I accomplished in the fourteen years was sixteen out of twenty possible points. Supposedly you cannot beat the simulator, but I knew some day I would do it. (Most pilots would score between eight to ten consistently my average was fifteen to sixteen). One of my goals since I was very small, in fact, twelve years old, was to beat the simulator. I felt that if a man programmed it, then a man could beat it. I went for a test run just to feel out the aircraft, and it handled very nice. In fact, it was the only simulator I had flown that so closely resembled the real aircraft that I flew it for about thirty minutes and really felt strong and alert. Soon the computer spoke.

"Commander Capuzzi, are you ready to take on the task force presented and save your civilization?"

"You're full of Lysino juice, Mack."

"Commander Capuzzi, are you—"

"Yes, yes, let's get on with it!"

I glanced over my head to see the time-spacer, a device giving you your location computations and enemy strength knowing this was my first move and the computer shot me down.

"You are destroyed."

"You devil you! You're a little more with the program, aren't you?"

"Timing is the essence of surprise, Commander."

"Sure, well, give me everything you have, lead bottom."

And he sure did. Before you could blink an eye, I had a bogy on my tail, one coming off my port and a support group in front of me.

"That's not fair, Mack."

"Anything goes, Commander. You should have been aware of that before we started."

I broke to my starboard side, cut the port engine, and when the bogy passed me, I cut him down. A second later, the port bogy was on a collision course with me. I didn't have time to fire the port engine up so I neutralized the ship for a moment, then put the starboard engine to maximum. That in turn headed the bogy in the path of my jet stream, and he went out of control into deep space. Soon there was an explosion.

"Well done, Commander, you have attained two points."

"Two points! That was worth at least six points, Mack."

"Hardly, sir, you still have the support group of eighteen aircraft. Get yourself out of this mess, Commander."

"What a mess, indeed."

I armed my rear and peripheral lasers and opened the bay for my proton torpedoes. Theoretically, I had only enough firepower for seventeen aircraft, if I didn't miss a target. The pressure was on. The first two bogies were easy, one on each side an easy shot for my peripheral lasers, but we both knew that, and soon I was informed of two bogies approaching head on and two from behind. Also, the more bogies shot down, the more complicated the attack patterns became until you were destroyed, theoretically, that is. I figured that I needed to get two ships hopefully without firing a shot and this was the perfect opportunity to do so. The first obstacle I had to overcome was to figure out which way they would run if I wasn't destroyed. My move would be to belly-up centrally through the middle of the attacking aircrafts, without getting destroyed.

First, I turned my peripheral deflector shield to stern and bow leaving my sides vulnerable. It was a chance I was willing to take. Next, I tried to shield at least one of the bogies on my stern by jamming the radar mechanism and flying slightly above my oncoming attackers. If the bogies followed me, the screen could be set up putting me in between the bow and stern attackers. My shields were taking a beating, and I decided not to fire back conserving my firepower. Then twenty-five kilometers away and closing fast, I let my shield down for a split second hoping to distract my opponents. With full power and my shields back to magnum force, I dived eighteen thousand feet in thirty seconds. For an instant, the h-force almost made me pass out, but soon I leveled off and recovered. Looking at the board, I found out that my plan had worked. The one rear bogy above me saw his oncoming comrades and flew hard to port, but it was too late for the bogy flying slightly after and four degrees below. The two attackers collided, and the explosion it produced hit the third oncoming aircraft and destroyed it also.

"Good show, Commander. You have destroyed three ships without firing a shot. That totals ten points destroying seven ships.

Thirteen ships left and ten points for a perfect score. You do know, Commander, is highly impossible."

"That's what you think, Mack. Don't get too cocky. I have plenty of firepower left, and you are really going to have to show me your best tactics to take me down."

"Yes, Commander. I realize that."

Since I had plenty of firepower now, I decided to be the aggressor. I could see ten ships on the screen, and within a split second, they scattered. I wasn't worried about the ones I could see, but somehow, the other three aircraft eluded my radar. Well, for now I had enough problems. I followed four bogies on the starboard attack grid. They flew tandem, one covering the other's six. They flew extremely fast, and I had trouble getting them in range until one looked like he had some engine trouble and slowed down considerably. But I was well aware of some of their strategy. Sometimes they would sacrifice one ship and try to destroy the oncoming bogy (which was me) by displacing radar and returning fire from my rear. I was just about in range for my phaser, but I had reached torpedo range first. Hoping they were going to take the bait, relying on my phasers to annihilate them, I fired a torpedo and once again neutralized my engines. At that moment, all three bogies passed me, and within ten seconds, I had released two torpedoes and riddled one with my double barreled nose laser. I veered to port trying to find the other bogies and not waiting around to see my hits. Soon, three explosions rang out, and I knew because of their proximity that I destroyed the attacking bogies. I then displayed the other ten bogies on my screen and then I heard another explosion—marking the decoy I had torpedoed earlier. I was still bothered though; two more bogies had successfully eluded my radar.

"Good. Very good, Commander. Four more ships and four more points. You now have fourteen points."

Two bogies split off, and I followed the other four since they still appeared on my screen.

"No time to talk now, Mack."

One ship was easy prey, and I destroyed him with a long-range torpedo, but soon I had three attackers coming in from all directions except my bow. Phaser blasts were bombarding me and they took their toll on my peripheral deflector shields. As they weakened, I faked a port roll and dropped a 180-degree turn to starboard that put one ship dead ahead and a phaser round took care of him. The phaser blasts were still exploding everywhere around me so I decided to fly through the debris of the ships I just destroyed hoping some of it would pick up some of the phaser rounds. One ship followed me right through, and three others kept abreast until I was through the debris. As I flew through, I had one more trick I was hoping they would overlook. I dropped an armed torpedo as I flew through the debris believing it would be ignited by the multiple laser blasts. Since the torpedo was masked amongst the debris, it would go unnoticed. As I cleared the fragments, I heard an explosion and soon there were only three aircraft left. All flew abreast the wreckage and they were quickly on my tail; I surely was in no mood for fun and games. One followed me through four rolls eating up my rear deflector shield hoping one more blast would make me vulnerable. My rear armament had almost completely destroyed his bow deflector shields and soon it would be the ship that broke down first. I didn't feel that I should be the one, so I cut both engines in a last ditch effort to let them pass and fired a torpedo that had the last bogies name on it.

Soon, he was destroyed, and I knew I wasn't vulnerable not because it would take at least fifteen seconds before the engines were cool enough to crank but it would take some time for them to turn around. I knew the other aircrafts were not within range because they didn't appear on my screen, but there was a bogy that was left I could not track, and it worried me. I put all deflector shields on maximum and waited. It seemed like the longest fifteen seconds I had ever spent. I waited and waited, expecting a phaser blast any moment. Ten seconds later, and I started to prime the engines. Then, two bogies appeared, and soon, I felt phaser blasts rocking my ship. At fourteen seconds, my rear deflector shield had been eliminated. As I started to fly again, my port shield was totally eliminated. I had to be the attacker now for only my starboard and bow shields were operative. I took off and did a 360 so sharp that I passed out for a nanosecond, but when I opened my eyes, I was directly behind the bogie. After releasing a neutron torpedo, I was redirecting my ship. The other bogie was now on my starboard side, which was exactly where I wanted him. My starboard shields took two hits, and then I hit neutral, which dropped me two thousand feet. As he flew over, I shot a heat-seeking rocket that he couldn't shake, and soon there was only one left.

"Very good, Commander, but as you are fully aware that there's one ship left and your rear and port deflectors shields are gone and the starboard side badly damaged. You have scored 19 points, and now you just have to contend with one more, and that's me. You do know you cannot—I repeat—cannot win!"

"You know, Mack, that depends on one thing, and you know what that is… It depends on who wrote the book! Think about what I just said, Mack, just think about it!"

"It is your turn to be destroyed, Commander!"

Soon, I had a laser blast on my starboard side, but no ship appeared on my radar screen.

"So this is how you win. Since I can't see you on my screen, I can't shoot you down."

"Your starboard shield is gone, Commander. Now, you will be destroyed—"

Before he could finish, I used afterburners and was gone. I could hear laser blasts behind me. Come on, this isn't fair. There has to be a way… Wait… Wait.

"Computer, magnify my scanner screen ten-fold, now."

As I gazed around the scanner, I could see some type of sigma wave directly behind me. Almost immediately, I initiated a 360 degree turn put full power on my bow deflector shield, and shortly after, I felt a laser blast directly forward.

"So I found you, but you must be exerting a tremendous amount of power to be almost invisible on my screen."

Soon, he moved slightly to port, and now with full power, I engaged my engines to follow that mysterious wave. Once again, a laser blast hit me directly forward.

"Now, I have you Mack, and I beat you… Yes, sir, I beat you!"

Before long, I fired two torpedoes and enough phaser power to destroy seven ships. Shortly, the computer darkened inside, and as I stepped out, a buzzer sounded with bright lights flashing everywhere. Smoke was pouring out of the top of the simulator. Instantly, Cappy came running down the hallway.

"Hey, Commander, what happened?"

"Cappy, I think I just beat the computer's attack pattern."

"You what? That's impossible. No one has ever done that before."

"Well, just think, you were here when it happened. That's history."

As he looked at the monitor on the simulator, he just stood in awe. "I can't believe it! How did you do it? I just can't believe it! We'll have to return this simulator to the aircraft museum. Put a plaque with your name on it. This is unbelievable! You're good, Commander, really good!"

I slowly walked over to the door, somewhat full of myself. "Oh, by the way, I'll need another simulator tomorrow, Cap."

"Yes, sir, it will be awaiting your pleasure, sir," said Cappy as he stood and stared at me scratching his head.

He looked like he was in some sort of a trance, not believing what just happened.

It was about 1330 hours now, and I was really starting to feel quite proud of myself. I told Derek I'd meet him at the rapper ball court right at 1400 hours, but I wasn't going to hurry anywhere right now.

That one was for you, Protector, God rest your soul. Thanks for all that perfect training you provided me with back in my younger days. You always told me I could beat that computer and you were right. I sure did!

What a wonderful feeling. Gamnon has provided me with such great feelings that I just might plan to stay here forever. What a laugh. I guess I'll have to come back to reality some day. Just then, Derek came walking down the pathway.

"Hey! How are you? That's a dumb question. You have a grin from ear to ear. What's up?"

"Your best friend just outwitted, outsmarted, overpowered, and defeated the undefeatable computer aircraft simulator. The computer started smoking, and Cappy came running as I modestly walked away. He couldn't believe I had beaten the simulator. No one has ever done that before today."

"That's great! You'll make headlines tonight. You've always told me you were going to beat the simulator one day, but I never believed you. You know if I would have programmed that simulator you never would have won."

"Oh really, I'll have to take you up on that."

"Anytime, pal. By the way, who's Cappy?"

"Oh, he's the old man who runs the aircraft simulator operations."

"I bet he still can't believe that you beat his machine."

"I feel so good. You better look out now. You are going to have a tough time taking me today."

"I know, but I'm going to give it my best just like you did."

That day was one of the best days of my life. We split two games, and I beat Derek in a tiebreaker by one point. Derek was still proud of himself for giving me a run for my money. By the way, he still won twenty tokens off of me. I just thought I was going to slaughter him. I was on such a high, but he played the best I'd ever seen and I was blessed to beat him.

I couldn't get that simulator off of my mind. I really wanted to get back to the apartment and tell Dawn, then see the headlines. It will be all over the communicators and the newspaper. I took a steam bath, a nice cold shower, then a short swim before returning home. I left the club and walked as fast as I could without working up a sweat, and when I got home, Dawn was waiting at the door. As I opened the door, she ran up to me and gave me a great big kiss and hug. When we were through, she looked at me and said, "Congratulations!"

"How did you know?"

"Are you kidding? It's all over the news and communicators. That news travels at the speed of light. How did you do it?"

"Well, that's my secret. If I told you how I did it, then I wouldn't be the best, would I?"

"You are afraid I'd show you up when I go down to practice."

"Are you kidding. Anyone can do it. It just takes practice and ingenuity."

"Well, I'm so proud of you, Joe. You just amaze me."

"Well, thank you."

Time seemed to go by very fast. Derek and I had been enjoying ourselves tremendously. We played sports every afternoon, and I was battling it out with the computer simulator every morning. They had rigged the simulator to self-destruct mode if anyone got close to beating it. I figured that out three months later, when I was very close to beating it again. At least I would go down in history as the only man who ever beat the unbeatable simulator. Dawn started going to the simulator in the mornings, but after about three weeks she began to feel the never-forgiving morning sickness we had read about in our training. She spent the rest of her pregnancy around the apartment in the early hours of the morning. Her afternoons were spent with Pamela and some of the other very pregnant women on Gamnon. Derek was learning more and more about the computer system of the Star Cities and with a little experimentation of his own he extracted precise data about our history that only Committee members had accessed to. He obtained some vague information on the Star Cities defense system, their enemies, research and development phases of weaponry and new to us a report on the remnants of the human society that still existed on earth today.

We both decided that it could be to our advantage to learn everything there is to know about ours and other known societies. It was hard to believe that our government had kept us so sheltered and repressed. We worked on the computer in our apartment for several days trying to avoid our partners knowledge of our mischievous ways. We worked only when they were out for the afternoon. Derek spent approximately one-third of the time reprogramming this computer as compared to Parrot. He attributed it to the knowledge he was gaining on Gamnon. I was so much more impressed with his job this time. His ability to make every connection without a mistake and every chip was replaced or relocated with such accuracy. His talent and precision were uncommonly acute.

"Wow, you are really getting good at this! What do you call it? Uh re-reconstructing?"

"That's a good word, but let's call it modification. Do you know how it was your goal to beat the simulator. Mine is to be smarter than this computer."

"Well, you're a lot smarter in my book!"

"Thanks, Joe, just one more adjustment, and she's ours forever to learn anything we want too."

"She. Why do you call it *she*?"

"Well, she's so delicate and sweet and compassionate, witty, caring—"

"Sounds like you're talking about Pam."

"Yes, I am, but that is why I call it she. She reminds me of Pam. I just can't get her off my mind."

"Sounds like you are stuck on her."

"I am, Joe, really stuck on her."

"Where does that leave me, Derek?"

"Oh come on, Joe. That's different."

"You better say that, you old dog."

"Oh you nut… Okay, it's ready and so are we."

"Great, let's get all of our questions together so we won't waste any time when she starts producing all this great knowledge."

"I can't wait, Derek."

"Me either, but it's getting late, and Dawn will be returning soon."

"Yes, I know. Same time tomorrow?"

"No, let's make it early around 0800 hours bright and early."

Dawn and Derek crossed paths shortly after Derek left, and soon Dawn was cheerfully calling my name.

As Derek was working on the computer, I was busily preparing our dinner. I had adjusted the lights, romantically, to a soft glow. Candles were lit on the dinner table. It was set perfectly without a utensil out of place. The table was fit for a king and queen, and truly I wanted to treat her as if she were my queen.

"Joe, where are you? Why is it so dark? Joe, where are you?"

"I'm in the kitchen."

"What's going on? What are you doing?"

"Oh, I have a surprise for you. You have been out all day, and I thought you might be tired, so I fixed dinner. This way you can relax for awhile, take a hot bath, and not have to worry about cooking for me."

"Gee, that's nice of you, Joe. In fact, that's real nice... and the lights."

We both looked at each other and simultaneously said, "Remember that night?"

We began to laugh, and soon she came over and gave me a hug and kiss. "Just hold me, Joe. Your body feels so good... warm, strong, comforting. You know I have this special feeling deep... so deep inside me, like it is in my very heart. A feeling I never had before I met you. It's a feeling of caring, wanting to be with you every minute of the day, holding you, looking, touching, embracing. Excited to come home because I know you'll be there."

"Yes, Dawn, I feel the same way, and I just can't explain the feeling. It is a comforting secure feeling, and I want it to become stronger and stronger. I do feel it move in that direction every day. It makes me stronger, more confident, and ever so powerful. It's a wonderful feeling deep inside me."

"Yes, it sure is."

"Well, it's ready. Let's eat, you can soak in the tub later. I am just starving."

"Me too. That shopping is really exhausting. Ha ha ha."

We sat and quietly ate our meal. It was so peaceful, just a wonderfully relaxing atmosphere. Soon, I broke the silence with a question that almost ruined our evening.

"Dawn, do you realize that in approximately one month, you will give birth to our baby, and our time will end soon after that?"

"Oh, Joe, I don't want to think about it. You know I've been so happy these past nine months. It's going to be real hard to go back to the way it was on Balem. It's kind of strange, but no one ever talks about their time spent here. It's like they never came over here. Do you think they block our memories or something?

"That's possible but how? Could it be drugs or computer probing? There has been a lot of talk about that computer XJ-621. They say it could erase everything in a person's memory or be selective to its elimination. Then they could reprogram you just like a droid, but that is only gossip."

"But they have been doing it for years, so it couldn't be the XJ-621. It has to be some type of drug, but how, Joe? How do they get us to take it? Is it gas, piped in while we sleep or is it an exit shot? Do you think they really do it? Can they do it? It's really kind of frightening."

"I'm sure they do it, Dawn."

"How do you know, Joe?"

"Well, I can't really divulge that information, but I will know exactly how it's done soon."

"Really, Joe?"

"Yes, ma'am!" My voice turned into a whisper. "I have a friend on the inside." I smiled.

"Did you ever think of how nice it would be to live together for the rest of our lives and have babies, two, three, maybe four all to our own to feel for, raise, protect and watch grow every day?" asked Dawn.

"Gee, that's a great thought, Dawn. You know it just might be possible some day. It just might be possible."

"Oh come on, Joe. It's just a dream. Where would we live? How would we survive! Impossible! Just im—"

"How do you like the food?" I interrupted.

"Oh, it's delicious, just great, but how would we survive?"

"Well, if it was possible, Dawn, since we are on the subject, would you take the risk involved to gain our freedom because it just might get us both killed or even worse, tortured, and then executed?"

"Oh, Joe, if it was possible, I would do it in a heartbeat no matter what the risk, no matter what the consequences."

As she raised her head to look at me, her eyes sparkled with a glimmer of hope. Her expression, her eyes, her smile showed me how she felt about me. What we both want is to be free to live together, fight together, and die together if need be."

"Let me have your hands, Dawn."

We both reached across the table and held hands tightly. Hers so soft and warm, mine so firm, but clamy considering what I was going to say next.

"Let's make a pact, Dawn."

"Sure, Joe, anything."

"Really, I mean a promise before God."

"Yes, lead us."

"Lord God, our Father and Creator, we will strive to be together and promote this excitement we have to grow and develop these feelings. We will become one being, giving, caring, comforting, and strengthening our lives. Our union will be above all except our relationship with you. Last of all, we will. Just then I remembered what my Protector told me just before he died, which up until this moment had no meaning. We will strive—yes, strive to be free."

I was contemplating.

Now, I know what he meant. He must have felt the same way about a person he met on Gamnon. Maybe, he remembered but was not willing to become free. Or maybe he was alone, his mate dying during birth or shortly afterwards. Many questions kept popping up into my head. He was a very brave, wise, and intelligent man who would have strived to be free if someone was there for him to be with, or was it me? He couldn't leave me to be raised by someone else? Why did he say that to me… How did he not forget Gamnon?"

"Joe. Joe, what are you thinking about? You looked like you were in a daze. Some kind of a trance."

"Oh, I'm sorry. What did I say, Dawn?'"

"Strive to be free. What does that mean?"

"Well, it means we will make our own decisions and plan our lives together. No more misconception and no more lies. We will know exactly what is going on in our life and live together as a family. Dawn, are you willing to believe in me and pursue our goal to strive to be free no matter what the cost? No matter what the consequences?"

"Yes, Joe, I am willing."

"So am I. Then it is settled. It is done."

She reached over the table still grasping my hands firmly, and we kissed each other sealing the oath to our union. This kiss deepened our loyalty and devotion to each other.

"And may the Almighty Creator be with us always keeping us safe and protected. Guiding our steps and showing us the way to freedom, amen."

"Well, the real challenge comes now, Dawn. I have to get a plan together, but that will come soon. Sooner than expected."

"How Joe? What are you talking about?"

"Well, Derek and I, actually, Derek has reprogrammed three basic Star City computers to give us every piece of classified information about ours and other societies. We also obtained current knowledge of any societies that exist as free nations, men and women united and living as families and tomorrow—"

"When did you—"

At that moment, Dawn pointed around the room as if to warn me of the Committees sensors probably located everywhere in the room.

"You don't have to worry about the Committee hearing anything, Dawn. Derek and I took care of that problem a long time ago."

"When did you do the reprogramming?"

"The first one was in his apartment on Altaur. That was the most difficult one to do. The second one was in our room at the Hall of Creation. Derek and I were roomies there. Derek and I... Well, mostly Derek has been working on this one for a while. Tomorrow we will find out even more about the existence of a new society."

"Society? What society?" asked Dawn.

"Oh yes, I never did finish my previous statement. We found out that a society where men and women live together really does exist. Derek is working on some questions right this moment. Then, we will formulate a plan to reach that society."

"You mean that this computer is programmed to give you classified information?"

"Now it is, with some modifications Derek worked out. See all the computers are filled with every bit of information available to man. You just can't retrieve the information as they stand now."

"Why are all the computers programmed with all the information?"

"Well, if Altaur is partially or completely destroyed, then there will still be computers available for the retrieval of information for rebuilding. I also think that they just don't want to lose all the knowledge gained over the centuries."

"Yes, but only give information to Derek and you. That's amazing. How did he do it?"

"Oh, he's a wizard at computers. We make a good team Derek and me… Just like you and me, and now hopefully, it will be the four of us. Will you talk to Pamela and see how she feels."

"Oh, I know how she feels. We've already talked about it… They have the same feelings for each other that we have for each other."

"Oh, am I the last to know?"

"Yep, you sure are!"

We both laughed for a second, and then Dawn got up to clear the table. "Can I learn some of our history tonight, Joe?"

"You sure can if you really want to."

"I really want to learn, Joe, as much as I can."

"Come into the living room. Just leave the mess. We can clean up later." We both sat down on the couch.

"Here we go. Tera?

"Tera!" Dawn said. "Where did you get that name?"

"It's part of our code," Joe said.

"Voice code for Joe, confirmed," Tera responded.

"Now, Tera, give us a detailed history of man from the time when progress was at one of its most rapid growth… about the year 2000."

"The beginning of the twentieth century, as time was recorded then, was indeed a time of rapid progression. It nearly led to almost total destruction and extermination of the human race."

We stayed up for a long time being taught our history, and soon, it was 2300 hours. It was the first time I was able to sit, relax, and digest all the information given to us. There wasn't one interruption the whole time. We learned everything that was available to the computer about the events that led up to the Great Macrocaust. It proceeded to tell us of the creation of the Star Cities and the Great War that led to the developement of the *Station America*. We also learned about Gamnon and all the events that take place from now until the baby is born. It also gave us information on our so-called reprogramming.

Sadness and great despair fell over us both, and we held each other closely. Some of the information given to us tonight I had heard but waiting for the rest of it until tomorrow seemed ridiculous. It was too important to take a chance on something interfering with our enlightenment. I figured I could fill in the blanks to Derek later.

"This is just amazing. I can't believe that this information has been kept from us for so long. It seems almost surreal."

"I'm going to ask some questions so Derek and I can formulate some sort of plan to reach the *Station America*. Tera, how are we suppressed and how does the Committee bring about the kind of amnesia needed to forget all that has happened on Gamnon."

"I'll bet it's the food, Dawn. That's the only thing that's different that we have in common. They must drug the food, but when? Where? We need this information."

"Affirmative. The food for all the citizens has been drugged ever since the Great Macrocaust. It suppresses the mating desire, suppresses physical urges, and produces a desire to be self-absorbed. It controls all the human emotions and there are selected drugs for each human emotion. The drugs are stopped only for the mating process. They start at the Hall of Creation decreasing the doses with every meal. By stopping the drug, humans retrieve their drive to mate, their emotions, and their memory rather quickly. They once again become truly human."

"Incredible, just incredible."

"Tera, at what point in the process of growth, harvest, or preparation does the drug become active."

"Why is this so important, Joe?" Dawn asked.

"Well, when we leave Gamnon, we are going to have to find food before it is drugged, so we can avoid the amnesia and alienation associated with it."

"The process of drug administration has to be done weekly. The drug is K-8126, and it is injected into the food by scientists at the warehouses before it is shipped to the stores and restaurants. If anyone questions the drug or processing, they are told it is a vitamin supplement that is needed in our diet because by artificially growing our crops they lack certain nutrients. The only people who know of K-8126 are the Committee members and the immediate supervising research scientists."

"Approximately, how many are aware of this food processing?"

"Seventy Committee Members and seventy-five supervising research scientists make up the indoctrination staff."

"That's going to be a major obstacle," Dawn said. "It's going to be really hard to retrieve food from the warehouse."

"Maybe there is another way. Tera, is there any other place that acquires food without K-8126?"

"Affirmative. Affirmative."

"I'll bet it's right under our noses. Right here on Gamnon."

Tera said, "Gamnon gets its food from a transport before K-8126 is processed into the food. There is a strict inventory performed to make sure the food has not been tampered with and on the Star Cities it exists in a certain section of the warehouses."

"Oh great!" sighed Dawn.

"What's wrong? That will be easy to deal with. In fact, Derek and I will take care of the food end of the plan."

"That's fine with me but how?"

"Not now, Dawn. Let's continue with our questioning. We will have plenty of time to make and review our plans."

"Okay, Joe. I'm just really curious. We will have to completely avoid the food."

"Where there's a will, there's a way. We will figure out a way."

"Tera, how did people live before the Great Macrocaust? How and why was our society developed in this manner and what is the purpose of this segregation?"

Tera said, "Back in time, men and women used to live together and function as one in the same, a unit called a family. These beings reproduce beings first called babies, then adolescent, then adults. The family all contribute to promote the growth and development of the unit, raising their own offspring. Special feelings keep them together for the rest of their lives here on earth. There existed classes of people, rich, middle, poor, and homeless. There were many different races, religions, languages, and governments. There was a group of scientists who predicted the Great Macrocaust and prepared themselves by designing a so-called perfect society. These men and women are the forefathers of your present society. One of the main reasons for the segregation of men and women was to eliminate crimes of passion, jealousy theft, and greed from the society. The main reason for the existence of K-8126 was to suppress human emotions and desires."

"What are emotions, Joe?"

"You'll see, we'll ask him next if he doesn't explain it, but for now, let Tera continue."

Tera continued, "The societies were developed to eliminate classes, greed, fear, compassion, love, hate, loneliness, and guilt. Everyone exists to promote their society or the one large family of similar people, the main principal being the same but the means and ways completely different. The society also contributes to its citizens by promoting growth and development of their technology and self-existence. People who don't produce for the benefit of all are exterminated. The scientific group tried to create a perfect society or utopia. It has existed over two hundred years. The brainwashing has proven very effective."

Joe asked, "What are emotions?"

Tera replied, "Emotions are a state of excited feelings of any kind. It is one of the fundamental properties of the human mind."

"Name some properties and explain them to me."

"Free will, which is the power of decision and choice. Free will was taken away after the Great Macrocaust. The power to express free will was eliminated from society. The society was drugged, K-8126, to remove it. Their will is now decided by the Committee."

"Okay, okay, I think I know about free will. What about other emotions?"

"Emotions were also to be abrogated, but it's extremely hard to eliminate all emotion from the human race. Examples of some emotions are the following: 1. Fear—a painful sensation excited by an expectation of harm or the apprehension of impending danger. The body reacts by releasing adrenaline from the adrenal gland, which increases heart rate. There may be sweating, agitation and definitely enhanced thought processes."

"I've experienced that, Dawn, have you?"

Dawn answered, "Yes, in my fighter."

Tera continued, "2. Hate—to dislike intensely or passionately. Extreme hostility towards or extreme aversion to."

Joe said, "That's the way I've felt toward the simulator. I wanted to beat it at any cost."

Tera continued, "3. Greed—having a keen desire to accumulate things of known value, hoarding, an eager desire or longing for something that is not yours. 4. Compassion—a suffering with someone, actions that help and encourage sympathy."

Joe said, "Gee, that's how I felt when my protector died. I guess something that tragic even K-8126 couldn't or wasn't strong enough to suppress. You know, I didn't eat for several days, either. Maybe, that's when my emotion started showing. In fact, I was even visited by a Committee member who practically made me eat. That's when I got over it, after I started eating regularly. K-8126 really must not last very long."

Dawn said, "I've never felt that way, Joe."

Joe replied, "It's all starting to make some sense now, isn't it?"

Tera continued, "5. Love—to regard with strong feeling. Passionate affection for another person."

Joe asked, "What's affection?"

Tera answered, "Affection—having kind desires and actions toward something or someone… feeling inseparable."

Joe answered, "Explain more about this feeling called love. You know, Dawn, I think this is the kind of feeling that I have for you."

Dawn expressed, "I feel the same way, Joe."

Tera explained, "Love is a devoted attachment to a person or thing. It can be felt between two people of opposite sexes. A special bond uniting them, caring for each other this bond can be felt toward the offspring of mating."

Joe interrupted, "Stop, Tera, stop. Did you hear that, Dawn? *Love*! I love you!"

Dawn replied, "I love you too."

Joe said, "That's the feeling! Inseparable, caring, united—the word is *love*! That's it! *Love*!"

Tera explained, "Emotions are a major part of the makeup of human beings. The supression of emotions is acquired by the act of desensitizing the society. The emotional state returns shortly after the drug K-8126 is eliminated from the normal everyday diet."

Joe said, "Can you believe it, Dawn? We have been drugged for many years now. We have literally been poisoned since the time of our birth. How cruel can they be. They have completely controlled our will. How terrifying."

Dawn replied, "It sure is!"

"Wait until Derek hears this. What is the result of this emotion, caring and binding of affection... this love?"

"What kind of question is that, Joe."

"Oh, I don't know. I'm just trying to learn as much as I can about this emotion called *love*."

Tera explained, "Love. In the records of the primitive era, there is no mention of this word. The Greek civilization used three distinct words for the one word translated *love*. *Eros* describes sensual passion and is commonly connected with human sexual activity. Fileo describes the intense caring of family members, sisters, brothers excluding sexual activity. Agape transcends both forms. It is self-denying, often sacrificial, and is unconditional. It is implied and illustrated in the commitment of a mother who endures laborious suffering in childbirth. Often seen demonstrated by warriors dying to save comrades in battle. Otherwise, it is not commonly observed. Among the monotheistic religions, it is a prime attribute of the Jewish and Christian God, who chose to come from heaven to interact with His creation made in his image, human beings."

Dawn said, "I can relate to some of that."

Joe expressed, "It blows my mind."

"Now, wait a minute, Joe. Didn't you say you would die to save Derek? Where did you get a thought like that? And you said you'd do anything to protect me."

"Yeah, but this agape thing would mean you'd have to love your enemies enough to die for them. I know I've never had that thought."

Tera continued, "Jesus of Nazareth is said to have embodied this love because He came and died an atoning death for the sins and failures of humanity in general, plus individuals personally. Jesus taught that God the Father was the embodiment of such selfless love and the Father, called the Godhead, decided to redeem, buy back from slavery, humans whose activities inevitably involved self-destructive behaviors. Jesus claimed He was God in the flesh, whose bloody death on a Roman cross and bodily resurrection from the grave provides salvation to anyone who believes in Him and His message. To accept Jesus as personal Savior and Lord creates a personal relationship with God that includes forgiveness of sins and assurance of heaven after physical death. Historian Josephus recorded an eyewitness who observed followers of Jesus with the words: 'See how they love each other!' The Christian movement is recorded to have lasted at least into the twenty-first century after Jesus's birth.

Dawn asked, "How could anyone, god or man, show that kind of love for everyone, even strangers?"

Joe said, "It is amazing. I guess that is what makes our God such a great and loving God."

"And we would be commanded to accept Him as Lord and Savior."

Tera explained, "No, it would be your choice to choose to accept Him or not. It's a gift from the Creator. A gift allowing you to be with Him forever after death. In primitive times, the result of the emotion later called *love* in some societies, described a male and a female deciding to spend their lives together, sharing, caring, and being united as one. They mated and made offspring who are a likeness of the two beings in love. They were called babies. These babies along with the now called parents or guardians made up the unit called a family. The woman birthing the baby was called the baby's mother and the male being involved was called the father."

Joe said, "Hey, that's what I am called, the father."

Dawn answered, "Baby, mother, father… It's all so special."

"Now remember, don't use that word outside of the four of us. We are the only ones who will know."

"Yes, I understand, but I'd really like to tell the other women."

"Tera, here on Gamnon what happens to this new being after it is born and deemed worthy to become part of the society?"

Tera answered, "After determination of sex and stability of health, the being is shipped off to its respective Star City. A predetermined, qualified, and respected protector will be provided for the development of that being so that being can grow and learn how to provide needed assets for its own society."

Joe asked, "Will the mating partners ever see the baby again?"

"No, that will be the end of the mates contact with the baby. No further interaction will be allowed, and that is imperative!"

"How and when do they separate the mates from the babies?"

"The separation takes place approximately one month after birth, assuring health and confirmed redrugging of mates."

"Redrugging, when does it start?"

"The drugging process starts while on Gammnon. It is slowly and discreetly added to the food, starting one month before the separation is to take place. By the time the separation nears, both parties are extremely interested in getting back to their respective Star Cities wanting to continue with their work and dedication to their society."

"How can they forget about their mate, their little newborn? Isn't it important for them to be together?"

"Besides the special drug, a long-term amnesia drug is added to the food approximately one month before separation. This drug erases the events that have taken place in the past twelve months. There is no recall, no one ever talks about Gamnon or the Hall of Creation, and the perspective societies exist as they have for all these years."

"They actually forget everything that happens, even the birth!"

"Affirmative."

Dawn interrupted, "That's horrible. What gives them the power, the right, the ability to manipulate everyone's lives?"

Joe replied, "I don't know, Dawn, but we are definitely going to have to find out how to avoid getting drugged, especially that last month. It's crucial that we start avoiding their food at least one and a half months before our seperation to ensure that we aren't being drugged and manipulated. We'll have to stock up with food relatively soon and eat sparingly, especially me, since you are eating for two. We'll have to talk to Derek and Pam tomorrow. We don't want the Committee members to get suspicious. Let's ask Tera if she knows the exact dates of when the drugging starts.

When exactly does the drugging process begin and give us an accurate departure day based on Dawn's conception date."

Tera answered, "Computing. Drugging will begin in forty-nine days, and departure is between the seventy-fourth and seventy-ninth day."

"Are there any other societies that survived the Macrocaust."

"Affirmative. There exist many societies that have survived since the Macrocaust. Several live on earth. One is called the Carthusians but not much is known of their societal organization. The newly formed Star Cities tried to exterminate them soon after the Macrocaust. They managed to eradicate 45 percent of the Carthusians but gave up their war in the year 2153.

"The Carthusians live on earth in a complex underground cave system. Food is very hard to grow on earth even now, but they have supplies sent to them by a common ally that exists upon an orbital Starship. It is totally self-sufficient providing its own food and everything needed for its people and that nation on earth. It was constructed over a short period of time, and several Starships have been developed since then. Its technological advances have not been monitored by the Star Cities. The Starship is named America; it first originated about twenty-five years before the great Macrocaust by a country that existed in the once-called North American continent. This country was known as the United States of America. These people live by a Constitution that gives them freedom of speech, liberty, justice, equality, and right to the pursuit of happiness. Men and women live together in a family unit. They give birth to new generations who are raised by their natural mates called parents. The

Station America now has many satellite communities existing all over the universe. Each satellite community has a certain function and is directly associated with the *Station America*."

"What special functions?"

"Every satellite contributes to one of the functions of the starship defense, agricultural, manufacturing, housing. Each colony meets with the starship annually to exchange goods and repair needed items. Every settlement is provided with a stock of supplies that will last seven years. They designed the mother ship so that if it is ever destroyed, they can replicate it by interaction among its communities."

"Who currently is commander of the operations on the *Station America*?"

"The starship is run as the country once was run, by elections, appointed committees, judicial boards, and many branches of the government. There does exist one man who has the power to make major decisions, and his name is Commander Joe Cavelli."

"Well, we have something in common. We have the same first name, and we are both commanders."

"Tell us about Commander Cavelli."

"High intelligence, bravery, great respect by his peers. He was once a pilot for the Star City Society. He fought in many battles, and his strategic planing helped win several intragalactic wars including major battles against the Carthusians. He then flew in an expedition that almost cost him his life. He went many days without food and remained on Tedron 6 for several months, living off what was available to him from the planet's own resources. He was deprogrammed after his drugged food ran out, and he experienced an entire range of emotions unknown to him. He then realized what the Star Cities had done to him. He would have died on that planet if not for a failed enemy navigation computer. A pilot in a fighter ship from the *Station America* landed on Tedron 6 after temporarily losing his orientation in a skirmish. The pilot helped Cavelli repair the navigational computer damaged in the commander's ship. He then followed the fighter pilot back to the Starship. There he became a loyal servant of the people and worked his way up through the ranks until he was elected commander in chief of the *Station America*."

Dawn said, "Joe, do you think we can ever meet someone from that starship?"

"You know, that dream just may come true."

"Do you really think so?"

"I am going to die trying. Dawn, let's make a pact together and vow to make every effort to pursue this dream of reaching the *Station America*. A pact to always strive to—I mean if anything should ever happen to separate us that we will strive to be reunited no matter what the cost. Let's say we will be bound by this great feeling called love. I love you and pledge my life to existing with you forever."

"I agree, I love you too, Joe, and I pledge to fight until death if need be in order to fulfill our vow to strive to be free."

"We have to realize that we will be outcasts—rebels toward our own society, and we are not so sure that America will accept us. If they don't accept us—"

Joe paused for a moment, trying to figure out other options that might be available.

Dawn broke the silence. "Joe, our doubt has to end here. Our faith in a loving and caring God will have to overcome any doubt we have. We have to believe it will all happen. I know there will be obstacles, but we have to have the strongest convictions, the strongest faith that it will all come true."

"You're right, Dawn. I've always known there was a Supreme Being that I could trust but never knew He loved us so much that He died for our transgressions and rose from the dead to prove his deity. So before our God, I relinquish any doubt in my mind about our commitment to each other."

"Thank you, my love."

"Tera, why has all this history of the past world and the existence of these other societies been kept from us?"

Tera replied, "The Carthusian society along with the world before the Macrocaust is designated as 'societies that failed to survive.' It came to be known as the 'black cloud' and never was to be recalled again. There was to be no input from societies that became mutated. Creators of the Star Cities aimed to completely abolish all previously known governmental policies and create a totally new entity promoting a perfect society."

Joe asked, "Have there been any escapes, or, as we would say, defections to join any other societies including the Carthusian and the *Station America* nations?"

"In the past two hundred years, there has been one escapee known to the Committee. His name is Commander Joe Cavelli, and it has happened within the last forty years. Previously there were 170 attempts—all were caught and executed."

Dawn said, "It doesn't look like the odds are with us."

Joe replied, "It doesn't matter. You have to believe it will happen. That statistic proves only one thing to me. It is possible for an escape to be successful."

"I do truly believe it can be done, Joe, with the proper resourses and a full-proof plan. With our desire to be free and a God who loves us and protects us together we can accomplish anything."

"That's right Dawn." He turned to Tera. "Tera, why didn't our society destroy the Carthusian nation?"

"The founding Star Cities' generation made a huge effort fifty years after the Macrocaust to exterminate the earth of these radiation-deformed people. The war lasted twenty years, but the Carthusians were smarter than anticipated. They entered the caverns and when retreating scattered for many kilometers, successfully ensuring their survival. It became extremely difficult to seek out and destroy every Carthusian."

"Where did they get food and weapons?"

"At first their weapons were very conventional, and they nearly starved to death. Soon they became allies with the society of people who created the *Station America*. They worked together for many years, and finally with the exploration into space, the two semi-states have become what they call sister societies. Now the *Station America* provides them with the necessary technology and supplies to survive and defend their society. After about ten years, the technology of the two societies finally surpassed the new Star City Utopians, and retreat to the Star Cities was inevitable. Once they retreated, the

Carthusians felt no need to continue their pursuit. They were finally comfortable and able to defend their homeland."

"Now, the important questions: How do we get out of here? What are the defense plans of the two Star Cities? How many border patrols? What are their schedules? Tell me everything you know about the firepower and locations of the main batteries and auxiliaries, and if they all tie into a main computer?"

The rest of the night was intense, and I made Tera repeat the information several times so I could write it down and study it. It was 5:00 a.m., and Dawn had fallen asleep on the couch. I picked her up and put her to bed, then went out to listen and study the defense plan several more times. I felt knowing that information fluently would someday become an asset to us. I also repeatedly reviewed the entire governmental and military structure trying to formulate a full proof plan for escape.

The next day went by very fast, and the sun peeking through the blinds gave off an array of different colors in the living area.

Derek called, "Joe, wake up! What are you doing sleeping in the middle of the day? Why are you so tired?"

Joe said, "What? What the—Who?"

"Joe, it's me Derek. Remember we were supposed to jazz up Tera for some information today. Oh, come on, jazz up Tera. That's got to be my best one in a long time. Let's go. Are you going to sleep all day?"

"Oh yeah, I was going to call you around 0800 hours. What time is it?"

"Eight! Top gun, you're just a little late. It's 1100 hours."

"Eleven hundred hours, I've been sleeping that long?"

"Yeah, why? Were you up all night or something? Joe, you didn't—not without me?"

"Yeah, I'm sorry, I couldn't wait. I was up all night memorizing the Star Cities defenses."

"Couldn't wait, right. Well, clue me in! Come on."

"Okay, okay, let me wake up a little first. By the way, Dawn and I vowed to reach *Station America* together or die trying?"

"Wow, is that something I should talk over with Pamela?"

"Do you love her?"

"Well, do you mean do I want to be with her forever? Care for her? Protect her? Yes, yes, of course, I love her. Is that what love is?"

"Yes, that's it. Does she love you?"

"I think so. She has definitely given me that impression."

"Well, don't worry. Besides I've taken care of that for you. Dawn is briefing Pam on everything. Yes, Derek, we are about to make it a team."

"Great."

"Did you review the history of *Station America*?"

"Yes and that's trouble. The only way we are going to be able to communicate with the starship is through the Carthusians."

"We are going to have to work on that plan."

"We could rig a computer to get us in contact with the *Station America*, but we have to know the time the ship will be in our orbit."

"That's going to be tough."

"How about the fuel?"

Tera replied, "It will take 184.5 gallons of propulsion fuel."

"Thanks, but ouch."

"Only a modified guardian fighter ship could hold that much fuel."

"What is the tank capacity of a normal fighter?"

"One hundred and forty gallons."

Derek said, "We will have to modify one of the fighters but where?"

Joe answered, "Wait. Let's ask Tera. Tera, do the Star Cities have any modified fighters available?"

Tera answered, "Yes, there are one hundred ships used in the Carthusian wars that were equipped with fuel tanks of 192.3 gallons. Although they have been used sparingly since the war, they haven't been commissioned in over a decade."

Derek said, "Oh great!"

Joe expressed, "That doesn't matter. Just let me get to one. I'll make it fly."

"Would a cruiser have that tank capacity?"

Tera answered "Affirmative. In fact, their fuel capacity is well over 192 gallons."

"How about taking one of those?

Joe said, "That would be nice, but they are so bulky and slow we wouldn't make it out of the landing bay besides there is not enough armament to reach America."

Derek said, "I guess I'll leave the air ships up to you."

"Tera, do the schedules of the guardian patrols change on holidays."

"Yes, a skeleton crew consisting of one-third of all patrol vehicles are on watch for the holidays. The remainder is used as security for the celebration. The rest are defense-ready, though, and can be called up and manned within twenty-five minutes."

"Great, that's when we'll make our break for the women."

Derek asked, "What? What, you are way ahead of me."

"Yes, that's right; I've worked up some of the plan already. In fact, I've been working on it for quite some time. I just needed a starting point, and now I have it."

"Why didn't you tell me?"

"I wasn't absolutely sure all of us would team up, and I didn't want to discourage the idea before it got started. Look, partner, I'm with you all the way, all the time. You should know that by now. We live for each other and die together. We take the risk at any cost. Okay, Derek, it's a pact, no more secrets, ever."

We both shook hands firmly, and as my other hand clenched the shake, together we vowed, "Forever."

Joe said, "We forgot to ask one important question. Tera, will we be accepted to live with these people on America?"

"Affirmative, the American society is willing to accept anyone who wants to join their nation. They live by free will and freedom of choice. It is a republic within a democracy. it was unique in the Old World."

Derek muttered, "Republic in a democracy."

"That is where the power rests with the people, ruling themselves directly or indirectly by choosing a representative group of elected officials."

Joe asked, "Is this freedom unlimited?"

"Personal freedom could be restricted by decisions of the executive president, the Congress or the court system. A person could not yell "fire" in a crowded theatre, for example. And everyone was expected to value human life highly, no matter what stage the life it's in; from conception to birth to dying and death. Each life is viewed as significant and precious because all were endowed by their Creator with the right to live. And Americans believe that they were born in the likeness of the Creator and existed to fulfill His purpose in their own lives. All of this was directly connected to the creation of a republic, a distinct form of governmental democracy."

"I heard that from my protector once but he told me that it was strictly forbidden to speak of it. He described to me a government of the people, by the people and for the people—a phrase from the Old World."

"Yes, that phrase was used by an American president, Abraham Lincoln, who was one of their most gifted presidents. His guide was the living word of God. It is called the Bible. A book written by men inspired by the Supreme Creator."

"Thank you, Tera. Download a copy of that book to my wrist hard drive. That way I'll always have a copy with me to use as my personel guide. Derek, can you update me on the computers that run the gun emplacements?"

Derek said, "Yes, I updated most of them and reprogrammed a good part of the main defense system myself."

Joe asked, "Are they all connected to a main computer or several secondary computers? What happens if we knock out one of the main computers?"

"They work like this. One computer manages one block in a designated area. That main computer controls all the firepower in that specific region—about twenty kilometers. If that main computer is destroyed, two auxiliary computers work together to pick up that area so each computer operates thirty square kilometers If both main and auxiliary computers are destroyed, it's broken up into four squares. It's impregnable in a three-dimensional area, completely protecting every parameter of Altaur. The more you knock out, the more computers that come into play. I'm proud of that system. I designed it, implemented, and deployed it."

"Did you have to make it so precise, so efficient?"

Derek replied, "That was my job, but I did leave a small loophole. I guess just as a matter of a trademark."

"You're inventive, I'll say that much for you."

"You don't think I would give away all my secrets, do you?"

"No, no, well, tell me how do we shut down an area of about four and a half squares so we can make a clean break for Balem?"

"Four and a half squares, wow! That's asking a lot."

"I know, but I figure, at top speed, that's the smallest area that has to be put out of commission for us to get off Altaur safely. Asking for four and a half, hoping to get two and a half is how it normally goes, Derek. I figure at maximum speed for four minutes we will be out of range of the perimeter guns and before the initial gun emplacement computers will be back online we should be already landing on Balem."

"The only way to accomplish that and give us a full four minutes is to reprogram the main computer. We will never be able to knock out enough squares."

"Oh, that's great. It's so well guarded. We'll never get near it."

"We don't have to."

"What is this, another one of your trademarks?"

"Yes, I do have to admit I got a million of them. Look, I have a handheld communicator that I can set on a certain alpha code frequency that will jam the computer, but it will only work for about five minutes. The computer is so sophisticated that it can change its code in five to six minutes."

"How did you manage to design that little communicator?"

"I studied under Dr. Neigh at the University. In fact, I studied there and worked with him on the new defense system."

"The one and only... You worked with him? I didn't know that!"

"Yes, sir, I most definitely did and don't think he didn't put any of his own trademarks in that system. I don't think anyone will ever decipher his weird trademarks but back to getting us out of here, the new fighters. Where are they?"

Joe said, "Good question. Where are the new modified fighters located?"

Tera answered, "The modified fighters are located in Sector 7 Bay 1234."

"Can you give me the computer code to enter the bays where the fighters are?"

"Yes, it's HR773057, but do you want the specific location of the new modified fighters closest to the area where you will be blocking the batteries."

"Are there more fighters somewhere else?"

"Affirmative. In Sector 27, Bay 1432."

"Well, forget the fighters. They're too far away. The four squares of laser battery locations needed to be blocked are in Sector 77."

Derek interrupted, "Sector 77?"

"Yes, that's where the laser emplacements have to be blocked. See from Sector 77. It's a straight shot to Balem and the fastest way. Don't forget it's all going to hit the fan once they figure out what has happened. And remember, theoretically, only two and a half squares would have to be blocked to make our escape. That should make our job real easy."

"Easier, well, less complicated. Okay, so we will confiscate an old Guardian fighter, and after you skillfully maneuver through the city."

"No problem."

"Then, as soon as we hit Sector 77 straight across the sky to Balem."

"Right but we will have to elude both Altaur and Balems' fighters.'

"Where are we going to land? And how are we going to avoid the sensors? Are we going to leave that up to Pam and Dawn?"

"That's right. That will be their job. They'll have to work that out."

"Are you sure they can do it? We are putting our lives into their hands. What if something goes wrong?"

"If they fail, we will know long before we land."

"I guess we will. Hey supposedly, the Star Cities are exactly alike. That will work to our advantage right, Joe?"

"Yes, which should make it fairly easy."

"Easier said than done."

"Well, anyway there are old landing bays that are located on the bottom floor just above the anti-gravity devices. When they built the new landing bays, the old ones were abandoned. We can fly there and blend in with all the old aircraft. Also, there will be all kinds of air traffic; along with our welcoming party."

"Sounds good, but can it be done?"

"I'm sure of it, with all that comotion being made we will just blend in."

"Well, let's get the computer code to block Sector 77, so I can store it in the memory banks of my communicator."

"Oh, I almost forgot about the code. That would have been a costly mistake. Tera, give us the deactivation number of the defense computer for Sector 77?"

"The deactivation number for the computer defense code for Sector 77 will be as follows: G52AR4y8721MO7LgL16L7A"

"Perfect, we're halfway there, partner."

"Sure. Next, we'll have to find the women once we land."

"Oh, Pam will be working on some sensors for them to wear. We will know exactly where they are once we are in range of the landing bays."

"We are gonna need weapons."

"Taken care of. There are some on the fighter."

"Perfect."

"Maybe, we can get a fighter from that store owner, with a little persuading that is. We can try that first and if it doesn't work out we will have to go to plan B. That is, hit Charlie up for my fighter. I just don't want to get him in trouble."

"You know, it will have to be done within a few days of returning because we won't be able to eat anything. Remember the food?"

"Wow! That's going to kill me! We are going to have to get some."

"I'm already working on a plan for that. We'll need some for the trip anyway."

"Okay, then what?"

Joe asked, "What do you mean?"

Derek replied, "How do we contact the Starship? We have no dates or times and we have to move as soon as we get back."

"Somehow, well have to contact the Carthusians. We can only hope they will be willing to help us."

"Somehow? That's pretty vague. That's the only part of the plan that bothers me. If we make contact and they don't help us, we're sunk."

"From that point, it's all ad lib. It's getting late. You better go home and tell Pam our plan, and I'll brief Dawn... Oh, and let's start stocking up on food. We need at least two weeks' worth. But remember, we still have to get our allotment. That last month and a half, we'll just have to destroy it."

"Say, I'm definitely not going to like that very much."

"We don't want them to get suspicious."

"Right. See you later."

Dawn came home shortly after Derek left, and both women agreed to whatever plan we felt would be successful. Time went by really fast after our talk with Tera, and that computer started to become a good friend. We went over defense plans daily and questions that kept popping up were answered promptly. Pam and Dawn were definitely looking pregnant now, and we both stocked up enough food so that we could eat somewhat normally the last month. Derek and I made some sacrifices and so did both women. All of us had began to lose some weight, and we started to worry about the babies, but the staff physicians assured us that everything was fine even though we weren't eating regularly and both Derek and I felt strong and in good shape.

One day at the simulators, Cappy asked me if I was sick. I guess the weight loss was starting to be noticeable. I said that I was just tuning up the old body, getting in shape. I had to keep up with all the youngsters coming up the ranks. He just smiled and looking at his own big belly remarked, "I used to look like you, Joe, but age finally caught up with me."

Derek needed to lose some weight, so he looked great, almost better than when he first came to Gamnon. Consequently, no one questioned him.

We were going to be permitted to nurture the baby for a short period of time after the birth and we, not being drugged, looked forward to the time spent with the newborn. Pam and Dawn each delivered healthy baby boys, and we started bonding immediately. We did notice that the mates of the newborns were starting to reject the little ones, and now it was our turn to put on a show.

"We joked around somewhat after the birth," Dawn said coyly, "that the little one looked like me."

Shortly before the separation, we talked briefly about leaving our baby.

"I don't know if I could part with him, Joe. He's so cute. I love him so much."

"I know it seems so difficult," Joe whispered. "I guess if we were drugged, we wouldn't have these feelings and leaving him would be alot easier."

"You're right," Dawn said. "We probably wouldn't care. That's so terrible!"

"Well, Dawn, maybe we won't have to part with him forever."

"What do you mean?"

"See this mark on my ankle. I have had it for as long as I can remember."

"What does it mean?" Dawn asked.

"I don't really know, but I can reproduce it pretty easily. We can mark him, just in case we have an opportunity to come back and look for him, someday. Who knows what the future holds for us."

"We can use Cryotron blue. It can't be removed and is easily available. In fact, I have some with me right now."

"Okay, Joe, but let's do it somewhere not very noticeable."

"Right, how about under his upper arm somewhere in his right axilla? No one would ever see it there. A month ago, I had talked to

Derek about making an instrument to inscribe the mark so we both made one."

Dawn and I along with Pam and Derek carefully inscribed a mark on our babies so even though they would be separated from us maybe some day we could be reunited. Soon, it was time to be split up, and Pam gave me a very small, highly sophisticated hand scanner that would pick up a sensor that she would place in the tiny holes in her ear lobes. I explained to her one more time when she was to block the radar scanner, and soon our plan was set.

Finally, it was time to enter the cylinder for our departure. We reassured each other of being careful not to eat the food, and with great confidence said goodbye both of us knowing it would only be a short time before we were reunited.

I could see Dawn's face just before we descended, and her eyes were bright with encouragement but sad with real concern. She blinked often wiping the tears away. The final expression was a very big smile, a wave, and a tear that ran slowly down her cheek. Soon, Derek was next to me, and both of us were extremely quiet over the absence of the ones we loved. As we looked at each other, we shook hands firmly reassuring ourselves that what lay ahead would prove to be the right choice and the priority for our mind-sets.

Soon, our lives would change drastically, fulfilling a need suppressed by a society that was ruthless in controlling every aspect of their citizens lives.

CHAPTER 7

Escape from Altaur

I fell asleep with no problem the night Derek, and I returned to Altaur, our beloved homeland, but my sleep was interrupted early the next morning. I reached over to touch Dawn who was still so fresh in my mind, saying warmly, "I love you!" Then I realized that part of my life just might never return. I felt so empty, lonely, fearful that I may not succeed and possibly never see her again. The thought of death in the process seemed so trivial. I looked at the clock, and it was only 0300 hours. I still had five more hours before my shift for Patrol started.

I went into the living area and turned on a soft light near the couch. Over on the end table was a book, I was reading before I met Dawn. The book intrigued me so much before Gamnon that I could hardly put it down. I picked it up, sat down on the couch over by the dimly lit end table, and started to reminisce through the pages I had wholeheartedly believed in. I skimmed through a couple of pages and soon I could remember the basic theme. I closed the book and gazed at the cover for a several seconds, then thought to myself, *What a farce!*

Through drugs and propaganda, they had controlled every situation in my life. I thought about throwing the foolish book away, but the wheels started turning. Joe, don't do anything suspicious. What if they check my trash? I'm sure they watch us for a while after returning just to make sure we are back on track. I surely would be caught and probably executed. I laughed a little and asked myself what is normal when you're drugged? I decided a walk might help so I opened the door and started to walk down the hallway. I noticed a gentle glimmer of light coming from Derek's living quarters. I'll bet he's having the same problem. I went back into my living area sat down for a second, then decided to go over and see if Derek was awake. I went down the hallway once again and knocked lightly on the door. I didn't even finish my second knock, and Derek opened the door.

"I didn't think you would hear me."

"Well, maybe I was waiting for that knock, Joe."

"I couldn't sleep."

"Me neither. Come on in."

As we walked over to the couch, Derek put his index finger on his lips signaling me to be quiet, then he pointed to the ceiling. Derek went into the kitchen and brought in a chair. He stood on it and reached up into the light fixture disconnecting a small wire.

"There now we can talk. I figured they were watching us, but I didn't know how it was being done. I checked out the place and found three more, but I keep the door closed on the bedroom and bathroom, and could you believe there's one in the shower?"

"Yes. Nothing would surprise me these days."

"Oh, there was one more on the patio. I'll just shut off the light. It is triggered by light and will shut down when the light goes out. We can talk out there. Maybe, they'll think you left and we can talk in private."

"I'm glad I came over here. I would have never found all of them. Are you sure that's all there are, Derek?"

"Yes, I did some cheating. I have this tiny little scanner. See, most of the time they are put randomly in the quarters. Even the men who put them in can't remember where they put them half the time, so they give them a scanner to trace them out."

"And how did you get a scanner Derek, no, no. I don't even want to know. Just tell me one thing, you didn't?"

"Yes, I did!"

"Oh come on, Derek. You designed them?"

"Sure, but they know that. Wouldn't they do something different for you?"

"Well, someone knows, but there are so many, inventors, Committee members, security personel, and engineers. Most of the time they don't know who does what."

"How do you remember what you have developed or what inventions you worked on throughout the years."

"See, everyone has a sign or trademark and when you cast the main mold you add it to the product. See, here is my sign."

"Does everyone do that?"

"Yes, sir, everyone! Here take it home with you and take care of your bugs."

"Let's go inside. It's kind of chilly out here, Derek."

"Okay, but we will have to trick them into thinking you went home. Their sensors will pick up your image again once we enter the apartment."

"In fact, go to your place now, open the door, shut the lights off, and close it again. Actually, rather abruptly, see, once they think you are asleep your system shuts down, conservation. I'll shut them off here, and in a couple minutes, come on back and we'll be able to talk—in the dark, that is.

I did as Derek suggested, and soon we were both sitting in his living room once again. The curtains were drawn, and the lights were off with only a small security lamp on in between us on the floor.

"We should be talking under candle light with Pamela and Dawn, right Joe?"

"Yes, I know. Speaking of Pam and Dawn, I just can't get Dawn out of my mind. I'm starting to miss her already."

"Yes, I know the feeling. My thoughts are constantly about Pamela."

"Derek, we can't wait any longer. Just think about it. What is normal over here? I'm not sure how I acted when I was drugged and brainwashed. The longer we wait, the higher the chance of one of us making a mistake."

"Luckily, the holiday is in two days."

"Yes, I don't know what we would have done if it was weeks away."

"Well, transportation is our first concern, armament our second."

"Yes, in fact, do you remember that hobby shop we visited on the way to retrieve your tools. You remember Hall of Creation fire drill?"

"Do I remember… How can I forget that escapade."

"I thought we were going to try to get your fighter."

"Well, don't forget. I want to try and keep Charlie out of this. Besides, those guys were up to something, and I bet you a million tokens that they could probably get us a new Guardian patrol ship."

"It would be less conspicuous. We'll take all our barter chips and offer them as payment. How much do you have, Derek?"

"I have about 150,000 chips."

"That's great. I have about 850,000 chips."

"What have you been saving them for, Joe? Oh, a special occasion?"

"Well, it can't get more special than this wild and crazy adventure."

"That's for sure, but do you think that's enough for a new Guardian fighter."

"It should be more than enough. You know I would settle for a slightly used C-32 or R-54 but nothing less."

"It sure would be nice to get a new Guardian ship, wouldn't it?"

"Yes, it would, but don't count on it. We'll just have to wait and see what's available and take the best ship we can get."

"It will probably be an M-73 fighter."

"Yes, probably! It's old but very efficient and armed to the max."

We both laughed softly, trying to ease the anxiety that was building in us. "What if he won't barter, and we can't get a ship?"

"We will get one, somehow, Derek! Somehow! We can always threaten them."

We have a little leverage knowing about their operation. We can get them in real trouble. And if they don't cooperate, we'll just have to use a little force.

There's no turning back now, no matter what happens. The women are depending on us and if everything fails we will just have to take my fighter."

"I know, Joe. I know."

"Listen, Derek, I'm going to find a way to spend the rest of my life with Dawn or die trying. We have to make that commitment. We have to be ruthless! No more negatives. It's confidence and optimism from now on."

"You're right, Joe. You're right. I'm with you all the way!"

"I knew you would be. Besides, we're too smart for these guys and if we run into trouble we'll just improvise."

We will leave 10 percent of our tokens in our account. Hopefully, they won't get suspicious. We'll get them tomorrow after work, maybe at closing, and if we're blessed, the Committee won't find out until after the holiday."

"Joe, what about food? I'm starting to get hungry. We ran out of real food—that is, untampered food—yesterday."

"We'll have to make a food run on the warehouse later today. I am pretty hungry myself. Let's meet at my apartment tonight at 0300 hours. We'll try to get enough for dinner and some dried food for the trip."

"With some healthy snacks we can go without real meals, at least, for awhile."

"Well, the Committee did some studies awhile back. It was some sort of survival in space study. They figured that the normal human being could go between eighteen and twenty-four days without food. But sleep, and water now that's another story."

"Well, we have plenty of water, and we can sleep anywhere. We'll be all right—oh, and we will have to be able to fit it all in our backpacks."

"I'm sure that can be done especially if we get mostly dried and snack foods."

"Well, in eighteen days, we won't need any of their food, one way or the other."

"Yes, I better get back just in case they have an infrared check tonight."

"Okay, tomorrow then."

"Oh, and don't forget to put those wires back together. Can you believe they don't trust us?"

"Ha! Ha! Do you blame them?"

"I'm glad you said something, Joe. I forgot about that connector. It must be the hunger. It's finally affecting my brain."

"Don't worry, Derek. I'll keep you in line."

"Thanks, see you later."

Morning came fast, and soon I was back to the old routine. Except this day was different. I couldn't stop planning and replanning. I knew we only had one shot at this, and the plan had to be foolproof. There was one problem I hadn't told Derek about because I didn't want to burden him with details. The system releases what are called interceptor ships once the defense system has been penetrated. They are the fastest ships developed for our city. Their main purpose is to protect the city during an invasion. They are also used to track and destroy escapees and black marketers. They are only used for these circumstances. The part that bothered me was they were unmanned and could be flown from base destroying our fighter by any means possible even self destruction. These ships were the reason there had been no escapes in so many years. Everyone had been eliminated. I saw one demonstrated a couple of years earlier. It occurred when a foreign supply ship entered our airspace. Knowing what I know now, I would say it was probably a transport from the *Station America*. They attacked the supply ship from every angle using laser guns, torpedoes, rockets, and even crashing into the ship disinagrating upon impact. The supply ship was destroyed and looking back; the ship was poorly armed and support fighters were scarce, consequently, the defense computers were no match for them and these interceptors ships annihilated the transport. It was inevitable that we were going to run into a bunch of them and soon after we leave Altaur. We must be prepared to defend ourselves. Our only advantage is they have a limited range, actually very limited. We do have one more resource up our sleeve and that is that I was well informed of where the interceptor ships were and where they launch their attack. Tera was very thorough in explaining the defense system.

The day went by rather fast, and it was time to meet Derek at my apartment and he was right on time as usual.

"Are you ready, Derek?"

"Yes, how about you?"

"Yes and I'm starving. Let's do it."

We headed for the warehouse, and I decided to inform Derek of our plan on the way. There is only one guard on duty at night. We could slip by him pretty easily, not even needing any type of diversion.

We got the plans and layout of the dispensary from Tarcon, Derek's home computer. We finally were able to reap the benefits of our hard or, should I say, Derek's hard work. He even gave us the exact placement of food items throughout the whole dispensary. We decided to get nourishing snacks and dinner items trying to exist on one good meal per day. Our plans were to jump the fence when the guard made his rounds, moving along the poorly lit dumpsters until we reached the entrance to the dispensary. Derek was then going to disarm the alarm system by inserting a certain magnetic card he had made to the specifications of the locking system and under the direction of our good colleague, Tarcon. Once the card was inserted into the key and a code applied, the alarm would disengage, then we'd enter a door code.

The reason it was so hard to enter was that each door had a separate code and the security codes were changed every week. But that wasn't really a problem and at dock 21, the area where shipments were delivered, once opened gave us direct access to the dried meats, fruits, nuts, snacks, and protein bars.

The door on the long dock was extremely well lit, but the locks were hidden in the shadows and could be approached secretly, and getting us through was Derek's job. His little computer could supposedly do it in forty-five seconds. Derek was just amazing with those computers. We sure made a good pair, a great team, but getting out could be a problem. All around the dispensary stood tall buildings, none of them with passages between them. The only other way out besides the way we got in was a small alley that ran behind the loading docks out to the main street.

The vehicles, which ran on tracks in the street, would just clear the tall buildings on each side. If we got caught between those two buildings, it was all over, even though, it would have to be our escape route if something went wrong. We walked alongside the fence waiting for the guard to get up for his rounds. Well, this began badly because the guard who was supposed to make his rounds every hour never did and fell asleep in the guardhouse. Now, our early morning excursion became somewhat complicated.

"Joe, we can't walk along this fence another time. The guard might wake up see us again and get suspicious."

"Well, I never figured on him falling asleep. We will never make it past the guardhouse with him in there. We'll have to provide some type of diversion."

I took out my laser weapon and on medium power started shooting the lights out alongside the vehicles hoping he would inspect the area and blame it on a power surge. After the third light was destroyed, the guard woke up and looked somewhat startled. At this time, we were across the street hiding in an entryway of a shop. He looked out toward the street then back at the vehicles. As he inspected them from the fence to the dispenser, he noticed that three lights were out on the vehicles nearest to the dispensary. Slowly, he put on his hat and reached for his laser. He put it in his holster giving us the impression that he really wasn't concerned. Soon, he was out the door making his way to the vehicle.

"Okay, Derek. Let's go, now! My stomach is screaming for nourishment." We climbed the fence, and soon, in a matter of seconds, we were on the other side making our way to the garbage bins. As we passed the guardhouse, we noticed some soft music coming from the slightly cracked window. Our eyes were on the guard the whole time. He never even looked back and it wasn't long before we reached the dumpsters. We worked our way down to within twenty-five feet of the entrance to the dispensary and waited for the guard to make his next move. For a moment, we lost sight of the him.

"Hey, where's the guard, Joe? I don't see him."

"I think he slipped around the vehicles. Just be calm and wait here a moment. He has to surface sometime."

We waited for about thirty seconds. Then, he emerged from the vehicles and walked over to check the entrance to the dispensary. If he looked real close, we thought he might detect us, so Derek and I slipped into the closest dumpster. The garbage bin sure had a pungent odor to it, and Derek felt he had to pinch his nose to stomach the smell. It was dark in there and in a certain way we were glad. A small opening did exist on the far end, and we could see the guard through it. We waited until he started back toward the guardhouse. When we no longer heard the guard's footsteps, we got out of the dumpster and moved toward the door. As we moved nearer in the dark, Derek noticed something on his right leg.

"Joe, check my leg. I think something is crawling on me."

"Yeah, me too. Those nasty slats. I hate those things. Give me your flashlight." Joe flashed the light on his legs and discovered about fifteen of them, but soon, they fell off and slithered away in to the darkness. I shined the light on my legs, and they too fell off. Slats are slimy black insects about the size of your middle finger. They live in all the garbage bins as a control specimen for the destruction of the garbage. They are very sensitive to light and are kept in groups of five hundred in each bin. Once they get too big or multiply too fast, little laser sensors inside the bin destroy them. They will try to suck blood if they get on you but are really no threat. They are just ugly looking creatures, but they actually digest everything, even bone, vegetable scraps, and hair. They live their lives out eating garbage at night. They relax in the daytime literally stuck to the bottom of the bin covered in garbage.

"Joe, I think you missed one on my back. He's biting right through my shirt." I shined the light up there, and sure enough, he was embedded.

"Oh, come on, Derek. They don't hurt much. Give them a break."

"Yeah sure, Joe. I hate those slimy parasites."

"Okay, let's go. This part is all yours, Derek. I'll watch and make sure the guard doesn't see us."

We waited for the guard to sit down again and prop his legs up to finish his early morning nap. We moved slowly up to the entrance and Derek put the card into the lock to disengage the alarm. I moved on to the shadow across from him next to a loading vehicle. Derek met me shortly afterward.

"That didn't take long."

"Thanks to Tarcon," Derek said.

"Now, if the guard doesn't see the disconnected light on his monitor, we'll be all right."

"He'll probably think it was another result of that power surge."

We moved quickly, but very quietly, down the narrow loading dock to door number twenty-one. Derek connected two jumper wires to the circuits on the lock and the computer started rapidly running through sequential numbers. After ten seconds, a click, then another at twenty-seven, and another at forty. The door clicked open.

"Oh, wow!"

"What's up, Derek?"

"Well, I calculated forty-five seconds, and it did the job in forty. How could I have made a five-second error?"

"Come on, you ham, let's go."

We both ran through the warehouse putting as much food in our space sack as we could carry. The space sack was unique in itself. It folded into a seven inch by seven inch square, and when it was opened, it would hold up to forty pounds worth of items and never break. It also had a thick nylon strap you could throw over your arms to use as a backpack, which seemed to be very practical. Tarcon showed us where the otherwise untainted food was kept, so there was no mistake in picking the right food. Soon, my pack was filled, and it was time to find Derek.

"Hey, Derek? Where are you?"

"Over here, behind the counter."

"Come on, Derek. Hurry, come on move it. We don't have all night!"

Derek's bag was full, but he was so hungry he was filling up pockets in his jacket and eating right there as he filled his sack.

"You're crazy, Derek. Let's go! And pick up your mess. Move it!"

"Okay, I'm nearly through."

I moved over to the door, and about fifteen seconds later, Derek comes running down the isle huffing and puffing with food falling out all over the floor.

"Let's go, I'm ready. I'm definitely ready," Derek exhaustly pleaded.

We moved toward the opening and checked both ways, poking our head out of the door to make sure the guard hadn't started to make any unexpected rounds.

As we moved cautiously and quietly through the darkness, we heard a small disturbance coming from the same garbage bins we were hiding in. We pinned ourselves up against the wall, waited a moment, then moved slowly toward the end of the dock. We quietly jumped down off the loading dock and hid there for a moment. Our eyes were clearly adjusted to the darkness, so we could clearly see the back of the vehicles.

"What was that, Joe?"

"I don't know, just wait here a moment. Hey, there's some movement over there, over by door 18. Look, Derek… Look!"

I motioned with my hand, hoping not to make our presence obvious, and soon afterward, we could clearly see the disturbance!

"It's just a cat, Derek. It sure gets the old adrenaline going though, doesn't it?"

"Yeah, let's go, Joe. I'm starting to get nervous."

We moved up toward the vehicles. Our initial plan was to reinstate the alarm, make our presence unnoticeable, and slip out the back way.

"Derek, you put the alarm back on, and I'll watch for the guard."

Derek slowly moved over toward the door. Then, all of a sudden, it hit me. We had moved out of the door so quickly that we forgot to close it. As soon as that alarm was established, we would be in deep trouble.

"Derek, Derek," I whispered loudly but to no avail. I quickly dropped the sacks and ran down toward door 21. I couldn't believe I had made such a crucial mistake. It just wasn't like me. As I passed door 18, it hit the fan. A light started flashing inside the building, and the alarm rang out loudly. I reached the door and slammed it shut. Soon, Derek came running down behind me carrying the two sacks of food. The alarm cut off instantaneously.

"What happened?"

"We forgot to close the door. Let's go. Come on, Derek. Follow me." We shimmied up a pole, threw our bags on the roof, and pulled ourselves up onto the roof.

"Get low and be quiet," Derek.

The moment Derek reached the roof, we heard footsteps on the dock: two Guardian patrol vehicles were riding along the dock shining their lights inside the building. Then, the building lights went on again. They seemed to light up the whole docking area. We lay low on the roof for about seven minutes, waiting for things to cool down. Soon, the lights went out, and the docking area went back to being pitch black. The Guardian ships left the area and the guard returned to the guardhouse.

"That was close, Joe. Maybe they thought it was a malfunction from that power surge."

"Power surge?"

"Yeah, the one we created."

"Oh yeah, Derek, wouldn't it be ironic if you received this alarm notice tomorrow at work? I can see it now: 'Dear Mr. Derek Johan, there seemed to be a power surge at dispensary 8562. Could you go down there today and check out the computer for possibly a malfunctioning circuit.'"

"I wouldn't doubt it, Joe. It's starting to get light out here. We better make our move, or we will be in real trouble."

We eased along the roof down to the last dock number 77. We shimmied down the pole and walked along the building to the alley.

We reached the end of the alley, and there was another gate. We made sure there were no Guardian ships patrolling, and Derek hooked up his computer to the lock once again. Soon after the third click, the door popped open, and we entered the street. We closed the door behind us and started walking home. After about seven blocks, we quit dodging patrol ships and walked as if we were on our way to work. There were many citizens out now, hurrying along to their respective duties. We entered our building about 6:30, with huge sighs of relief. We started to eat some of the food, which really hit the spot, and I did some reminiscing of the previous night's mission.

"Derek, are you sure the guard didn't see you after that alarm started howling?"

"Yes, I'm sure he didn't because as soon as I pulled that card out, it startled me so much, I jumped to the shadow immediately and crawled to the sacks. Besides, he didn't leave the guardhouse until I picked up the sacks."

"I'm really glad you saw the sacks. That could have been disastrous. Let's destroy that card. We won't need it anymore."

"We'll find out more about it when the news report comes out around 10:00 a.m. That should give us the whole story."

"Let's prepare a real meal, Derek. I'm tired of just picking at this food."

"You mean you actually pick up more than travel food? Interesting."

"Yes, I wanted to make this meal that I really thought was very tasty, and you know, the ingredients was just seconds away from all that dried travel food."

It took me about forty-five minutes to prepare the meal. It really took me a while to arrive at the recipe that Dawn had made for me. I even brought out the crystal serving tray, something I kept just for special occasions. Crystal was considered very elegant, and it was very valuable on Altaur. The only place it could be found was in high-class restaurants on the Star Cities. It was a very beautiful piece and so delicate I was actually afraid to display or use it. My beloved Protector handed down this platter set to me, and it had been among certain Protectors for a very long time.

"The crystal, Joe? This must be a special occasion."

"It sure is and wait until you taste this dinner."

I opened the platter slowly and watched the expression on his face as his eyes caught a glimpse of the preparation I had made for him. Shortly afterwards, I was enthralled in laughter. His expression was so odd and so exaggerated that I thought his face would be permanently disfigured. His nostrils flared with his eyes wide open, and his brow wrinkled. Then, his mouth dropped to the floor.

"What is that stuff?"

I couldn't stop laughing hysterically at the face he made, when I uncovered the dish, and it took me several minutes to recover from his expression. Then, Derek started laughing, and before you knew it, we were both on the floor in tears.

"I sure wish I had a camera to catch that expression. It was a once in a lifetime revelation. It was frightful enough to scare the committee members right out of their cassocks."

After that comment and at that very moment, Derek abruptly stopped, and pointed to the ceiling lamp where he found the microphone in his room. We both got silent, and I motioned to him that I'd forgotten about that thing, but the chance of it being on was 1 in 1,000.

"Let's eat. I'm pretty hungry."

As I started to serve this food, Derek reached up and disconnected the bug He obviously had something on his mind.

"What's up, Derek?"

"I don't want to keep it off long, so I'm going to ask you straight away. What made you decide to go to the roof?"

"Well, there are two reasons: first, there are no entrances to the building from the roof so logically there would be no reason to check it. The second is it was a flat roof with a two-foot wall around its perimeter. Perfect for hiding."

"How did you know about the design of that warehouse? Tarcon never gave us that information."

"That's right, but after the third time reviewing the blueprints on Gamnon, I noticed the information and thought it might become useful in case we needed plan B, and we did."

"Needless to say, you were right."

"Let me hook up that bug again."

Derek reached up and reconnected the receiver, and we both sat down to enjoy our odd looking food. For a while, we hardly said a word, and before long, we were both so full we could hardly get up from the table.

"Well, how did you like it, Derek?"

"Oh, it was delicious, but I still can't get over how it looks. It's the kind of dish you would like to eat with your eyes closed."

"Yes, I know the feeling. I felt the same way the first time I saw it."

"Where did you find this recipe?"

"Well, you know every recipe has a story behind it. This was a long story, and when we get some time, I'll sit down and tell you."

With that comment, I looked up and pointed to the microphone in the ceiling.

"Oh sure. Well, I best be getting home. We have a big day tomorrow, the holiday and all."

"Yes, it sure will be quite a day. A day we will always remember. You better get some rest. Take care."

I went over to clear the table, and as I was about to carry the platter and the dishes over to the sink, I realized that, either way, by tomorrow I would be gone for good or indisputably dead. It really didn't matter whether I washed them or not. I went over to the sofa and lay down for a short while, then got up and decided that I should go through my personal things. I knew there were a couple of things I wanted to take with me tomorrow. One of the items and most important was a medal that my Protector gave me before he died. He achieved the highest awarded intragalatic medal available to men in our society. There were only four other men ever to achieve this award. Two men were known within the society, and they were very intelligent, brave, wise, and very much respected. The third man in our society was, until recently, the highest council member. He had just passed away. The other man who acquired the medal has never been spoken of and his whereabouts are unknown.

My Protector had known him once and told me that he was a very special man. He said that if I ever had the opportunity to meet him, I should feel very honored and privileged. He said that I should wear the medal when I felt a need to be brave and strong and that it was his right to give the medal away at his death. I sat down for a moment, contemplating the most wonderful times spent with my Protector and decided that this was the time to wear the medal. I would wear it under my flight jacket and wouldn't remove it until we reached our destination. There were a couple more items I thought I'd secure but they all seemed so unimportant. I finally decided that the medal would be the only extra weight I would take, as it reminded me of my beloved Protector. I decided to leave the rest of my belongings here; this would become a new life. I felt sure that I was making the right decision and for the first time in my life I felt a peace of mind. I lay down on the bed and fell fast asleep. It was the most restful sleep I had in a long time.

The day quickly turned into night, and it was time to prepare my mind for next day. I finally got things squared away and called Derek to make sure he was getting prepared. Our talk was short and vague, as we figured the lines would be tapped. We both fully understood each other's intentions. Still tired, I was back to sleep, and morning once again came very soon. I woke up very refreshed, jumped in the shower and started to get my thoughts together.

There was one thing that bothered me, and that was I wasn't sure I could trust those men at the hobby shop. I decided that it was a long shot, but I'd just have to take that chance. I just needed to have an alternative plan just in case this one fell through. It's important to have an alternate plan; that's what my Protector always told me. My shower was slightly longer than usual, being tied up so deep in thought, and I figured it was going to be my last one for a while. Next, I went into the kitchen and started to make breakfast for Derek and me. I knew Derek wouldn't prepare it himself, and soon he would be knocking at my door. The smell of breakfast cuisine filled the apartment. Derek was over just as I set the table, and not much was said as he entered the apartment and walked directly over to the table. In fact, not a word until he sat down and started to fill his face!

"I'm so hungry, I could eat a horse."

"You could have fooled me, Derek. By the way, what is a horse?"

"Oh, it was an animal on Earth many years ago. You know big, long tail. They used to ride them, I think, back in the dark ages."

"Slow down, Derek! What's your hurry?"

"Sorry, it's just so good, and who knows when we will eat again."

"Are you packed?"

"Yes, sir, my boxers with the hearts on them, toothbrush, pair of socks, and some sweet-smelling aftershave."

"Boxers with hearts on them?"

"Yes, Pamela made them—oh no!" Derek hurriedly pointed to the ceiling.

"Don't worry, it's disconnected. I figured it wouldn't matter after today is over. They won't check it out until after the holiday anyway."

"I hope you disconnected the right wire, or they'll be all over us holiday or not."

"Yes, sir, just the way you did it the other night."

"Great! If it's done wrong, the main alarm raises cane at central. Anyway, they would have been here by now. I'm glad you had a good teacher."

"Sure did. Hey, maybe I could teach you how to fly someday."

"What, no way, after this trip, I'm going to keep my feet firmly on the metal of some big Starship… some huge Starship."

"Well, you'll have to fly it, if something happens to me."

"Hey, nothing is going to happen to you! Do you hear me? And don't talk like that."

"Hey, we still go through with it, even if one of us doesn't fare too well, okay? Agreed?"

"Sure, Joe."

"Anyway, once we pick up Dawn and Pam, and all are on board, she can fly it if something happens."

"Yeah, that's a relief, it's not the flying that worries me, it's evading those laser blasts and neutron torpedoes once we get into the air."

"No problem, Derek, just get me in the air, and I'll handle it from there."

"Sounds good to me." We ate breakfast and once again stuffed ourselves. "You really enjoy eating, when you think it might be your last meal, don't you, Derek?"

"Last meal or not, I sure do."

"Well, let's go down and enjoy the festivities of the holiday. We might as well have some fun before we make our debut. It will give everyone a chance to start feeling real lightheaded."

We put on our packs and went down into the streets where everyone was having a great time. The narrow streets were lined with streamers and confetti. There were parades, food stands, spirit houses, games, refreshments, and competitions everywhere. The food smelled so good, but we knew we couldn't try any. Maybe that's another reason we ate so much. Many of the citizens were dressed up in all kinds of different costumes. This was the most important, most celebrated holiday of the year. It symbolized the birth of the Star Cities many, many years ago. The competitions included flying skills, primitive weaponry, a laser shooting contest, hand-to-hand combat and many other events. Medals and reward tokens were given out to the best performer in each event and the events would go on for hours.

I remember the time I won my first flying competition. There were two of us left in the final turn, and my competitor had won it some seven years in a row. This was my first competition. He was very brave and an extremely quick decision maker. His reflexes were the best I'd ever seen. I knew it would be a real accomplishment to even get a chance to compete with him let alone beat him. This was the main event of the holiday and the streets were completely evacuated. Everyone usually goes to the spirit houses, and a communication system is set up all over the city for them to watch the competition. Most of the citizens saw the competition from closed circuit scanning, and the winner receives the highest civil award, plus reward tokens which amount to a very healthy sum. The course consists of a pattern pre-picked by the judges and unknown to the pilots. The course is given to each pilot just prior to the start. It's logged into the computer, and ultimately you are guided by it. The main objective is to fly the course which maneuvers though the city under bridges over and alongside buildings and down alleys without wrecking your ship, which subsequently meant death. The best time along with total points won the competition. There was one catch though; you had to be at least nineteen years of age which was the only rule. Needless to say, every pilot tries the competition at least once by law, and some compete regularly, although there were no stipulations after your first competition to continue. It also gave the

Committee insight into weeding out the bad pilots and choosing the good ones for the Air Force squadron. There was spectulation that year that the path was too difficult for me because of my age and lack of experience, and only 10 pilots were predicted to live. There were twenty-five pilots that year, and only two died but three were seriously injured. There was one maneuver on the course that proved to be fatal for the two pilots.

You had to fly under a walking bridge between two buildings then up over an arched transport bridge, then down through a tunnel pitch black and very long, then, around a tall seventeen story building, and fly upside down through another short tunnel. Then, you had to right yourself, flip sideways between two close buildings, and then straight across the narrow finish line. The main problem that was the cause of most of the injuries and all of the fatalities, was that once upside down, to right yourself, you had to maneuver down, judging from inside the ship because you were upside down, up was down. If you tried to right yourself by going up, which is normally the right procedure to do in space, you would actually be going down and crash into the street. The tunnel needed so much concentration that once you maneuvered to right yourself there wasn't much of the race left to finish. It was said the city wide course was too dangerous and we had an over abundance of pilots, but that was just scuttlebutt. It definitely was a dangerous course, and if any of us had known the course before the competition sign-up, we would have all refused.

"Joe, are you implying that they wanted to get rid of some pilots!"

"Well, Derek, I'll leave that up for you to decide."

"You know after all the information we have acquired, I wouldn't put it past them."

"Those poor guys. To lose their lives over a peace time competition, not fair."

"Yeah, I'll never forget that race. You were brilliant."

"Well, sometimes I wonder how I did it," Joe solemnly spoke. "Talent, my boy! Talent!"

"That upside down maneuver nearly did me in. Sometime I think that just one millisecond and they'd just send me home in a PVC coffin."

"Yeah, bet I could have carried you home in my pocket. Thanks, Derek."

"Your time was three seconds, no 3.0216 seconds, faster than anyone, and you were the third competitor to sign up. You were brilliant. Besides, we can finance our trip now because of that little win."

"You're right about that. Let's go."

We walked through the crowded streets and held interesting conversations with several of our comrades; enjoying some of the contests too. Soon, we were right in front of the hobby shop where we had hid from the Guardians. It seemed like ten years ago. We walked into the shop, as two comarades of my flight class of 2280 were leaving.

"Hey, Joe! What's up? Been a long time. You still flying?"

"You got it, Stephen, every day. It goes with the job."

"Yeah, I guess it's a living. What sector?"

"I'm in the Air Force now. What about you?"

"It's 5216. It's like being on the other side of the universe."

"See ya. Don't take any chances out there!"

We walked around the store for a couple minutes waiting for it to clear out wondering if it ever would be void of window shopping customers. As the last customer left, Derek walked over to the door closed and locked it and put a closed sign in the window. I moved to the back of the store and confronted the owner.

"How's the laser business, Mac?"

"What are you talking about? Hey, what are you doing? Open that door!"

"Sir, you are just closing for the day, so just relax."

As we worked our way to the front of the store, he moved behind the counter and boldly remarked.

"What do you fellows want? I'm losing business here."

"That's just what I wanted to hear, old man. I need a new Guardian fighter with extensive firepower on board. I figured you would be the one able to get one for us."

"Who me? Why?" He slowly walked to the far end of the counter and started to lean on the corner, slipping his right hand under the counter. He looked me in the eye, and before he could free his hand, I had drawn my weapon and aimed it straight at his head.

"I wouldn't do that, sir! Now put your hands on the counter!"

"Don't be so polite, Joe."

He put his hands on the counter, but I failed to look down at his feet for an alarm button. It was set off under his right foot.

"Now, sir, the ship!" I said, still pointing the laser at his head.

"I'm a respectable businessman. Do you think I'm just going to give it to you?" I reached into my pocket and pulled out a large number of tokens.

He moved closer to the pile of chips, and I moved back from the counter. "Oh yes, that's a healthy sum of tokens. I think I could move you in the right direction. Let me see here. One thousand... Two thousand."

"Quit stalling and produce, or I'll use this laser. Don't try my patience!"

"Hey, Joe!" I heard Derek call from the door.

"It doesn't look good over here!"

"What? What's going on?"

"There's a squad of Guardian troops, and they are headed this way."

"You bum, an alarm!"

"Come on, Derek. you too old man you're coming with us."

"What, no way! You can't make me, you are surrounded."

With that remark and the setting on my laser handgun fixed on maximum power, I shot a laser blast to his left arm piercing it through charring the edges of the wound. The store owner, surprised by my actions, became very cooperative.

"Whoa, Joe! You shot him!"

"Like I said, 'I'm not messin' around'. Now you listen to me, old man! I know you run weapons out of here, so there has to be another way out. If you don't want to run around town with nine or ten laser holes in your body, you better get us out of here. I mean business! See, I'm also a businessman. Now move it!"

We went through a door behind the counter just as the Gardian patrol reached the front door of the shop. There were a couple loud knocks, and then the door quickly flew opened and slammed into the wall with the sound of broken glass hitting the floor.

"Through here! Come on."

"Can you lock the door behind us?"

"Yes, yes. Now, let's go and hurry. Hurry!"

He reached up and hit a button on the wall just above the metal trap door, and we ran down about fifty flights of stairs rather quickly. They led to the old cargo bays that were used for repairs before our new transports were built. As I ran down the stairs with my laser in the upright position, held by both hands, I switched the power to stun. As we reached the door to the bay, I turned and shot the storekeeper.

"Joe, did you kill him?"

"No, no! Why would I kill the old man? He is just stunned, just stunned. Let's go."

"Go? Go where?"

"Follow me. We have to resort to plan B. You know me, Derek. I just pray to God that we don't get Charlie in any trouble."

We ran through the bays, Derek totally unware of our direction, and finally, nearly exhausted, he demanded some answers.

"Hold it, Joe! I'm beat. Where are we headed anyway?"

"Okay, we'll stop for thirty seconds, just enough to catch our breath then we are off again. Did anyone ever tell you, you ask too many questions?"

"Yeah."

"Who, Derek?"

"Pamela."

"That figures, just calm down and follow me—plan B, landing bay 90."

It was completely dark all through the bays, and the only lighted areas were in the hallways leading to the stairwells that headed up to the street. There were remnants of old cargo planes and fighter ships that lay all over the floor, which made it somewhat slower going.

"Good thing you have a small flashlight, Joe. It looks like you thought of everything."

"I hope so. Look at these old ships… You know, a good pilot could still fly these old ships and be competitive with the latest model."

The ships were covered in a gel-like substance used to protect their metal from deteriorating just in case they were to be recalled for active duty. The bays and ships were just forgotten when the latest models came out and the new bays were built. We maneuvered around the bays for about seven minutes until we came to bay 77.

"Let's stop here for a moment."

"Thanks, Joe. I thought you nearly forgot about me."

"We can't stay here for long. We have to stay on schedule for that radar jamming over at Balem. We don't want to disappoint the girls."

"What radar jamming?"

"Dawn is going to jam the radar, so we can land."

"When did this come about? Have you spoken to her? How, Joe? Was Pam with her?"

"No no, we made these plans on Gamnon."

"Gee, I'm glad you thought of that radar. Joe, how are we going to contact them?"

"Pamela gave me a scanner that she made on Gamnon."

"They will sense those receivers. The ones in her ears, right?"

"Yeah, once I turn it on, we will be able to tell exactly where they are, and I hope they will still be in the same place waiting, when we arrive."

"Why didn't you just tell her what bay we were going to land in?"

"Since the bays were the only part of the two cities that have been rebuilt, I wasn't sure if they were numbered the same. Don't worry, the sensors will work fine. Besides, what if we can't land at the bay we agreed upon?"

"I never thought of that, Joe. I am glad that you were in charge of the plans."

"Also the workers were still building certain bays while we were on Gamnon. There were just to many *ifs* for us to be exact about too much of the plans."

"Okay. Now what, Joe?"

"Let's go borrow an Air Force ship."

"Well, I hope that's easier than trying to buy a new Guardian ship!"

"Oh come on, Derek. Let's go!"

"Okay, it sure sounds good to me. I'm ready!"

We entered bay 92 and ran to the hallway leading upstairs to the city. We entered the street, and to my surprise, we didn't see one Guardian patrol. We walked two blocks and headed for bay 90. This was my bay and inside was my ship, *The Striker*, I have been flying for seven years. It was also the same ship I won the race with two years ago. I put my card into the bay door and the door opened.

Two pilots walked by, saluting as they passed, and off to the left was good old Charlie sitting at his desk nestled in the guardhouse. Charlie was a true gentleman; his position as security guard for twenty-five ships went back many years. In fact, he was a security guard when my Protector was flying. I liked Charlie very much. He was a quiet, old man with white hair and an average height but built very strong. He was extremely healthy for his age and weighed about 230 lbs., all muscle. His muscle mass was close to mine, and he must be at least 40 years my senior. I was hoping I wouldn't have to fight him since our friendship was very strong. He has known me since my first flight, and I considered him one of the closest friends I had in the work place.

"Hi, Charlie! How are you doing?"

"Hey, Joe, who's your friend? And what's up? You are definitely in the wrong place. All the excitement is upstairs."

"This is Derek… Derek, Charlie. We go way back. I just wanted to show him my ship." Charlie looked at me rather oddly, and I could sense his curiosity.

"What's up, Joe? You are the worst liar! Give it to me straight."

"You're not going to like it, Charlie."

"That's nothing new coming from you. Come on, what's up?"

"I'm taking the ship, and I am not coming back."

Charlie, who was sitting at his desk, never changed his expression or tone of voice. "I appreciate your honesty, Joe."

He acted as if it wasn't such a bad idea, like the thought had occurred to him several times before, but being too old and not knowing where to go, he just let the thought pass. He got up and walked over to the door of his little building.

"Well, he was right, that old geezer."

"What, Charlie?"

"Oh, old David, your Protector. He told me one day you would do this crazy thing, and he was right. I'll be hanged. He got me from the grave."

"Okay, just sign here so I can stay out of trouble. If I was somewhat younger, I would go with you, Joe."

"I know you would. Thanks a lot, Charlie, and thanks for not asking any questions. I sure am glad I don't have to fight you."

"Ha ha, you crazy kid. Hey, Joe, here… You might need another one of these."

Just then, he took his holster off and threw it over for me to catch. I handed it over to Derek and looked at Charlie.

"Don't worry. I can get around the gun. Now get out of here."

I looked at Charlie for about fifteen seconds staring, reminiscing, and smiling then I went over and shook his hand.

"I'll never forget you, Charlie," I said.

And his reply was "Me either, son."

We both hugged and firmly shook hands. As I walked away, I thought it pretty strange the word *son* had come up once again. I wondered about that word. The only other time I heard it was on my Protector's death bed. Both men knew they would never see me again. I couldn't figure it out.

"Charlie…"

"Get out of here, Joe. Good luck!"

I walked over to the ship looking back at Charlie trying to instill a detailed picture of him in my mind. I was really going to miss the old man and his stories. Derek was already inside the ship and as I approached the entrance I heard Charlie yell out once again.

"Good luck, boy! Good luck!"

The ship was in excellent condition, fueled up, and clean as a whistle just like he had done for many years, but for some reason, it appeared extra clean. I knew when we left the bay we would have to advance rapidly because the computer would pick up an unscheduled flight. That, in turn, would alert the Guardian defense system. It would take approximately fifteen seconds for them to converge. The reason we would stick out like a sore thumb is not so much our presence but the fact that we would have to arm our weapons. If we tried to sneak through unarmed, it takes approximately fifteen seconds to arm; there would be no time to arm our weapons for a confrontation if we were noticed as deserters. The only way to make it was to be fully armed with defense shields engaged leaving the bay. As we primed our engines, armed our weapons and prepared for takeoff there were few words between Derek and me. It seemed an uneasy atmosphere for a moment, but it passed.

"You okay, Derek?"

"Yes, I think so? How about you?"

"Yes, I'm fine. Now listen, Derek, once we get airborne, a lot of situations arise very rapidly. When you speak, speak clearly, decisively, and only about pertinent facts pertaining to our immediate situation. Leave out the garbage and no hot-dogging it. It's very important!"

"I'm not quite sure what you mean, but okay. I'll try to keep it short and sweet."

"Thank you, Derek. Let's arm the weapons and perform a security check. Main switches on, internal lights on, energy defense shields check, front and rear computer check, lasers and weaponry on, navigation computer check. Coordinates logged in and programmed, gunnery motion front and rear 180 degrees, engines primed and ready, lasers zeroed…"

The security check took a full thirty seconds. The ship was theoretically and realistically a completely dependable and very durable machine. There were places for a pilot and copilot side by side and a rear and lower gunner in the stern plus a place for a navigator when needed.

Sleeping quarters were lengthwise and bunked directly behind the pilot and copilot on opposite sides of the hallway. Behind the sleeping quarters, which were long but not very wide, opened up a small living area, and believe me, it was very small. It was a round area about fifteen feet in diameter. On either side of the circle were wings and fuel storage. Below the center of the living area was the lower gunner's hole and to the rear of the circle, directly behind the pilot was the rear gunner. I guess the only description I could give of the outside was a fat marquise diamond with wings and a pot-belly. All armament was housed inside the ship so the lines outside were extremely streamlined. It was a big fighter compared to the old two-seaters, but very versatile and agile in the right hands.

"Okay, Derek, let's do it. Charlie, are you listening?"

"Sure am, Joe!"

"Give me thirty seconds, then hit the alarm, call the Guardian Patrol and scream bloody murder."

"Sounds good, take care! I'll sure miss you, boy."

"Me too, Charlie."

"Take it high, lookout below, and don't take it too slow!"

"What the does that mean?" inquired Derek.

At that moment, Derek was G-forced back in his seat, and we were gone.

"How do you do that? Joe."

"Turbo boost, Derek, and remember no questions."

It wasn't very respectful and totally against the law, but it would give Charlie a cover for our departure. The force of turbo boost would invariably burn up the bay making it nonoperational. I was pretty confident that Charlie would be out of harm's way in his little guardhouse.

"Well, they will sure remember that. Anyway, Derek, hold on."

"I hope we don't have to do that again. My head is still in the bay."

Within seconds, I headed around the southwest corner of the city proper.

The city moved by so fast that everything peripherally was just a blur. The colors from all the festivities appeared with such vivid intensity that it startled me slightly, but as they blended together like a rainbow, my mind again quickly began to focus on reality. I decided to give us some more time by taking a shortcut to the area we needed to go to exit our position on Altaur. We flew low within one hundred yards of the street and the sound from our engines must have been heard on Balem.

The buildings seemed to close in on us, and it took quite a bit of concentration to keep from plastering us all over the place.

"Oh no, Joe, look out!"

"Shut up, Derek! Just shut up!"

"Okay, okay, but I'm closing my eyes. Wow, that was close."

I could vaguely hear Derek talking under his breath, and I understood none of it because I was concentrating on saving precious time by evading large buildings. There came a point where I approached a small building just about four hundred yards in front our ship and nowhere to go but up. At this speed we were sure to collide so I sharply decreased our speed, pulled back hard on the glide-wheel, then hit the turbo boost. We cleared the building, but not enough to keep the ship from shaking violently.

It was the closest I had ever had come to a loss on a tactical diversion. It was a little to close even for me. I proceeded south, soon afterwards, flying adjacent to the defense batteries. The scanner showed Altaurs' Guardian forces approaching.

"Joe, bogies on our starboard rear quarter."

"From space above or from around the bays. Derek, be more precise!"

"From the bays, Joe, the bays!"

"How far behind us, Derek?"

"Approximately thirty five clicks, Joe."

"Okay, hold on! Here we go!"

"I hate when you say that! Here they come, Joe, and let me tell you they are moving fast!"

The only consolation was that since they were coming from the bays, even flying at full throttle the Guardian patrol vessels were too far away to intercept us. I had a few seconds to make a strafing run on the batteries just adjacent the bays. I didn't need both the fighters and the batteries converging on us at the same time. Without any explanation to Derek, there really wasn't any time for it; I flew around the Hun building and decided to make a run on each battery, ending my run by taking out the ammunition depots. Each battery had one, and there was also a larger depot that contained ammunition for all the batteries in sector one. That is the battery I was looking to destroy. I figured by hitting the ammunition depot I could blow out the whole set of batteries defending the escape route.

I continued a strafing run on the gun batteries hitting the target precisely in the right spot, then shot straight out to the escape path with four Guardian bogies right on my tail. I hit the power boosters, cranked it up to full throttle, which put us about fifteen miles out, and the bogies couldn't keep up with us. I then did a 180-degree turn and headed back toward the batteries. Just as I entered the city, the batteries let loose with a mirage of torpedoes and laser blasts. My plan was to lure the four bogies back toward the batteries hoping the batteries would eliminate one or two of them.

"Here we go, Derek!"

"Go? Go where? I don't know what the blazes is going on!"

I was directly over the ammunition dump, and the enemy ships were going through a direct assault by their own batteries. I hit the last battery with a neutron bomb, igniting the battery next to it and soon the consecutive batteries started to explode. A direct laser blast to the 5th battery one more neutron bomb to the ammunition depot, and soon 7, 8, 9 and 10 were lit up like roman candles. Now the last objective, the tractor beam. With it still intact, we would have to redistribute all our weapons power to the turbo boost and we would be defenseless.

"Joe, they're right on our tail. Scanner readings say two thousand yards and closing… closing fast. There are only two bogies, Joe. Running them through those batteries really helped us out by eliminating a couple of the assailants."

"Rear deflector shield up, Derek."

"You're kidding, they've been up ever since we started. Double-check."

"Yes, sir. Shields are up. They've locked and are ready to fire, Joe. They've fired two torpedos."

As soon as Derek got the word *fired* out of his mouth, I rolled to the portside, dived toward the city, and split two buildings with a sound that was probably heard all over Altaur. Seconds later, the projectiles hit the buildings just behind us.

"That was close, Joe!"

"Close doesn't count, Derek!"

I pulled up out of the city and flew 45 degrees to port, straightened her up but for only about three seconds, then 30 degrees starboard and the tractor beam lay just ahead.

"Derek, I'm going to laser this tractor beam, but to make sure, key it in on your computer and drop me an egg right down its mouth."

Several seconds after Derek sent a neutron bomb targeted at the tractor beam)

"You did it!… There she goes, Joe."

There were flames behind us and our success was evident. "How much distance does that give us, Joe?"

"It should give us a 3000 foot hole which will be plenty of room to escape." I made a 180-degree turn back toward the tractor beam. I skimmed the gun implacements, then at the center of the beam made a sharp 90-degree turn toward Balem. The tractor beam was wide along the batteries, then tapered off.

It was pie-shaped, actually more like a cone-shaped on a three-dimentional scale. The other tractor beams alongside this one crossed at certain places but could be avoided if carefully maneuvered. At the very end of the beam, it was possible for for only two ships to squeeze through safely. I decided to increase our speed to keep the Guardian ships well behind us. The risk was well worth the reward. The only problem we would have was if the other tractor beams would overcompensate for the destroyed one and leave us only enough room for our ship to to go through. That situation would be difficult at this speed but not impossible.

"Derek, give me an update on our companions."

"We have two Guardian ships behind us and two others converging from sectors 7733 and 7737."

"Derek, the bogies from those sectors will be too late to cause us any trouble. We should be out of here by the time they arrive."

"I would truly appreciate it if they didn't crash our party, Joe."

"Me too! We are going to have to be careful when the other two arrive. Derek, when they get in close proximity, use your own discretion with the laser anti-aircraft weapon. I'm counting on you for a little help."

Shortly, I heard Derek start firing, in between several laser blasts to our shields. They were close. I decided to push the ship to its upper limit, fearing that was going to be the only way I could make it through the hole without company.

I could feel laser blasts hitting our port defense shield, and the shots were getting numerous and more intense, and I knew our shield was starting to take some real damage.

"Derek, I need help on this port shield. It is starting to weaken."

We were moving very fast, and once I maneuvered around the adjacent tractor beam, it was a straight shot through the hole. The hole had diminished from the three thousand feet to about one thousand feet; in fact, to a point where I was forced to enter at somewhat of an angle. The radar confirmed the fact that we did have close to a four-hudred-foot clearance on each end, but it was the shape of an oval the widest part being vertical instead of horizontal, and at this speed, it was going to be a real challenge. Our port defense shield was weakining and needed rest from those two fighters converging off our port side. With a few more hits our shields would not have time to reinforce themselves. Our port quarter bogy was really getting to be very annoying. Then, all of a sudden, the blasts from the patrols stopped. My concentration was back, and I had complete control of my senses once again. There was not a single hit, which meant we were getting close to the hole in the tractor beam, and our bogies were getting concerned about the size of the hole themselves. One other option I could have considered was that Derek could have iced those two bogies. Also our defense shields started to regenerate which would help us on the other side. "Derek, did you get him?"

"Yes, sir! Only one though."

"It couldn't have come at a better time."

"Yeah, but this other one is giving me some trouble and the two from the city are making headway. They will be here soon."

"Don't worry about them, Derek. We'll be through the hole before they can do much damage, and if they don't watch what they are doing, we are going to have some fireworks when they approach that hole."

"Now Derek, I want you to listen very closely. We have a problem up here!"

"What? What problem!"

"Just listen, our hole is vertical instead of horizontal. In order to get through I am going to have to fly horizontal until I am very close to the hole then turn sideways, but as we go through, the ship's momentum will spin us in a circle several times after we clear the tractor beam."

"Several?"

"Yeah, I'm not sure how many before I can get control again so buckle up and close your eyes when I say or you'll lose everything you've eaten in the past month."

"Oh great! I don't like this, Joe!"

"We have no choice."

"Just get us through that blasted hole. I'll be fine!"

We turbo-blasted for seven seconds. That put us well ahead of the intercepting ships. Consequently, they were out of range, and I was calculating the odds of them getting through the hole. The chances all three would make it were slim.

"Here we go, Derek! Hold on!" About three seconds later, I angled the ship up ninety degrees. I thought I might have overcompensated, but it all happened so fast I was through the hole and spiraling out of control before I could give it another thought. As we entered the hole, there was a bright eruption of light brought about by the walls of the tractor beam closing in on our engine exhaust. I backed down on the engine speed trying to control our spin. Suddenly, by reversing the starboard engine, I hoped it would reverse our spin enough to get us out of the spiral. After five more seconds of spinning and nothing working, I turbo-charged my starboard engine. It slowed us down enough for the power thrust of both the starboard and port engine to work. Before long, we were flying straight except we were upside down, something I really enjoy doing.

"Joe! Joe! If you don't straighten me up, everything inside is going to be outside!"

"Okay, Derek! Here we go!"

"I just don't like it when you say that, Joe."

One more port power thrust, and we were right side up once again. "Status, Derek! What's up back there?"

"I see one flash, no two flashes of light, two ships—oh man, Joe! One more! They all made it, but two are fading fast. They must have slowed down tremendously to get through the hole. It will take them some time to get up to full speed. All three are still on the radar screen."

"Okay, Derek, hang in there! I'm going to see what's up ahead."

Our forward scanner showed a thick meteor shower to our Southeast. Just then, I heard Derek put up our port defense shield clear his guns and start firing. I felt two good size blows to our port side.

"Man, Joe! He just won't get off our tail!"

"Derek, put full power to our starboard shield. I figured since that starboard bogy wasn't dropping several neutron torpedos, that a Condor 85 was eminate."

"He'll cut us down in seconds if he sees our port shield down!"

"Just do it, Derek! And just trust me!"

I then dropped to a sixty-degree dive and took on a heading of southeast; once again, I turbo-boosted the engines.

The bogy on our port side fired. It really didn't matter because we were well out of range of the torpedo and its sensing capability. I did feel one more extremely heavy blow to our starboard defense shield most likely a Condor 85 double power neutron torpedo. We rocked for a second and then, the ship stabilized. The C-85 would have blown away half of the ship under normal shield power, and Derek and I would have been miles apart by now probably in little pieces but his attack plan was text book and I knew what was coming. "Dang! Did you call that one, Joe? You don't have to worry about me questioning anything now. In my book this is a new life 'cause mine would have been over with that torpedo. No question about it."

"Well, you better hold on to your trousers Derek 'cause we are going through a meteor shower in approximately fifteen seconds."

"What! Are you crazy?"

"I hope they think I am."

"Have you ever flown through one?"

"No."

"Don't tell me no, Joe."

"No, not really, just in simulation."

"I told you not to tell me!"

"If I am correct, they are just as crazy and will follow me in. Derek, once we get into the shower I need you to come forward to relay computer coordinates for me." It was really innovative how the gunner seat could be reallocated. It was the last and latest invention. The gunnery seat along with the navigation computer, scanner and radar, would break away from its rear position, spin around then track along the hallway and snap into a copilot position.

"Why don't you put it on autopilot?"

"Autopilot would reduce our speed tremendously. I can do it manually if you can give me some coordinates. We can take some hits providing our bow defense shield is intact. So, as soon as we enter the meteor shower, we switch to full power on our bow and stern defense shields, okay."

"Got it, but won't they try it manually also."

"They'll have to, Derek, and believe me, they better be great pilots plus have an extremely competent navigator. Ready?"

"Are you kidding? I will never be ready for this?"

Derek quit firing and put his computerized radar scanner on 180 degrees before he disengaged to come up to the cockpit. His first coordinate was obtained just before he snapped into the copilot position.

"Pretty good, Derek!"

"Just drive Joe, 46SW, 38W, 26SE, 50 SSW, 30NE."

Derek really started to collect the coordinates very rapidly and his skill helped us to avoid all the larger meteors. Our defense shield took care of all the smaller ones.

"Derek, when you get a chance, check our scanner, and identify our bogies."

"Joe, you are amazing! I always wondered how you beat that computer on Gamnon. Now I know."

"Thanks, Derek."

"A collision, Joe, one bogy down."

"52E, 62SE, 45NE, 2pSW."

"Joe, look straight ahead. Are we going to make it?"

Just ahead there were two large meteors, one slightly larger than the other, and they were headed for each other extremely fast. Once again, I had to fly sideways through the two and hope the collision between them, subsequently, didn't produce enough force to push us into another meteor. But I knew the ships behind me would have a tougher time than me. I hit the turbo charge for a split second, not knowing what was on the other side of these huge meteors. We were through directly and once again in a mess of meteors.

As we pulled through, I had to reduce our speed by half and bank hard left in order not to collide with another meteor or hit one hard enough with our defense shield to push us into an oncoming one. We could feel the defense shield get a mirage of small meteors, but we were holding course, and I soon had her under control. We then heard a large explosion—obviously the interaction between the two large meteors.

"Derek, check the scanners. I want to know what is going on behind us."

The ship started to shaking violently for about three seconds from the after shock. "We had to have gotten one of them."

"We got two, Joe, one was sandwiched between the meteors, the other was destroyed when the explosion of the ship sent the port meteor flying into the other Guardian ship passing slightly below the meteor. I guess they didn't figure on the explosion, Joe, but we still have one bogy on our tail."

"One on one, I like that! That evens up the odds real quick."

"Wait a second, Joe. Let me increase the area on my radar. Sorry! Thought there was only one bogy. There's one following the meteor storm at a ninety-degree angle from the northeast. In fact, he's just outside it waiting for us to pop out."

"There go those odds! Derek, we are going to have to take this one in the meteor storm. It will be a lot easier one on one, once we are out of here."

"Any suggestions?"

"Yes, you are going to have to go back and take care of him."

"But what about the coordinates?"

"Our deflector shields are going to have to take the brunt of this. Give me the infrared scanner. The eyepiece, Derek, I can't take my hands off the contols. At least I will be able to see what's going to hit us."

He moved the scanner arm in front of my eye and reentered the rear gunner turret. It took a few seconds to get my eyes adapted, and in the meantime, I could feel the meteors bumping our defense shields. Derek was firing away but to no avail and the storm was getting somewhat thinner now so I had a chance to think once again.

"Derek, we're coming up on a fairly good size meteor. I want you to try something."

"What? What, I'll try anything. I just can't get a clean shot with all these meteors in the way."

"We'll have to use them to our advantage."

"How? What do you want me to do?"

"When this one passes, wait until it gets close to the Guardian ship and send a neutron torpedo right at it. Maybe the shrapnel caused by the explosion will hit the Guardian ships and at least damage part of its defense shield."

Derek waited and let the large meteor pass just until it was in direct line with the Guardian ship. He fired a neutron torpedo directly hitting the meteor. A few seconds later, there was the collision of the meteors and another explosion.

This second explosion threw us off course enough to shove us into a small meteor damaging our starboard defense shield.

"You did it, Derek, but I didn't think it would take them out. You know the explosion threw us off course enough to ram a meteor. Our starboard defense shield has been damaged. One more hit without time to regenerate, and we are going to have to keep him on our port side."

"Yes, I know. One more hit, and we won't have a starboard shield."

"We will be out in about seventeen seconds, so be prepared for immediate interception."

"Wait! Wait, Derek! I think I have an idea, listen. Set one of those timed neutron bombs and when I say drop it, let her loose, okay? I am going to drop it and turbo boost out of this shower. If they have been tracking us, they will follow our coordinates as we exit the storm. Maybe, just maybe, we can get him!"

"Ten, nine, eight, seven, six, five, four, three, two… Now, Derek! Now!"

We dropped the bomb just inside the storm, hopefully making it undetectable.

It appeared that they followed our coordinates, just as I predicted. "Joe, they turbo-boos—"

Instantly, as they locked in on our coordinates, we heard an explosion. "Well, Derek?"

"We caught them by surprise, all right, but we just eliminated their defense shield. Not bad, Joe."

"The whole shield? Be specific, Derek!"

"Port, starboard and stern, oh, and it looks like one of their engines is failing. They are losing power."

"Yes, sir, Derek! We got them. They'll have to return to base."

"We did it! Joe, we did it!"

"Don't speak too soon, first check the scanner and don't forget we still have to pick up Pam and Dawn and you know they will be ready for us. I think our trouble is just beginning."

"Scanners all clear?" asked Joe.

"Yes, and with another expert pilot on board things should run a little smoother.

I won't have to be copilot anymore, and with more tech support, we will be cruising. "Yes, I can't wait to see them."

"Let's change course to a heading of 305 NNW, a straight course for the Star City Balem."

"Now, we have to execute the next phase of this complex, strategical plan."

"I hope the women will have that radar down before we get there."

"They have to. It's the only way we can get into the old bays undetected."

"Hey, why didn't you tell me about the tractor beam?"

"I didn't want to bombard you with a lot of insignificant, unnecessary details."

"What! Are you crazy, unnecessary... insignificant... Kind of think that the tractor beam was slightly *major*!"

"Would you have had second thoughts if I told you about everything?"

"Second thoughts, me? You've got to be kidding. Well, do the women know when we are coming? What's our next plan of action? When do we contact them?"

"Slow down, Derek, I'll contact them soon, and they'll shut down the radar."

"What are you going to do if they don't, Joe?"

"Well, we will have to go to plan B."

"Plan B? Again, it would be nice for plan A to work for once. Plan A is?"

"Pamela made these communicators that work on an extremely high radio frequency. Didn't she explain them to you? They have two coded messages, one for eliminating the radar in our sector and one for when we have landed so that we will be able to find out where they are. I'll send it in about ten minutes."

"It sounds too easy, Joe. What's the catch?"

"There shouldn't be one."

"What if it doesn't work?"

"Quit being pessimistic, Derek. If it doesn't work, we will be forced to improvise and find them our own way."

"That would be just great. That's probably the way it will turn out."

"Well, what would life be without a challenge?"

"Easy, I'm sure!"

"What, Derek?"

"Oh nothing, Joe. Nothing."

We cruised for about seven minutes, and I tried to organize my thoughts just in case Derek was right, and our plans had to be altered. Soon, it would be time to initiate the sensors for the radar. The communicator appeared to be working great.

"Okay, Derek, check and see if the radar is still functioning."

"No it's off. No, wait, it's on again. Did you send the message?"

"I sure did."

"Well, send the signal again."

"It's constant, Derek. They should be reading us loud and clear. Anything yet? They'll be picking us up here shortly."

"Joe, we are getting really close. They better do something soon or—"

"We are in range, Derek. Is the radar down yet?"

"Yes, it is down—no, wait, it's on again. No, it's off now. What's going on?"

"Perfect. Just perfect."

"Just perfect? You're not making sense. Isn't it suppose to stay off. What's going on, Joe?"

"That's the signal. Dawn said the signal would short-circuit the radar, so it would look like a legitimate malfunction."

"Talk about being left in the dark. Why doesn't anyone tell me anything?"

"It's now or never. Good work, ladies. Let's do it, Derek!"

A voice informed them from the landing tower, "We have problems with radar tracking. Follow the normal routine, and we will notify you when repairs have been made."

This was great. Something was finally working smoothly. The radar jamming had been successful. No one approached us probably for two reasons. First, the ship we were arriving in was exactly like the ship they used for defense. Remember, that everything was exactly the same as on our Star City. Second, we came in very passively, using the same entry code as their patrol ship, which was extensively explained to me by Dawn. Our ship, as long as voice contact was not requested, would go virtually unnoticed. We just had to sneak into the old bays undetected. We circled the city trying to look inconspicuous and when the signal was strong enough we would switch to voice communication with the girls. It would I hope narrow down our search range.

"The signal is strong enough, Derek. I am going to give it a try."

"Dawn? Dawn, come in."

"Joe! It's so good to hear your voice."

"Yours too! Is Pamela there?"

"Yes, sir. Use bay PS 43. It should be coming up soon. We'll meet you there."

"You got it! See you soon, out."

It took about one minute to get to the bay, and we decided to make one final check of our surroundings before landing.

"Derek, check our scanner, and see if there are any ships nearby."

"It's pretty clear, Joe. In fact, the batteries are even unmanned. There's not a soul near that bay."

"What, Derek? Not a soul? No life forms anywhere?"

"No, why?"

"Derek, listen up. That's really strange. The defense batteries are never unmanned. This just doesn't feel right. We got here too easy. Listen, be prepared to make a quick exit if this doesn't pan out. Start checking the scanner for life forms, Derek, and don't take your eyes off it until we see the girls, I don't like it... I just don't like it!"

"Here we go!" No sooner did I enter the bay than Derek came across the ships communicator.

"Joe, we have ships converging, and there are life forms everywhere."

"Man, I knew it. Hold on, Derek. Here we go!"

"I hate when you say that," he said.

I expected something, so I disengaged the engines upon entering. We were coasting in neutral, and halfway in, I hit the ignition accelerator in reverse mode. It seemed like we never even entered.

A engine turbo blasted in reverse is usually uncontrollable, but I jammed the engines forward immediately, and within several seconds, we were flying up over the city coming around to follow a circular pattern around the bays.

Almost immediately, eight converging Guardian ships were within striking distance, and before you knew it, we were taking laser blasts on our starboard and rear defense shields. We started at bay PS 43, and, as I came over the city and down once again to the bay area, we were at PS 403 and receiving heavy fire. The laser blasts were bouncing off everything along the bays and many of the laser rounds were ricocheting off the outer frames of the buildings.

"We're going in, Derek!"

At that point, I flew inside the bay and started to use the landing bay as a shield from our pursuers. Four ships followed us in and the others circled around the outer perimeter as we flew from bay to bay. Several were coming toward us from the other side of Balem too. We were definitely in the heat of the battle now.

"Hey, Joe, I have just about had enough of this game!"

"Me too. It's time to even out the odds, Derek."

"I'll say! What are we going to do?"

"Just hold—"

"I know, I know, just hold on. Hold on."

It appeared the whole squadron would converge on us at bay 203 so I increased my speed, and at bay 200, I banked hard to my starboard side and hit the turbo-chargers. As soon as we hit the atmosphere, I saw blurred pictures peripherally of the converging ships now on the port and starboard side of us. Then, there were a barrage of laser blasts and several explosions. At that range, a direct hit by a full-power laser blast would penetrate a defense shield and destroy a ship.

That took care of a couple, I thought.

"What was that, Joe?"

"According to our scanner, they just shot down several of their own ships caught in a crossfire."

"Good thing you hit the turbo, but rather risky coming out from the bay area. How sure were you that we wouldn't burn up from the heat of the turbo?"

"Not very sure, Derek, not very sure at all."

As we talked, I turned the ship around and headed back for Balem. "Back for some more, Joe?"

"Why not? I don't have anything else to do. How about you?"

"No, not really."

"Besides, that gave me an idea. Look, Derek, we are all the same, right?"

"Right, but what does that have to do with our situation?"

"Well, think about this scenario. If we get back into that shooting gallery, and all of us have the exact same defense fighter how are they going to know who is shooting whom. Somehow they have to mark our ship. Our question is how?"

"I wonder if that is how they, you know, that kind of make sense. Take a couple pot shots here and there see how they react. Do you think it will work?"

"You never know until you try. Besides, Derek, what do we have to loose and have I failed you yet today?"

"No, but there's always a first time."

"Okay, it is our turn to play the game. Deflector shields intact?"

"Yes, sir!" Just then, a laser hit our port defense shield.

"Derek, check the scanner and see what shields they have up. Maybe that's how they distinguish our ship."

"You got it, Joe. They are using every shield except for the rear shield. It's down. So that's how they mark us."

The laser blasts started to increase and now from almost every direction.

"Shut it down, Derek. We have them now. We'll can play that game too." As soon as our rear deflector shield was shut down, the laser blasts stopped.

I flew right into the middle of the main squadron and, with full power, began shooting at the backside of another ship, hoping she would eventually put up her rear shield. She didn't so I pulled up behind the ship, followed her for several seconds and fired aiming straight at the communication center located aft and to the left of the engine. Once destroyed, she had no choice but to put up the rear deflector shield or be totally destroyed.

It worked. The pilot put up her rear shield and headed out of the pack presumably retreating to its own bay. We did have a bit of luck because it headed back toward the bay, where Dawn and Pam had been sending the strongest signal. We followed her all the way around to bay 86 when we decided to make our move. I backed down pulled up into a steep backward 180 and came up behind another Guardian fighter who with a series of laser shots once again knocked out the communication center and she raised the rear defector shield.

They took off in the other direction with several determined Guardian fighters pursuing. I don't think any of them knew whom they were shooting at. I continued along bay 95 through to bay 67 and dodged inside once again. Behind the bays were storage areas, and Derek was just the right person to break into the old storage bays. What amazes me was he did it right from inside our ship using several complicated coded messages. He said it was pretty easy, although sometimes I think he's pretty modest about his talent. Once inside the bay, we closed the door and shut down the whole electrical system. That way with all the rubbish in these old storage bins, they would have a hard time detecting us.

"Well, that was fun. Now what? How are we going to find the girls?"

"We still have one more trick up our sleeve, Derek. See, Dawn and I prepared ourselves in case the ear probe malfunctioned nullifying our plan. Pamela designed a personal sensor, which I surgically implanted under Dawn's arm inside her right axilla. It's very small so we were able to use our first aid kit at the apartment. The sensor can be detected from one of several transmitters. My armband and the communicator Pam made for us will also work as a personal tracking device and the frequency used is antiquated. She used the frequency of the old radio waves. There is only one drawback, though, being that small the battery doesn't last very long, so we have to do this rather quickly."

"Joe, you had everything figured out, didn't you," replied Derek.

"We really put some thought into every aspect of this escape. We had to, Derek, these guys aren't stupid, and remember, there has only been one escape. I've been praying that we are number two. We sure tried to give us several options. Now we will wait until dark, so get some rest. The transmitter is working great. In fact, I don't think they are far from here. They have definitely moved from PS43, though. It may be a trap set by the Guardian forces. Charlie probably had to tell them who took the ship which is fine if it kept him out of trouble. Maybe that means he's still alive.

"What happens after we get them?"

"I'm not exactly sure, but we will be back out there rather quickly, right in the thick of it all. Then, we will have to figure out how to contact the Carthusians. They are our only hope, but for now you better get some rest."

"Sounds good to me, Joe. Mentally I'm exhausted."

"Yes, me too, but I'm going to keep an eye on the transmitter tracking the girls and try to formulate a plan. I'll wake you up when they've stopped long enough for us to home in on their location. We'll trade off until dark."

"I'm going to look around in here, first."

"Derek, let's stay aboard. I'm sure they are looking for life forms all over the place and the metal on the ship shadows our life forms. Besides, there shouldn't be anything out there anyway."

Derek retreated to the sleep area, and it didn't take long for him to start snoring, assuring me of his ultimate relaxation. I let Derek sleep for a long time, and soon the signal from Pamela became strong and stable. They had definitely moved them but not far from bay 43, and now they were stationary. It was about two in the afternoon, and I woke Derek up around four o'clock.

I did a systems check on the ship and, after formulating a plan, decided to rest.

"Derek, wake up. It's your watch."

"What? What, oh thanks, Joe. I really needed the rest. Anything happened?"

"Two Guardian ships passed by, but they were moving pretty fast. I was surprised they didn't wake you. Obviously, they had other things on their minds. Dawn and Pam are stable now. I'm pretty sure what sector they are in."

"Get some rest, Joe. You can tell me the plan later."

My body was drained and my mind fatigued, and it didn't take long for me to pass out either. I slept solid for two hours, and soon it was my watch once again. Derek returned to bed with an "All's well on the western front." I don't know where he gets his sayings, and I sat at the control panel, my mind once again spitting out tons of different information. I started to review my plans over and over, revising them in case of a crisis, trying to calculate all the angles and considering all the possibilities.

I even thought of the worst scenarios, like capture, punishment, even torture, and death. But I figured death was inevitable, and if they were going to be my executioner, then I would have the courage to try anything to achieve our ultimate goal, the *Station America*. It began with my strong belief in the integrity of our plans. I considered several revisions, until all angles were covered with every bit of information attainable which made my decisions and the execution of our plan flawless so far. It was the confidence I needed to continue on.

I also pondered about why Pam and Dawn were not at the position we first picked up their signal. Were they lying in the morgue now, executed, or just sitting in a holding tank? Why did they move? Did they get captured? If that was the case, I was hoping they would be held captive in the high security prison ultimately waiting to be executed in public later. I'm sure Balem would like to make examples of them to deter further attempts for escape, but that would be the best scenerio because at least they would be alive. That, in turn, would give me the opportunity to rescue them, but if they were dead the plan, our work, the goal would all be forsaken. I quietly prayed for their safety.

"Father, you are a loving God and care for your children. You are sovergn and in control of every situation put forth upon men. Whatever your will demands becomes a part of the history of man. I ask you now to protect Dawn and Pam whenever they are and give me the oppurtunity, through your grace and mercy, to be able to locate them, plus, give me a plan for their rescue. Secure our relationship, bless the unity that you gave us through your love and work out this plan for their deliverence. We will give you the praise, honor, and glory for all that You do in our lives because that is what we were created to do. Amen."

CHAPTER 8

The Rescue

Time seemed to pass very quickly having no interruptions from the enemy, and shortly after my rest, my mind started to work overtime. I repeated the plan several times inserting possible obstacles. My thoughts had started to become confusing, and soon my obstacles outweighed my confident plan, but still I was willing to try nearly anything to achieve my goal. I reassured myself of my abilities and the confidence needed for our game plan. Then, I realized I hadn't had anything to eat in about twelve hours. I went over to the cupboard and reached up for some freeze-dried meat sticks. No sooner did I touch the bag than three other bags of crackers, hard rolls, and biscuits came crashing to the floor.

I looked over at Derek who didn't waste any time closing his eyes and falling back to sleep. He never even finished waking up. The Guardians could have executed him right there in the bunk, and he probably would have never known it. I picked up my mess and put three meat sticks in my pocket. I walked up to the control room and decided to put the radar on to check out our situation. I believed that the short exposure time of our power surge would not give them enough time to precisely pinpoint our location. The radar quickly showed me two Guardian aircraft as they headed out toward space and indeed in somewhat of a hurry.

Plus, there were two Guardian ships at the edge of our screen, traveling close to the old bays. I figured they were just trying to isolate our position. Feeling fairly safe, I decided to walk out into the storage area and check out our situation. As I walked out the door, I turned to look back at Derek, and suddenly, I realized the trust he had in me. Flying all over the place, barking out orders, following my plans precisely and doing everything I commanded. I felt proud to be treated with total respect by someone who was so well educated and respected by our society. He truly was a great man, and I would do anything to retain his respect and friendship. I turned and walked down the ramp. It was so quiet and peaceful. It just didn't match the excitement the confusion, and the destruction that was so evident a few hours earlier. I walked over to the door, listened for a moment, and quietly opened it. The hallway was dark except for a small light that peeked through a small window on the door to the landing bay. I walked over to the door checking just for video security equipment. I reached the door, opened it quietly, and walked into the bay. There was a heavy dew settling in on the bay floor depicting the high humidity present in the sky. Through the dew, I could see the glitter of particles used to give the city buoyancy in the sky.

The moon started to come up over the entrance of the bay and accentuated the already fluorescent floor. It gave an appearance of the fourth galaxy, Tetron 8107. This galaxy had an infinite amount of highly luminous stars. It truly was a magnificantly beautiful sight and the most rememberable event I ever saw looking through the astological telescope at school. It was such a beautifully eloquent display composed by our Creator. I decided to bring myself back to reality, and since things were very quiet, I put my scanner on to see it could locate the women.

"Come on, Pamela, I'm counting on you and these scanners better still work."

I pushed the scanner button, and instantly, they appeared on my tracker screen display. Before long, their bodies were pinpointed, and I was correct in assuming that the rest of Balem was a mirror image of Altaur. It looked like they were located right in the middle of a detention block. I had a real strong feeling that the difficult part of our task was about to be performed. I shut the scanner off and reviewed my plan. For the first time, I felt that I had the confidence to perform the task. I strolled back to the ship to inform Derek of our plans. On the way, I decided that if I were to tell Derek every detail of the plan, he would end up asking 1,500 questions, and we would never get to execute it. So, I decided just to take him through it blindly again. He did so well on the last impromptu that I felt I'd be better off having him unaware of our future plans.

"Derek! Derek, wake up you old dog! It's time to move on! Derek, let's go!"

Derek jumped out of the bunk and landed straight up on his feet, a maneuver I had never seen him do before today.

"Hey, Derek! Slow down, it's not an emergency."

"What? Where? Joe, what's going on?"

"Sorry, didn't mean to startle you."

"I was in such a deep sleep that I forgot where I was and what I was doing here. Gee, it's a real eye opener when reality sets in. What's up?"

"It's time to get the girls."

"What's the plan?"

"I'll inform you as we go."

"Here we go again, another impromptu. You always leave me in the dark."

"I'll set the automatic sensor alarm. If someone locates or tampers with the ship, we will know about it. It will be transmitted through my laser, wrist device. It also can be used as a homing device just in case we are separated, disoriented, or simply lost. Here you take this wristlet. I always keep an extra one on the ship."

We walked through the hallway and out into the bay making sure no one was around. The night was so still and black you could hardly see your hand in front of your face. The overcast sky blew a cool breeze through the landing bay and the whistle it produced was kind of unnerving. The only way to move around in the bay was to use my infrared visual nighttime optics lenses. Once we put them on, everything was in full view. The objects were red but very distinguishable. I used them frequently on patrol so they were nearly second nature to me, but Derek seemed to have some trouble focusing. We walked slowly around the outside wall of the storage bay. The bays extended about one hundred yards from the storage area, and nothing marred the entranceway out into the atmosphere.

The bays were kept completely organized, nearly every piece of equipment came from the storage area. The equipment was easily accessible but also very well contained. During an attack, everything was kept in the storage area just in case the bay was attacked and damaged. Similarly, fighters could land quickly be refueled and repaired most efficiently and returned to battle promptly. The storage area, even larger than the bays could hold up to eight fighters comfortably. Also, they could house the weaponry and repair parts for all of them, together with the tools, machinery, fuel, and housing facilities for the crews. The scope of the bay area was so extensive that it made up nearly the whole lower level of Balem. The storage and bay facicities made up 70 percent of the total lower second floor. The other 30 percent housed the power generator and was located dead center of the facility.

This demonstrated the most secure area of Balem. It appeared as the center of a pie with the slices being the storage bays. There existed three levels, one below us and one above. Now, out of the isolated storage area, we could hear workers below us very clearly. Since the layout mirrored those on Altaur, the new bays and storage areas were being built just below us. It always puzzled me why the middle level was built first, unless they knew of bigger and better fighters that would need bigger and better equipped storage areas and landing bays. It's probably phase two of three phases. I have no clue what plans they had for level three. We could go undetected as long as we stayed on level two so off we went working our way close to bay 37. There we would have to enter the facility to reach the women.

"Here it is, Derek. Are you ready?"

"Definitely! It's about time. We've been sneaking around down here for thirty minutes."

"Not really Derek, it just seems that long. They should be up above the old landing bays. If I'm right, it will put us right smack in the middle of the detention center."

"They should be? If I'm right? You don't sound very confident, Joe."

"Well, you never know what lurks behind closed doors."

"Who said that, Joe?"

"I don't know. Who really cares?"

"Now, give me the bad part, Joe. What floor, seventy-seven?"

"No, not quite, thirty-three is the floor."

"That gives us just enough time to get up there and then get caught coming out, if you know what I mean."

"That's why they made it that way. Supposedly, they can secure the area before the elevator reaches the bottom."

"Oh great, so how do we—no, how do you—propose we get to the thirty third floor and out undetected. Never mind, you will show me when the time comes."

We ran up a long stairwell and somewhat winded stopped at the door on the landing located on the third level. The door was very large, big enough to give a good size crew room to escape a bay being destroyed. There was a small window in the center of the door, which enabled us to see into the hallway of the main structure. I opened the door rather gingerly and waited until two Guardian patrol personnel walked by the door. They always patrolled in pairs. As soon as they passed by, I released the door. The noise was muffled but loud enough for them to notice a disturbance. We hid behind the door and as it opened toward us our identity was completely concealed from the stairwell. They entered the door with lasers in hand. As they reached the stairs they split up, one going up toward the city and one going down to the old landing bays. We had predetermined which one we would attack and Derek drew the short straw. It was his job to take out the Guardian going down the stairs.

The Guardians wore a certain poly-metallic armor that covered them from their head to their toes. The material was kind of unique because it resisted laser blasts, at least single shot blasts and was very flexible. The armor conformed to anybody who put it on. You could be 6'3" and 240 pounds or 5'6", 110 pounds, the same set of armor would fit you. I never looked into the theory behind the suit, but from what I gathered, it depended on the molecular structure, super heated to a relative temperature of about 210 degrees Celsius, and then instantaneously cooled to minus 135 degrees Celsius. That produced an elastic very durable multi-layered rubber like substance. It was highly resistant but independently conforming to any body type or build. The boots were made out of the same material as well as the gloves. They were also very lightweight, rubbery, comfortable, and highly protective. Their protection extended over the entire body, and the gloves went passed your elbows. It was nearly impossible to get burned in the suits unless the temperature reached close to 150 degrees Celsius. The Guardian fighter pilots had similar uniforms, but they were gray in color as compared to these light green suits.

Around the head was a helmet. It was made of a stronger not so flexible material. It was somewhat awkward, as it didn't conform to the body. It stopped short just below the skull in the back, leaving an area of about three inches unprotected. It was designed for some mobility in turning the head. The front extended down past the neck to the top part of the chest. The chest shield extended from the top of the shoulder to just above the hips; there was a back plate also. The helmet electronically covered vision from ear to ear. Peripheral vision was not impaired, and the visor was capable of deflecting any weapon known to man. The helmet also came close around the ears and amplifiers were inserted into both sides. The helmet fit snug and proved to be very efficient. It had the ultimate protection and comfort, superb amplification for hearing, and a wide visual field. They could also hear a wide variety of frequencies especially at both ends of the spectrum.

Fortunately, Derek and I knew about their equipment and were prepared to act in a manner as to be undetected by them. Looking at two Guardians standing side by side from two different Star Cities, one could not tell who was who. Perfect for my plan. The situation presented us with two Guardians facing away from us as they entered the stairwells. Their most vulnerable weakness was right in our path. As they took the first step the click from my laser made the Guardian going down the stairs turn and prepare to fire. The other Guardian going up the stairs felt the direct hit from my laser and fell to the ground stunned. In one smooth motion, Derek was in the air making an attempt to disarm the Guardian. His momentum violently forced both of them down the stairwell to the landing below.

The Guardian's weapon flew out of her hand and down in between the stairwell. I could hear it bounce off the railings of the floor below. She reached for another weapon fixed to her thigh, but I sharply aimed my laser and hit her somewhere on her forearm. The force was strong enough to disarm her, but the armor was keeping my laser shots from penetrating her body. Derek was now back on his feet and ran toward her grabbing her arms and slamming her into the wall. His next move was tearing away her helmet and initiating a double combination right hook and upper cut straight to the jaw with a jab and backhanded fist punch. She slithered down the wall in complete confusion, hit the floor and passed out.

"Good job, Derek. Hey, that was a great combo."

"You like that, huh?"

"Well, phase one completed. Next, we penetrate the system by wearing their armor and helmets. That's the only way we'll be able to get to Dawn and Pam."

"As we changed clothes, it finally dawned on Derek that we were dealing with women now."

"Hey, Joe, these women are tough. You know she nearly killed me. I just don't like the idea of hitting a woman. I think of Pamela every time I see one and punching them out just doesn't seem right."

"I know, Derek, but we have no choice."

As soon as we were dressed, we tied and gagged both Guardian patrolman and took them down to the old storage bays. We tied them up to one of the super structures feeling that they would be found soon after our escape.

"Okay, up we go Derek." We reached the top of the stairs, and I slowly opened the door and listened for footsteps or any other sign of activity.

"These helmets are great, Joe. I can hear footsteps, but they are very faint."

"Now remember, Derek. These are women so don't say a word or you will be using that famous right cross again."

I opened the door a little more and heard a door slam with strong footsteps coming toward us. They sounded like they were very close to our position so I closed the door slowly and within five seconds there appeared two more Guardians walking by our door. Shortly thereafter, I opened it again and it was clear. We stepped out into the hallway, quietly closed the door and started walking down the hall. We set our lasers on stun and continued to walk slowly trying to look inconspicuous. We passed several patrols going the opposite direction, and soon we were at the end of the hall. A squad of Guardians were high-stepping in cadence and soon passed us, saluting the uniform I was wearing. It must have been a high-ranking officer, at least, I wanted to think that for the moment. We just returned the same salute trying not to raise any suspicion.

"Joe, I think you're an officer."

"What do you mean think? I am."

"I mean in this woman's army or whatever we are part of over here, Air Force, Guardians, whatever."

"I hope that rank comes in handy helping us to get out of here."

We walked and walked, it seemed like forever, up one flight of stairs and past two doorways. Once again, up one more flight, then down the hallway following the homing device that was working perfectly receiving the women's signal. We finally reached the elevator, and soon we would be waiting to enter the detention area.

"A piece of cake, Joe."

"Don't get too confident we haven't even found them yet."

The elevator finally made it, seeming to be the longest elevator wait I have ever had. It opened and a droid greeted us from inside.

"What floor, please?" Before the droid had spat the phrase out, I stepped in front of it and pushed the thirty-third floor.

"Just like an officer! Just 'cause I am a droid doesn't mean I can't operate this primitive elevation device. What a menial job for such an intelligent droid like me. I just can't understand why they gave me this job. What a stupid job. I should be doing something important!"

I chuckled under my breath. I could hear Derek laugh a little too. I leaned over to him and whispered, "The person inventing this little droid must have been ultimately frustrated with his job."

run out. It will be almost impossible for them to find us. They will be on their own now. We won't be able to help them."

Shortly, we all met down at the entrance to the detention center. "Okay, Derek, let's go."

We removed our helmets to reassure them of our identity. "How are you ladies doing?" asked Derek.

Pam and Dawn were surprised to see that the guards who stood before them were actually Derek and I. They were so excited to see us.

"We didn't think you would ever find us. My homing device just ran out!"

"Well, we found you! We still aren't out of here yet, though. Let's go!"

We moved toward the elevator, the two of us still presenting our disguises. "Derek, what are we going to do with this creature?"

"Creature? He is human, Joe, and he looked like he needed a break. We're stuck with him, for now. At least, we know he'll be on our side until we get out of here. That may work to our advantage."

As we all waited for the elavator, you could have cut the silence with a knife. Finally it arrived; we entered and push the nonstop button to the first floor. We quickly reached the first floor and immediately a loud alarm began to ring throughout the building. All the elevators stopped; luckily, we're already out and moving toward our destination.

"Gee, Joe, we just made it. A couple of seconds earlier, and we would have been descending the elevator shaft."

As the alarm rang out, citizens, guards, and Guardians hurried throughout the first floor. Despite the circumstances, we continued to keep our pace and guard our prisoners as if we had real orders to carry on with our business. About halfway back to the ship, we turned down a long hallway toward the storage area. As we entered the long hallway, we could see flashing red lights spaced out about every twenty feet. The sirens were still blaring and security was running everywhere. One-third of the way down the hall we were approached by a Guardian.

"Papers, please, we are under red alert. I have to see your papers."

I fumbled around in my chest armor for a few seconds. Then simultaneously, we both drew our lasers. I managed to get a quick shot off before the officer and hit her hand. The laser fell to the ground, and I then launched a left hook to her helmet, which threw her up against the wall. Soon, I followed with an upper cut to the jaw now exposed with the helmet rolling down the hallway. I heard two other shots hoping they were from Derek's laser. I spun around and threw off my helmet to increase my field of vision. I fell to one knee and fired upon a charging Guardian. I could hear the laser shot buzz by my ear. The hallway seemed to be filling with Guardians now. I turned to Dawn and threw her my extra laser. She was on one knee now, and it wasn't long before I heard her laser fire repeatedly.

Now, Derek without his helmet on proceeded to take the lead.

We started moving down the hallway quickly but cautiously. We passed several hallways that ran 90 degrees toward our bay, and Guardians seemed to be everywhere. Moving quickly, we passed three adjacent storage room doors without any trouble. Then, out of the corner of my eye, I saw a small utility door open and a laser stick out of the crack in the door.

"Dawn! Dawn!" I shouted.

She didn't realize what had happened so I took two steps forward and leaped directly in the path of the laser. The laser blast hit me directly in the chest and threw me right on top of Dawn. Derek saw the laser about the same time I did and turned and fired hitting the laser and putting a large hole in the door. The laser dropped to the floor and the door slammed back into place.

"Joe! Derek! Come quick. He's dead! He's—"

"What, Dawn? Don't jump to any conclusions. I'm fine. I'm glad it hit me in the chest and not the head. I would have been a dead man for sure."

"Let's move! shouted Pam!"

The laser blast did hit me directly, but I still had the Guardian chest plate on. It took the brunt of the blast leaving a black-charred hole in the armor. As I regained my posture and stood up, Dawn quickly hugged me.

"You saved my life, Joe! I love you so much!"

She quickly and firmly gave me a reassuring kiss on my cheek, and let me say that a cool, calm feeling rushed through my body.

"Let's go, I'll guard the rear! Go, Derek!"

We moved rather quickly now. The halls were swarming with security. I could hear laser blasts in front of me, and I had my share coming from behind. It sure was getting hotter by the second. Soon, we reached the end of the hallway. Derek looked around the corner and down the next hallway. Just then, two laser blasts hit next to his head and small pieces of the wall fell on him. He quickly moved back behind the wall trying to protect himself and shouted back at me.

"Joe, I need some help up here!"

"What, Derek, I'm pretty busy! What's the hold up?"

"There are two, maybe more down this back hallway. I can't get a clear shot at them."

Before Derek could get the words out, Dawn handed Derek two small silver and red balls, Joe had just passed to her.

"Try these. Just roll them down the hallway, and they will do the rest."

"Where did you get these?"

"Oh, it's my secret weapon. I always carry four or five in the handle of my laser. Stand back, they have a helluva punch."

Derek rolled the two balls, one right after the other with different velocities, and within three seconds, there was an extremely loud blast as fire shot back toward the wall where Derek and Dawn were concealed.

"Holy Moses, Joe!"

"What were in those things?"

"I'll tell you later. Let's go!"

We all moved down the hallway running past four or five Guardians who lay dead on the floor. The halls were all charred black from the explosion now and two doorways along with several paintings and an entry way were ablaze. Smoke billowed out into the hallway behind us, giving us some added protection. About fifteen seconds later, and we were at the storage bay adjacent to our ship. Derek had gone passed it, and it wasn't until I came upon it did I beckon him to return.

"Derek? Where are you going?"

"This isn't it. Is it?"

"Sure is! That's the last time I let you lead."

"Oh, I thought it was the next one. I wasn't too far off."

We entered the stairwell and immediately met resistance. A security guard was coming down the upper stairwell and she fired two shots, both narrowly missing me. I hit the floor, and Pam, who was just behind me, took out the descending Guardian. Soon, everyone was in the stairwell and moving quickly down toward the storage bay.

"Joe, this place is crawling with security and Guardians."

As soon as we reached the landing, we stopped and I quietly told them to rest, and I would see if anyone was in the storage area.

They squatted down next to the door, and Joe quietly stood up and looked out the small window to see if there were any Guardians moving about the bay.

"We can wait for a moment here and try to catch our breadth."

"Joe, do we have this storage bay to go through before we get to our fighter? It can get pretty messy if we meet resistance," remarked Derek.

"Well, we are close, and it can't get any messier than it has been. Let's take this armor off. Maybe we can pick up some speed."

As soon as we slipped off the armor, I took another look through the window and the area was still clear of Guardians.

"Now, we have to move quickly so try to keep up with me. Let's go!"

The door swung open, and we all took off running. We passed the storage bay and Joe ducked into the next hallway. They all passed him for a second, stopped, and retreated back to the hallway but Joe was gone.

"Joe, where are you? Joe, come on. This is no time to fool around."

Just then, Joe put the lights on which shown back into the hallway, and as we walked through the entryway, there before us was our fighter.

"How did we get… Joe, what's going on? You son of a gun, you knew exactly where we were going."

"That stairwell wasn't the original, you old hound dog. This is the back door, isn't it? See, I wasn't wrong, was I?"

"No, not exactly! Just thought we'd take a shortcut. I figured we might meet more resistance, but I concluded the risk was worth it. Besides, someone has to take control and lead this group."

We all entered the ship and took our positions. Dawn and I sat in the cockpit, and Derek and Pam moved to the rear guns. I would be in charge of flying and Dawn would be in charge of weaponry and navigation.

"Hey, Derek, I don't know why you invited this criminal to come along."

"We don't know if he's a criminal, Joe."

"Yeah, well, strap him in to the navigator's seat and we'll deal with him later."

"I'm taking care of that now, and I will find him something to eat. Who knows the last time he had any food."

"Hey, Derek, we are going to need you to man that rear gun as soon as possible."

"Dawn, check the scanner, and see what's out there waiting."

"Yes, sir." I started the engines and figured that the sound would attract a handsome number of Guardians at our door.

"Well, it looks clear, Joe. No, wait… It's starting to get pretty crowded especially in the hallways next to the bay."

"These are loud engines. You think, in this day and age, they'd invent one that doesn't make any sound." Just as I said that, a subtle laugh came over the headpiece.

"Derek? What's that for?"

"That wasn't me."

"Was that your buddy back there?"

"Yes, it sure was. My name is Eric."

"Oh, do you know something I don't know?"

"Possibly… uh… most likely. Yes, probably."

"Well, Eric, I think I'm going to like you, that is, if we ever get out of here. Where are you from, Eric?"

"I'm from earth. I'm one of the remnants of the radiated genetic monsters the famous Macrocaust left behind. Just a wonderful time in the history of man."

"That's what I thought, Joe, and if we are going to reach the *Station America*, Eric just might be able to help us, or at least guide us to someone who can. Maybe, he knows someone in the Carthusian nation. That would be to good to be true!"

"Good thinking, Derek. That's probably the best idea you have ever had."

"I thought it was a pretty good idea... Hey, what do you mean the best?"

We both laughed for a couple of seconds, and I figured it was time to get out of there before the whole Guardian army was knocking at our door.

"Dawn, what do we have out there?"

"There's about fifty approaching on foot, and some Guardian ships in sight."

"Well, there's only one thing to do, Dawn. As soon as I get maximum power out of these engines, you blast the door away, and I'll get us on out of here."

"Everyone ready?"

"Let's do it!"

"Now, Dawn!"

At my command, the door blew open shattering into a million pieces. Shrapnel was flying everywhere and Guardians were running in all direction. I then put the throttle to maximum and hit the turbo charger, and we were out of the bay in seconds.

"Joe, I didn't know you could go from standstill to turbo charge."

"I really wasn't sure myself, Dawn, I've only done it once, and that was when I left Altaur. Needless to say, this one was a lot smoother. Besides, I do have a few tricks up my sleeve."

It wasn't long before I heard Derek come through the communicator. "Joe, we have five bogies on our tail, approximately fifteen miles away, and boy are they moving."

"Interceptor ships or Guardian patrols?"

"Interceptor ships, five to one."

"Those are not very good odds with interceptors. You just try to keep them busy and play defensive, Derek. Dawn, put 75 percent of our deflector shields on our tail, and I'm going to try to use the ruins on Earth to our advantage. Eric, we are going to need your help on this one. Where's the largest and closest city on earth with high buildings we can use for cover."

"The coordinates are already locked in on our navigator, sir, and if you'll put the chart on your screen, you will receive the coordinates promptly."

"Nice work, Eric! I'm liking you more and more every minute."

Soon, we were on a direct path to old Seattle, one of the major cities in the United States before the Great Macrocaust. Derek and Pamela were staying busy in the back, and the interceptors just seemed to be somewhat annoying at this point.

"Put the bow scanner on, so we can evaluate our course and locate all of this rubble scattered throughout the city," Dawn said.

As we flew close to the ground, the city became more massive, and our path grew more compressed. Most of the buildings were just refuse, but many of the steel-framed larger buildings were partially erect.

"Joe, we have an interceptor right on our tail, and I can't get him. He's good, real good! I mean she's good! We have one coming up on the starboard side too. You better do something quick."

"Derek, they are unmanned. That is why they are so important to destroy. Those ships are flown from a computer back at base and will stop at nothing."

"Dawn, redirect all our power to the rear and starboard deflector shields. I hate to do it, but we're going to have to take a chance. Dawn, what is going on up ahead? Is there any cover we could use to our advantage?"

"Joe! Joe! We are taking a beating back here. I need some help, now!"

"We have an overhead concrete walkway across the street, but it's only fifty meters from the ground, and half of it sits in ruins."

"Dawn, give me the dimensions of this ship."

"Height, four meters. Width seventeen meters. And length eighteen meters."

Just then, our object detector alarm went off. The guidance system promptly said three miles and closing two miles."

"Can we make it, Joe?"

"We'll have to make it, Dawn. If we go over, that starboard bogy will cut us to pieces and that doesn't take in consideration the other four coming up fast"

"Dawn, we have enough width but with the rubble will we make it?"

"Barely, Joe, barely! It's going to be tight."

Without warning, a rocket hit our starboard side. The impact pushed us four degrees to port but the shield held. Two laser rounds followed.

I slowed our speed to two-thirds power for five seconds, then up to full throttle, I regained my speed. That was enough of a delay for the starboard interceptor ship to pass us by. As we regained velocity on the engines, he slowed down, but he moved two hundred yards in front of the us. One of the other interceptor ships pulled up in order to avoid a collision and went to port. He circled around and was about five hundred yards behind us and approaching fast.

"Good move, Joe!"

"Now, it's your turn, Derek! You have to keep it busy and its mind off what we're going to do next."

"What's that? Forget it. I don't want to know. Just do it and fast!!"

"Joe, if they hit us under the bridge, it will throw us right up against the building on the port side. There won't be anything left of us."

"I know. That's why we're going in at full speed."

"Full speed, I hope you're good, Joe!"

"More than hope and better than good!"

At that point, we were twenty seconds from the bridge. I slowed to half speed until I saw a reaction from the interceptor on the guidance screen. They slowed, not fooled by the move this time. That's what I figured, though, and as soon as our starboard bogey launched a torpedo, I regained full power. It seemed like a blink of an eye, and we were under the bridge. Regaining full power that fast lowered my starboard wing about six degrees something I figured would happen, except I just wasn't sure to what extent. As we passed under the bridge, I tilted my fighter slightly to port. I could feel some drag on my starboard side, and I knew we were scraping the underside of the bridge, but we were still in one piece.

"Joe, we are leaving a trail of sparks back here. What's going on?"

Debris flew all round, most of it behind us. The walkway was fairly wide, but we were through before you knew it. I switched on our rear view, so Dawn could report on our enemies. Once we were clear, I flew straight up over two short intact buildings. Then I banked port, slowed to two-thirds and maneuvered through some tall buildings. I again picked up more speed. The interceptor ship on our starboard side misjudged the distance between the two buildings and the walkway, which was connected to it, and at full power banked hard to port. The strain on the attacker's internal rudder mechanism, subsequently malfunctioned, and they couldn't compensate by coming around once again hard to starboard. They crashed right into the remains of the builing adjacent to the walkway. There was a violent explosion. Steel and concrete were flying everywhere, and the rest of the building started to collapse. The attacker who was one hundred meters behind him couldn't avoid the explosion. The force propelled it into the building and back to the other side of the walkway, and there was another explosion. The two buildings and the walkway were now reduced to fragments of steel and cement with flying debris everywhere.

"Great shot, Joe! Two birds with one stone, not bad."

"That's an old saying, Derek."

"I used to read a lot in my younger days. Something to do with hunting."

"Hey Joe, we're not home yet!" Pam shouted.

"We have three ships closing in fast at two o'clock."

We had barely escaped the city going south and sure enough, they just wouldn't leave us alone. I pulled up to twenty-thousand feet and to the south southeast was a tall mountain range.

"Maybe, we can lose them in those mountains," I said.

"Eric, you wouldn't, by any chance, know anything about those mountains, would you?"

"Funny you should ask! I grew up in those mountains."

"I am so glad you decided to come along for the ride."

"You're glad. I'm beginning to wonder what I got myself into hitching a ride with this crew. It's like you have nothing to lose and believe me I really didn't want to die."

"It's funny you should say that. We really don't have anything to lose."

"Are we still on full deflector shields, stern and starboard?"

"Yes, sir," Dawn said.

"Okay, put full power on port, starboard, and stern and leave our bow open."

We flew down into a valley and skimmed the inside of a steep cliff, trying to avoid their scanners as we moved down the range. It wasn't long before they found us, and our gunners were having a hard time eliminating the threat. Another rocket hit our port side throwing us about thirty degrees to starboard and extremely close to the cliffs on the other side of the ravine. I tipped the starboard side up and barely compensated for the shock, and the force made me sway starboard side down, then up, then down again. I knew we were way too close to the sides of the cliff so I pulled my starboard side up to nearly ninety degrees and headed for the middle of the ravine We ended up just grazing the contour of the cliffs approximately twenty meters from the edge. In an aircraft going at this speed, well, it even made me uncomfortable.

"That was too close, Joe!" Dawn screamed.

"I know, I know. Now calm down. What's the damage report on that port deflector shield? Is it still intact?"

"We have a hole in the shield about two meters in diameter."

"Derek, did you hear that? We have to be careful to protect our port side."

"Yes, sir, I'm on it!"

underneath the ship, and I fought to gain control of it. The ship swayed back and forth.

"I can't keep her steady! We're losing power."

"Altitude, Dawn?"

"Eight hundred meters."

"What's the terrain?" I demanded.

"Derek, keep an eye on the bogy. I'm going to drop the fuel tanks and our weaponry payload just before we land. If we're lucky, they'll think the explosion was us."

"The scanner shows a very lose sandy bottom about fifty feet deep. It must have been a river bed before it dried up."

"That's deep enough. If we can drop our payload and make them think we've exploded, I think we can bury ourselves without any problem."

"It's our only hope, Joe."

"Is everyone all right back there?" Joe asked.

"Yes, somewhat shaken but fine. Most of the damage is on the exterior. We're not even getting any smoke back here, Joe."

"Good. We're smoking like crazy outside!"

Smoke was bellowing out of the port side of the ship, and fires started every few seconds. The fire extinguisher system was intact, and the fires were doused as soon as they started, which gave me confidence in the ability of our ship to survive.

The interceptor ship was closing with continual laser blasts, now, to our stern. They did keep their distance though fearing an explosion.

"Altitude, Dawn?"

"Three hundred meters and falling fast."

We banked hard to starboard, flew around the last hill of the mountain range, and for a brief second, lost visual sight of the interceptor.

"Dawn, drop the tanks and payload now!"

Smoke and fire raged through the small trees below after a loud explosion. "Did that sound like us blowing up?"

"I hope so," Dawn said softly.

"Prepare for landing—crash landing, that is."

We lost altitude fast, and all I could see on the viewer was the loose sandy ground coming up fast.

"I sure hope this stuff is real soft."

We hit hard with a force that carried us deep into the sand. Soon, the ship was completely covered, and we didn't stop for about thirty meters. It felt like seven miles, but we eventually came to a stop with no explosions, and everyone secure in their seats. The sand muffled the smoke and actually helped confine the fires on the exterior. That sand probably saved the ship and gave us a bonus of great camouflage too.

"Is everyone okay? Derek?" Joe asked.

"Yes, sir, we're fine."

"How about you, Dawn?"

"I'm good, Joe, just a little shaken up."

"Are our life support systems intact, Dawn?"

"Yes, sir, and the damage report will be in soon."

"Eric, everything okay? Are you still glad we brought you along?"

"Yes, and may I say glad to be alive, well, and on solid ground," Eric replied.

It probably has been awhile since he was on solid ground, I thought to myself.

I sat back into my seat resting my head on the rear mounted head rest exhausted from the mental concentration I needed to control the ship. Dawn unbuckled her safety strap, leaned over the cockpit, and put her arms securely around my chest. She looked into my eyes and kissed me and then hugged me tight. It brought back the memories of Gamnon. They were such great memories.

"Dawn, cut all power, with some luck their scanners won't detect our position. They should track us to our ground debris, if they pick us up at all. I hope the explosion was enough to the fool the sensors on that unmanned fighter."

For a period of about ten minutes, we heard a lot of commotion above us. Ships kept passing by every minute or so checking to see if the explosion was our ship or just the payload, but we hadn't been captured so it appeared our plan worked.

"Dawn, check the radar screen and see what's going on up there?"

Dawn used a weak auxiliary power to turn the radar on, hoping if any ship was in the area it wouldn't pick up our signal.

"It's all clear, Joe. There is not a ship within fifty kilometers from here. I think we fooled them."

"Let's go back and see what the rest of the crew is up to."

We got up and went to the stern of the ship. There were some areas that were damaged along the way, but it appeared there was nothing damaged that couldn't be repaired. We would just need the equipment. Derek and Pam were sitting together, and Eric was across from them. They were eating and drinking, and it looked like a normal social hour at our apartment."

"Well, we did it, at least for now. That food looks good, Derek."

"Well, join us, Joe. We would be glad to have you."

"Sounds great. We'll sit tight for a while, relax, rest, and nourish our war-ridden bodies. We'll keep the radar on. If a ship approaches, we'll go back on weak auxiliary. We're going to need some time to figure out what we are going to do next."

"Have any ideas, Joe?"

"Don't ask. Getting shot down was not in my plan."

"How about a real meal, Derek? Eric?"

"It sounds good to me," they both said simultaneously.

"We'll whip something up," Dawn said. "Come on, Pam, we have work to do."

"I'm really hungry," Derek said.

"You're always hungry, Derek."

"I can't remember what a real meal tastes like," Eric said.

"How long were you there, Eric?" asked Joe.

"Oh, about three years."

"That's a long time to be in prison."

"You're not kidding, Derek."

"What did you do deserve that sentence?"

"Oh, I really didn't do anything. I was just out working and was picked up.

I think they had planned to study me. At least, that's the way it appeared in the beginning. They spent almost every day taking me to the lab and examining me."

Then, they seemed to lose interest. Anyway, I was out one beautiful evening looking for some radiated wood. See, I'm sort of a scientist, and we've been doing a lot of research with radiated wood. It seems to make great fertilizer. Can you believe it? I was picked up looking for what they use to call refuse. The wood once ground up increased plant growth rate by four, so we could produce four growing seasons in the time it took for one previously, and the best part is there are no side effects. The only problem is collecting it. It has to be cut in sizes we can harvest, and you can't touch it without special gloves, or it will give you severe burns. We also used it to run our generators.

"Anyway, I had found a very large, highly radiated area, just as a Guardian patrol ship flew by. I was too stubborn to give it up. They surrounded our team picked us up and took us away. The first two years were pretty bad. I missed my family. Then, after I accepted the fact that I might be there until I die it got much easier. It feels good to be back on solid ground. I have a good feeling about being home and I'm sure there are a couple more people who are going to be very grateful. By the way, what's going on with the four of you. You sure made some people pretty angry at you," Eric stated.

"You can say that again, Eric. Joe, you tell him. I'm exhausted," Derek said.

"Well, it all started on Gamnon," I stated.

"Oh yes, I have heard of that place where that extremely bizzare mating process is required of you for the purpose of, what is it, promoting your society?"

"Yes, that's it. We decided that we would like to spend our lives together. So the brilliant Derek Johan reprogrammed the computer in our flat to give us and only us any and all information concerning the past, present, and future, that we could use to help devise a plan for our escape. Our ultimate goal being the *Space Station America*."

"*Space Station America*, huh?"

"Yes, I hope if you can direct us to the right people, that is, once you find your way home, we can reach our goal. I do have to admit that it was very selfish of us to kidnap you fully intending to use your services. Actually, it was only a backup plan, but it looks like we already have used up all of our options."

"We sure have, Joe."

"Are you familiar with the *Space Station America*, Eric?"

"Why sure, but do you know that it passes by only twice a year, and that it is only in our orbit one time. We only need it once a year to bring special supplies, unless a request is made for some particular necessity."

"Once a year. That's not what the computer stated."

"Well, it used to be much more often, but our society has developed into a much more self-sufficient, high-tech community unless things have changed since I was captured. They orbit and send in transports once a year."

"When is the next supply ship?"

"Well, let me see if my calculations are correct, then they should have sent supplies about nine to ten months ago."

"Yes, thirteen, I think?"

"You know I haven't had an accurate recollection of time in a while."

"Derek, remember when we were in the hallway going to the Hall of Creation, and we saw that strange alien fighter? He just played games with those Guardian ships. There was really no contest between them. In fact, he looked like he was just having fun during the whole ordeal."

"That sounds like them," Eric said. "Usually some older fighters escort all the transports in because they are slightly slower than the Star City fighters. Their technology far surpasses that of the Star Cities but they still send fighters as a precaution. The transports could very easily make it on their own."

"When is the next communication date? It must be coming up soon."

"Yes, if I had to guess I would say within three month."

"Sorry, Derek, I keep forgetting. We don't have a ship that can hold enough fuel to reach them. Well, then, I'll have to design a modification for this ship if we can figure out how to get it out of this sand. I've been working diligently on some experimental designs for a new fighter back on Altaur. With a machine shop, the right equipment, parts and some time I can modify—"

"Dinner is ready," called Pamela. The women started to bring out two large trays with all kinds of food.

"That all came from our supplies?" I asked

"Where else do you think we got it, Joe?" Dawn replied.

"Come to think of it, that was a pretty stupid question. It just looks so different. It even looks good."

"Really, anything would look good," Derek said. "No offense girls, but I am famished."

"Well, it's not much," said Dawn, "but we really didn't have much to work with, mostly freeze-dried foods."

I opened the covered platter in the center of the table, and it looked like a delicious roast.

"Dawn, where did you get a roast?"

"Derek, we didn't get anything like that, did we? Is it a mirage?"

"Nearly, it's processed from a package of dehydrated meat, and some homemade coreal sauce. We just added some water."

"But, Derek, we were only supposed to get—"

"Did you really think I was going to just get that garbage that you told me to get? I threw a couple extra goodies in my bag as I raced along the aisles."

"You're crazy! You lugged that stuff all day at the festivities and never once complained?"

"Sure, if I asked for sympathy, you would have left it, right?"

"Yes, I sure would have."

"Aren't you glad I didn't ask?"

"I sure am!"

We all sat around the table and ate. Afterward, we felt rested and a lot more relaxed than we had been in the past few hours. I have to admit my mind was totally blank for a good while. It was over quickly, though, and as Derek and the women cleaned up, I sat down and started to talk to Eric about some future plans.

"Now, Eric, back to business. Does your society have any airship defense systems, supply ships? Maybe, we can borrow some parts."

"We have a small force, but many of the ships are old and not really used any more. We really don't need them."

"Do you think your people will help us reach the *Station America*?"

"Of course, our society mirrors that of the *Station America* and all of our principles and teachings are exactly the same. Freedom to choose what you want to do and when, where, or how you choose to do it. There are no secrets in our society. We believe in freedom of the press and freedom of speech. Our principles and concepts are based on the principals and ideals of the United States of America. Do you know what that governing body stood for in its day?"

"Not really. We had so much information to learn and many plans to make for our escape, I can't remember alot from that history lesson. I'll sit down and learn more about your society and the *Station America*'s community once we get the ship straightened out."

"I will too," Derek said.

"I didn't think you were paying attention, Derek."

"Come on, Joe. My ears are always listening, acquiring, learning, and storing important information."

"Eric, do you think we can get this ship out of this sand and repaired it in time to meet the *Station America*?"

"Certainly, very easy in fact. We'll have to do it at night, though. There are too many Guardian patrols out during the day and it has to be done soon or the sand is going to fall away from the ship and expose your identity."

"How about fuel?"

"It's available and there's plenty for your needs. Our highly skilled machinists can make repairs. We can use parts and ideas from our Defense System storage facilities. The *Station America* helped us set up a very complicated and unique defense system. They came to our need when your society tried to exterminate us."

"I remember bits and pieces of the history surrounding the extermination of earth people, the Carthusian nation. We were lead to believe that our armies were successful."

"Another lie. Your society is just full of them."

"You can say that again, Eric. We could hardly believe what the computers were telling us after being deceived for so long. Eric, how are your people going to react to us? Is there any hostility toward our society now? I wouldn't blame them if there was, after what we tried to do to you."

"That happened a long time ago, and we have helped others, from different earth sectors, to reach the *Station America*. There was a huge inundation of newcomers when the supply ships were running two and three times a year. The newcomers tapered off abruptly about seventy years ago. We haven't had a successful attempt since that time. It's a nice feeling to know that there are still people out there who are willing to take the risks to become free."

"Well, count on this trip being successful because we are going to make it, and we will do whatever it takes to achieve our destination."

"You certainly have the confidence. I guess that's what got you this far, along with some blessings and pretty good talent for flying. It's good to see that the desire and drive to be free has never been completely suppressed. I guess as long as we can retain our human emotions and our reluctance to be repressed, we will always strive to be free."

"Eric, a very dear and very important person in my life once told me those same words. Strive to be free... He told me that just before he passed on to another life. I'll never forget him."

"He must have been a great man."

"He was. He surely was."

"Gee, Eric, we sure got off track for a second. What happened toward the end of the Carthusian War."

"Oh yes, we did very well toward the end of the war. We shot down many of your fighters. We started to defend our people and cause, with superior technology acquired from our good friends on *Station America*. Your people began to lose confidence in their ability to defeat us and finally ended the war. They went back to the Star Cities, let's say, with their tales between their legs."

"The America nation must have had incredible leaders throughout the years. Who leads the *Station America* now?"

"A man named Joseph… Well, it's Commander Joseph Cavelli, but he is such a humble man that he just wants us to call him Joe. You remind me a lot of him."

"I like his name, all right. Do you think I can learn more about him. He sure sounds like an interesting man."

"Sure, when we have some time, Joe, but I'm really tired now. I definitely could use some rest."

"Oh, I'm sorry, Eric. I just get carried away sometimes. We can all use some rest, right, Derek?"

"Sounds good to me, Joe."

"Eric, you can sleep up front in the navigator's quarters. There are some larger beds back here we can use."

"Sounds great, Joe. I'm sure you guys would like some privacy. Good night and thanks for the ride."

Derek and Pam went to the port compartment, and Dawn and I took the starboard. Dawn turned the light off, and we both laid down on the bed.

"It sure feels good to lay down," said Dawn. "It sure does. I'm exhausted."

"Joe, do you think we made the right decision in leaving our people and seeking a life together."

"Dawn, what's wrong? Are you having second thoughts?" I turned and held her close to me. "I love you. I couldn't have it any other way. My life would have been meaningless on Altaur without you. Are you really having second thoughts?"

"No, no. I love you too, Joe. The feeling becomes stronger every minute I am with you. But I have never been so close to death before and it really hit close to home today. One minute you are alive, happy, and in love, and the next minute, you could lose everything. I'm frightened, Joe. I don't want to lose you. Sometimes I just think of the great times we had on Gamnon. How wonderful they were. I just cherish those memories every day."

"Yes, but if we continued to eat the food back home, we would forget all about those memories. You would forget about me, this beautiful relationship we share together, our baby."

Tears appeared on her cheek, and her emotions penetrated deep into my heart. "Dawn, it's going to be all right. We are together now and forever. No one is ever going to separate us."

I held her close and wiped the tears from her face reassuring her that everything was going to be just fine. I tried to give her confidence and support even though I, myself, questioned some of our actions. There was silence for a short period of time and then I regained my own confidence. We held each other tight, tears now, showing even on my own face.

"Don't worry, Dawn, when we're together, the strength we have multiplies tenfold. Together we are strong, but separated we have nothing. Hold me, feel the strength, the confidence we have together."

"Thanks, Joe. I do love you and my strength grows continually. I truly love you."

There was silence once again, for what seemed like a very long time. Then she said something that tore my heart in half.

"Joe, they took our baby!"

"I know. One day we will get him back too, but right now, we have to achieve our goal of becoming free. Gaining the liberty to have another baby one that no one will take away from us. Free to have five or six babies or even ten."

"Ten! Are you crazy! Well, maybe we could have six."

We both laughed and held each other tight. We kissed and hugged, and as the warmth of our bodies drew us together, we fell fast asleep in each other's arms.

We woke up early the next morning feeling very refreshed and ready to tackle the upcoming conquest. Derek and Pam were already up, and the aroma of some very appetizing breakfast filled the ship.

"Good morning! How did you sleep?" I asked.

"Like a rock, Joe. That is the best night's sleep I have had in ages."

"Did anyone wake up Eric? I hope he can help us get out of here."

"No, I'll go check on him," said Pam.

Pam came back from Eric's sleeping quarters excited and disturbed.

"Joe! Joe, he's gone! He's not in his bunk."

"What? Slow down."

"Well, I knocked on his door, and no one answered so I slowly opened it and found his bunk empty. In fact, it looks like he didn't even sleep there. The sheets aren't even turned over, the towels are all dry, and nothing is out of place in his quarters."

"Now what, Joe?"

"Just calm down, Pam. Dawn, could you get me a cup of coffee, please."

"Why sure, I'd be happy to," said Dawn.

"How could you be so calm, Joe. You know he could be getting his people to come and capture us. Maybe, even use us for experimentation. We really don't know him very well."

"Come on, Derek. He seemed pretty grateful to be rescued, and remember he did say that his people would help us."

"He probably felt that it was better to reach his people at night. There are too many patrols out in the daytime, and they are sure to be doubled for a couple of days. At least, until they truly believe we were destroyed in the explosion."

"That makes sense, but why didn't he want to take one of us with him?"

"Well, he probably travels faster alone and maybe he didn't want to endanger our lives. Besides, did it really look like we wanted to be bothered with anything last night?"

"Well, you are right about that, and I am sure he was anxious to see his people again."

"I think we should sit tight for a couple days and have some R&R until this mess blows over. And believe me, a couple of days are not going to matter. We have all the time in the world and we can't very well leave the ship and try to find him. We'll need this ship to reach *Station America*. I am going to assess the damage on the inside, then work on my new plans to redesign the ship for our long journey."

"Okay, and I will go up top and see how much camouflage we really have going for us, and by the way, Joe, see if you can figure out how much firepower we are going to need for the rest of this trip. Hopefully, we can get it. You know like neutron torpedoes and more timer mines."

"Don't worry, Derek, if we can't get fire power, we will just have to outsmart and outrun them. Probably more of the latter than the former."

"Yes, you can say that again. Pam, want to go topside and check things out?"

"Hey, don't forget we are not on holiday here. Be careful and don't wander out too far. Stay within sight of our position and be sure to watch out for Guardian patrols. You'll have to use the escape hatch in the aft gunners section. According to our external computer sensors, the sand is not as thick there."

Derek went back to the gunners section to access the hatch entry, with Pam following close by him. As they reached the hatch, they noticed some sand on the floor directly under the hatch.

"Well, Eric's no dummy is he, Pamela. He found the best way out too."

As Derek opened the hatch, some more sand fell down into the ship, and the bright sun filtered through some branches and rocks that appeared to be placed on the hatch door. Derek proceeded to exit the ship being very careful about exposing himself to patrols outside. Once they were out, the hatch was closed, and they put more sand, branches, and rocks all around it. As we stepped into the wooded area adjacent to the sandpit, we looked back to try and locate the ship.

"Look, Derek, you can't even see the outline of the ship. That sure was a great idea to try and dump here."

"Probably more like some great piloting and a true blessing. It's a good thing there are some rocks and branches signifying the hatch entrance or we would have a hard time finding it."

"Yeah, it sure looks like Eric doesn't miss a trick. He must be coming back, or he wouldn't have stopped to close and hide the hatch. I'm really starting to like him."

"Me too, Pamela. I hope he comes back with some help."

"Hey, Derek, what's that over there?"

"Where, Pam?"

We walked over to a small opening in the forest.

"Those are beautiful. Do you know what they are, Derek?"

"Yes, those are daffidills. There were many different varieties of flowers before the Macrocaust. Most of them were destroyed but some very pretty, very durable species survived. The tall plants are called trees. Some history lesson I received a long time ago in a musty-smelling old place that gave me some insight on the botany of the world. These trees can grow up to 180 feet high and these flowers, they really smell great... Smell them."

"Oh yes, they smell wonderful, and you know it matches their beautiful color. It's amazing how the earth has still survived after all the destruction our ancestors put it through during the Macrocaust. It looks like the radiation couldn't destroy everything. We are thankful for that."

"But you should have seen it before the Macrocaust, Pam, flowers, trees, ferns, and bushes—they were everywhere, and everything was so green. Flowers were every kind of color you could imagine. People used to give flowers as gifts. Isn't it amazing. What a change from this dry old gray and black rock. But with these flowers and some small trees that I've noticed, I think the earth is on its way back to beauty and elegance."

"I'll bet it was just beautiful."

"Yes, it sure was, or at least from what I could tell from the pictures Parrot showed us and the books I read."

"Hey, listen."

"What, Derek?"

"That's an engine. We better hide, and we need to find some good solid rock to nestle up to. If we don't, their scanner will pick up our body heat. Over there, Pam, it looks like a cave. Let's go, it will be perfect."

As we got to the entrance of the cave, the engines got louder and louder then they faded off into the distance.

"That was close, Derek, too close for me."

We had entered about fifteen meters into a cave, getting in far enough would deny the scanners the opportunity to pick up our body heat. All of a sudden, something wrapped around Pam's leg and started pulling her toward the inside of the cave.

"Derek! Derek, something's got me! *Help!*"

Derek turned and drew his weapon. By now the creature had another tentacle-like appendage around her waist strapping her left arm to her side. She fell to the ground and grabbed on to a limb secured by some rocks. But the creature was too strong and her grip was slipping away. Derek aimed and shot a laser blast just on the other side of Pamela but the appendage held fast. Two, three, more laser blasts ripped through the appendage severing it in half but the other appendage still had a firm grip around Pamela's waist. Then another appendage and another came forward.

"Help! Derek, help!"

The back of the cave was pitch black, and Derek couldn't see any other part of the creature. He aimed the laser to the back of the cave and put the computer on rapid fire and completely exhausted a power pack into the rear of the cave. A loud roar bellowed inside the cave. Another tentacle wrapped around her chest.

"Derek, I can't breathe!"

Derek reloaded his laser and once again sprayed the inside of the cave then aimed it at the tentacles, which were now close together. Another tentacle was severed, and a roar ripped through the cave. The grip loosened and the remaining tentacles pulled back into the cave. Derek ran over to Pam, picked her up, and quickly approached the entrance to the cave.

"Pam, are you all right?"

"Yes, Derek, I think so. What was that thing?"

"You got me? I never saw it, but it sure didn't like my laser."

As they sat down just in front of the cave, Derek felt something grab at his leg this time. As he turned, the creature was in full view. Pam let out a scream, and Derek drew his weapon once again. Pamela followed with hers; they both aimed and hit the creature right in the head. The creature slowly moved outside the cave's entrance, and now as it let loose fell back, hit the ground, and tumbled down the embankment right next to Derek. The creature rested in a crevice at the bottom of the embankment now as still as the rocks around it.

"Look at that thing, Pam! He is huge! He must be almost four meters high, and his tentacles reach out a good fifteen meters. I don't know how I could have missed hitting him. He must have been back behind some rocks in there. His tentacles did all the dirty work. Look at that, he has a mouth or beak or something nestled inside the group of tentacles. Hey, Pam, this looks like… Oh, what were they called? They lived in the sea before the Macrocaust… Octo… Octopus! That's what it looks like."

"Wow, I'm glad I didn't live back in those days," Pam said.

"No, they were very friendly, in fact kind of playful, and their size was one-tenth the size of this thing. Gee, the effects of the radiation were phenomenal. Look at the size of it. Hey, these were found in caves under the water. He must have been protecting his den. Pam, let's go back and see what he was protecting."

"Are you crazy? Come on, Derek! No way am I going back in there."

"No, they usually only had one animal to a den and their protection of it was… well… like their whole purpose in life."

"Usually! Usually!"

"Oh, come on, Pam. I have a lighted projectile. We'll throw it deep in the cave. If there are anymore, we'll leave. Come on."

"It's a good thing I love you. I sure wouldn't do this for just anyone!"

We drew our lasers and slowly moved to the entrance, continuing cautiously.

When we reached our previous position, I took the projectile and threw it up toward the top of the cave. The projectile was made to be shot from the laser or to be thrown, and it had very sticky adhesive on the latter side past the handle. When it touched a surface, it would stick, and the light lasted for twenty-four hours. As I threw the projectile, Pam held a small spool of wire attached to it. We could then retrieve it later to recharge it. As it stuck to the ceiling of the cave Pam felt something again grab her ankle and start to pull her towards the rocks.

"Déjà vu, Derek, here we go again!"

But he was much smaller than the creature previously and a laser round next to him scared him so much he just moved back behind some rocks.

The cave was now very bright inside, and you could see pretty far into the cave. We didn't see any more large octopus and proceeded further in. Just past the projectile, the cave opened up into a beautiful underground oasis. Light from outside penetrated through several holes on top of the huge cave. It was spectacular. Over on the far wall, it was approximately 1,800 meters from us, there was a large waterfall, starting at the top of the cave and flowing to the bottom where it formed a small river. The river in turn flowed into the middle of the cave producing a beautiful lake. The lake took up most of the cave, but around its edges were trees and flowers, ferns, and bushes that extended about forty meters from the banks of the lake. Raindrops fell from the rocks making up the top of the cave. It was a fine constant drizzle that covered the whole inside of the hidden valley. The water was crystal clear and animals could be seen stirring about the banks feeding on the vegetation. We stopped and sat far above the lake. At the end of the cave, the entrance to the oasis looked down into the valley, and there was a gradual slope leading down a hill that made it easy to descend if one so desired.

"This is so beautiful, Derek. I can see now what he was protecting."

"It really is spectacular, Pam. Look, the heat from the thin layer of rocks over the valley produces evaporation then when it hits the rocks above it produces condensation and gives you rain. It must rain nearly every day, and I'll bet the nights are quiet with just the sound of the waterfall. It must be a very deep lake with some type of runoff to the outside. That waterfall is dumping tons of water into the lake, but the lake never changes. This is unbelievable. You know, Pam, the earth looked like this before the awful Macrocaust. There were trees, flowers, plants, and animals everywhere. Clear lakes, mountains, waterfalls, and green valleys existed just like this valley. It's beautiful, just beautiful. Hey! Let's go for a swim. What do you think, Pam?"

"Sounds great, but what about the animals?"

"Oh, we're bigger than most of them and we will keep our lasers close by just in case we need some protection, but I'm pretty sure they won't bother us. Look right below us. There is an area with no trees. I guess this is how the creature came up to the cave. He created this path over time. Anyway, we can reach the lake this way and check the water for radiation. Maybe, we can drink it." We walked down the path and in a very short time we reached the lake.

Pamela checked for radiation and found it all clear. We took off our clothes and waded into the lake. The water was cool and refreshing.

"This is great, Derek. Come over here and hold me. This is like a dream come true."

"It sure is, Pam. It sure is."

They held each other close for a long time. They both felt like they were in Paradise. The aquatic life seemed to stay away from them, and they played around, jumping, diving, chasing, and just wading for what seemed like a very long time. Their situation and previous lives just seemed to just fade away. They were so happy.

"Oh, Derek! I could stay here forever."

"Me too! It's quite tempting, but we better get back. They will be worried if we don't return soon."

They got out and sat down on the grass for a short period of time.

"Pam, I don't regret anything I've done. If I die tomorrow, I'll feel like my life has been fulfilled. Being with you has made me very happy."

"Me too, Derek!" They held each other tight, feeling the warmth of their bodies penetrate deep into their souls.

"Well, let's go back. I am going to take a sample of this water back to the ship. We can test it there to see if we can drink it."

Derek bent down to fill up a small container with water.

"Derek, you know I have never been as happy as I have been these last two days. We have really..."

"What! I thought that is what we just got done talking abou—"

Just then, Pam pushed Derek into the lake clothes and all. She turned and ran to the entrance of the cave.

"Hey! Why you—"

"Last one back is a rotten potato!" she exclaimed.

"That's not how it goes! It's a rotten egg. You just wait until I catch you."

As Derek came out of the forest, he could see Pam entering the escape hatch. He ran as fast as he could, opened the hatch, and jumped down the entrance. As he hit the floor of the ship, he realized that he'd better camouflage the hatch or the reflection of the sun off the metal would stick out like a sore thumb and be seen for miles. He quickly went back up the hatch gathered some rocks, grass, branches, and mud from the forest cover the hatch and then quietly proceeded to enter the ship.

"Hey, Pam! Where are you? I can hear you laughing."

"Joe, where is she? Did she tell you what she did to me?"

"She told us all about it. Let me have that water sample, Derek. You can take care of her later."

"Oh, here it is, Joe. It was beautiful, just beautiful. You won't believe your eyes and with a full moon coming through that cave tonight. It will be like heaven on earth."

"Sounds great! Dawn and I will go out later. Now, let's see what we have here. If this water is good, we are truly being taken care of by our Creator. It will prove that He provides for our needs. That's for sure."

"Joe, have we just run out of water?"

"Yes, we have a couple emergency drinks left but not enough to sustain us for very long. We really need drinkable water."

"Oh, and watch out for giant octopus, Joe."

"What, octopus? That's strange."

"I'll tell you later. I am going to get her good this time," Derek said.

He had a small cream pie in his hand and believe me it was amazing how he kept making things appear out of his pack. He started sneaking around the ship looking for Pam.

"A cream pie, you got to be kidding me."

"How did you get, oh, forget it. I don't even want to know. I don't know how you do it, Derek, but you are sure coming up with all kinds of stuff. What else is in that sack?"

"I'll never tell."

"What are you going to do with that?"

"I am going to put it right in her face."

"You've got to be kidding and ruin that beautiful pie. Give me a piece before you get crazy."

"No, no, I am not really going to do it, but I'll sure scare her right out of her pants."

"Not a bad idea. In fact, sounds like fun!"

"You devil you. Now come on, Joe, help me."

"Keep me out of this one… Oh it could get awful messy!"

"Hey! There they are… in the galley… over by the stove. Hey, Joe, watch this!"

Derek moved very quietly, and with the girls looking in the opposite direction, not realizing his intentions, he approached the door to the galley. All of a sudden, they turned and caught a glimpse of the pie now racing toward them.

"No! No, Derek!" they yelled in unison.

At that moment, they charged Derek both of them tackling him right in the middle of the galley. The pie flew up into the air just above their heads and landed with a splatter of cream filling everywhere, mostly all over everyone's face. They sat there all laughing just amazed at what just happened.

"Are you guys crazy? I was bringing it in to serve to you!"

"Oh yeah, Derek… Right!"

"Come on, Derek. Do you expect us to believe that wild statement?" said Pam.

Just as the words came out of her mouth, Joe walked up to the three of them just lying in the middle of the floor.

"Derek, what happened? I thought you said we were going to eat that pie?" Derek looked up at me as if to say, "Well, it just didn't turn out like that."

"Oh, Derek, we are sorry."

At that point, they both apologized and started to wipe up Derek's face. Pam started kissing him apologetically and somewhat passionately.

"But, Derek, you really—"

"Joe, just leave. Can't you see the pie is gone, and there is nothing you can do about it? Are you guys really sorry?"

"Oh yes, Derek, yes!" they exclaimed.

"Is there any way I can make it up to you, Derek?" asked Pam."

"But, Derek, I thought you were going to scare—"

Derek cut me off at that point and motioned for me to go to the other compartment. As I turned around, I mumbled to myself, "Gee, he is really going to enjoy himself. I wonder if he has another one of those cream pies."

"Well, it's time I get back to work. Let's analyze that water and see if we can drink it without too many ill effects."

It took a while to run all the tests on the water, but the time was well spent because the water was nearly free of impurities. With a small amount of K:333, which we had plenty of; this water would be just as pure as our water on Altaur. The reason for such good ground water could have been explained easier by Eric, except Eric wasn't around, and I could only speculate that either the radiation had dissipated in the area or the mountains protected the area enough to allow enough radiation to eliminate contaminates but not enough to do much damage directly to the water. Derek, now all cleaned up walked through the door curiously waiting for my results.

"Well, Joe? How does it look?"

"Perfect, Derek! With just a small amount of K:333… perfectly drinkable."

"No R:3, S16, or K21?"

"No, nothing else."

"That's great!"

"Yes, I sure wish Eric was here. I'd like to know a little more about this area."

"It's getting dark, Joe, and I hope he'll be returning soon."

"Oh don't worry, Derek. He will be back and remember, we helped him, and he'll return the favor. Have a little faith."

"I hope you're right."

"I am Derek, I am. I have a good feeling about Eric. He'll come through for us. Just give him a chance."

"Dawn, how would you like to take a walk and see what the earth really looked like before the Macrocaust... Oh, and collect a couple gallons of water too."

"Sounds good to me, Joe. I'll get the water containers."

"Derek, you and Pam stay here, and when Eric comes back, send him down to the valley. I'd like to see him as soon as he arrives.

"That is, if he arrives."

"Don't worry, Derek, I have full confidence in him. He'll be back soon."

"I guess I just don't trust someone I don't know very well," replied Derek.

"Well, you better get used to trusting people you don't know because from now on we won't know anyone at all."

"Yes, I guess you're right, Joe. Have fun, I'll send him straight away. Hey, Joe, since I have to keep busy, let me see those fighter blueprints you have been working on. Maybe, I can contribute something to redeveloping the main computer system."

"Sure, they are in the drawer under the cockpit but don't make too many changes until I am sure of the design."

Dawn and I had no trouble finding the entrance to the cave even though dusk was slowly setting in. We both entered slowly. Several bird-like creatures flew by us searching for the dead carcass of the creature Derek and Pam killed. We had noticed several small rodents attacking the corpse just before we entered the cave. It sure didn't take long for the scavengers to react. We walked deeper into the cave noticing Derek's emergency light still illuminating the once dark cave.

"Oh, Joe, I am so excited. You know if our life ended right now, it wouldn't matter to me. I love you so much I feel my life is complete."

I reached for her hand and squeezed it tightly.

"We are about to witness something probably no one except Pam and Derek has ever seen before this day."

"It's wonderful Joe, and I'm the happiest woman in this universe. I am here in love with someone I'll spend the rest of my life with experiencing a free and beautiful world. A person could not ask for anything more."

"You are right about that, Dawn, but we aren't completely free yet. Freedom is just around the corner, though. I can feel it."

As we reached the entrance of the concealed valley, we stood in awe and amazement. The valley was even more beautiful than Derek described it to be.

"Oh, Dawn, Derek didn't give this world justice. It's magnificent."

As dusk settled, the orange glow from the sun filtered through the holes in the rocks. The colors changed from orange to red. Then as the sun left our view, the moon shone brightly as it peered through the holes in the cave. The water down below glistened from the moonlight streaming through the holes in the ceiling and the waterfall hitting the lake sparkled like a star filled night.

"You know, Dawn, you may be right. We may have just found freedom. I could live right here for the rest of my life. You know, maybe, this can be an option. If the *Station America* is unreachable, unattainable... This just may work or, maybe, when we reach America we can convince them to let us start a colony. With their support it wouldn't take long to become self sufficient. We can start a whole new family, yes, and maybe try to find the rest of our existing family. Dawn, I see a bright future here. But one step at a time, right?"

"Yes, one step at a time. First, contact America, and then maybe we start our own little America.

"Hey, look, Dawn, there goes a raccoon and look over there, in the clearing by the lake, four elk."

"Elk, Joe, how do you know what these animals are called. We were never allowed to study about life before the Great Macrocaust."

"A library, that's where you can learn about anything in the universe."

"Library, you had access to a library? What is a library, and how can you learn anything in the universe from a library?"

"Yes, Dawn, and it's hard to believe what came about from it all. Suppressed societies, brainwashed into thinking their way is the perfect way. It is so sad. I am so happy that we made a decision to break away and strive to be free. I think I am finally beginning to understand what the phrase means."

"Yes, me too, Joe."

"Strive to be free. Freedom sure feels good."

We sat there for a long time and just held each other gazing into the moonlit lake. We felt such a relaxing peace. The water seemed to stand still. The trees made no movement and the air was cool and serene. The animals were gone now, and it was the most relaxing moment I had ever experienced.

I felt totally free, my own person, reminiscing about my old life. We turned and looked at each other. For a moment, I felt a peace that surpassed any other feeling I had ever had. It was like a heavenly, comforting type of feeling. Not a word was said, just smiles, a hug, a deep feeling of love, togetherness, and fulfillment... freedom. I raised my hand, and she put her cheek firmly against it. I brushed her smooth, silky blonde hair from across her face, and we gently kissed each other, feeling a presence of warmth, love, and passion.

"Dawn, I am deeply in love with you, and I am confident in the decision we made to be together. If our lives ended at this moment, we would be together forever."

"Joe, my love for you grows deeper and deeper every hour we spend together. I don't regret anything we have done. My love for you is sincere and everlasting. We are blessed to be able to achieve the freedom and love we set as our goal. Thank you for all you have given me. My heart will be yours forever."

We embraced each other, and together we felt a strong bond growing between us. It truly was the most wonderful moment of our lives.

CHAPTER 9

The President

The night was very still, and as the moon lit up the darkness, shadows were cast everywhere. The night was filled with brilliant stars, glistening with an array of sparkling city lights. Predators could be seen hurrying along hoping to fill their bellies with some form of nourishing substance. The sandy ground, where the fighter lay, was starting to settle and an outline of the ship was becoming very evident. Derek walked around the ship, trying to shovel sand around the contour. As we approached, Derek turned and drew his weapon.

"Derek, wait! It's Joe! What's up? You are really jumpy."

"Can you see what is happening? I don't know when it started protruding from the sand, but a Guardian patrol ship flew overhead about thirty minutes ago. I thought you might be a landing party."

"It's really starting to show, isn't it?"

"Yes, sir, and if Eric doesn't come back, soon, with some help you better start formulating a plan. You realize by sunrise tomorrow, we are going to be sitting out like an oak tree in a prairie field."

"A what?"

"Oh nothing, just something I put together from some literature I read down in the basement."

"I know what a basement is," Dawn added.

"You could give me a hand, Joe. There are some tools over there."

"I am going to see what Pamela's doing. Be careful up here. You never know what's going to sneak up on you, right, Derek?"

"Right, Dawn, right."

"Joe, if Eric doesn't come back this evening or by morning, we'll have to abandon the ship."

"Yes, I know. We'll have to blow it up. I hope they won't come looking for us. Hey, Joe, where are we going to go."

"If who doesn't show up?"

"Hey! What the—Joe!"

Eric somehow got close enough to Derek to scare the life out of him. I was behind Derek trying to shovel sand around the contour of the ship and we never heard him approach. But it wasn't just Eric. He had fifteen other men with him, and we didn't hear a thing. I looked up at Derek when I heard him shout, somewhat startled myself, but I regained my composure rather quickly.

"Eric, how you doing?"

"Fine, Joe, fine."

"How did you do that… How did fifteen of you do it without a sound? That's unbelievable, really incredible," exclaimed Derek.

"Eric, good to see you! I knew you would come back."

"Joe, don't you realize what he just did, isn't it? Amazing how?"

"Well, Derek, we've been sneaking up on people for years now, I mean years. Just look above you, real close, Derek."

"Well, I see sky and stars and the moon is pretty low in the sky over there."

"No, Derek, directly above you, are there stars?"

"Why no. There is a void directly above us. In fact, a rather large void, now that you mention it."

"Henry, this is Eric. Could you display a little light for a very brief moment."

"Yes, sir, straight away. It's all clear tonight. Nothing on the radar."

All of a sudden, hundreds of lights flashed directly above us outlining a aircraft ten times larger than our own ship.

"What! Joe, look at that! It's a ship, but it doesn't make any noise. Any noise at all! Isn't that amazing?"

"Oh, just one of our old inventions."

"Well, Derek, Dawn told us to be careful that we never know what will sneak up on us."

"Yeah, Joe, she was right."

We all laughed for a bit, and Eric explained that he'd been looking in the area just a short time before the heat sensors picked up our bodies. It was an extremely short time before Eric had recovered our ship and secured it to the transport. Before long, we were in the entertainment room, meeting Eric's people and learning more about the Carthusians, comparing technology and just having a great time. Eric told us of several countries that survived the Great Macrocaust and how they all got together and formed several nations, how the Star Cities tried to defeat each nation then secretly steal their superior technology, how many of their people died and were disfigured during the war and that the radiation caused permanent genetic defects; and how the Carthusian society survived with the help from the *Station America*.

He explained how their society decided not to build fighter ships to send against Altaur, but to build a defense system impregnable to all forces. Their national policy prohibited aggression or conquest. He explained that they had one squadron of fighter ships and a workable prototype of a new fighter graphically displayed in their defense system. He also noted that if they were needed, four squadrons could be built within forty-eight hours by different sectors of the Carthusian nation. Pilots were trained on high-tech simulators and all of them rotated through the *Station America*'s Air Force.

He explained how their days are really nights and that 99 percent of their activity occurs during the dark hours of the night. He explained to us that their purpose was to rebuild the earth in their own way, mostly underground like the cave that Derek and Pam found earlier. Carthusians built it!

"You know, Eric, if these silent ships were equipped with weaponry, you could easily destroy the Star Cities with a carefully executed plan."

"Oh, Joe, we could have destroyed them many years ago, but we are not an aggressive race. We feel rebuilding is more important than destruction and devastation."

"And we thought we were the ultimate power, how ironic is that?" replied Joe. "And minimal fighter aircraft! Derek, I can't believe that a defense system could exist without them. That's not our rationale for defense."

"Joe, our society does not believe in aggression and conquest. Collectively we have decided against those principles, remember?"

"It's amazing. Joe, I just can't believe that we were so naive," Derek remarked. "Well, it's just that you were not informed of the situation, not that you were naive."

"That sounds a lot better, doesn't it?"

"Eric, I am sorry about all of the questions, but I have to know one thing."

"What's that?"

"Well, who invented the device for the silent ships? He must be a real genius. Is he still alive? Can we meet him?"

Eric just smiled as he got up from the table and moved toward the spirit bar. "Derek... that little... Derek... Eric's the genius. He designed that ship."

"What are you talking about, Joe?" Derek asked.

"Don't you see, he invented the silent transport, that little rascal. He is full of surprises! Incredible!"

"I'm sure glad we brought him along. That's a plus for us that we didn't count on."

We all got another spirit, and Eric offered to take us up to the bridge.

"I thought you might be interested in seeing how we operate from the helm. It is somewhat different than your ship."

Eric, Derek, and I entered the elevator. The women were escorted to the ladies entertainment room and were shown where to get cleaned up. We told them we would be back soon. It took about twelve seconds to reach the bridge, and as soon as the door opened, the room just enthralled us. The technology was astonishing and somewhat overwhelmed me—something that I, Joe Capuzzi, thought would never happen. The bridge was oval-shaped with a large screen running completely around the room. You could see a 360-degree panoramic view of the outside.

The ceiling was also a screen, that viewed either directly above or below the ship. Computers were set up one next to the other completely surrounding the screen all around the oval wall. In the center of the room was a large oval table that showed a three-dimensional holograph of the surrounding atmosphere and topography relayed to it by the ship's sensors. In the center of the holograph was the ship we were in. All this was produced with a series of laser lights and input from the surrounding computers. It showed enemy ships—strengths, weaknesses, and formations; it also projected a logical pathway that each intruder would take. Several voice modulators sent out repeated coordinates, arrival times, speeds, and elevations above the surface of the earth. Guardian patrols were strictly monitored, and radar positions plotted continuously. Movement on the surface of the earth was analyzed, and all information was stored in the main computer's memory banks. There were about twenty-five people diligently working at their job hardly noticing the invited guests.

"Where are we going, Eric?" I asked.

"Well, if you will look at the screen behind you, you'll see our destination."

"Right there," Derek pointed.

"All I see is water and more water."

"Good camouflage, isn't it?" Eric said.

"Sure, for a fish," Derek added.

We all laughed, and shortly afterwards, Eric explained how the entrance to their home lies deep within the vast ocean we were viewing.

"See, Derek, we can enter anywhere in the water and reach our destination from any point. That way, if we were followed, they can't really pinpoint the real coordinates of our base since the ocean provides great camoflage."

"That's brilliant," Joe said.

"So if you were being followed or even chased, you could enter the water at fifty or even a hundred kilometers away and even if they tracked you for a while, with the depth of this ocean, there is no way they could follow you home."

"Yes, you're right, but there is a way we can be tracked. We have developed a way, but I think it will be a long time before the Star Cities attempt research in that field. It has taken us many years to refine the technology."

"Did you work on that invention too? Are you sure you aren't someone real important in your society. I keep getting this feeling that you are a lot more important than you say you are! In fact, I'll bet you are real important, Eric."

"Well, I didn't want Balem to really know who they caught, so I've played dumb for quite some time. I'll tell you this, Joe. My title is president, and I was elected to run things on earth for a while. The citizens were mighty pleased to see me. In fact, you escaped renegades are now being praised as famous heroes."

"I thought you were a scientist and were out collecting woods."

"Well, Derek, I am and a ship commander. The day I was captured I was out looking for that highly radiated wood called U7171428 or U-717. It's wood all right, but a wood that provides our society with needed energy. See, U-717 is the only kind of material we can use to fuel our generators. It lasts a very long time, but it is very hard to find. In fact, now there are only seven scientists who know where to look for the material."

"You'd think as highly sophisticated as your society is that they could have found a substitute. Oh, you said something about fertilizer too."

Funny you should say that because I just found out that shortly after I was captured an energy substitute was being developed that was ten times more efficient. "At the time, I was captured there were only two scientists who knew how to find the wood in large quantities that is, my father and I. We had just started a training program, but the scientists were not skilled enough to perform their duties.

So after the seven scientists were able to escavate the material there were plenty of qualified people to take care of the new mineral excavation. I would never have to worry about it ever again. We all have learned to make sure qualified professionals represent each field and that training new personel is important to governing a society. But, you know, I have learned two important lessons from my experience. One is not to go collecting wood, and the other is not to go out in the daylight unprepared."

We both laughed for a second, and then, Eric took command of the ship by moving toward the center of the bridge and studying the three-dimensional tactical board.

"We sure could have used one of those boards on the fighter. With one person studying the board our defense plan would have been flawless."

"It sure would make things easier. Well, Derek I just want to tell you that taking Eric was the best idea you have ever had. How the Creator has really blessed us on this trip is amazing! It's like He had it all planned out."

"Eric would have just rotted away in that cell. It's a good thing they never really knew who you were, or they would have definitely taken advantage of your knowledge and position."

"Yes, like we are going to do, Derek?"

"Well, it's different with us because he has the right to refuse to help us. Anyway, this freedom he believes in is the basis of their society. He is obligated by his belief, but I think he will help us because he chooses to and not because he has too."

"Yes, but does he have really anything to gain for all his trouble?"

He already gained the most important reward and that was his freedom which if I might add was some of our doing."

"You are right about that."

I looked up at the depth guage, and it read "125 feet" and I didn't even realize that we were submerged. Soon, the water got very dark, and the computer screens on the bridge gave us a clear picture of an extremely dark underwater course. The lights on the bridge consisted of only the computer lit screens and the oval laser map. We started to move laterally, and it seemed like quite a distance although our speed was extremely hard to judge.

Just ahead showing up on the laser map, and the forward screen projection were a series of lights. They seemed to appear out of the deep black ocean, quite abruptly. We could only surmise that communication between the bridge and the landing bay initiated the landmarks. As we drew nearer, the lights illuminated an extremely large entrance, large enough to put seven of these transports out to sea in a hurry. Just inside of the lighted entrance we started to surface. As we entered the bay area, the ship broke water, and the rush of water over the ship reminded me of that beautiful waterfall we found near our incapacitated ship. The ship came to a halt and people started leaving the bridge very rapidly.

"Hey, Joe, come down here for a minute," Eric shouted.

As we walked toward the laser map to once again greet Eric, all the screens lit up. It was the most spectacular sight we'd ever seen. The lights beneath the ship were brightly shining, and the water was crystal clear, you could see several hundred feet. There were hundreds of different kinds of fish, in many different shapes, colors, and sizes, and they were all swimming in every direction.

"Eric, this is beautiful. Where did all these creatures come from, and why didn't they perish with everything else on earth," asked Derek.

"Come from? They've always been here. The radiation never penetrated the water. All these species survived and are doing quite well, and believe me, this is just a small portion."

"That's spectacular and so beautiful," Eric.

"I figured you would enjoy it. For the life of me, I can't understand why your society doesn't capitalize on the treasures found in the sea. Our research has brought us an abundant amount of food, water, nutrition, salt, chemicals, and much more. This entryway and part of our living facilities are fabricated from technology we learned from the sea. And as you can see, it's quite impregnable. What do you think, Joe?"

"Well, I guess they feel that they can survive without the sea, stupid pride, lack of ocean biologists! By the way, Eric, where did we enter the sea?"

"We flew out into the ocean, circled back, and entered about seventy-five miles from land. You couldn't see the approach because of the dark night. There was no moon so with the atmosphere being quite dark when we submerged, it was impossible to see. As part of our defense plan, we built this base initially for our escape route, but it turned out to be a great entrance, and the escape route is now by land. Oh, and by the way, they are called marine biologists."

"Well, whatever they are called. I just cannot understand why we have abandoned the sea. It sure seems odd for such a perfect society... yes, such a perfect society."

"You know we went directly to the sea after the great Macrocaust. That's how we survived— the sea providing for our food and caves along the coast a safe place to live. Well, caves fabricated by men. We drilled through rock and shale to great depths and established small societies under the surface of the Earth. We explored the great sea from beneath using it as our camouflage for protection. Soon, we found underwater caves, and we built underwater cities taking sea water and producing air and pure drinking water. Before long, cities arose, and our technology surpassed any other post-Macrocaust society, even yours, Joe."

"And yes, all of this evolved through the help and assistance, not only in technology but manpower as well, from the *Station America*."

"You sure have opened my eyes, Eric."

"Me too," said Derek.

"I think we are all amazed," said Joe.

"Eric, I just have one question. Do you really eat those animals? They look pretty weird to me, and what are those other things moving along the bottom?"

"Those other things as you call them are called crustaceans, and they are very tasty," Eric said.

"I'll have to try it before I will believe that, Eric."

"You will, Derek. You will."

"Oh, man, I just walked into that one."

"No, Derek, you jumped in with both feet," Joe said.

"Let's go find my friends and see what's on the agenda for tomorrow."

We departed the ship in amazement, and that feeling continued as we walked through the large caves. From the ceiling of this main loading dock hung hundreds of pointed spikes. Eric told us that they were formed from melted rock. When the entrance was cleared, some of the rock overhead had to be melted to obtain a large enough area to house the transport ships. The ceiling must have been several hundred meters high and the pointed spikes hung down between twenty-five and forty meters from the ceiling. As the dock was being built, the cool air rising from the ocean water, cooled the melting rock forming the spikes. They reached all across the ceiling, the larger spikes being in the center where it took the most heat. As the spikes branched out to the sides, they got significantly smaller. Their color ranged from cerise to copper then to a light sorrel. Another phenomenon of sea water and super heated rock was that depending on the heat needed to make the entrance many brilliant colors lined the floors. It sure was impressive. We walked through the landing bay and entered a small tunnel behind the storage compartments.

"Eric, your society is so new to us. Everything about it is astonishing to me, but I have a feeling that you know everything about our society."

"You're right, Joe. We monitor your society's actions very closely."

"They can't know everything, Joe. There's got to be something they don't know," exclaimed Derek.

"What about the festival, Eric?" Derek asked.

"Which one, Derek, you have several well-known celebrations?"

"The big one with the special event," he responded.

"Oh yes, the race, the race. Derek, is that what you are alluding to? The race Joe won seven times? I'm aware of that celebration, and he hasn't lost since he flew in his first race. There were sixteen deaths involved in those races. Joe is a real celebrity on Altaur."

"How could you know that, Eric? Even I don't remember how many deaths occurred in those races. Do you know, Joe?"

"He's right, Derek, sixteen, but our society only recognizes fourteen. Only a handful of pilots know of the other two deaths."

"Mac Sandler and Skippy Henderson, they were listed as recovering. Two of your young pilots were told to assume their identities in order to ensure the annual continuance of the race. Most pilots are not publicly known at least by photograph. Their reputation sort of precedes them. They were the best until Joe came along. Both were lost in the same race, and the publicity would have ruined the tradition. The games they play with their citizens' lives. So they altered the replay video showing both pilots ejecting before impact. It was done quite well, I may add. But in reality, they hit buildings, and both went down with their ship. Joe won the race and the Silver Badge of Excellence, right, Joe?"

"That's right, Eric. I saw them hit, and there was no time for ejection. Several of the contestants were briefed after the race and sworn to silence. You must have some great intelligence."

"We do. We have the best. I knew about you before you escaped, but I wasn't sure it was really you. I did an intelligence report on all of you when I went back to my base last night and the computer identified the whole lot of you. Through my brain scan, our computers can pick up vivid pictures from my brain and ID them with the correct names which lead to all kinds of information. So by visually seeing you and recording it unconsiciously, we obtained complete profiles of your past."

"Also, we have been getting many disturbing reports lately. That is in the last year or so. Obviously, I didn't know, but our scanners showed a false alarm, supposedly a fire in the Hall of Creation, a real disturbance. A pilot beating a computer simulator that was unbeatable, a small quantity of stolen food and a stolen fighter, not to mention the ruckus you made escaping, or should I say, leaving your society."

"You mean you have been monitoring our whole journey?"

"Well, not me but our computers and defense staff, and let me say you have been pretty impressive."

"That's unbelievable, Eric. Your society is extremely efficient."

"Yes, we are, but for the longest time actually up until now, we had no idea who was making all that trouble up there."

"Eric, I need you to find out one thing for me."

"Certainly, Joe. What's bothering you?"

"I had a dear old friend who helped us escape mostly by looking the other way and I had to turbo…"

"He's fine, Joe. He was safe in his guard house when you hit the turbo blasters, and they believed his story. They also finally realized who was causing all the commotion, and let me say they were not pleased. In fact, your identity has already been replaced, and there were quite a few who were willing to assume your identity."

"We sure pulled it over on them, didn't we, Joe?"

"Well, Derek, we're not there yet, and the most difficult part of our mission has yet to come."

"He's right, Derek. The next part of your plan, whatever it is, will have to be done on your own. We can't support your escape, at least physically, and don't expect any assistance from *Station America*."

"The *Station America* has a very old, extremely complicated treaty between your societies. They agree to respect each other's airspace, which sometimes is disregarded, amusingly by *Station America*'s pilots, who are then reprimanded for a short time for their escapades. Also, they cannot interfere with runaways."

"We're not going to give up, Eric, until we have achieved our goal or we die trying. We've all agreed it's success or death."

"Yes, I realized that very soon after our acquaintance. You're a very determined group of people. Enough talk for now. Follow me and we will nourish our bodies so our minds can think clearly."

We met the women after landing, and as we walked toward Eric's home, many tunnels branched out laterally, and it was somewhat difficult to get our bearings. It turned into a complicated maze, and without Eric's direction, we would have been lost.

There were many people hurrying about opening doors, shuffling around the tunnel and most of them, probably 98 percent, had some form of visible radiation scars, mostly about the head and the neck moving down the arm. There were several with hand malformations."

"Eric, does everyone have radiation scarring?"

"Not all. Probably 97 percent have some noticeable radiation scarring. We are thankful the genes and chromosomes that make up our internal organs were strong enough to survive, but many outward physical feature genes and chromosomes had severe damage. We are grateful it has not scarred our internal organs to the point of shortening our lifespan. We are perfectly normal except for our outward physical appearance."

"Actually, to be like you would be abnormal or as they used to say 'funny looking' to us. It seems kind of unusual to be physically perfect, that is, something like you. The four of you would be physically perfect to us. We all have grown accustomed to our appearance. It's strange how under different circumstances normal is abnormal and vice versa."

As we entered a long hallway, Eric motioned to us to proceed; a sweet odor filled our sense of smell. The hallway was long and very poorly lit. On each side of the entrance were stone statues of some sort of animal. I think they were lions, but I'm not really sure. The hallway demonstrated the same material as the others, square metallic panels that lined the ceiling and walls. Instead of the long fluorescent lights filling the center panels of the ceiling, small lamp posts were placed every fifteen feet or so.

The lamps were filled with a unique gas that once a flame was put to it glowed with all kinds of soft colors. The hallway was very soothing and peaceful. As we walked down the long hallway, Eric told us that this was the entrance to his home and that the pleasant smells coming from ahead would be explained when we passed through the upcoming door. We reached the door, and Eric started to give us a detailed description of the unique door that lay ahead.

"This door was made from a metal, very difficult to obtain, that before the the Macrocaust was very precious and valuable. It was called gold. This door was solid gold and in its time would have been worth millions of the once well-known monetary currency. Now, because of it's weight it served no purpose. If it weren't for its brilliant shine and unique color, it truly would have no value at all. In fact, because of its weight we nearly decided not to use it.

"But it was artistically foraged, and on its surface was a picture book of history describing the world as it exists today. The Star Cities, all of earth's societies and *Station America* were the drawings presented to us. After the etchings, there was about a 1,500-word description and explanation of the Great War and its consequences to mankind."

As we read the inscription, an empty feeling overtook me. The feeling was also evident from my dearest friend and comrade. Even Eric showed signs of grief and sadness.

"Every time I read the inscription, I get the same empty feeling," Eric said. "It doesn't matter how many times I read it, it just tears me up inside. It makes me wonder what this world would have been like without all this hatred, this Macrocaust, these mutations. What would I have looked like, what kind of work would I be doing, where would I have lived, what hobbies would I have enjoyed. Who would have been my friends, my neighbors... You, Derek? Joe? Would I have any enemies? These questions will never be answered.

"You would think after so many years, I would just walk on by but I don't. I read the words every time I pass through those doors. It hurts... It really hurts. The mirrors we look into are a constant reminder of what the human race did to us. The radiation bums, the chromosomal damage. Did you know our race used to be your size?

"There was a number of 'little people' on earth before all this too, but they couldn't survive. Throughout time they disappeared. Now, we are taller than the average human with large hands and feet. In fact, our whole society tends to be rather large and most of our citizens are very tall."

Just as Eric finished, the massive doors in front of us started to open. They were slow and meticulous as they opened but as the crack began to expand between the two doors a bright light shone through, lighting up the whole length of the hallway. As we walked through the doors, it opened up into a beautiful tropical garden. Flowers, trees, shrubs, and a brilliant array of colors that produced the most beautiful picture we had ever seen. There were waterfalls and small ponds with small animals hurrying about their business.

"Eric, this is so beautiful." Pamela sighed.

"I just can't believe what I am seeing," said Dawn as she just stood there staring at all the beautiful flowers.

"And, Eric, the smells are wonderful, so fresh and sweet," Pamela exclaimed excitedly.

Eric just smiled, looking so proud and honored to show us his garden. "But you know, Joe, we don't have it so bad, and once I'm in the garden, I completely forget what was written on that door."

"You're amazing, Eric. You are just amazing," replied Joe.

"Here, ladies," Eric stated as he took both their arms and guided them through the garden.

"These are roses and those are marigolds, petunias are over here, and these here, well, let's just call them buttercups."

"Buttercups, that's a funny name," Pam said as she looked around the garden in complete amazement of all the color and diversity of the flowers.

"Yes, ma'am, it sure is a funny name."

We walked around the garden for a good while, our hunger leaving us for a brief moment. Eric decided to go check on a time for dinner and once he excited the door at the end of the garden, another man and woman dressed in a brightly colored uniform entered the room. They remained there the whole time as we walked around the conservatory. As we approached the door, they came up to us saying it would be their honor to show us to our rooms.

In the rooms, Dawn and I found a clean change of clothes, which even to this day, I never figured out how they knew our size. I guess it must have been that computer scan they did on Eric's brain. They also provided us with showers, steam rooms, massage tables, snacks, and refreshments. It wasn't long before we were escorted to the massive dining room, which was elaborately decorated with the same metal that made up the historical door at the entrance. There was a long table, and many people were hurrying around it setting plates, arranging flowers, and placing large platters of food everywhere. We were placed at our seats, and Eric sat at the head of the table in somewhat of a higher backed chair displaying his respectable position in his society. After we were served and consumed our food, the conversation turned to relationships.

"Do you know its a normal human emotion to want a person of the opposite sex to be with you? I too am in love with a very special lady who means the world to me. She is loving and caring and really looks after me. You will meet my wife later this evening. She is a very busy lady, and since I've been gone, she has been running the show down here, but as soon as I'm filled in and get rested for a couple days. It's my job again. I have a lot of catching up to do, of course, with her guidance."

Our meal was very elaborate, and it ended with a tasty dessert and fresh coffee. Derek, Eric, and I moved to another room in their house while the girls left for their quarters to relax. As we entered the room, Eric called his study. He offered us a beverage which Derek and I were glad to accept. The study was a fairly large room and bookshelves filled with books ran the length of the room on both sides. There was a ladder that rolled down the breadth of the shelves, which was used for the books on the upper level. A large desk was placed in the back of the room, and it had papers, letters, documents, and maps scattered all about its surface. There was a large window behind his desk. In fact, the whole wall was a clear window, and it overlooked Eric's beautifully designed garden down below. We all sat down, Derek and I on a large couch, and Eric on a chair next to a reading lamp.

"What's the ball next to you, Eric?"

"What, this over here? It's a globe, and it demonstrates the Earth before the great Macrocaust. These books at the base is a summary of the earth's history, its populations, achievements, and geography. In fact, everything you could possibly want to know would be in those volumes."

"The earth was a pretty big place, wasn't it, Eric?"

"It sure was, and the population, well, there were over five hundred million people just in our country called the United States. The country of China had over seven billion."

"That's hard to fathom. Just about all those people perished. Right, Eric?"

"Well, it's hard to say because communication has been practically nonexistent, but from what these societies have written down on records right after the Great War, roughly seventy societies are still in existence. The last census totaled around seven million people, but that probably has increased by now."

"Nearly total destruction. What a pity. You wonder how 'mankind' with such intelligence could be so asinine," said Derek.

"Eric, how did you obtain such an accurate census if the communication was so bad?" I asked.

"The *Station America*, Joe. The Starship's records contain much more accurate information. We don't bother accumulating data about the other societies on earth because at this point in our development it really doesn't concern us. But we do know that the information is available, and we can communicate with our sister society *Station America* at any time."

"Eric, I don't mean to be insulting, but do the people *Station America* have any deformaties or scarring associated with the radiation fallout?"

"Ha ha ha. Are you wondering if the *Station America* people are abnormal like us, Derek?"

"Well, not abnormal. Don't forget we are abnormal down here. I didn't want to upset you."

"Ha ha ha. No, they are normal like you, Derek. You'll have nothing to worry about."

With that comment, Derek turned as red as the brilliantly colored rose Eric showed us in his garden.

"Now, I have a surprise for both of you. This is something I am very proud of and not many have seen it… probably because I just finished it before I got captured, and only my voice recognition could open the electronic lock on the door. I will tell you one thing though. Many people will be able to obtain a voice to log in now, and I'll never be so selfish again. It really bothered me when I was in prison to think that I might never be able to return, and all my work would be locked up in this room forever."

Eric was really appreciative to be back home and quietly walked over to a large metal door, and once the lock had clicked, the two immense doors opened. As the door opened, we could see a whole universe in front of us. Suspended from the dome-blackened roof, brilliantly displaying planets and star configurations, were the two Star Cities, Gamnon and the *Station America*. They were all meticulously detailed and scaled down to match the size of the room. They all moved extraordinarily slow, and the constellations all changed with the movement. Small ships were electronically launched from each suspended entity. A computer would design a battle or chase scene, which would be relayed to each ship. The detail and accuracy of the launches, and the dynamic battles were amazing. Then, at the command from a very sophisticated computer, there was a reenactment of our very own escape.

"Eric, how did you get all the information needed to reenact our escape?" asked Derek.

"Well, most of it came from our tracking centers, but I did manage to get some information from your ships computer. I put it together when you were relaxing in the garden and preparing for dinner. That's not all. Sit down in the center of the room, and after the reenactment of your escape, the computer will at your own command give you any information you desire about our world, the world before us, and your world. The dome will be your panoramic view, and the computer will visualize any information you desire."

"Joe, this is better than Parrot, Tarcon, and Tera."

"I'll say, and it's readily available. We'll meet here every night, as often as we can, at the end of our day and learn about our new life. Eric, would you be able to join us and along with the computer provide your insight and wisdom?"

"I will be honored to assist you, anyway I can."

"Great, Eric! Just great!"

We walked out of the room and back to the study to refill our glasses. "It's so nice to relax and not feel the stress of being shot at all the time, right, Derek."

"You can say that again. This is the safest I've felt in several weeks."

"Eric, I do have one more question. I hope you're not tired of me asking all these questions, are you?"

"No, no, Joe. I understand your curiosity. Actually, I expected alot more questions than you have asked."

"Well, we'll catch up. Once we enter your Dome of Knowledge."

"My what? Dome of Knowledge… I like that. That's what I'll name it. Your question, Joe?"

"Oh yes, Eric, how did you achieve, or, acquire all of this? The palace-like accommodations, the position among your people… Everyone on our Star City has the same facilities, and I can bet that everyone's residence here is not like yours."

"You're right. The accommodations for most of the people are very nice, but they are very conservative. It's mostly owner preference. You can have a very nice residence or just a plain and simple one, depending on your money and other things as well. Me, I was elected to this position."

"Elected?" Derek asked. "What does that mean?"

"I think it means someone put him there," remarked Joe.

"Well, let's just say I was chosen by the people, and it all came about from people choosing a candidate, then voting. There were two others who ran for this position. Most of the people, in fact, we needed 57 percent to win, voted for me. We have a ballot booth, and people privately cast their ballot. It's called the democratic way, based on prewar doctrines in the country that used to be called the United States of America."

"So how long does the position last?"

"Ten years. That is as long as I pass a mental and physical test. You can run for two consecutive terms, but traditionally, they have only stayed for one. You have to be thirty-five years old to run for election. After my term is up, we move to another home, which is usually close to this home here, for advisory reasons. Those accommodations are very nice but not as elaborate as these quarters. The next president, after voted into office, will move here. Did you know before the Macrocaust they voted every four years? Seems like a really short term. Campaigning takes up most of your time during election year."

"Campaigning?"

"Oh yes, it's persuading people that you are the right person to govern them. It's very important especially these days, as incorrect decisions could expose our whole operation. It could be disastrous. Take you, for example, in my cell, I had to decide whether going with you would enhance my return, and decide in a very short period of time. I'll have you know I was willing to die if my decision was wrong, in fact, I would have never returned if my brain scan turned up a negative report on you. You surely would not have liked that decision. See, your rescue might have been a plan for you to build my faith in you, then as I lead you to my people, who knows… invasion… war… maybe total destruction!"

"Wow, when did you decide that we were really trying to escape?"

"When they shot us down. It really appeared to me that they tried to destroy you, but the brain scan verified your identity which in turn confirmed your intentions."

"They sure did try to kill us!" Derek said.

"I sure got off track. What were we discussing? Oh yes, leadership… elections."

"Once they pick a president, the people have a full year to decide if they like his leadership or not before he can continue his work as Commander. Something like a probationary period. If they like his work, he stays. If not, he's out the door. Actually, a Committee decides whether you stay or not. It's called a House of Representatives. See the people elect representatives to make their decisions for them. They represent the majority from their district so ultimately they are making a vote based on the decision from that community. Its really not difficult to learn, and you will learn more in the Dome of Knowledge. Yes, I like that name. I really like it."

"How long have you held this position Eric?"

"Trying to guess my age, huh, Derek?"

"No, no, Eric. I didn't mean any disrespect."

"Oh, lighten up, Derek, I was just joking with you."

"Lighten up?"

"Relax, Derek. I think it means relax," Joe said.

"Let me see, the House of Representative reviews my position every four years, and I have had one review plus three years. I would say seven years and that is including the time I was in captivity. My wife assumed the position in my absence, but I was reinstated as soon as I made contact with my people so, yes, seven years. The next election will take place in three years, or when I die or become incompetent in the eyes of the House of Representatives. The vote has to be an 85 percent in favor of resigning my position as president. They were pleased to see my return. Also my wife and child were very pleased to see me. My wife will show her gratitude and delight with a very special banquet celebration tomorrow evening."

"Sounds great, Eric."

"Sounds great to me too," replied Derek.

He pushed a button on top of his desk, and two men came to the study. "These gentlemen will show you back to your quarters so you can rest for our event. They will then escort you and the women to the dining area when it is time for the celebration."

"I am sure glad you provide us with these house guides, Eric. I could get lost around here pretty easy," Derek said.

"And you wanted to be my navigator, no way. You stick to computers."

We all laughed quietly as we proceeded to walk to our quarters.

Later the next day, the women appeared for us to escort them to dinner.

"Wow, Dawn, you look great!"

"Thank you, Joe. It felt so good to take a nice hot bath… although the tub was a little long."

"Ha ha, that is to be expected. Well, are you considerably impressed with their society? I hope we have enough time to see everything, but if we don't, the Dome of Knowedge will help us tremendously."

"The what? The Dome of Knowledge?" she inquired.

"Yes, Eric created it. I will tell you about it later, but it's suffice to know that we can acquire any information we desire in Eric's study. In the time we will have here, I think we will be able to get a good understanding about our society, Eric's people and the culture of the *Station America*. Tomorrow, Derek and I are going to start on the ship. It really needs a lot of work, and I have plans for a couple of modifications. Oh, before I forget, remind me to tell Pam that I'd like her to work on some scanners for me. I am pretty sure that she can adapt them to our needs."

"Did you meet Eric's wife, Catherine, yet, Joe?" asked Dawn.

"No, not yet, but from what Eric says this dinner she is organizing is really something special."

"The women who escorted us to our quarters speak very highly of her. She's very educated and has done most of her studying in the field of human relationships, raising offspring and is a specialist in women with families and careers. She has written seven books, and all of them are well respected in their society. I have a feeling we will be learning a lot from her."

"Yes, I think we will be learning a lot from everyone here. We really have so much more to learn. I am definitely going to enjoy our little stay here."

Soon, we were on our way, and before we knew it, we were being seated for dinner. The table was rectangular in shape and extremely well decorated. It did seem kind of odd though because we were all seated on one side of the table with Eric and his wife in the middle. We sat for a while, enjoying a light dry spirit then without any announcement, the wall directly in front of us started separating and, shortly, we were in a large ballroom where hundreds of people had gathered. They were eating, drinking, and dancing. Special servers were everywhere dressed in black long-tailed suits, white shirts, and shiny black shoes. An orchestra was playing in the background and the ballroom was lit up with twelve brilliant chandeliers placed all around the room. Tables surrounded the dance floor, and it appeared that everyone was having a great time. As the walls stopped, our table slowly moved to the front of the dance floor, and everyone in the room grew silent. Then, as Eric stood up, the applause started and continued for a long period of time.

"Dear people of the Carthusian nation. It has been of great fulfillment in my life to be reunited with my people. At one time, I had given up hope of ever being once again the leader of this great nation. Then my friends seated here at this table on their flight to freedom comforted my soul and replenished my hope to be reunited with my family and friends. I owe them my life, and I am happy to honor them as our guests here tonight. I would also like to thank my beloved wife, Catherine, who on such short notice, has prepared the festivities for tonight's celebration."

Eric then introduced us one by one and reassured his people to come forward and socialize with us. He then sat down and ordered some more spirits for us and motioned for the orchestra to continue playing. It was surprising, the number of people who came up to talk to us. In fact, dinner was delayed for a while so that everyone could spend a little time with us. Believe me, I, thought, we had a tremendous amount of questions. This crowd was just as inquisitive about us as we were about them. We learned a lot from all the conversation that took place that evening.

About seven o'clock, dinner was served, and it was delicious. We all agreed that it was the best prepared and most appetizing cuisine we have ever tasted. Shortly after dinner, the orchestra stopped playing and the servers wheeled out and filled the dance floor with odd looking tables later described as gambling tables.

Eric explained their functions and assured us that the games were not only challenging but also fun. He said it was a long-standing tradition and held at every banquet. He supplied us with an exchange currency and a good explanation of the games. Forty percent of them were computer oriented, and the other 60 percent consisted of games played with some strange looking "poker cards." To this day, I cannot figure out how they received that name. These games continued until the early morning, and when the crowd quieted down at about 5:45 a.m., more food and coffee was served. Then the currency which as Eric informed us was not real; was used for an auction in which the people bought food, supplies, and clothing for the less fortunate in their district and donated by well-respected businessmen.

"Eric, we have had a great time and really appreciate the celebration Catherine prepared for us, but I can hardly keep my eyes open."

"Me too, Joe," Dawn added.

"I understand," Eric said. "I guess it has been such a long time since I have had so much fun, freedom and celebration, the time had just eluded me. I didn't realized how much I really had until I lost it all. It's amazing what solitary confinement can do to you. But most important to me was the love I had lost. I thought about Catherine every conscious moment I had in that cell and dreamt about her in my sleep. We have been married now for over thirty years, and our devotion and love for one another is extraordinary."

"*Married*, Eric. What do you mean by that word?"

"Oh, I am sorry, Dawn, Joe, excuse me, that was very inconsiderate of me. Marriage is a ceremony that is performed before God, our supreme being. You devote your life to each other and you are bonded to that person of the opposite sex for the rest of your life. You create offspring and live as a family. The whole ceremony centers on the caring, giving, loving, and uniting of hearts. It's the same feeling you, Dawn, have for Joe and, Pam, you have for Derek, together with their feelings for you. This special band we wear around our third finger on our left hand represents our marriage. You have been married too. Maybe, not by ceremony, but in your hearts bonded by the living God, and that's what really counts. I had some rings made for all of you. Marriage is a special gift given by God. You know, I prayed every night for the Lord to give me one more chance to live free again. You see, I was frustrated with my life and I had to learn the hard way how much it really meant to me.

"The pressure of my position as current president and the stress of raising and dealing with my family—it was all about to destroy me, so I accepted a risky challenge. By being the leader of my nation and taking charge of the mining project, I gave up my responsibilities to my family and to my people just to acquire new reserves of U-717 energy cores. It was pretty selfish of me not to include them. I led an expedition deep into unknown territory. I believed patrols didn't exist in the area so I lightened security. It wasn't long before a patrol caught sight of us. Three were killed and two captured. Two other citizens, a well-known scientist and a lab technician, died in captivity. It was all my responsibility. You know I never gave up hope that someday I'd be free. I knew it in my heart that the Lord would help me and sure enough in his own way and His perfect timing, he did… and let me also say that I am thankful, extremely thankful. Now, I am rested, strong, stress free at my work and I feel I can teach others to be the same. I am very happy man now and will never lose sight of everything that I lost, thankfully, for only a short period of time. Well, enough for now. I can see exhaustion in your eyes. We will have plenty of time to talk. Now, off you go we will meet again, and it will be my honor to present all of you with the rings."

We were once again escorted to our quarters.

"What a great party, Joe, and the rings. They represent the love we pledged to have for each other, and it will show everyone the way we feel," Dawn said.

"I know it's a great symbol of our love. Eric and Catherine are truly special people. I really have grown very fond of them," I replied.

"You know, I just can't understand why our society would want to eliminate such nice people."

"That is amazing, Dawn," said Pam. "It really convinces me of how wrong our society really is."

"Well, we think it is wrong, especially to drug all the citizens and suppress the society like they do, but you know the leaders really believe it is the right way to live. After all, this way did fail at least once. Right, team?" I said.

"Oh come on, Joe," said Pam.

"Joe, you don't really mean that, do you?" asked Dawn.

"Ha ha! Just trying to stimulate your brains on this bright and early morning."

"Get out of here, Joe. Hey, we'll see you later on today. Good night, or should I say good morning! Oh well, come along, Pamela. I am exhausted. See you later."

The living quarters were very comfortable, and the time it took Dawn and I to prepare to go to sleep was about thirty seconds. As we lay down together holding each other close I had such a calm, comfortable, relaxing, even peaceful sensation come over me, a feeling of fullfillness. That same peace I had felt once before, a peace that transcends all other feelings, a peace that only our Creator could give me. Soon, we were sound asleep.

CHAPTER 10

The Modification

By the time I crawled out of bed and became part of the living again, nearly twelve hours had passed. Everyone had gone about their business, seemingly not even remembering the wonderful celebration just twelve hours earlier. Even the girls who had been up now for about four hours acted like the celebration never occurred. It wasn't long before they started telling us about the wonderful time they had with Catherine while we were asleep. They went shopping, sightseeing, and they learned new ways of the Carthusian culture. They seemed more excited than they appeared to be when we met, the very first time on Gamnon. Soon, without a word, they were gone once again with Catherine, this time for nourishment, which didn't sound like a bad idea.

I went over to meet Derek, whose quarters were just across the hallway.

There was a server who escorted us to the dining area, and Eric was there waiting. "Good evening, gentlemen. I figured the first place you would like to visit would be the kitchen."

"That was a good guess, Eric. I am starving."

"Sit down and loosen your belts. The food is well prepared, and there's plenty of it. Then, Joe, before you start working on your ship I would like to introduce you to my son. He will be very helpful in adapting your ship for your next journey."

"Son?" asked Derek. "I didn't know you had a son."

"Oh, I'm sorry, fellows. You know we have been so busy talking that I forgot to tell you that Catherine and I have a son. He is a very bright young man, and we are quite proud of all the accomplishments he has made already."

"You mean, you honestly get to keep them?" asked Derek.

"Keep them? Why, of course! In fact, it's your responsibility to teach, nourish, comfort, and protect your offspring. They stay with you until they can provide for themselves. Then, they take spouses, and the family cycle begins once again. Oh, here he is now. Chuck, come here. I have some friends I want you to meet."

"Yes, sir," replied Chuck respectfully.

"His real name is Charles, but we all call him Chuck. In fact, he feels Charles is a little too formal. Derek, Joe, this is my son, Chuck. I have informed him of your destination and also provided him with a computer diagram of your ship. That should help to make your modifications easier. Now, you can draw them out before you start to work. It's always good to have a plan."

"Honored to meet you, Joe, Derek. I am very thankful to you for bringing my father back to us."

"Eric, I don't mean to be disrespectful, but Derek and I can handle it, and besides, isn't he a little young?" whispered Joe.

"Ha ha. How old are you Joe and you Derek? Besides, don't forget he is my son, my creation, and believe me, he is somewhat smarter than I was at his age."

"Why, thank you, Father."

"No thanks needed, son. It's true."

"But, Eric, can't you help us?" Derek asked.

"I have many responsibilities to my people, and it's going to take me a good bit of time to catch up on all the events that happened during my captivity. Besides, I'll be spending a lot of time with you in the Dome of Knowledge. Remember every night after dinner, and, by the way, who do you think invented the silent underwater transport ship that you arrived in two days ago?"

"Well, I thought you did," I said.

"Me too," echoed Derek.

"Me. Ha ha ha. Come now, I never said it was me, remember. I just smiled."

"No, I guess you didn't actually say you did… You mean Chuck invented it?" I asked.

"Of course, he's a whiz at stuff like that."

"You've got to be kidding! He's so young."

"He will be twenty-three on his next birthday."

"Twenty three!" exclaimed Joe. "He looks about fifteen."

"We start our children's schooling at a very early age, and they go all year with only three weeks of vacation. They learn fast and progress with lightning speed and children who are like Chuck, that is gifted, progress at even faster rates. Chuck has been working in his profession for seven years now and the ship is only one of his many inventions."

"Gifted children?" asked Derek.

"Okay, I know just where to start our first lesson tonight. We will start with terms and their definitions. Our society is exactly like *Station America* so the terms are the same. You will learn much from my study."

"Sounds great to me!"

"We'll be there and on time, Eric. Chuck, are you ready to go and work up some designs for this ship? Check out our damage? We have a lot to do."

"Yes, sir!"

"You don't have to call me sir. Joe will do. See you later, Eric."

We walked through the solid gold door again and Chuck took us back to the docking area. He proceeded to get instructions from a man dressed in a white suit and helmet. The man was directing some workers on where to unload a shipment. When he finished, he turned and talked to Chuck for a few minutes and then pointed off to his right, an area next to a large open storage facility. Chuck proceeded to walk over to us and informed us that our ship was located in the last storage area, Bay 77.

"Bay 77 is the bay where your ship is located. Father must have directed them to that bay because we assemble our transports there. It is thoroughly equipped with all the tools and instruments we need to modify your ship. Also the ammunition bay is close at hand. Joe, the ship is in pretty bad condition. Have you seen it since we pulled it out of the sand?"

"No, I haven't. I didn't really think about it. We've been rather busy enjoying ourselves."

"I wish we could supply you with a fighter, but ours are really antiquated. Your ship is the first new fighter I've ever seen. I've studied them in class but was never fortunate enough to ever see one physically. Actually, I'm kind of concerned about adapting our ammunition to your ship. The ammunition depot is where we reload the fighters that come from the *Station America*. About the fighters, I was never really interested in their cabilities or weaponry but that still doesn't mean I don't know about them. I have studied their design and have also worked up an analysis on your ship. Maybe, together we will be able to come up with something unique. The supervisor really believes that it is beyond repair. But I believe that there isn't anything man has created that can't be fixed or modified."

"Don't worry, Chuck. the only way we would get discouraged is if we opened that bay door and all we saw were ashes. Even then we would find a way."

"Hey, Joe, why don't we wait for one of their transports to make a shipment and just go back with them?" asked Derek.

"Sounds good!" exclaimed Chuck. "But they won't take you. It's forbidden for them to pick up runaways. They figure sooner or later they would pick up spies sent to infiltrate their society. Besides the only way they will accept you is if you make it on your own. Secondly, a transport isn't due for awhile. There's Bay 77. Joe, put your hand on this faceplate on the wall next to you."

As soon as I put my hand on the plate, Chuck walked to the other side of the large door and scanned his identification card. The door slowly opened.

"There must be two people to open this door, one with an identification card and the other with a computerized hand print code. Joe, you and Derek both have handprints coded into the computer, so there shouldn't be a problem getting in. If you come alone, the supervisor will have to help you get in. Remember, two of you have to be present for this door to open. I will issue some identification cards for all four of you when we return this evening."

As we walked through the large doors, the room seemed to expand to an enormous size. Our ship scarred and battle worn was positioned in the center of the bay. The size of the bay made it look like a little toy. The ship was completely black, partially from the hit we took and subsequent fire and partially from the black coal like sand it sat in for hours. On each side of the ship lay a row of computers strategically positioned for repairs. The back of the bay was filled with different kinds of machinery some of which I was familiar with and some completely foreign to me. Scrap parts hung on the wall adjacent to us and cluttered the floor all the way up to the computers and over to the left was a machine shop equipped with presses, drills, molecular brushes, and cutters. In fact, it was equipped to make any imaginable part known to man. Over to the left of Derek was an accumulation of all sorts of metals and plastics in all different shapes and sizes.

As we walked closer, the ship looked even worse than we could have imagined.

Even though the damage was superficial, I wondered how extensive it truly was.

"Joe, I didn't think we took on that much damage. It sure is hard to tell from the inside of the ship."

"Yes, but I knew we got hit pretty hard when I lost power. It takes a direct hit on the engine or extensive exterior damage to drop like we did… like a rock. Well, it looks like we have a lot of work to do."

Chuck went over to a switch on the wall and engaged it. Fans started to blow and air-conditioning started to filter up from the vents located all over the floor. Derek and I took our shirts off, preparing for a major cleaning and proceeded to hose down the ship. As soon as we started to identify real metal, my confidence came back. It took us several hours to clean up the outside so the damage could really be assessed."

"Well, she's clean. Chuck, you look at the engine. Derek, get on those computer scanners and evaluate our internal damage. I am going to walk around her and check out the body damage. The front of the ship was pretty tore up from the impact into the sandy area. It was obvious some large rocks were in our way."

"Joe, Derek!" Chuck beckoned from the other side of the ship. "Here's the shot that took you down. Actually it was the impact from the first blast, then a piece of shrapnel from your ship tore loose and hit the igniter. The initial hit destroyed the first igniter, and the shrapnel damaged the second igniter."

"No wonder we fell like a rock," said Derek.

"No wait, Joe. This doesn't look right. All three igniters are wired together. That doesn't seem right!"

"It's not... Let me see, Chuck. Well, I'll be a—Derek! Come here!"

"What? What's up?" exclaimed Derek.

"Look, Derek! Someone sabotaged our rig. Chuck, check that third igniter. It's under the engine, up toward the right."

"It's blown, Joe."

"So it wasn't the shrapnel. They wired our igniters together. Wait, Derek, remember how they were just waiting for us when we reached the ship I mean they were all over the place. They knew... They knew exactly where we were hiding the ship. They wanted to shoot us down. They probably videotaped it to show everyone."

"And it is pretty strange that ship kept pounding our port side. They must have rewired it, while we were getting the girls."

"They are sneaky. They used us, Derek, and they won. At least it's going to look like that to everyone else. They must have jammed the frequency on my wrist device because I never got the alarm."

"At least, they think we are dead. That may give us an edge."

"Well, the first thing we are going to do is rewire the igniters and change their location. If they recognize us on our next little trip, they might use the same tactics. We will be prepared this time."

"Yes, sir."

"Hey, Chuck, can you get me more speed out of these engines?" I asked.

"Well, from what I can tell so far, I think I can increase your speed about 45 percent."

"Sounds great and with a little increase in our firepower that just might give us the edge we need. Derek, our numbers will be painted bright red. I want them to know who they are dealing with so brighten up our insignia too."

Time went by fast, and soon we were into our second month. We worked every day, Chuck on the engines, Derek with the computers and interior, and I on the body armor and defense armament. Many days we worked right up to our history session with Eric. The girls would bring us some dinner, and we would eat while we worked, sometimes in the oddest of positions. Derek and I spent many a night returning after the history session finishing up projects we felt couldn't wait for tomorrow. The women spent most of their time with Catherine but they also chipped in helping to clean and restore the inside of the ship. Catherine taught them so much about living together with men that there were some obvious changes going on. They really took care of us during this time of detachment. Most of the time, I would come back to our quarters completely exhausted. Dawn would prepare a hot bath and give me a soothing massage before bedtime. Almost always during the message I would just pass out. She really understood my feelings and encouraged me to achieve my daily goals and reassure me of her confidence in my work.

Chuck helped tremendously throughout the rebuilding of the airship. We were amazed at the knowledge and ingenuity he showed us. Chuck was very intelligent and knew so much about aircraft that we let him design most of the modifications. He told us that he always wanted to design a fighter ship but never had the opportunity since his society had no use for such offensive airships. It was a dream come true for Chuck and a blessing for us because he actually cut our rebuilding time by close to one third. In fact, sometimes I wondered if he slept at all. We would come in at seven in the morning, and Chuck would have already put in a good two hours worth of work.

One morning, he suggested that we relocate the engines. Using his design, we would be able to obtain more speed and increase the maneuverability of the ship. After running the design through the computer Derek found, theoretically, he was right so we changed them. He also designed seven styron core blaster pods and positioned them very carefully, three on the top and four on the bottom of the ship. He promised me that he would show me their function on the trial run. He was getting very excited about the new ship even more so than Derek and me. After we decided to reposition the engines, I helped Chuck as much as I could. The equipment available to us was so sophisticated that it also helped us to work more efficiently.

"Chuck, you know back on Altaur, it would have taken up to a year to do the work we're doing in two months. It is incredible. Your technology is so advanced. I am really impressed."

"Well, thanks, Joe. These engines will probably give you about 50 percent more power. That should be enough to outrun ten interceptors."

"But I thought you said we could only get 45 percent more power?"

"Well, Joe, I guess I was wrong."

We both laughed. Then Chuck explained the thruster he added to the engines. "Joe, I have installed a new thrust mode to your ship. The button is located on the steering mechanism in the cockpit. It produces a super burst of energy that last for about ten seconds. See, I added this fuel injector to the engines. When the button is pushed a supercharged fuel is injected into the engines simultaneously giving you a fifteen hundred-kilometer-per-hour thrust for roughly ten seconds. It will get you out of anywhere in a hurry."

"What's the name of the fuel, Chuck?"

"It's called xeron 77, and the tank will sit on the underside of the ship in between three plates of carbothroxine composit. It is virtually impregnable. Even upon an impact crash, it will not explode. It is fully contained."

"How many times can I use this mode and how often can I use it."

"Well, the tank contains twenty-five thrusts, which will be plenty and you need to let the engines cool down after a thrust. The coolant Segron 33 provides for the cool down phase. It takes approximately fifteen seconds to cool down the engine enough for a subsequent thrust. In fact, the button will not reset until the engine is cool enough. It's like a protective device so your engines won't burn up. I have also doubled your fuel capacity."

"What about the weight?"

"Well, I didn't actually double the weight. I just made your engines more efficient. The actual fuel capacity is slightly larger, but it lasts 95 percent longer. See, I added this little device here that takes the vapor from the exhaust and redirects it to these injector sites. Once that happens, I can cut the fuel injector volume in half without losing power and besides it cuts out that extra fuel tank that we would have to mount. It then is expelled through these exhaust distributors, obviously in a weaker state."

"You're incredible, Chuck, and I'm impressed with the knowledge and design you have put forth on this ship. How many more surprises do you have for me?"

"Just a few, Joe, just a few. Here's another feature I think you will like. You should be able to achieve 97 percent of your speed on two engines as you could on three engines. On the control panel, there's a red light that flashes when any of the engines are damaged or completely destroyed. If it fails to provide the proper thrusting power, the engine will be expelled from the ship automatically, or you can expel them manually if you need to do it quickly, thus decreasing your weight reasonably fast. With this power mode in place on the remaining engines, your speed should be brought back close to normal. These power boosters will not engage until an engine is expelled from the ship.

"I'm thankful for that."

"I have also installed what I call an equalizer. This is all automatic, Joe, so you don't have to worry about a thing. In fact, Derek is working on the computer that will handle this modification right this very minute. Now, the equalizer starts once the damaged engine is expelled. Let's say your starboard engine malfunctions and is disposed of, then the middle engine moves out on this track here, and thus becomes the starboard engine. This balances out the power once again. If the starboard and middle engines are damaged, the port engine moves to the center, thus balancing power and retaining great maneuverability."

"How much power do you lose with two engines destroyed?"

"Not much, see as each engine breaks away, more power is generated to the remaining engines, and because you lose a bunch of weight your power and speed is retained. Of course, three engines work more efficiently, and as you decrease the number of engines, the work is increased on the remaining ones. Also, fuel efficiency drastically decreases with one engine, if the same speed is desired you increase your fuel consumption, but by decreasing your speed, your fuel will last longer. Just remember, if you are still in a tight spot the engine will perform for you. You just have to realize that each time an engine fails you, the time to remain functioning decreases, directly proportionate to fuel consumption and stress on the remaining engines."

"You are amazing, Chuck, but are you sure I can fly this machine? It's definitely different than the one I am used to."

"Oh, don't worry about that, Joe. I have taken care of that for you."

"How?"

"I adapted our simulator, well with Derek and Pam's help, for you to practice your flying. Actually, it will allow both you and Dawn to adjust your skill level to the new fighter's maneuverability and fire power."

"So the simulator has the firepower on it also, Chuck?"

"It sure does. Derek was able to reconstruct it off your ship's computer. It should be ready this evening, and you probably can work on it after supper."

"Sounds great! I haven't flown in some time. I really need to brush up on my skills. Dawn and I will start this evening. Is it set up for a copilot?"

"Sure is. I thought it would be best to work together, and then you can anticipate each other's moves."

"Well, our days will really be full now. Even though the ship is nearly done our history lessons can go on forever. Between the simulators and our lessons, we'll put in a full day's work, every day."

"Joe, pull up on that igniter until I plug in the tandem switch."

"You've got it, Chuck. By the way, is there anything these engines cannot do for us?"

"Well, they can't make breakfast or dinner well maybe dinner but definitely not breakfast."

"Ha ha, you are crazy, absolutely crazy."

"Oh, there is one more function I forgot to tell you about. Actually, I think I told you we'd wait for the trial run, but since you'll be using the simulator, I better tell you."

"What's that?"

"This ship can hover. The seven thrusters placed on the top and bottom of the ship are strong enough to hold you in midair. You know if you want to do some sightseeing or something. They also allow you to take off in very tight places. Oh, they have another feature too. Say you are being pursued and you just can't shake them for that matter, and believe me, there probably is at least one or two just as good as or better than you at the helm, especially those computer pilots."

"Not likely, Chuck," replied Derek.

"I guess he hasn't heard of that computer I beat on Gamnon," I whispered to Derek.

"I like that confidence. Okay, let's say there is one pilot just as confident in his ability as you are and you just can't shake him. What you do is take the ship to top speed and then turn the upper thrusters on. That switch automatically cuts the engines acceleration putting the engine in a neutral drive. As the thrusters kick in you drop significantly anywhere from 2,000 to 2,500 feet. Then, the thrusters automatically shut off and put your engines back into acceleration. It happens so quickly that you only lose about one-tenth of your acceleration power. Soon, you find yourself in pursuit, and as you slowly regain altitude you can take him out where he's most vulnerable—his belly."

"I sure would like to try that one out."

"Well, you can. It's all programmed in the simulator. There are other features, most of them insignificant for your purposes, and there are a couple of them that are purely theoretical. They will all be explained in the introduction provided by the simulator."

"Maybe, we can try them out on our test flight."

"Sounds great!" Chuck said. "Joe, I'd love to be on board, but I'm not sure that my stomach can take the regular maneuvers, let alone the experimental ones."

"You will do fine. It's really not bad at all. Maybe, you can fly it with me."

"No, I'm just the designer. I leave the flying to you older, more experienced guys. That's it, Joe. They are all ready. I am very pleased with these engines. Now, the real trial will be the test run, and let me say this, Joe, I am just as confident in the performance of the engines as you are in your piloting skills."

"And me, I'm confident in both of you, whatever you are doing," said Derek.

"You've convinced me, Chuck. I am fully assured that they will pass the test run. But we have much to do before we try them out. We better think about supplying our ship with firepower. We sure are going to need it. I think most of our stores were depleted on our last excursion," I replied.

After careful consideration and testing, we found out that the ammunition was completely compatible. We first decided to add one laser and another torpedo bay to the bow. That would give us two torpedo bays holding twenty neutron torpedoes total. We kept the rear laser and torpedo bay the same except for increasing the rounds for the laser gun from one thousand to three thousand and increasing our torpedoes from five to ten. The torpedoes were powerful enough to explode near the enemy ship and still disable or destroy it. Laser guns would take repeated direct hits to destroy their ships, but they were somewhat more powerful than the old ones. Also, Chuck installed rocket launchers on both the starboard and port wings. They would house twelve rockets each. The rockets have a longer range than torpedoes and are also used as a defense mechanism. If a neutron torpedo has been released or a rocket been fired and has been picked up on our radar, these rockets can be directed by the computer to engage the oncoming target. What we had done was double our firepower, and since we were able to produce more power out of our engines thanks to Chuck, our speed and maneuverability would remain the same. We also decided that if we couldn't reach our destination with that much firepower, we didn't deserve to get there. Our next concern was the defense shields. We had to get more power out of our defense shields since our hits would probably triple if they sent a large number of fighters against us and that would mean changing the onboard reactor.

As soon as they picked us up on radar, identifying this new ship as not one of there fighters, there is no telling how many attack ships they would launch. The abuse our shields would take would be close to three times the normal amount and our reactor would overheat if not modified.

First, we relocated the defense shield device. We moved it from the bow to the center most point of the ship. That way, it would take a direct hit to damage the whole system. In fact, a direct hit on the defense shield would completely destroy the ship. We would reinforce most of the ship with a new compound that was as strong as the metal covering on the outside of the ship and, then, beef up the core reactor to handled the increased attacks.

Chuck had some of the workers install the metal. It was all done from the inside, and it was sprayed on like you would spray paint. We completely stripped the inside, reinforcing every structure we could see. When it was all done, the ship contained four seats: the pilot, copilot, and two rear gunner seats. A storage area for food and emergency equipment lined the hallway connecting the rear and forward compartments. Beds, gallery eating area, table, chairs, latrine, and everything that could be removed was removed.

Chuck also installed a device that could redistribute the defense shield power. A screen was located in the lap of the co-pilot who could change the power of the defense shield to fit the occasion. Let's say, for example, that two bogies were drawing fast to port with another directly behind but off in the distance. The copilot could put 85 percent of the power to our port shield and 15 percent in the stern and then redistribute the shield power with the push of a button. If the enemy was in all directions, the copilot could equalize the power to all shields. Dawn would be in charge of our defense shields and also the defense rockets and torpedos would be her responsibility.

Next, we had to eliminate all hatches and reinforce our one and only entrance hatch. There would be no emergency hatch since there would be no where to escape to in space. We decided to either make our desination or die trying. The new entrance would be between the two laser guns in the nose of the ship. We would have to crawl along a short tunnel to get inside. The door to enter the ship would actually disengage by raising and extending along the nose. It would reengage by a method of hydraulics and seal tight. From the outside of the ship, it would appear that there was no entryway.

"Well, Derek, now that we are through with the design, I am glad I never showed Chuck my plans for a fighter. Their technology far surpasses anything we can dream up. Chuck has sure made me humble. I thought we were the most sophisticated society alive, at least, that's what they led us to believe."

"What are you trying to say, Joe, that you finally realize that pilots are human too. We all know that, although I do admire your confidence. If you didn't have it, we wouldn't have gotten this far. Just keep in mind that Chuck designed it, but you are going to fly it. And let me tell you that flying is the most important aspect of this whole crazy plan. No one can get us there safely except you, Joe."

"What Derek?" asked Chuck.

"Oh, nothing. I was just talking to Joe about our plan that's all."

"Joe, there is one more device, and I am not sure if you'll need it, but we installed it anyway. It's called the antifixator. The interceptor ships have the capability to attach a tractor beam. Actually, it would take at least five interceptors ships located in five different directions. They can actually stop a ship in midair as long as the ships are strategically positioned. Once they find out your destination, they can position the ships to intercept you. This device scatters the tractor beams that are dispersed onto a ship or another object but only small tractor beams with low power can be dissipated. Their technology was experimental as of last month, but I wasn't sure if they had progressed since then to make it operational."

"It looks like you have done your homework, Chuck. You have taken into consideration every problem we could run into along our path."

"We also have some special fire resistant garments that will be issued to you. Your ship could be completely on fire and as long as it lands you will be perfectly safe. We've removed all the lights and the only wiring will be in the two compartments and some overhead running lights in the hallway. There's only one thing that bothers me, Joe, and that's all this firepower. There is no way you could dump it, if you take a good hit. And if it blows, they will hear it all the way down here."

"That goes with the territory, Chuck. We will need every bit of it to make it to the *Station America*," I replied.

"How much food are we going to take?"

"Derek, Derek, always worried about your stomach. I think the one storage compartment will hold enough rations for about six days. If we somehow get damaged but not destroyed and are able to drift in space, our air supply will only last five days."

"I guess that will be enough food, then, won't it?"

"Sounds like it to me."

"So I think that does it, Chuck."

"Yes, we have attained the maximum amount of power so the ship can maneuver without breaking up. We supplied the ship with the ultimate amount of weaponry and have given it the utmost in defense protection. I think we have done a great job."

"Well, two to three weeks on the simulator, and we'll be ready to take her on a test run. After that we just wait for the *Station America* to come close enough for us to reach them."

"That's assuming our test run is satisfactory, right, Joe?"

"Sure, but I am confident, how about you?"

"Yes, sir, I can't wait."

Dawn and Pam entered the repair and assembly bay.

"Hey, how's it coming along?"

"Great, Dawn. In fact, Chuck has pleasantly provided us with a simulator to practice on since the modifications have really changed our ship."

"The outside is slightly different. How's the inside, Joe?"

"There has been a considerable amount of modifications. The inside has really changed Dawn, but we have prepared it for a journey that will be much more difficult than the one we have already made. Chuck has furnished us with a much more efficient ship."

"Well, guys, let's take a look," Pamela said. "Guys, that's a new one from you."

"Not around here, Derek, just some normal colloquialsm."

"You girls didn't waste any time fitting in around here."

"We sure didn't, and it's ladies, not girls," proclaimed Dawn.

"Wow, they sure are learning fast! Wouldn't you say, Chuck?"

"They sure are, and for your information, *ladies* is the term for highly sophisticated, mature, and experienced women."

"Well, Chuck, it looks like we are falling behind on our social etiquette."

"They are just passing us by," said Derek.

"Yes, they sure are," I said.

"Passing you by, we left you guys back on the Star Cities a long time ago."

"Oh no, they've been hanging around with Catherine too much. I can tell," Chuck exclaimed.

"You can bet your bottom we have," exclaimed the women simultaneously.

"Bet your bottom?" asked Derek.

"Slang," said Chuck.

"What is slang?" I asked.

"Just some more local dialect," replied Chuck.

"Okay, ladies, how about a tour. We'll show you what we've done so far and what has to be done. Then, Dawn, we'll have to work with the simulator and when we're ready, a test run, right Chuck."

"That's right, and it shouldn't take you long to master the modifications."

"Well, we are trying to modify it to meet our needs for this one trip. Except for the engine work and the increased firepower we are going pretty primitive. Derek and Pam, you will be our rear support, Dawn and I will pilot the ship. Everyone will follow my orders, and if I get wounded or killed, Dawn will take over. Agreed?"

"Agreed," Pam said.

"Agreed," Derek reiterated.

"Dawn, you will not leave your post under any circumstances. If something happens to me while you are gone, the ship will be destroyed. If I've been hit and appear to be making irrational decisions, Dawn will take command. Derek and Pam will have to make repairs. Derek you will be responsible for identifying bogies and keeping our stern free. Both will man laser guns, but Pam will be our first person for damage control. If she is injured, we will have to increase the power on our rear defense shield to help you out. If we have extensive damage and both of you are needed for securing repairs, we will fly evasive maneuvers and give you 75 percent of our shield power for the rear defense shield.

"If at any time a computer malfunctions we will resort to manual operation. That is, if Derek or Pam cannot repair it within a reasonable amount of time. Our test flight will involve use of all engine modes and the firing of all designated weapons insuring proper usage, guidance and aim. On the test run our targets will be stationary and our ability to arm, lock, and fire effectively will be imperative. If we engage a Guardian ship at any time we will have to destroy her, that is, after we scramble any communication between their ship and any of the perspective Star Cities. So far they think our ship has been totally destroyed, and I want it to stay that way as long as we can. Our trial run will be set at dusk and the main portion of the test will take place at night."

"Do you really think the test run is necessary? If we are spotted our chances could greatly be impaired."

"I thought about that, Derek, but we have so many modifications and different armament, if we get up there and it fails we're dead without a doubt. We have to test our work. Chuck will take us out of here in the transport and accompany us on our run, by his own request. We will adapt a chair at the navigation computers. Is that all right with you, Chuck?"

"That's fine, but are you going to give us time to work out the bugs?"

"What do you mean, Chuck?"

"Well, the test run should be soon, just in case some of the modifications need adjusting. The *Station America* will be at it nearest point in approximately thirty three days. We will be able to tell with more accuracy once she arrives in our area. I think we should leave two weeks for minor repairs and adjustments."

"Okay then, we will set a date for the test run in nineteen days. How's that, Chuck? Do you agree?"

"Sounds great."

"Then it's set. We'll need a couple more days to put the finishing touches on the fighter. We will rearm her the night before and immediately put her in the transport. Any questions? Then let's go get a bite to eat. We haven't done that together in weeks."

"Eric and Catherine will be happy about that. You know we all haven't had dinner at the same table since we started the repairs."

"Has it been that long? Time sure flies when you're having fun," said Chuck.

At that statement Derek and I looked at each other, thought for a brief moment, and together excitedly said, "Slang!"

Everyone laughed, and we all walked back to the living quarters together. It didn't take long to clean up, probably because we were so hungry. As we walked into the dining room, Eric and Catherine looked pleasantly surprised to see us all together.

"Come on in. We're so glad to see all of you."

"Yes, we are pleased to have you all for dinner. It's just like a family reunion. Sit down. Help yourselves."

"I hope we will meet again after your departure," said Eric.

"I'm sure we will," I said.

"Positively," replied Derek.

"I remember another man telling me the same thing. It was some time ago. He's a strong man about my age. In fact, he is the Captain of the *Station America* and his character, integrity, and bravery are unrivaled. We spent a lot of time together many years ago. We worked on several projects here on earth. In fact, he was from your world. He was and still is a very good friend of mine.

"We communicate when he comes into our orbit, but his duties keep him aboard the *Station America*. I have visited him several times on *Station America*, but our visits always seem too short. Together we helped designed the new Starship, the one he commands now. I also helped to design the engines, develop the fuel, and design the agricultural department, along with some noted scientists."

"Do you mean there have been other *Space Station Americas*?" asked Dawn.

"Oh, of course. There has been a *Station America* community for over two hundred years. The old ships become outdated and over populated. They update them every fifty to seventy-five years. This one, we built not long ago, is the biggest and has the most sophisticated technology of the chronicle. There's no other spacecraft like it. It houses about one million people and has the capicity for five hundred thousand more. You can also add modules to the exterior compartments which was not available in the past. It's a beautiful ship, and I am quite proud to have been a part of its creation."

"That was a fantastic dinner, Catherine. We all appreciate the generosity, guidance, and assistance your whole family has given us," I remarked.

"You are quite welcome, but remember I have a lot to thank you and Derek for, because Eric would still be rotting away up there in that old detention center. Our family could never repay you for your rescue."

"Well, let's just say that up until now everything has turned out for the best all around, but one more task, and I hope we can be just as happy as you two are right now."

"Our love is forever with you, and I pray every night for your safety."

"Thank you very much, Catherine."

The next nineteen days were spent diligently at the simulator, while Chuck checked and rechecked the modifications and rearmament of the ship. Derek and Pamela worked hard on their battle simulator, and, to all of our surprise, both had achieved a high score on weaponry and defense analysis. They were much better on scoring hits and felt much more comfortable on the guns and torpedoes. Slowly but surely, we were getting prepared. Dawn was working extensively on the new radar, and soon, she had it perfected. The simulators really helped and the night before the test run we all got together, discussed our objectives, and ran through the trial run. As we turned out the lights, we all felt confident about our responsibilities for the trial run. The ship was armed, and the next morning, we would eat a light breakfast check the ship out, practice on the simulators and take a short nap before our excursion.

Derek woke up about one hour before our departure and came over to make sure I was getting prepared for the next highly intense couple of hours.

"Joe! Hey, Joe!" Derek rapped on the door of our quarters. "Are you up? Are you ready? This is Derek. Open up!"

"Who else would it be?" I exclaimed.

As the door opened, I stood there in my skivvies and bright red house shoes. "Come on in. I'll be ready in a moment. Dawn, are you ready?"

"Yes, Joe, I am. I'm going over to get Pamela. We will meet you at the ship in thirty minutes. Soon after her words ended, the door slammed, and Dawn was gone.

"Hey, Derek, did she go?"

"Yes, sir."

"I didn't even get a kiss. How weird. What could be on her mind? I'll be out in a minute, Derek."

"Okay, let's go. Chuck called me earlier. He's already at the ship."

"Well, Derek, they sure can't leave without us now, can they?"

What could have been on her mind. It must have been important. She never leaves me without giving me a kiss, I thought.

***

Dawn knocked on Pam's door, and soon, they were together preparing for their upcoming event.

"I am starting to get pretty excited, Pamela. How about you?"

"I am too. I can't wait to get aboard the ship. They've been working so hard to get it prepared for our journey."

"I know. They have been putting in some long days. Pamela, I have something important to tell you."

"What's that, Dawn?"

"Well, I went to see Catherine yesterday, and she took me to one of her physicians."

"What's wrong, Dawn. Are you sick? Are you going to be able to go with us? What's the matter?"

"Oh, nothing like that, Pam. I'm just pregnant again."

"What! Seriously! Oh, you are not... Really Dawn! Wow, I can't believe it! Well, congratulations! Are you excited? Have you told Joe? How far along are you?"

"Slow down, Pam, slow down. I am barely six weeks, and no, Joe doesn't know, and we are not going to tell him until the mission is over, and yes, I am very excited."

"Why not tell Joe? He will be really excited."

"Well, there are a couple of reasons, even though I am not sure they are good ones. The first, is I don't want it to interfere with his judgment. Like giving up and surrendering when we get into trouble. We definitely will never see each other again. The second is he might leave us behind, believing it is too risky to take a chance on both of our lives. I know he would come back for us, but I don't know when. It could be a year or so, maybe longer. No, Pam, this baby is not going to interfere with our plans. Now, you are going to keep my secret, aren't you?"

"Of course, Dawn. I'll keep your secret. At least from Joe."

"No, Pam, if Derek knows, Joe will find out. No one is to know except for you, Catherine, the doctor, and me. I must have your word."

"Okay, Dawn. You have my word but only to the point where it doesn't interfere with our mission. Agreed?"

"Okay, that's fair enough. I really can't expect much more than that."

***

Derek and I finally reached the ship. Chuck was working on the storage compartments. Remarkably, he was putting the final touches on our fighter. After he was finished, all three of us made a final inspection of the new ship.

Everything was checking out perfectly, making the time for our departure right on time. We all decided to skip dinner, feeling it was best for our stomachs and the three of us proceeded to meet Eric back at his home.

We met Eric and Catherine in Eric's study, and he extended his best wishes for our flight. He also reassured us that the trial run would go perfectly and not to fear. His confidence in Chuck's work and our ability was remarkable. The women met us there shortly afterward.

With all the people in the room, it would seem there would be conversation everywhere, but the room was silent. Eric sat behind his desk; Catherine and Pam were on the couch in front of him. Chuck was standing at the far wall reading some type of literature on engine modifications and Derek and I sat in large armed chairs one on each side of the couch. Dawn was sitting half on and half off the arm of the chair I was sitting in. The silence was eerie, and if it wasn't for the sound of Chuck shuffling papers, you could hear a pin drop. No one made eye contact, and everyone seemed to be in their own little world. I could hardly stand it anymore. But I, just like the others, was rehashing my job once again, probably for the hundredth time. I felt fully confident of the ship's ability and my skill in flying it. I also felt that everyone was prepared and skilled at their own jobs and responsibilities.

I guess it was just that unnerving fear that happens to everyone before a flight. The fear that something will go wrong or someone will make a mistake. I thought mostly about navigation. If detours had to be taken would we have enough fuel to perform our job? Theoretically, they could move us all over space and never land a direct hit and still defeat us. I was sure not to indulge the others with my only real concern. But soon, the ice was broken as Chuck mentioned his plans to join us on our test run.

"Well, it looks like the kind of adventure I have been looking for."

I turned and looked at Eric, and it was obvious from his expression on his face that Chuck never informed his family of his plans. Without a word, Eric looked at me very concerned. He seemed torn between the danger and his pride for his son—between his son's safety and the glory of his adventurous spirit. "It's his ship. he designed almost all of it. He deserves the right to be on her for her maiden voyage," Eric said.

But the dangers, combat, capture... maybe death. Eric never had to say a word. I could see it in his eyes that he wanted me to make that crucial decision.

"Well, Chuck, it wouldn't seem right to leave the chief designer on the ground, especially when you have designed just about the most efficient fighter that ever existed. It's only fair that you see your work in action. Besides, if anything has to be changed, it would be to our advantage to have you aboard—that is, if it is all right with you, Eric."

"You make a strong case, Joe. I can see it would be a grave mistake for me to keep my son from this important mission."

"Yes, there is always room for improvement, and if I am aboard, it will be easier for me to work out the details. Time's a wasting. Is everyone ready?"

I got affirmations from everyone including Eric and Catherine, and before long, we all were walking out the door toward the ship. Eric and I were the last to leave the study, trailing some fifty feet from the others.

"Joe, I appreciate you asking me to let the boy go. I have a lot of respect for you for considering our feelings. That's important to me."

"Well, Eric, you're welcome, but your not knowing about Chuck's decision was a surprise to me. I thought from the way he talked to me that he had discussed his decision to accompany us on the trial run, with you."

"No, he hadn't, but that's like Chuck. He did the same thing to me when he invented the silent transport. I guess this one is different because it involves confrontations that we really don't know what the outcome will be. He could possibly lose his life."

"Don't worry, Eric. We definitely will not be taking any chances. But you realize that if we are detected we will have to defend ourselves and most probably have to engage and destroy the enemy vessel."

"Yes, I realize that, Joe, I am not worried with you being aboard. You remind me so much of my close friend, Joe Cavelli, the commander of *Station America*. The similarity is astonishing."

"Well, Eric, here we are. Now you can see the workmanship of your son."

"Oh yes, she looks a little different than when I first saw her," replied Eric.

"She sure does."

"Well, good luck, my boy, and be careful."

"Yes, sir."

I was the last to board but only after making one more final outside check of the ship. Everyone was secured in their seat. I sat down and proceeded to go through the inside system check.

"Dawn, all systems go?" I asked.

"Yes, sir."

"Are we secure in the stern?"

"Affirmative," Derek said loud and clear.

"Dawn, let's crank up the number 2 engine and get us over to the transport. I've got to check on one more system."

"Straight away, Joe."

Dawn proceeded to take us over from the storage bay to the transport on dock 33, and I made sure the tracking sensor was synchronize with the forward computer.

"Joe, where's the transport?" Dawn asked.

"Well, it should be… Chuck, what's going on?"

"I have a little surprise for you, Joe. I designed the engines to be waterproof and pressure resistant in water to three hundred meters. We can just take off all by ourself. These engines will run underwater just as they perform in the atmosphere.

"You're kidding! These engines will function underwater?"

"They sure will."

"Well, how did you make—Forget it, Chuck. I am not asking another question. I am just elated with your dedication to our ship and our cause. We will never be able to repay you for all you have done."

"Forget it, Joe. I have really enjoyed it. This project was the most fun I have had in a long time."

"Here we go. I guess I better set her down easy in that cold water. Let's try our lower blasters and see how they work."

We engaged our underside blasters, which raised us off the dock about fifteen meters. I moved us slowly forward, engaging our number two engine, which lies right in the center of the ship. As we hovered over the water, a strange feeling overtook me. I have never flown in this medium and wasn't sure how the ship would respond. We slowly disengaged power on the blasters, and within seconds, we were in the water, sinking slowly.

"How about some speed, Chuck, get us moving in this stuff."

"Directly, Joe. We will move rather slow until we reach the entryway and then gain speed "Derek. Any leaks back there?"

"No, sir."

"Chuck, is our bearing 245 degrees at a 45-degree angle to the surface?"

"Yes, sir, everything is A-OK," Chuck answered.

"Depth, Dawn?"

"One hundred meters… eighty meters, sir."

"Scan the surface for foreign aircraft, Dawn."

"Forty meters, and all is clear, Joe… Hold it, Joe," Dawn added.

"Cutting speed to one-third. Dawn, what do you have?"

"Two Guardian patrol ships moving south by southeast at a high rate of speed and radars off."

"Intercepting?"

"No Chuck, probably close to dinner time."

"Okay, all is clear. Enemy ships fifteen kilometers south of our position."

"Good work, Dawn, and your ship has passed its first inspection. Chuck, good work on our long range radar scanner. Okay let's go, full power."

Quickly, we exited the medium and were in the air. "Okay, two rolls to dry us off, and we are in business."

I rolled her fast twice and headed in a north by northwest direction. "Altitude, Dawn?"

"Nine hundred meters, and it looks clear. It sure is good to see the sun again."

"You can say that again, Dawn. Now let's see what kind of power we can muster up."

We hit full power, and the ship ran great except for some slight vibrations coming from the rear wing rudder. Chuck reassured us that he could take care of the problem with about three hours worth of work and four tritacon stabilizing brackets. We cut our speed after a short period of time and headed for the mountains. We varied our altitude between two hundred and four hundred meters maneuvering in and out of the valleys. We took her to one hundred meters and increased the speed to challenge her maneuverability.

"She feels good, Chuck, and she handles beautifully," I said. "Dawn, let's warm up our night scanner and navigation system. The sun seems to be setting fast, and the shadows produced by these mountains are making nighttime appear somewhat earlier than we had predicted."

The front scanner was working just perfectly and many objects that would go normally undetected were showing up bright and clear.

"Okay, Derek. It's time to try out our fire power. I will be selecting targets for both of you. You just follow the computer, and when you get a visual, do your stuff. Try some manual shooting too. You never know when the auto fire computer is going to shut down or be shot out."

We practiced using every weapon both manually and computer driven. All worked with precision. I put her through a rigid flying test doing every maneuver I could think of at the time. She ran extremely well, which was better than expected. "Chuck, what's the fuel consumption?"

"Not too bad. In fact, somewhat better than I predicted."

"Dawn, how are the scanner and navigation computers working?"

"Fine, just fine, Joe."

"Good. Now let's really put her to the test. Just north of here is the old city of Seattle, right, Chuck?"

"Yes, sir."

"Dawn, plot a course and work up a test route from the computers memory banks. Once you have it, give me a visual of the course. Chuck, buckle up tight 'cause this one will really make your stomach feel like it's in your throat. Let's enter at an altitude of one hundred meters, and increase the speed from one-third to three-fourths. Listen up. We need to be ready for anything, crew."

"Descending, Joe, we are now at one hundred meters and three-fourths power."

"Okay, put me on visual, so I can see what we will be up against."

At that moment, the eyepiece moved into place, and I was looking at the old city right before us. This test would really show us how maneuverable the ship would be. We finished the course in about thirteen minutes going from three-fourths to full speed, flying over buildings, under bridges, through alleys, flying vertical and upside down.

We flew through partially standing structures and did 180-degree turns consistently, at maximum speed. Dawn took her through once too and was really impressed with the way it handled.

"Okay, Derek, let's try a torpedo run, and remember once the target has been visualized, you have two seconds to fire, or they will have burned us."

We flew, once again, close to the ground. Then I banked hard to starboard, and Derek fired on the target. He destroyed the shop and everything next to it but was a little sluggish on his firing.

"Derek, you have to fire a little qiucker!"

"I know, Joe, I know. I was off a full two seconds, and that is unacceptable. I'll have to work on it some more in the simulator."

"You will get it just keep up your tenacity. That's not bad for a computer geek."

"Well, Chuck, she gets an A+ for the trial run, and she handles beautifully."

"She sure did, Joe, and I can say this with great confidence that she performs perfectly under your control. You really have the touch."

"Thanks, Chuck. Well, Dawn, activate the short distance scanner and put the coordinants in the navigation computer that will get us back to the underwater fortress. Also, put on the defense shield just in case. Two to one bow to stern."

"Scanner set, coordinates logged in, shields on."

"Okay, then you take her on in. I am going to look around in here for defects. We can't be that perfect."

Dawn took control, and I inspected the inside of the ship. Everything checked out fine except for a small amount of water I noticed along the hallway. I traced it up to the storage compartment and noticed a small puddle at the bottom of the lockers. I brought it to Chuck's attention, and he assured me it would be taken care of when we returned. Just as I made my way back through the hallway, a voice came over my headphones.

"Joe, I need you back to the cockpit. We have a bogy following us. Derek, Pam, to your battle stations."

As soon as Dawn ended the warning, I made it back to the cockpit. "Okay, Dawn, fill me in."

"We have three bogies, two off our port stern and one directly behind us. Joe, they have fired a laser blast."

"Forget it. Our shields will take care of that hit. Dawn, I want you to scramble all frequencies and block communications."

Just then, another laser round hit our port side.

"Sir, I did that when our radar picked them up, and I am assuming that's the reason for their agitation. I also evened out our defense shields."

"Good job, Dawn."

"You're right about the laser hit, Joe. They are just bouncing off. Now, they are forming a strategic battle formation, Joe."

"Okay, crew, it's about time we really found out what this bird can do."

I banked to starboard and cut the engines to one-third, and without warning, I banked hard to port and cut the engines to one-twenty-fifth, just as a torpedo sailed by our stern.

"Joe, they have launched another torpedo, and we are receiving continuous laser fire off our port side."

"I am going to full power. Dawn, I want a continuous status report on our altitude."

"Joe, that torpedo is close!" exclaimed Pam.

"It sure is, Joe! I can see it coming directly behind us, and, Joe, if I can see it it's way too close!" screamed Derek. "One thousand meters… Five hundred meters… Come on. Joe, do something!"

I headed straight down toward the earth at an angle of about 45 degrees.

"Five hundred meters, three hundred… Joe, you have to pull us out of this dive, or we will break up, Joe! One hundred meters!" screamed Dawn.

I rapidly pulled her nose up, hit the thrusters, and within seconds, we were climbing sharply to five thousand feet. Suddenly, an explosion followed.

"Chuck, she maneuvers really well, and the power is tremendous," I commented. "How's everyone's head and stomach?"

"Pam is a little queasy, but I am fine, Joe," Derek said in a slow, crackly voice.

"I am fine, too," Chuck said.

"Radar reports, Dawn."

"They are eight thousand feet directly behind us, all three—no wait, they split up."

"They are so predictable," I said calmly.

I headed to a higher altitude and did a 180-degree turn heading straight for the bogy which was originally on our stern. As I brought her to full power, I was in firing range, and as soon as I leveled out, fire is what I did. I fired one torpedo that hit dead ahead. It took out their defense shield. Soon after, I launched another torpedo, I followed with two rockets and ten laser blasts along the same track. The lasers hit first, then the rockets, further weakening the auxiliary defense shield and the following torpedo completed a direct hit destroying the ship. Soon after the explosion, we felt some laser blasts to our port deflector shields.

"Joe, they are both on our port side!"

I descended to earth at three-fourths speed. Then I flew through the mountain ranges for a while, trying to put distance between us and at the same time equalizing our defense shields. Then, I spotted a great opportunity to try out our blasters that Chuck recently applied to the top and bottom of the ship.

"Chuck, what is the width of that pass directly in front of us."

"The entrance is about forty-five meters wide and, Joe, the sides of that ravine is full of loose rock. In fact, any loud noise will bring down the walls which are about seventy-five meters high."

"Dawn, with the modifications, how wide is this ship? And, Chuck, find out where the rock is most likely to break up."

"Well, the pass is two thousand meters long, and the sides are really unstable around nine hundred meters inside the pass."

"Joe, the ship is twenty-five meters wide," Dawn reported.

"That gives me ten meters on each side. Chuck, is that forty-five meters the closest it gets along that range?"

"No, sir, it opens up to sixty meters then back to twenty-five meters at the point of the unstable rock."

"Derek, how you doing back there?"

"I have taken out the bow defense shields of the trailing bogies, but they are coming on strong and closing fast. They are now on auxillary power."

"Okay, Derek, hold on and cut the firepower. I'm going to try something."

"What?" Chuck asked.

Before I could answer, we were gaining altitude in preparation for a 180-degree turn.

At the end of the turn, which put us about three hundred meters from the pass, I directed a straight path, flying low, to the entrance of the canyon and increased the engine throttle to full power.

"Derek, are they still back there?"

"Yes, sir, right on our tail."

Within seconds, I had entered the pass so fast that the wings caught drafts from the base of the pass and started to sway up and down.

"Hold her steady, Joe," I said to myself.

As I steaded the wings and leveled her off, we approached the five-kilometer mark. "Derek, did they follow us?"

"Yes, sir, but the rear bogy must have skimmed the sides of the pass. He went down and exploded seconds after he entered."

"Good, two down and one to go."

"Dawn, how long to the unstable surface?"

"Two hundred meters." I cut speed to half at about one hundred meters from the unstable rock and quickly turn the ship vertically. At this time, the bogy had closed in considerably and started to fire continuously with laser blasts to our stern. Derek started to return fire.

"Joe, I can smell this bogy back here. Any closer and I'll have to get another place setting and invite him to dinner."

With that remark, I reached the loose rock and promptly engaged the top and and bottom blasters simultaneously. Within seconds, rocks flew in every direction and right into the path of the oncoming Guardian ship. I disengaged the blasters leveled her off and hit the turbo thrusters. We were out of the pass in three seconds.

"Joe! Joe! I am going to kill you, you son of a gun! That was just too close… way too close!"

"What's the matter, Derek? Did we get him?"

"What's the matter! How about you coming back here and cleaning up the mess I left in my pants! Yes, we got him. Rear radar clear."

We all laughed for a minute. I think mostly to relax and release all the stress that was built up during the maneuver.

"Now that was exciting!" said Chuck.

"That was terrific, Joe," Dawn said.

"Thanks, Dawn. Well, Chuck, I'm sure she passed the test now. Let's get her home, Dawn."

"There's one thing that's bothering me though. Dawn, did you pick up those ships on the radar or on the short distance scanner."

"I picked them up on radar, Joe."

"That doesn't seem right. The scanner should have picked them up sooner than the radar. The radar is for long range detection. The short distance scanner should have picked them up and warned us long before the radar reported them.

"Derek, when did you notice the enemy ships?" asked Joe.

"I didn't notice them until I put on my weapon's computer."

"My scanner screen has been clear. In fact, it was clear the whole time."

"Chuck, you'll have to check out the rear short distance scanner."

"Sir, I was in the process of checking them when you asked, and it appears that it has malfunctioned."

"Chuck, I'll tell you something now. I like the way you work. How would you like to accompany us on our journey to freedom? Do you think Eric and Catherine would mind?"

"Slightly sir, just slightly. The way they responded for this test run shows me the only way I could go would be to stow away. I'll get on the scanner as soon as we dock, and don't count me out yet, Joe!"

"Thanks, Chuck."

We reached the bay without any interruptions, and let me tell you that we were all happy to be back. I was glad that we had the encounter, now that it was over, because it really did put the ship to the ultimate test. Subsequently, I felt she was ready for our dangerous mission, and everyone was truly prepared to perform their duties.

CHAPTER 11

The Last Escape

I talked Chuck out of working on the scanner that evening. We all retired for about an hour and met in the study to discuss our run. Soon after, we sat down to a great meal. Derek, Chuck, and I were up early the next morning, once again working on the ship to repair the rear scanner and assessing the damage we took from our excursion. Chuck also fixed the leak we had found in the storage locker. Chuck, feeling responsible for the malfunctions, checked and double-checked the whole ship to make sure everything was operational. He was very thorough, and I was glad to see that he took the time to meticulously inspect the entire ship. Chuck stopped in to see us after his full day's work and apologized for the malfunction.

"Chuck, don't worry about it. We are all fine, and you have to expect some malfunctions on a new prototype. Forget it. Besides, we have everything fixed and operational now, and that's what a test run is for—to work out the rough spots. Believe me, I was relieved to know everything went so smooth."

"Yes, I know, Joe, but what if we never engaged the enemy and just came back with an A+ for the test run. If Dawn didn't notice those Guardian ships on the long range radar, they would have had a computer lock on our ship and that would have been it. I could have killed everyone."

"Well, Chuck, that didn't happen, and besides, if we were all killed, would you have really cared? I certainly wouldn't be in the position to care. Would you? In fact, I really wouldn't have cared at all."

We both looked at each other smiled, and within seconds, we were in a state of laughter. After further discussion, I finally convinced Chuck to move on with his work and forget the ordeal. He left shortly afterward, and it was clearly noticeable that he felt better than when he arrived at our living quarters. The time had flown by, and it was very late. I went into the kitchen and poured a glass of cold water. It tasted so good, and I stood there wondering why I never thought about how refreshing it could be. I thought that if we were killed I would never enjoy another glass of water. How simplistic, something taken for granted, that we hardly think about, being so important now.

I went into the bedroom to find Dawn on the bed, and the acoustical weather machine was set on a spring shower with birds chirping in the background. On occasion, you would hear raindrops hitting a window pane methodically setting a nice comforting sleep pattern. I glanced over to look at her and found her in an angelic like sleep. Her arms were tucked neatly under her pillow. Even though the sheet covered her, you could see her beautiful body. I stared at her for a moment then lightly kissed her on her forehead. She was so beautiful, and I was thankful to the Lord for bringing us together and providing us with the strength and love to undertake this dangerous mission. It felt good to know I couldn't lose. If we made it to *America*, we would live as a family, together forever. If we happened to get killed, we still would be with Him, who made and perfectly matched us together, for eternity. I slowly walked around the bed and laid down trying not to disturb her sleep, but she felt my gentle presence and lovingly those wonderful words flowed from her lips.

"I love you, Joe, so much, so very, very much."

I reached over to hold her close to me, kissing her gently on the cheek. "I love you too."

She smiled and said, "Joe, even if we don't make it to *America*, we still will be together, right?"

"We sure will, Dawn, so we can't lose. It's a win-win situation." She moved closer to me, and we embraced. "Dawn, I am going to give it everything I have. We are going to make it."

"I know you will, Joe. I believe in you."

As we kissed, her lips sent waves of contentment through my body, filling me with such a wonderful feeling of delight. It was a beautiful night, one that I would remember for the rest of our lives. Morning came too soon, though, and I woke up to the most appealing smell coming from the kitchen. I got up and entered the living area.

"Good morning, Dawn."

"Hey, Joe."

As I walked in the kitchen, she turned from the stove and held me close.

"That's really nice of you to fix me breakfast, but you really didn't have to go to all this trouble," I said.

"I know, Joe, but I wanted to. I love you very much."

"You are so affectionate, Dawn. I love you too. I just want you to know I'm going to get us to *America*."

"Thanks, Joe. I really do appreciate everything you are doing."

We both sat down and ate breakfast hardly saying a word to each other. Just as we were cleaning up the breakfast dishes, we heard a loud knock at the door that briefly startled us.

"That must be Derek. Well, got to run. I'll see you later, Dawn. I love you."

I went over and open the door and was surprised to find Eric standing there. "Joe, we have made contact with *America*! They are willing to accept you, but as I said before, you'll have to do it on your own."

"That's great news, Eric. So when do we make our move?"

"They said at their current speed, it will put them in position in about thirty six hours. You'll have a period of three hours to make your rendezvous."

"Three hours, Eric. That's not very much time especially if we run into trouble."

"It will have to be, Joe, they have a treaty with the Star Cities and believe me, it involves large distances between them, the Star Cities and us. Also there are time restraints between the Star Cities and how long they stay in the earth's orbit. You will have approximately three hours to make your escape."

"Theoretically, two hours and thirty minutes should do it," said Joe.

"Oh, and considering fuel consumption, you can't make to many detours."

"I know, and they won't help us, right, Eric?"

"Well, they aren't supposed to—the treaty, you know—but if you get close enough, I have a strong feeling you might get some help from my old friend. I just can't say how or when for sure. Oh and Joe, after you leave, there will be definitely no communication from us to you or *America*. We will give them departure codes and the only transmissions will be what we hear from your link with *America*. We will keep your secret as long as we have scrambling capabilities. Once again, your fuel consumption is going to be critical."

"Yes, I know, and there is no more room for spare fuel is there?"

"No, Joe."

"Do Derek and Pam know?"

"Yes, they are at the ship. They said to have you meet them there as soon as you can."

"Is Chuck at the ship?"

"Of course, I wouldn't be surprised if he offered to accompany you."

"What do you think about that, Eric? Chuck is brilliant, and I sure could use the extra help, but if you are against it, I'll demand that he stays here with you and Catherine. I'm sure he is needed just as much or more here and that will be my reason for him to stay."

"I love him very much, Joe, but he turned into a man a long time ago, and his decision will be accepted by his mother and me. You know what I would do if it were me twenty years ago."

"Yes, sir, I sure do, Eric."

I told Dawn the news, and we both went down to the ship along with Eric who seemed really concerned about what his son's decision would be. As we entered the storage bay, we found them all waiting at the entrance to the ship.

"Well, you have all been informed of our contact with *America*. Chuck, we will need to take out all the storage compartments and rig them for fuel. I am hoping to have fifty more gallons of fuel."

"What, Joe, fifty gallons! Fifty gallons! No way I can possibly give you thirty, maybe thirty-two, but that's pushing the weight dispersion factor, and I hate to mess with that equation. If you start messing with that, you compromise our speed and maneuverability."

"It's imperative to have more fuel, Chuck. Do what you can."

"Okay, I'll see what I can do. Oh and, Joe, I am coming along just for the ride. It's my privilege you know. I'm responsible for... It's my design."

"Oh, fine and, Derek, I want one more engine inspection especially on the ejector mechanism, reload the weaponry, and fill her up after Chuck finishes. I'm going to map out some navigational charts so we will be able to relay our route, in code, directly to *America*."

"Oh fine. Are you all right, Joe? Did you hear what I said?"

"Yes, Chuck, now get on that extra tank. Move it! We leave tomorrow evening and everything has to be ready."

"Yes, sir."

"Thank you, Joe," Eric whispered.

We all went about our business, and Dawn and I decided to go over our stragedy. "Dawn, how long will the *Starship America* be attainable once we enter space?"

"Once in space, there's a period of about ninety minutes. That gives us a small window for combat and some minor detours before we attempt to land, only if we are not shot up too much and our fuel isn't exhausted. After that time period, we won't have enough fuel to continue, and they will be changing directions, heading deeper into space. If everything goes on schedule, we should still have about forty five minutes in the area of the Starship before all this happens. If we haven't made our approach and successfully landed, we'll be captured or all die together. Let me just say I will not be captured and put on exhibition for treason."

"I agree, Dawn. We all make it together or we die together. There is no other way."

"By the way, Dawn, is that a practical or theoretically explanation?"

"I know theory and reality are eons apart," Dawn answered. "Theoretically, we will not have very much fuel left once we reach our destination, but practically speaking with a little conservation it can be done."

"Okay, then that does it, Dawn. Calculations are done now and it is time to relax. I know exactly where to go. Come on." I went down to the storage bay where I found Chuck vigilantly reorganizing the inside of the ship.

"Hey, Chuck, come down here for a couple minutes. I want to talk to you."

As he crawlded out of the nose of the ship and stood before us, I met him, leaving Dawn a few yards behind me.

"Chuck, I need to borrow a small shuttle, and can I get the coordinates to that place where we were shot down. I have got to see it one more time."

"Okay, Joe, but be careful. We can't make it without you and Dawn."

"Don't worry. From what I hear, your little shuttles are highly evasive and fast enough to out run anything a Guardian ship can throw at us."

"Well, it should. I designed it. There's one over in storage bay 57. In fact, it's mine so be careful... Hey! No scratches or anything, okay."

"Sure, Chuck, thanks. See you later."

With the coordinates neatly placed in my belt, we walked over to Chuck's ship. "Hey, Dawn, I know a place we can go for a short while. We both need to relax and our mission is just a short time away. Chuck gave us permission to use his ship. Come on, I know exactly where to go."

We entered the ship, did a quick preflight check, filled it up with fuel, and within minutes, we were slowly moving out toward the underwater entrance. As we hit open water, I set in the coordinates Chuck gave me to put us right back where we were shot down. It was somewhat different this time though, because we were able to land near the cave opening and engage a camouflage mode on the ship. Its concealment was so good that even from a few meters away its true identity was still brilliantly disguised. We walked over to the entrance of the cave, and as we entered, we heard a Guardian patrol pass by at high speed. We walked through to the entrance of the now called Garden Paradise—the name that I came up with on our way there. It was once again a breathtaking sight, so peaceful and relaxing. The stress we had experienced throughout these past few months just seemed to dissapate. Reality was shortly forgotten, and our minds seem to fuse together with the beauty, the solitude, and the freedom. We both lay down on the soft mat of grass nestled between several tall hardwoods. We closed our eyes and could wholeheartedly feel the true meaning of freedom.

"Joe."

"Yes, Dawn."

"The events of the last year or so seem so unbelieveable, almost surreal. It all happened so fast, sometimes I wonder why me? Why us? I never dreamed it would go this far, and I would be sitting in a place as beautiful as this with someone who makes me feel so special inside. And I have such a wonderful feeling for you, a feeling I never even knew existed before I met you. My life was totally uprooted, I produced a living being, and I nurtured feelings in me that I've never known. I decided to give up my strong beliefs and give my whole life to someone I never knew existed. And here I am in a beautiful paradise wondering what the future holds for us. It's kind of frightening. I'm starting to get really scared," said Dawn.

"I know, Dawn, especially when we don't know what the future holds for us. But I do know the time we spend together is such a precious time. I don't regret a decision I have made concerning us, and I feel committed to my feelings for you. The part that bothers me is that I have to fight and even kill my comrades. The guys I grew up with and fought beside, guys that I have great admiration for, and now they are my enemies. It's really strange how events happen… Our lives have changed remarkably."

"They sure have, Joe. They sure have changed."

We sat for a long while, reminiscing through our short time spent together, never doubting the decisions we have made. We talked of the future even though we weren't sure of what was in store for us. It was a time of laughter, concern, planning, and relaxing. The atmosphere was calm and still. The air seemed fresh and crisp. The thought of building our future right in the spot where we lay was so inviting, but it soon passed when we spoke of people like us living the way we want to live. The adventure of space, the conveniences of a new society, and the challenge of a new life together, all gave us the encouragement we needed to pursue our goal. We could very well be happy together here living with the earth society, but we really wanted to be with people of our own kind. We would always be considered out of place, even though we were normal humans. We would be living in a world where normal was abnormal. Sooner or later, their society might even reject us. Who can ever be sure? History tends to support the tragedies that befall the human race. There will always be prejudice, persecution, anger, and hate, no matter how hard a society tries to avoid it. Our goal was set, and variation was not an option. We have a mission, and Derek and Pam are depending on us to accomplish our goal for their freedom too.

"Well, Dawn, it's time to go back. It's getting late."

"Yes, I know. Just a couple more minutes Joe. It's so beautiful."

"Okay, but we need to return soon. Maybe, we will come back some day. Who knows what the future holds for us."

"I hope so. I just love this place."

After a short while, we returned to our ship. Several patrols flew by which delayed our departure. I wondered if detachments were increased for the next few days because *Station America* would be in the vicinity soon. I remember doubling patrols because of the presence of an alien ship in the area, but for the life of me, I can't remember the reason. The ships were so far out in space, there was no real threat. I accepted the assignment though and performed my duties as if it were a real threat. It just amazes me to think of everything that was kept from us. It instills tremendous disappointment in me and for a society that is so highly respected by their citizens.

We returned to the dock without incident and met Pam and Derek coming from the fighter. We exchanged a few words, parted, and returned to our quarters. We hoped to provide our bodies with the long-needed sleep and relaxation. We slept soundly that night and long into the morning, but the time sped by fast, and by noon, the four of us were ready to tackle any situation that should arise. Both Derek and I were very confident of our abilities and desires to move on to a successful mission. Pam and Dawn seemed somewhat nervous, but they each said they were ready and willing to accept the responsibility given them.

Once dinner was over, the time seemed to creep ever so slowly, trying our patience. We discussed the plan once more and felt fully assured of its success. We didn't see much of Chuck before or after the planning session, and he showed barely any emotion during the discussion. He did reassure us of his ability to stand his post and perform his duty. About two hours before our departure time, we all met at the ship for one final check. As we finished our examination, Eric and Catherine came down to see us off. As they walked down to the ship, I could see Eric carrying something at his side.

"Hello, Eric, Catherine, how are you today?"

"Fine, Joe, thank you," Catherine responded with energy in her voice. "Joe, we wish you all the luck in the world, and may God be with you."

"Thanks, Eric."

"We thought a crowd would be inappropriate at this time and felt a small send off would be more appealing, but I have something here that has become a custom among our people. When a vessel takes a long journey and the travelers might not be around for some time, we present the captain with a special gift—something to keep you comfortable on your journey. So as a representative of our people I give you these pilot's boots."

"Well, thank you very much, Eric. It's a wonderful gift."

"It is also customary for the representative to put the boots on our very good friend as a good luck charm. Sit down over here, Joe."

I walked over to an old wooden box we had used for the repairs on the ship. Eric took off my old boot and proceeded to put on the well-tailored, black-laced leather boot. As he put the left boot over my foot, he noticed a small mark on the lateral side of my leg, a few inches up from my ankle. He leaned over to look at it more closely.

"Joe, where did you get this mark?"

"Well, I am not sure. I have had it ever since I could remember. I thought my Protector put it there, but the reason was never given to me, and I guess I just never asked. Why?"

Eric looked closer and his eyes lit up like a full moon on a clear, still night. It was a symbol he knew quite well, but he quickly regained his composure and nonchalantly finished the ceremony.

"There we are, a perfect fit, good thing I got Dawn to measure your feet when you were asleep."

"So that's how you made the right fit. It looks to me like a conspiracy."

We all laughed briefly, and at that moment, the small hangar was filled with people. They were quiet and well organized, and the warmth and friendship was felt deep in our hearts. The five of us all talked briefly with Eric and Catherine, and then we exchanged hugs and proceeded to the ship. I turned and glanced at Eric, and I could see his eyes turn glassy and a small tear fell gently off his cheek. He moved closer, and we shook hands firmly just before I entered the ship.

"Thanks again, Eric. We will meet again someday, somewhere, I promise."

"I know we will, son. I know we will. I'm looking forward to it already."

We entered the ship and took our positions. Eric and Catherine moved to to the side of the storage bay, and we went through the final system check.

"Joe?"

"Yes, Dawn."

"Did you see Eric's face when he saw your mark? How strange, it's like he'd seen it before. I thought he was going to say something to you."

"Yes, I know. That was very strange."

"Joe, the coordinates are plotted in the navigational computer, sir."

"That's great, Chuck, and forget the sir, okay. It's Joe from now on. Now listen up. I don't want any hesitation when I give you a command. We are a team now, and if you please, I am in the driver's seat."

"Oh, come on, Joe. You have to be kidding," replied Derek. "Drivers seat?"

We all laughed for a second, realizing that it would probably be the last lighthearted moment we would have for a while. Soon, we were at the dock, and within seconds, we were in the water with quarter power, making our way to the entrance.

***

Back at the dock, Eric stood, as still as a statue, staring at our ship in a state of reminiscence.

"Eric, Eric," Catherine said. What's the matter? What was that symbol on Joe's ankle? It was pretty obvious that you recognized it by the way you reacted when you saw it. Have you seen it before?"

"I just couldn't tell the boy, Catherine. I just couldn't jeopardize his mission, his decision making, and fill his mind with even more questions."

"Tell him what, Eric?"

"That symbol was put there by my dearest and closest friend, and I just couldn't tell the boy for fear it would alter his judgment. I wanted to tell him so badly I could hardly stand it. His father put that symbol there just before they took the child back to serve on Altaur. His father after marooned and rescued by an American fighter made it to the Starship. He spent many years aboard the Starship moving rapidly up through the ranks and now he resides as commander-in-chief of *America*. That's Joe Cavelli's son!"

"Oh Eric, you should have told him. We have to contact the starship *America* now and transfer the message."

"No, Catherine. We can't. It might impair his father's ability to make the correct decisions also. No, we will not interfere, but we sure are going to track their progress. Yes, indeed, and Catherine, Chuck is going to be fine. He is in good hands. He made some hard decisions. This probably his hardest, but they have the best chance with him onboard. With the Lord's help, they will make it. Now, it is our duty to pray for them. We must leave it up to the Lord."

***

Inside the new and improved fighter, the crew prepares for the insuing battle. "Derek, be prepared for combat as soon as we break through the water. We have no idea when this escapade will start," I said

"Dawn, engage defense shield."

"All shields engaged, full power."

"We will proceed at half-power until we break the surface. Then I will jettison us up with full power. So be prepared. Is everyone ready?"

"Ready back here."

"Me too!" said Chuck.

"How about you, Dawn?"

"I'm ready Joe. Let's get on with it."

"Depth, Chuck?"

"Two hundred meters… one hundred meters… fifty meters."

"Engine 2 disengaged, engine 1 and 3 to full power."

Within seconds, we were out of the water and high into the atmosphere. "Course one-five-zero, altitude five thousand meters."

"Good, Chuck. Hold steady on the course. Dawn, check the scanners."

"Speed, Chuck?"

"Full speed."

"Clear, Joe, gravitational field weakening," said Dawn.

"Derek, radar readings below."

"All clear."

"Dawn, check outer space."

"Air Force ship, five kilometers port side, outer space, we've entered the cosmos. Air Force ship closing, asking for identification code."

"Send one, Dawn. Who knows maybe he'll—"

"He fired a torpedo, Joe. Two thousand meters."

"Derek, take out the torpedo."

"Pam, launch a rocket whenever you are within range."

"Two kilometers."

"Come on, Derek," I said silently to myself.

As soon as Pam launched a rocket, I heard an explosion reassuring me of the confidence I had in her ability.

"Dawn, scramble the communications."

"Done."

"Got 'em!"

"Good shot, Pam," shouted Dawn.

"Well done, team. Cutting speed to three-fourths."

"Joe, three bogies dead ahead, coming fast ten kilometers, and they are launching… Three torpedoes launched."

"Holy Moses. Come on, Dawn, you have to pick them up sooner."

"Yes, Joe, I'll try."

"Hold on. Chuck, how far is the earth's gravitational field?"

"Seven kilometers."

"Torpedoes, three kilometers."

"Derek, Dawn, man the radar and scanner. Navigation is secondary. Chuck, you monitor our course. I'll get us back on track as soon as I can."

"Full speed."

"Torpedoes two kilometers."

"Earth four kilometers."

"Here we go."

"Earth two kilometers. Joe, that's too fast. We'll bounce off that field like a tanker ball!" Chuck said as he shifted uneasily in his seat.

"A what?" exclaimed Derek.

"One kilometer. Pull up, Joe!" exclaimed Dawn.

"Here we go. Turbo thrusters. Hold on."

The thrusters hit so hard it forced everyone back hard into their seats, once again. "Great modification, Chuck. That extra power is awesome. Here we go back on our original course."

"Our bottom temperature is rising, Joe."

"Got it, Chuck. Dawn, give me a report on those torpedoes."

"Three hits, Joe... on the earth's gravitational field that is."

"Derek, How many bogies out there and where are they?"

"Three, two right on our tail, Joe, and coming fast."

"Derek, Pam, how about giving me a little breathing room up here. Where is that other bogie? Dawn, I need to know now!"

Just then, two rockets hit our starboard defense shield, rocking the ship.

"Thanks, just where I want that third one... Hold on."

I cut my speed to half and hit the lower blasters. I waited until they they both disappear off the scanner, which only took a few seconds, and then I hit the upper blasters, fired two torpedos and four rockets on a target lock. Within seconds, I banked hard to starbo chasing the third bogie.

"Joe, those two are gone. Where did they go," shrieked Dawn."
"They are destroyed, Dawn. I need to know what's ahead of us."

As I banked three degrees to starboard, I ejected a torpedo off the port side and discharged two rockets, directly in front of me, using the ship's target guidance system.

"Joe, they are all off the screen!" bellowed Derek.

"Do you have them, Dawn?"

"Well, I had them. He was directly in front of us for a second. Now he's gone. Is our radar screen clear now, Dawn?"

"Yes, Joe, all clear."

Just then, an explosion shook the ship, an aftershock confirming the kill. "Course 150, Chuck."

"Joe, you are not going to believe this, but there are five bogies directly ahead of us, seven scattered off our perimeter and three approaching our stern."

"They must be doubling patrols because *America* is in the vicinity."

"But why, Joe, do they know we didn't die in that river bed?" Chuck asked, worried.

"I don't know, but we're going to have to go back for a short time. Chuck, plot a new course to Balem. We are going to have to redirect our approach now. It's obvious they are still looking for us."

I made a 180-degree turn, rolled the ship to right ourselves, increased our speed, and headed back to earth.

"Are they still following us," Derek.

"Yes, sir, twenty kilometers, static *V* formation, speed constant. It looks like they'll follow us back and make their move once they have narrowed down our destination. They will be all over us once we reach Balem."

"Dawn, jam the frequencies. We have to keep the Star Cities in the dark."

"No transmissions have reached the Star Cities so far, but I am running out of time. They will be able to communicate in about forty-five seconds," Dawn replied.

I knew our Air Force was really good, I thought.

"That's fine, Dawn. They won't need to communicate. We will be right in their backyard by then," I replied.

"Joe, what are you going to do?" asked Dawn.

"I am going to try and lose them or destroy them in the city."

"Fly through it?"

"Well, sort of."

"That's suicide. It's not like the Seattle run!" exclaimed Dawn.

"Yes, it is for him, Dawn. He's been playing cat and mouse since he was just a youngster. Maybe, the territory is somewhat different, but the game remains the same, right, Joe?"

"You got it, Derek."

Within seconds, our coordinates were logged into the computer, and we were on our way at full speed. I was guessing that they wouldn't expect us to head back to Balem. Since their defenses wouldn't be expecting us, I figured we could run them into their own city, and once we lost them, we could plot a new course to break away from the city and intercept the *Station America*. Once we were in the city, radar tracking would be difficult for the ensuing Air Force ships. There's just too much interference.

The only way they can pursue us is by visual contact. So I flew right down the main concourse of the city and my hunch was right. There was absolutely no resistance coming from the city. By the time they figured it out, it was too late for them to react. The main defense system was useless because activation would jeopardize the pursuing ships and the citizens out in the street. It would also engage a nearly unstoppable chain of events that would involve numerous crossfires from their security guns. They could possibly destroy most of the city, if they activated it.

"Dawn, keep an eye out for Guardians approaching head on. Derek, keep me informed of the rear actions, and for heaven's sake, keep on firing. Chuck, do you have the new course?"

"Yes, Joe, and it's been logged into the navigation system."

"You'll have to pick up the course on the northwest side of Balem."

Before he could get the words out of my mouth, we were flying over two very tall buildings, then down a street and banking to port, once we cleared the power generators. I continued heading toward a narrow passage down by the main power plant. Our rear defense shields held fast, but if they weren't rested regularly, they would disintegrate.

"Joe," Derek said, "I got one, but we have two on our tail and two behind them."

I turned the ship on its side and maneuvered through a long alleyway disengaging our rear defense shield so it could replenish its power hoping they wouldn't follow us.

As we ascended to an altitude above the highest building, I reengaged our rear defense shield, turned 180 degrees, and reentered the alley.

"Derek, how many are still with us?"

"Two, they followed us right into the alley this time. They are about one thousand meters and closing."

I cut my speed and went vertical toward the end of the alley collectively engaging the top and bottom blasters. The power from the engines threw us off course slightly, but by that time, we had cleared the alley. Behind us were the remnants of two large buildings, and the two Guardian ships were caught up in the rubble. Moments later, we heard explosions and the ships failed to appear on our short distance scanner.

"Good show. Even I didn't know how those blasters would react on stable buildings, Joe, and I developed them."

"I wasn't quite sure either, Chuck, but I figured as long as we were close enough to exit the alley, if we were thrown off course I could compensate out in the open. Oh, I also dropped a neutron bomb out our rear bay."

"Joe! We have company again!" shouted Dawn. "And we're about to take some flak off the port side—"

Before she could finish her sentence, I had banked hard to starboard.

"The torpedo missed us, Joe, but we have one dead ahead."

As we approached the overhead walkway crossing the street, I ordered maximum speed and the Guardian pilot veered hard to port, with me right on his tail gaining fast. Three laser blasts, a hard bank to port, a firing lock, five more laser blasts, two rockets, and that ship was no longer a threat.

"There's just one left, approaching fast on starboard quarter."

"Chuck, set our course because as soon as we lose this one, we are out of here, forever."

"Yes, Joe. I'm on it… It will only take a second."

I banked hard to starboard and flew behind three tall buildings. Afterward, I flew down through a park and right past the Guardian command post.

"Dawn, where is the communication center?"

"It's in Sector 2, position 1R, which is the sector we just flew over, but I didn't see the communication center," replied Dawn.

"Where did they put it?"

"I remember now. It's about three kilometers west of here. There wasn't any room after they redesigned the emergency generators, so it was moved."

"Well, that's the only discrepancy we've found so far in the two cities. Derek, what about our shadows?

"Still with us, but they're not in range yet!"

"If we disrupt the communicator, they will have a hard time relaying our position. The only way they could find us is with the ship's scanner and the range of those communicators is minimal especially flying through the city. I think it's worth it for us to pay them a visit."

We turned west, and before long, we had a visual on the communication center.

"If we knock out the towers and the transmitter units, we can move through the city camouflaging our escape. There's the tower, and right below it are the transmitters."

"Where are they?" Dawn asked.

"They're under the main tower encased in tritactium 8577—that is, except for the bottom of the bunker its just plain tritiam. At least, ours are."

"That stuff is practically impregnable. How are you going to destroy them?" asked Dawn.

"The only way is to punch a hole with our lasers just in front of the transmitter. Make the hole deep enough to tunnel below the transmitter then on the second pass drop a neutron bomb down the hole under the floor of the bunker."

"Joe, we don't have time for two passes. This bogy is right. At that moment, we took heavy fire on our stern."

"Joe, our shields are weakening, and I can't get a sustained shot on him."

"The hole is nearly made, Derek. Hang in there."

As soon as the hole was deep enough in front of the tritactium 8577, I throttled to full power and started 360-degree turn aiming for a second pass. The Guardian ship banked to port and, once its crew saw our intentions, moved to intercept.

"Joe, he's right on our tail! A firing lock is imminent from our port bow."

As I leveled off, I hit my bottom thrusters and decreased my speed by half. Before long, the approaching ship, not having time to compensate, was under us and passed right by us. I unloaded a heat-seeking rocket, and as they gained altitude to reposition, the rocket hit him in the belly and destroyed his ship. I flew starboard and made another run for the transmitters. Within a short time, we had a firing lock, and I dropped a five-hundred-pound neutron bomb right down the hole. By the time the bomb exploded, we were five kilometers away. Our rear scanner verified destruction of the target, and by the time the scanner verified our kill, we were right back into the thick of things. Dawn reported five new targets, dead ahead and moving straight for us.

We just flew through the middle of all of them, and they didn't have time to engage. Within a millisecond, we were four kilometers behind them banking hard to port eluding the four rockets they had fired from ther rear portals.

"Well, you know, if this weren't for real, I would bet my life this was a movie. Where did they all come from? Son of a gun! Okay, Derek, get ready because the fox is about to become the hound. It's about time we changed to the aggressor. The communication channels are down, and except for visual, no one knows where we are or what course we are going to take."

I veered hard to port and was in hot pursuit of the first Guardian ship I saw. The others regrouped and were trailing a good ways behind us. I soon had a firing lock on the enemy and fired four laser shots and two rockets. He veered hard to port and kept on going, increasing speed and pulling away from us.

"They must have all their defense power on their rear shield. Easily done with no pursuit from any other direction. Well, we can take care of that!" He continued the same heading until he was on route back to the city.

"He's going—"

"Back toward the city."

"Yes, Joe, how did you know?" asked Dawn.

"I think he's trying to take me at my own game. Dawn, give me a firing lock on the first tall building in his path. Put the torpedos on computer guided navigation and as soon as you have the firing lock on the building and the ship is five hundred meters away fire a proton torpedo."

"Affirmative. Lock. Fired!"

Soon, there was a large explosion and then a second explosion. I flew hard to starboard after the torpedo was fired.

"Joe, what happened?" shouted Derek. "He's gone! What happened to him? There is so much debris down there, I can't pick him up on the scanner!"

"I just jumped the gun. Instead of firing at him, I hit the building in front of him and with just his rear shield up, and no time to compensate he ran through that rubble unprotected. Give me a fix on the other ships, Derek. We can't waste time rehashing."

"One dead ahead, two port and one starboard."

"Okay. Now hold on I am going to make a pretty stressful maneuver. Chuck, set our course to follow the ship on our starboard side, and let me know if the ship dead ahead comes up on our six."

"Course 130."

"Okay, where is he, Chuck?"

"He's right behind us, Joe."

"Okay, half speed. Now, as soon as he slows down, I want to know, Chuck."

"Not yet, three kilometers, two kilometers."

"Come on, slow down."

"One kilometer."

"Five hundred meters, okay, Joe. He slowed to half-speed."

"Here we go. Turbo thrusters are on, so hold on."

I flew wide open toward the starboard ship. At three hundred meters, I quickly pulled the ship straight up, my goal being twelve thousand meters and dropped two timed neutron bombs in the process. Our ship rose at an 85-degree angle, and it shook and vibrated so much I had to really hold her steady to make her climb straight up.

My stomach was lying on the floor, and my head throbbed incessantly. I was concerned about my crew.

"Everyone okay? Report."

There was a huge explosion, and the ship started to shake once again. I leveled her off at twenty-five thousand meters and slowed our speed to half, finally regaining control of the ship. "Dawn and Chuck are fine. How's everyone in the back?"

"I am really nauseous, Joe, and Pamela needed a barf bag, but we are all right now."

"Sorry, Pam. Derek, give me a report on the four ships."

"I see three bogies, one headed away from us, one trailing slowly, and well the other is just kind of sitting there. Their engines were damaged according to our scanner. The other ship was wiped out. In fact, there's a lot of debris down there."

"Joe, I have some bad news."

"What've you got, Chuck?"

"Well, that maneuver burned up several of the components of the device that keeps the engines running in sync."

"Oh, man, what kind of power can you give me?"

"Well, full power on the port engine, half out of the starboard, and a quarter power from the main."

"Joe, he is starting to come on strong, ten degrees on our port side."

"Okay, well, we can't outrun him so we are going to have to outsmart him"

"Chuck, give me half-power on both outer engines."

After a 180-degree turn, I took a nose dive and headed straight for that ship. "Dawn, fire lasers from both sides. I'm going to have to scare him."

"What, Joe?"

"Just do as I say, Dawn."

Dawn started firing even though we were slightly out of range. I headed my ship on a collision course straight for him.

"Derek, I think the appropriate word is *banzai*. Banzai!"

"You son of a gun! You are going to bluff him. I hope it works."

"Dawn, open a channel of communication with that ship."

"Okay, Joe. Whatever you say. It's open, Joe."

"Okay, Derek. In unison, banzai! Banzai!"

Both of us started screaming at the top of our lungs, and Dawn sent it throughout their ship.

"Joe, they are cutting speed!"

"They have changed course, Joe!"

"They're running away."

"I knew they thought I was crazy!"

"It worked! It worked, you madman. I love you! I love you, old dog you!" screamed Derek through the headphones.

"Okay, Dawn, how's it look out there?" I asked

"Except for that sitting duck, it's all clear," Dawn answered.

"Chuck, do you think we can find those parts on Balem? We have to repair the engines before we make our break for *America*."

"They are pretty standard parts, Joe. We should be able to find them pretty easy."

"Joe, if they have given up the pursuit, we can just set us a course for *America*, right?" exclaimed Chuck.

"Yes, that sounds good to me!" said Derek.

"I am up for it!" Pam said.

"That would be fine, except don't forget about the Air Force. If I'm not mistaken, they are out there somewhere ready to intercept us. All these ships were Altaur and Balem Guardian fighters, correct, Dawn?"

"Yes, Joe, except for the Air Force fighters that followed us in from space."

"We would never make it without making repairs, Chuck."

"I have some parts right here, but there are a couple more that I will need. I'm not a 100 percent sure they will be on Balem, but if they aren't, I can possibly try to rig up something from the tansports in the old storage bays."

"Okay, we go back to the old landing bays. Dawn, can you find us a shop that will carry the parts we need. Check their inventory on the Internet?"

"There's a machine supply shop close to bay 17. The parts are there."

"Okay, set a course through the city. No, wait, maybe we could sneak in from underneath the city under the cover of this moonless night. Our approach will be from the west. They will probably be pursuing us from a course based on where we were last sighted. We can plot a course to *America* later. Maybe, they will think we headed out into space. They sure wouldn't believe that we went back to Balem, now would they? And besides on the radar, we all look the same."

"That's right, Joe," remarked Chuck.

"We can just follow one of their ships in. We can use their normal landing approach pattern since I'm well aware of how that's done," said Joe. "Okay, let's go see the mechanic and maybe even fill her up!"

"Man, you are crazy," whispered Chuck.

We dove to just above the earth and approached Balem from the west. The cover of darkness gave us a great veil visually, and since our ship reflected the same image as their own ships on radar, we felt safe just moving in at one-fourth speed. A couple of ships passed us, and soon they were in front of us, but the black night covered our ship completely and made it impossible to identify us. It never seemed to cross their minds that we might come back to Balem. We landed within minutes, but we could only get to bay 27. That made our shop just a little farther away than planned. We pulled her back into the storage bay once again and locked her up tight.

"Chuck, you check out the shields and see if there is any more damage to the engines we don't know about, then give me a list of parts you are going to need. Dawn, you route us the easiest way to the shop. It doesn't necessarily have to be the quickest way. I'd rather sacrifice some time for fewer people. We want to get a minimum amount of exposure, and we are definitely willing to gamble some time for that. Also, find out the security system of that shop. That will be helpful. Pamela, you find out where we can replenish our weaponry and get us some more fuel. Derek, give me our course and the time we should intercept *America*, calculate our fuel consumption and see where we stand. I am going to shut my eyes for a brief moment and come down out of the sky. Derek, go get our hand weapons and pass them out."

Within five minutes, I received all the information I had asked for. The crew had been amazingly thorough. We gathered outside the ship.

"Joe, our fuel consumption will be 1,400 gals of Z-18603 or 1,200 gals of Z-18213. I am not sure which fuel is available on Balem."

"Dawn?"

"We have Z-18603."

"Good. How much do we have in our tanks, Chuck?"

"Our main engine has 460 gallons, our starboard engine 500 gallons and our port engine 500 gallons. That gives us 60 gallons extra. It takes 650 gallons to intercept the Starship—that is, if we plot a course from our position in a straight line directly to *America*. Of course, our fuel consumption will jump dramatically once we engage the enemy."

"Good work, Chuck. I hope we're not any longer than thirty minutes. Can you repair the ship in fifteen minutes if we get the parts."

"Joe, if you get the parts, I'll repair the ship in ten minutes. Just get me those parts, and we will be as good as new."

"Great."

"Pamela, what have you got for us?"

"I have some good news and some bad news, Joe. The closest amunition depot and fuel supply are directly above us. There's a storage arsenal directly above and fuel reserve above bay 26."

"It's a good thing Z-18603 is not combustible until TAC 300 is added to it. We'd be sitting under a bombshell."

"That's the bad news TAC 300 is found above bay 35."

"Yes, that's bad news. Well, let's forget the fuel. We won't have time. We will just have to get out of here and use the quickest path. Thanks, Pam."

"Okay, Dawn. Let's have it."

"Joe, there are three routes, two are pretty secluded, and one is right down main street. We are sure to raise an eyebrow taking that route. The shop is only four blocks away, and the security system is pretty primitive. It can be bypassed by attaching a Fuiller relay switch to the activator below the alarm sensor shorting out the track condensor. It's pretty simple."

"That's great, Dawn. Okay, here's the plan. Chuck, you'll wait here and prepare the ship for the new parts. Have you found any other damage?"

"No, Joe. Everything is functioning properly."

"Good. Dawn and Pam, you two will go get the parts. You'll be the least conspicuous since we are definitely the wrong gender. First, all of us will go upstairs and surprise the guards at the arsenal. Dawn and Pam, you'll change clothes with them and enter the back alleyway to the shop. Now remember, if you get in trouble go to the streets where there are a large number of women. You can easily get lost in the crowd. Derek and I will transport the weaponry down the elevators and replenish our stock. Dawn, how many guards are posted at the arsenal?"

"Usually four. Two at the door and one at the outside desk and sometimes one in the back of the armory. They are all heavily armed."

"Derek, we will go directly behind Dawn. Dawn will take the one out at the desk, and Derek and I will take the two at the door. Lasers on stun. We will tie them up in the back of the arsenal then retrieve our ammunition. Everyone ready?"

"Yes, Joe," echoed Pamela and Dawn in unison. "We're ready."

"What about the one in the back of the armory," said Derek.

"We will take care of her later, but remember, she is not always there."

We went up the steps to the upper level. Dawn opened the door and stepped out into the hallway, turned, and fired at the guard at the desk. Derek and I were directly behind her, and before the other two guards could aim their weapons, they were laid out on the floor. Pam and Dawn made a quick change, and within minutes, they were out the door and moving down the long corridor, which entered out into the city.

I assessed the unfolding game plan: the first part of our plan went very smooth, the guards were neutralized, and the women were on their way. We should have the ammunition loaded by the time they got back, and I hope it would only take Chuck ten minutes to

repair the ship, and prayfully, the women wouldn't run into any problems. "It's imperative that we don't get followed coming back," said
Dawn. "If we do, we'll have to lose them or redirect their pursuit."

"Yes, I know. Even if it means our capture."

"That's right, Pam. But let's not think about that. There's the
alley. Let's go and be quick about it."

The alley was very dark. There were Dumpsters lined up behind
several shops; otherwise, it was fairly clean. There was a small security
light above the entrance of each shop. The alley was desolate except
for three to four women gathering under a shop light at the far end
of the alley. It wasn't long before they soon disappeared into the street
beyond the entryway. Now it was clear, so we moved quickly but
discreetly though the cold, dark alley. Several times as we passed the
shop lights, I felt uneasy. If patrols blocked both entrances, we would
have no escape, and it would be shoot to kill. They would never take
us prisoner after destroying so many of their fighters. I didn't tell Pam
what I was thinking about, putting my laser hand gun on kill, feeling
what she didn't know wouldn't hurt her. It also might make her feel
uncomfortable. As we reached the end of the egress, the city started
to come to life. We waited there as citizens passed by, then when all
was relatively quiet we began to move closer to our objective, which
was now less than seventy-five meters away. Everyone was minding
their own business, and it looked very similar to any normal night.

We tried to look inconspicuous as we walked along the street
when two Guardian patrols came around the corner, lucky for us,
they were moving quickly and on the other side of the road. We
moved up the street, stopping every so often, to make it appear to
look like we were just window shopping. As we approached the
oncoming crossroads, a Guardian patrol hurrying along the sidewalk,
came toward us. They saluted and crossed the street before coming to
close to recognize us. Shortly afterward, we approached the machine
shop, but to our surprise, there was a lot of commotion outside the
front door. We ducked into a nearby alley.

"Dawn, what's going on? There must be twenty citizens out
there and half are Guardians."

"I don't know, but it's not good and look, Pam. They are checking everyone's papers. We will never make it past that checkpoint."

"Hey, look over next to the machine shop? They are hauling boxes of lasers and scoped sniper rifles from the commissary."

"That must have been a front for a weapons operation."

"I can't believe it. Out of all the shops in this city, a bust has to be going on right here. Can we go to another shop?"

"Afraid not, Pam. There's no time, but this just might be the diversion we need. Let me see… We can enter the drain in this alley and get across the street. There should be an air vent just above the security light over the door in the alley behind the store. I can put you on my shoulders and you can slip into the shop, get the parts, and we can leave the same way."

"What about alarms?"

"There shouldn't be one in the vent. At least that's what the computer said."

"Besides, with all that commotion out front, the alarms should be off inside the shop."

"Are you sure about that. It's going to be a real mess if those alarms aren't off."

"Sure enough. Let's go."

We entered the drain, and there was enough room for both of us to crawl, one behind the other, but if you were claustrophobic, you would have had a real problem. It was pitch-black except for a small light just ahead of us. We moved slowly along the drain pipe trying not to make any noise.

"Dawn, the smell is getting a lot worse, and what is that hissing sound."

"It's water, Pam, and where do you think we are in a candy shop?"

By the time we reached the main line, the smell was awful, but we quickly moved through the shallow water-filled drain and up to the other side of the tunnel. The main line was lighted, and what we saw was not very pretty. As we moved down the other drain, it once again got dark, but the smell was not as bad. That sure didn't make it any more pleasant.

"Why don't they deodorize that place? It's really a putrid."

"Well, Pam, they really don't expect anyone to go trouncing around through it now, do they?"

"I guess not."

We checked the alley to make sure it was clear. Then we made our move. "Now, Pam, unscrew that light bulb before you enter the vent, and put the cover back over the vent once you have entered, just in case someone passes by."

"Where will you be while I'm risking my life?"

"I'll be inside the drain. If something goes wrong and you have trouble when you reach the vent, I'll come out and help you get down. Now, one more time, do you know where to get the parts?"

"Yes, Dawn. Don't worry."

"How long will it take you?"

"Once I get in a matter of seconds."

"Well, don't dilly-dally around and get out fast," said Dawn." Okay let's go."

I lifted Pam up on her shoulders, and Pam proceeded to unscrew the bulb. Then, still standing on my shoulders, she popped the vent open, entered, and replaced the cover. I moved back inside the drain. Pam proceeded along the vent, which was slightly smaller than the drain but much more pleasant smelling. She went past one vent and soon came upon another.

As she peered through the vent opening, she could see patrollers hurrying about the street. She opened the vent and jumped to the floor. Suddenly, an alarm rang through the building. Pam ran right to the area where the parts were, gathered up more than what was needed, shoved them into a bag and ran for the vent. As she reached the counter, she saw a patroller open the door and shine the light over toward the counter. As she turned on the light, Pam rose up above the counter and fired. She made a direct hit, and because the laser was on stun-mode, it kicked the patroller two meters backward in the air and out through the door. The noise was overwhelming, and before anyone else entered, she shot out the overhead electrical box, shorting out the whole shop. Then, she jumped up, opened the vent, and crawled in. As she moved away, she heard more patrollers enter the shop firing their hand lasers. As she reached the outside vent, she heard many footsteps outside the shop's alley entrance. Then, there was a laser blast, and several guardians entered the building. Pam lowered herself along the outside wall, holding onto the inside latch of the open vent. Then with one hand, she replaced the vent and dropped to the alleyway. She ran over to the drain cover, opened it, threw the bag in, and lowered herself in while replacing the cover. The alley quickly filled with Guardians, and the noisy scene quickly mirrored the situation in front of the commissary. We moved toward the main pipeline once again.

"Did you get the parts?"

"Yes, Dawn, I sure did, but how was the alarm set off?"

"Most likely, it was a laser alarm set up by the patrol after the bust, about eighty to one hundred beams probably crosslinked the whole shop."

"What, Dawn, you knew all along?"

"Well, I wasn't sure. Sometimes, they don't set them up in adjacent shops, and I didn't want to scare you."

"Did you go right back into the drain after I entered the vent?"

"Well, yes, I had to. I didn't want to take a chance of someone entering the alley."

"You are right about that. Oh, that smell," Pam said.

"Well, get used to it because we are going to have to make it our escape route."

"Do we have to?" Pam pleaded.

"No, we can go up top smelling like the sewer, and once we pass one citizen she can announce where we are to the Guardian patrols. That is, if the patrols don't smell us first."

"Okay, I get it," replied Pam.

We moved down the main sewer line for about ten minutes, trying to visualize where we were up on the street and coordinating it to our position in the sewer. We did fine until we came to a large opening where the drain branched off into seven smaller lines.

"Now which one?" asked Pam.

"We must be close. These drains must branch off to the storage area and repair bays. Now we just have to find out which one to take," said Dawn.

"Maybe Derek and Joe can help us. Let's see if we can contact them."

"Joe, this is Dawn. Can you hear me? Joe, can you hear me? Come on, Joe, where are you? Over."

"You are coming in loud and clear, Dawn. Are you okay? We were worried."

"We ran into some trouble, and we need help."

"What's up?"

"We are in the sewer system, and we reached the main line that branches into the bays. At least, we think that's where we are. There are several branches. We need some help finding the right tunnel."

"Okay, hold on."

It seemed like we waited for eternity, but soon, Joe responded. "Joe, what's going on? Are you there?"

"Yes, Dawn, we have a plan, but we needed time to move our ship so we could reach the drain. Now listen up, I want you to knock out all of the lights."

"What?"

"The lights, then, look down each drain and come to the one that's lit at the other end. We are going to light up the tunnel for you with the ship lights."

"Sounds good."

They proceeded to shoot out every light in the sewer system that they could see. "Okay, all the lights are out. Turn on the light."

"Okay, they're on."

"Joe, we have a problem."

"What, Dawn?"

"There are three tunnels that are lit up. Do they all lead to you, or are they all separate?"

"Hold on. Derek will check the computer."

"Dawn, they all go to separate bays."

"Wait, Dawn," Pam said. "I hear something."

"Hold on, Joe,"

"Now what. I can't stand it when she puts me on hold. Come on, Dawn. Talk to me!"

"Joe, it was nothing. Now what?"

"Well, we have another plan, but you are going to have to move once we do this cause we are going to make somewhat of a commotion."

"Listen. Chuck has been working on the engines, and he has removed the nonfunctional parts. Once we get the parts, we can be out of there in ten minutes, so you will have to hurry."

"Dawn, someone's coming! Someone's coming!" cried Pam.

"Joe, whatever you have to do, you better do it fast 'cause we are going to have company soon."

"Okay, listen. We are going to start the engine over the hole. You find out which one is throwing heat like a furnace. Once you know, call us and we will shut her down."

"Start her up, Chuck," I said.

As he started the port engine and moved the ship over the hole, Pam fired a laser shot back up the tunnel. They both heard a splash, but knew that more would follow when the patroller was late to report. Pam moved in front of each branch and soon found one throwing out heat.

"That feels good, Dawn."

"That's the one, Pam, I can't wait to get out of this smelly drain pipe. Joe, we have it. Shut her down."

It took about thirty seconds, and we were taking the drain off the bay floor as the girls popped out, one at a time.

"Wow, you two smell awful!" Derek said pinching his nose.

With that remark, Pam threw the bag of parts to Derek, and they both started to move toward the entrance of the ship.

"Wait, not on my ship, you don't. Take them off, now!"

Soon, both were down to their underwear and began running toward the ship. Derek had already entered the ship to give the parts to Chuck. The women made me get to the opposite end of the ship which I reluctantly agreed to do. Dawn went back to replace the drain cover, and when she turned to go back to the ship, she met Joe coming around the wing. He had a smile from ear to ear. At that point, they both started running, slightly embarrassed, toward the entrance of the ship, trying to cover as much of themselves as they could.

Derek came walking down the ramp a couple minutes after they entered the ship.

"You caught them, didn't you?" Derek asked.

"Yes, sir, running up the ramp, and let me say that it was a real pretty sight. They are both so beautiful. Pam, she was kind of red in the face. Hey, how is Chuck doing on replacing those parts?"

"When I left him he was stuck between the xeron fuel tank and the main computer."

"I can hear Guardians in the tunnel, Derek."

"We can drop a grenade down there," said Derek.

"No, no, let's just put the wheel of the ship on the cover. That should hold them in, and it will be a while before the rest of the patrol gets here."

We proceeded to move the ship once again. Within minutes, we were all in the ship. The women were cleaned up, and Chuck just got done putting the finishing touches on the burned-out engine parts.

"Dawn, check the outside of the bay. Is everything still clear?"

"Yes, Joe, scanners are clear."

"Are we ready, crew?"

"All affirmative?"

"Chuck, can we get full power?"

"Sure can, Joe."

"Shields up, Dawn."

"Joe, we are getting some company now," replied Dawn.

"Shields are up, Joe."

"Here we go."

Dawn opened the bay doors, and we exited with the ship at three-fourths power.

The patrol ships were close but still approaching the bay. As we left, I hit the turbo boosters, and they followed in pursuit.

"How many, Derek?"

"Two right now, Joe, and it looks like they have fired up the tractor beam and are aiming it right at us."

"How do you know that, Derek?"

"Oh, just a new little invention that Chuck has come up with recently."

"Thanks, Chuck. When did you have time to do that?"

"Well, I nearly had it working before we left. I just needed a little more time, and this little excursion gave it to me."

"This is a good time to try it out. Engage the tractor beam disperser."

"Derek, when they attempt to achieve a lock on us, let me know and I'll give them some real flying."

Laser blasts hit our stern, and I could hear Pam return fire.

"Joe, that second patrol ship is moving to starboard, and the other one is coming fast. Joe, they are trying to lock in with the tractor beam."

Just as his words came out, I banked hard to port and increased power on the main engine to full throttle. The starboard ship followed increasing its laser blasts and firing a neutron torpedo, but the Balem pilot forgot to check her coordinates, and within seconds, she slowed down only to be trapped in her own tractor beam. That slowed her up enough to make her chase invalid, but we still had one ship on our tail and a torpedo locked in on our stern.

"Joe, the torpedo is closing fast, and so is that ship. Believe me, it won't take long for me to see the whites of her eyes and that 'got you' grin on her face."

I hit the upper blasters slowed to one half and watched the torpedo fly right by us, and then I fired a heat-seeking rocket along the path of the torpedo and banked hard to starboard. Soon, a loud explosion, and I knew my rocket hit its target. The Guardian patrol ship was now closing fast on our starboard side. I pulled our ship hard to port and hit full power leaving a timed neutron bomb behind. The ensuing ship was not fooled and banked hard to starboard to avoid the bomb. Before long, there was another explosion.

"Dawn, did we get her?"

"No, Joe, but the radar is clear, at least from the city."

"That worries me. She has to be somewhere out there."

"Where did she go? Check below us, Dawn. That's the only place she—"

"Wait, wait, there she is, and she is real close. She's coming up right under us, and she aiming right at our belly."

"She's firing, Joe. She's firing."

Shortly, we felt several laser blasts to the underside of the ship. We started to shake violently, and it took me several seconds to steady her.

"Chuck, set our coordinates for the *Station America*. Derek, I am going to do a 360, but I am going to dive to do it. Your best shot is going to have to be when you are on your head. You will be completely upside down when she passes by us."

"Joe, have you ever done this before?"

"Derek, just get her will you? You too, Pam, keep firing."

I cut the speed to half and took a nose-dive to a course that put us all at a 45-degree angle heading back toward the city and then a 360 and we were on our heads. Derek and Pam just kept firing, and as soon as we completed a full upside down maneuver, we all felt an explosion that rocked the fighter.

"All clear," Dawn said. "Joe, can you get us out of this position I'm nauseated."

"Hold on, Dawn. That's odd you usually don't get sick."

I turned the ship upright, and after my head stopped spinning, I banked hard to port and increased our speed to full power as we flew deep into the upper atmosphere.

"Chuck, are we on course?" I asked.

"Yes, Joe. We will make contact, physically that is, in one hour if we cut our speed by a quarter. That will give us more time to make our approach."

"Dawn, all clear?"

"Yes, Joe."

"Okay, Chuck, I am going to let you have it for a while. Keep us on course."

"Straight away, Joe."

"Now, Dawn, about this no-pursuit from Balem. No pursuit at all? Check the radio frequencies and scanners and see if a squadron has been launched from Altaur. Keep the scanners on, and open the main computer to check all communications. Someone will be after us. I just know it. Derek, you take care of our pursuers. Dawn, try to contact *Station America* and let them know we are coming. Chuck, cut speed to three quarters."

The ship was cruising nicely, and not an intruder was in sight according to our radar. If we didn't run into any meteor storms or any electrical disturbances, we would be right on schedule.

"Chuck, what is our ETA?"

"Approximately fifty seven minutes, Joe."

"How about scanner range and communications?"

"Well, we can't pick them up on our scanners, but they should have a good bearing on us. I hope they try to contact us before we get in firing range."

"They should, Chuck. Your dad was supposed to send a message to them as soon as we left earth."

"Derek, any activity behind us yet?"

"No, it's clear back here, Joe."

"Maybe, they gave up on us," Pamela wondered aloud. "Maybe, but not likely."

"Derek, check all quarters on the radar, and as soon as we are in range of the scanner, check the other side of *America*. I wouldn't be surprised if they tried to sneak up on us from the other side."

"Got it, Joe."

"Joe!" cried Dawn. "Joe, we have established contact with *America*!"

The whole ship grew silent, and then I could hear Derek and Pam joyfully acknowledging the communications.

"Joe, I can hardly believe it! I always knew our dream would come true, but the reality of hearing their voices really gives me hope. It's really going to happen I'm starting to get excited! I can't wait!"

"Well, we're not sitting inside having tea yet, but the communication is a great sign."

"Joe, I picked up a squadron, no two squadrons, one in sector 3, and the other in sector 5."

"How far, Derek?"

"They are both about one hundred kilometers from *America* and closing at half speed." "Half speed! They must have had a tanker out there. They will have plenty of fuel and time to waste it with a refueling tanker close by. Chuck, how far are we?"

"About 150 kilometers, and at three quarters speed, we'll be there at the same time."

"How about full speed?"

"With the fuel consumption as it stands, we wouldn't make it. We would end up twenty-five kilometers short with an empty tank."

"Man, too bad we couldn't refuel. That would have been great!"

"Joe, *America* is holding at frequency 9973.69977.3."

"Oh yes, *America*. Let me have an open line, and pipe it through the ship."

"Will do, Joe."

"This is the… the… freedom ship calling Space *Station America*. Do you read?"

"*Freedom* ship? I like that," said Pam. "I like it a lot," said Derek.

"This is *America*, *Freedom* ship. We have visual scanner tracking your ship and compute an arrival time of approximately fifty-five minutes thirty seconds, at present speed. We have been monitoring your activity and progress through long-range probes. You are an amazing group of people. We have been cheering you on ever since our transmission from Eric on the colony of Earth. We are looking forward to your arrival and will generously welcome you as our guests. If you increase your speed to maximum, you will embark long before our unwanted company, and it will also make your approach much easier."

"Affirmative, *America*, but we have a fuel problem. Three quarters speed will be all we can achieve if we want to make a house call."

"It looks like you'll be in the thick of things, then."

"Yes, sir, but where there is a will there is a way, and let me say that we have the will. We will do whatever it takes to achieve our goal of living free and having the liberty to choose our destiny."

"*Freedom* ship, you have already come farther than many others who have tried to accomplish this task. We welcome you with open arms, but as the treaty states, we cannot. I repeat cannot assist you. A war would be unavoidable if we assist you in any way."

"Affirmative, *America*. We are quite aware that your position is neutral. Please give us the coordinates of a landing bay equipped for heavy battle so we can adjust our approach."

"We have many battle equipped landing bays that can be jettisoned if major damage is encountered. We will relay these coordinates to your navigational computer.

"Is there any way we can receive these coordinates in code?" asked Joe. "Negative. Our codes are only known to colonies of the mother ship and the earth society."

"Yes, we are aware of that, but we have with us a member of the earth colony Chuck, President Eric's son, is aboard and has assured us of his ability to decode the message."

"Affirmative."

"Chuck, start working on that code as soon as possible."

"Right Joe, I'll have it decoded straight away."

"We have one more communication to relay to your crew. It will also be a coded message."

"Affirmative. It will be decoded. May I speak to the commander?"

"This is the commander speaking."

"Sir, my name is Joe Capuzzi, and, sir, could you give us some information on formations and numbers of Air Force ships we will be up against when we reach your starship?"

"You are a very efficient young pilot, and you seem to be very confident in your ability. You remind me of someone I knew many years ago. He was a great friend I miss him very much."

"Well, sir, I had to be efficient and confident, or we would never have made it this far."

"True son, true. Well, Captain Capuzzi, we can give you all the information you need without breaking our treaty with the Committee. From now on, all our transmissions will be sent in code so our communication will be private, and the Air Force cannot monitor the final approach to our landing bay.

"Yes, sir, and thanks, Commander."

"Chuck, will you receive all their transmissions."

"Yes, Joe, it's all taken care of."

"You adventurers have a ways to go so get some rest. You will need your strength and agility. We will monitor your progress and the progress of your enemies. We will keep you informed of any change in course, speed, or numbers. We will resume our coded transmission in ten minutes. Rest my friends, rest... Over."

"Joe?"

"Yes, Chuck."

"I'm pretty sure I can adapt our computer to decode the transmission and voice them over our communicators."

"Sounds great, Chuck. That would benefit all of us."

"Joe, those coordinates are coming through," said Chuck.

After the coordinates came through, a second coded message was received.

"There is one way we can assist your needs. If your ship enters the neutral zone, a zone close enough for the Starship to take on external damage from enemy attacks, we can protect our interests by assisting your vessel without violating our treaty. That distance is one thousand meters. Now, they can still fire upon both of us, and we can protect our interests but only within that distance from our ship. Our hands are not completely tied."

"That's good news!" I said. "Okay, everyone try to stretch, relax, and clear your minds. We will need all our strength and agility in the next hour."

"Dawn, you take first watch, keep an eye on fuel consumption and give me a report every ten minutes or so. We better put her on automatic cruise. You never know, we might be able to save some energy."

"Yes, Joe, I'll put her on cruise control, directly."

"I've got to close my eyes for a while. They are really burning."

"Rest, Joe. I'll take it for now."

"Thanks, Dawn. I'll be able to think much clearer once I get some rest."

CHAPTER 12

REM

The ship became quiet soon after the last transmitted message. The stillness around us was unnerving, but I knew everyone was trying to rest and prepare for the reality that was forthcoming. My mind was exhausted, and my body paid the price. Every muscle hurt, and my eyes were on fire. I closed them momentarily and put on some rare classical music I always carried with me. Beethoven, Mozart, it was so relaxing. It was a great feeling to know I could close my eyes and not worry about who's on my six, coordinates, we are outnumbered, bogies, torpedoes, the responsibility of four passengers lives. As I closed my eyes, I could hear the navigational computer clicking in our updated coordinates. The engines hummed ever so softly. With the lights dimmed and the stars outside glimmering through the narrow windshield the ship became so peaceful, so calm, so relaxing. Soon, I entered a deep sleep, a dream state…

"We have a long way to go, Joe."

"Yes, Dawn, I want you to know that no matter what happens I love you, and nothing will ever change that feeling."

"I love you too, Joe, but what if only one of us makes it to *America*—that is, alive. One… alive—"

"Derek! Pull the fire alarm. It's our only chance. It will be a great diversion. Look! Look at that ship. It outmaneuvers our fighter like he's just playing with him. What finesse! I'd sure like to fly one of those birds. Gee, this line is so long… It's a boy!"

"Joe, it's a boy."

"Dawn, this is like paradise."

"Derek, they are in the detention area."

"Chuck, what's our course? How far is *America*?"

"Dawn, what's our arrival time?"

"Nearly one hour."

"Derek, any pursuit off our stem?"

"Yes, sir, two interceptor ships, and they are closing fast."

"Dawn, speed and distance."

"Seventy-five kilometers and full power, four minutes, and they will be within range."

"Chuck, can we get more power out of these engines?"

"I can give you light speed, but it will drain our fuel supply. Other than that, we are at top speed."

"Light speed. We would have passed *America* yesterday."

"Pam, check our fuel reserves."

"They are in range, Joe."

"Dawn, I want the computer to monitor all movements of the interceptor ships… changes in speed, course, and direction."

"Four hundred kilometers, Joe."

"Now, one to starboard and two on our port side."

"Chuck, what is our actual speed?"

"Fourteen hundred kilometers per hour, sir, and that is maximum for this ship. I can try to get more, but it makes this aircraft very inefficient, fuel consumption triples, we will lose maneuverability, and she shakes like crazy making it hard to control."

"Range of that Air Force fighter, Derek."

"Three hundred kilometers and closing."

"Joe, they launched a torpedo."

"Okay, Chuck, give me full power on the engines. That's way too far to launch?"

"Joe, we'll run out of fuel. We'll never make it."

"We can't go any faster without eating up our reserve."

"Come on, Chuck, more speed… Just give me more speed."

"Yes, sir. Whatever you say, sir."

"Dawn, see if you can contact the *Station America*."

"*America*, transmit… Transmit. This is *Freedom* ship calling *Station America*. Come in."

"*Freedom* ship, this is *America*. Can we assist you?"

"Sir, this is the captain of *Freedom* ship. We need to get an idea of what we are up against, once we enter your neutral zone. Our scanners aren't strong enough to position the enemy."

"Sir, we are surrounded there must be one thousand Guardian ships around our perimeter. It is impossible for you to land… I repeat, impossible."

"Derek, both Altaur and Balem don't have one thousand fighters all together."

"Who's protecting the cities? This doesn't make sense! Air Force?"

"*America*, can you repeat your message. How many fighters?"

"Enter the forward bays. They are the only ones operational."

"What? I asked for fighter information!" Chuck lock in the coordinates once they are decoded."

"Sir, everyone heard the transmission."

I began to toss and turn, and later, Dawn told me she wanted to wake me up, but she knew how badly I needed the rest.

"*America*, can you assist us in any way?"

"Negative. If we assist you, we will violate our treaty with the Star Cities. It will be the excuse they need to start a full-scale war. We can release ships to monitor your progress. That's all. *Freedom* ship over and out."

"That's just great, Derek. Did you hear that garbage?"

"Sounds like we will be pretty much on our own, Captain."

"You can say that again. Well, crew, let's get prepared."

"Dawn, give me the position of the fighter ships on our stern."

"Holding steady, sir, but I had to increase our speed somewhat to stay out of torpedo range. Are they Guardian ships. No, they must be Air Force fighters."

"Chuck, what's our fuel status?"

"Running at this speed will give us about fifty-five minutes for combat once we reach *America*."

"That should be long enough because if we can't land within fifty-five minutes we probably won't survive anyway."

"Wait, that doesn't sound right. Fifty-five, that's too long. I know we don't have enough fuel for that amount of time. Chuck!"

"Joe, *America* is on our scanner now," said Dawn.

"Derek, how's our stern?"

"Just those interceptor ships on our stern. All else is clear, Joe."

"Let's have a visual on *America*, Dawn. Interceptor ships. That can't be. Their range is limited to the Star City area. Could it be Air Force?"

As *America* appeared, the ship fell silent. It's size was enormous and you probably could fit two Star Cities inside her round earth shape appearance. It was covered with different colored lights, and defense weapons could be seen scattered all over the sphere.

There were also large areas of softly lit, well-defined, armored mounted bulkheads. They designated the primary defense modules for the *Station America*. The landing bays were stacked one on top of the another corresponding, relatively speaking, to the earth's equator. There were a series of lights on the top and bottom of the landing bays. As we approached, all the bays became dark except for the one our coordinates were set on. The overall ship appeared just as Eric had described it to us… very impregnable… extremely technological."

"Joe, we have two fighters coming in at two o'clock."

"Hold on. Here we go!"

I banked hard to starboard, hit my upper blasters, and dropped fifteen hundred meters. I heard laser blasts ring past our ship's bow.

"Dawn, give me the maximum speed we can enter the bays and at what distance we have to stop."

"*America*, this is *Freedom* ship. Give us the maximum speed we can attain for our approach and the distance we have to land once inside the landing bay."

"*Freedom* ship, you can approach at quarter speed you'll have fifty meters."

"That's a really short landing. Is that all the room we have to land?"

"Do you have nets? I repeat, are nets available?"

"Affirmative."

"Bogy ten, three, four o'clock and, directly astern," cried Pam.

"Full power, Chuck."

"Yes, sir."

"Joe, I am going to need some help back here," exclaimed Derek. "They are tearing up this ship and it won't be long until—"

"There's just too many, Joe! Too many."

"Joe!" Dawn cried. "Two torpedoes dead a-stern!"

"Hold on! Here we go!"

I cut the power, put the ship in neutral, hit my upper blasters, and as I regained power, banked to port. The torpedoes passed us, along with the two fighters from our stern, but the drop in altitude put us closer to the two bogies from four o'clock. As I banked to port, I shot a rocket and dropped a timed neutron bomb, and within seconds, the explosion detonated. One Air Force ship was destroyed, and one was disabled, abandoning his pursuit."

"Dawn, where are they?"

"They are approaching our stern, Joe."

"Chuck, all deflector shields on our stern now!"

"Affirmative, Joe!"

"Dawn, keep me informed."

"Two intercepting dead ahead, two lagging behind our current pursuers, and three approaching at ten o'clock."

"Chuck, full power! I see *America.*"

"Full power, Joe!"

America came up fast in our viewer, and soon we were flying right under it and coming up the backside, trying to lose our attackers. As we cleared the topside, I headed back toward our original position flying upside down and running directly into the three ten o'clock bogies.

"Report on our defense shields."

"Yes, sir, Joe, they are weak. We are taking a real beating on our stern."

With three laser blasts, a dropped neutron bomb, and a 180-degree spin, the two Air Force ships were destroyed, and we were upside down headed into space. I banked hard to port, cut power to half and entered an approach toward the landing bay.

"Chuck, cut our speed to half. If we can take the abuse for ten kilometers or so, we can cut our speed to one-fourth and approach the bay. With a little luck, we might make it on our first pass."

"Joe, we are really getting hammered back here. Our stern defense shields are starting to diminish fast."

"Dawn, divert some of our shield power from the bow to reinforce the rear shields and pray they leave our bow alone"

"Yes, sir."

"Joe, there's the bay!"

"I can't cut our speed. The gunfire is too heavy. Prepare to abort."

"Abort, *Freedom* ship. This is *America*. Your approach is too fast."

I banked the ship hard to starboard, flew extremely close to the *Station America*, in fact, close enough for our fighter to knock down probe sensors and waste disposal ducts. We flew alongside *America* for about ten kilometers, flying close enough to confide in her protection. We nevertheless took significant laser blasts, and as soon as we cleared *America*, there was a torpedo blast that shook our ship side to side almost starting an uncontrollable spin.

"Joe! Joe, what hit us?"

"Chuck, damage report."

"Everyone's okay, but our port shield has been eliminated, and I can't readjust our remaining deflector shield. It was a direct hit. Our main computer has malfunctioned and our radar screen is breaking up!"

"He must have been hiding behind *America*, just waiting for us."

"Joe, he never did appear on our battle scanner."

"Chuck, how are the engines? Are the rear scanners working?"

"They're fine, Joe, so is the radar, but fuel is getting to be a problem."

"Joe, three bogies at ten o'clock off our stern."

"Get them, Derek. I am going to make another pass at the landing bay."

Derek fired brilliantly and destroyed two oncoming ships before they could release a torpedo, but the third was a little too much for him. He set a timed neutron bomb, but not before a constant high-powered laser blast that broke the shield and hit Derek's cockpit directly. There was a loud noise, and Derek was thrown up against the back wall of the cockpit. He then fell to the floor just two feet behind the cockpit. He landed face down and blacked out from the hit.

"Derek! Derek!"

There was a loud noise, remnants of the timed neutron bomb.

As Chuck tried to assess the damage, with our defense shield depleted I veered to starboard redistributing our defense shield for two more attackers and cut our speed to one-fourth for the final approach.

"Chuck, how's Derek? Report! Report!"

"He's dead, Joe! He's dead!"

"Dead, he can't be… We have been together too long!"

My heart was broken. I felt empty inside… alone… despondent. It was like a part of me was gone. I couldn't think straight. Then, three laser blasts off our starboard side.

"Joe! Joe!" Dawn cried. "Our starboard shield is gone! A direct hit, and we are history, Joe."

There was another laser blast off our bow.

"Position, Dawn, position."

"Three clicks to reach the landing bay."

Laser blasts kept pounding away at us. My life just seemed to pass before me.

When I first met Derek and became such good friends… our reprogramming antics… fire alarm… Parrot… Dawn and a son… emotions… beating the simulator… Dawn in the cylinder… Tera… freedom and Star Cities… history… escape from Altaur… Balem… Gamnon… Eric and his family… the ship… love… Jesus… our right to choose… the paradise…

Derek's dead.

"Joe, we can't make it. It's still two kilometers away!"

But I lost focus. Our desire and ambition to reach *America*. Derek's is no longer with us. How worthless this whole adventure was now.

The empty feeling I felt in the pit of my stomach. Why did he have to die? The anger for our enemy… for Derek. Why did he have to die? Why?

"Joe, we're getting close."

The ship started to shake and vibrate nearly out of control. "The landing bay doors are opening."

Then, there was a blast to our stern.

"I can't hold her. She's veering off to port!"

"Come on! Hold on! Hold on!"

"Power, Chuck. I'm losing power! Chuck!"

Then there were multiple laser blasts.

"Chuck!"

"Fuel, Joe! We are out of fuel!"

"No! No! We are too close! Please, dear Lord, please!"

CHAPTER 13

The Battle

"Joe! Joe!" Dawn screamed. "Wake up! Wake up!"

Dawn unbuckled her safety straps and jumped out of the cockpit to move closer to Joe. Shaking him, she tried to arouse him. Joe startled out of his deep sleep with eyes as wide as quarter chips and his heart racing as if he was in a firefight. He started grabbing at Dawn with uncoordinated movements.

"Fuel… Fuel… Port side. What's the fuel status? Hold on, Derek."

"Joe!" cried Dawn. "Wake up, Joe!"

"Oh wow, what a dream," replied Joe.

"Are you awake?" exclaimed Dawn.

"Yes, well, now I am, yes, I'm okay."

"I could hardly wake you," she said.

"I had a bad dream, a really bad dream."

"Tell me, Joe. Tell me about it."

"*Freedom* ship to *America*, come in."

"Later, Dawn, get the Starship. I need to talk to them."

"Sure, Joe."

"Chuck, how does it look?"

"We still have some trailers, and now we show some activity around the Starship. I can't tell how many as of yet."

"Keep me posted, Chuck."

"*America*, status of activity on your port bow."

"We recognize seven vessels. They entered our airspace quickly so there must be a cruiser close by. They sure are covering all their bases. It looks like you'll have a heck of a welcoming party. They should be visible on your scanner as they position themselves under the Starship."

"We are picking up their activity and are preparing for our forthcoming battle. Keep us informed of any new developments, over."

"Okay, let's make sure everything works. Derek and Pam, check your weapons. Dawn, check the external doors on our neutron bombs and torpedoes along with our total weapons system. Chuck, check the circuitry on our engines. Let's make sure the coordinates for the bay are in line with *America*'s. Check out our blasters and make sure the engine detachers are operational."

"Lasers functional, Derek?"

"Check. Mine are working properly."

"Pam?"

"Armed and ready."

"Chuck? Dawn?"

"Okay, Joe, okay."

"Here's how we stand, seven vessels are in pursuit from our stern, seven vessels at our bow and—"

"Joe, we've got three on our port side and two from our starboard side... Well, a couple here and there actually the odds are around twenty to one, and as it stands right now, I don't think many more will change the odds. Actually about pretty even wouldn't you say, Derek?"

"Sounds about right to me."

"Joe, look! Look at the scanner. I have never seen a cruiser like this one. It's moving slow at about thirty kilometers from the starship. Look at it! It's huge!"

"Chuck, Derek, Pam turn on your viewers. Can you identify that ship?"

"No, sir, not me. No, Joe, I've never seen one like that."

"Computer, scan and analyze."

"The Star City ship is the new cruiser. Six basic turbo charged engines bilaterally, cruising speed of this engine system is five thousand kilometers in forty-five minutes, and it is heavily armed with defense batteries."

"That's pretty slow, Dawn. It must be the Corsair I read about on Gamnon, but I thought it was just in a development stage."

"Triptilion exterior. Very durable... defense armament is 7,733 laser guns, 5077 torpedo bays, strength of shields 4-3771 aconites... defense shield activated. Pretty strong shields with a great computerized defense system. Give me some defense options, Chuck, and how many fighters can it deploy."

A calm silence filled the communicator.

"Joe, it can deploy four hundred ships in about an hour, so they will probably throw fifty at us at a time, or it would get pretty crowded out there. I'll check for information with *America*... *America*, this is *Freedom* ship, come in. Acknowledge. Are you there?"

"Reading you loud and clear. We have been monitoring your conversation. Will have all available data on that cruiser shortly."

"It has a pretty strong tractor beam, Joe. If they catch us in it, the disperser won't work. That will be real bad news."

"Derek, what is going on back there. Give me some good news."

"Rear forces still at seventy kilometers and holding steady. They are just waiting to make their move, Joe."

"Dawn, what's ahead?"

"Same number starting to close toward us at seventy-seven kilometers. *America* is twenty kilometers directly behind them."

"Chuck, let's take her slightly off course and see what they do. Change course to 175 degrees 6W-32."

"You got it, Joe. Course changed to 175 6 West-32."

Hopefully, this should give me an idea of their attack plan. If they changed course with us, they would hit us as they stand. If they scatter, we would get it from all angles. I preferred they scatter because once we broke their line, there would be crossfires and it would be hard to recover. We would only have to deal with a few behind us, but if they changed course, that means they'll send everything they have right at us and evasive maneuverability would be compromised. I predicted their course to be the latter and about five minutes later…

"They are changing course and are steadfast in their formation," Dawn said.

I know these guys. I've worked with them for years, I thought.

"That's just what I expected. How predictable they are. Chuck, get us back on course. They'll try to hit us head on and hard with everything they have so lets get ready for some evasive action."

***

Meanwhile on *America*.

"Commander, the *Freedom* ship has changed course to 175 degrees 6W-32. Shall I send a transmission?"

"No, Lieutenant. Let's see what he's going to do. If he's smart he'll learn their attack plan from this maneuver. If they change course and maintain formation, they will probably try to hit them head on. He's showing some great tactics. I remembered using that same maneuver over fifteen years ago, and I'd use it again if I were in his position. Good move, young fellow. Now read their strategy and get back on course. I'll bet he plays a mean game of chess."

"Back on course, sir."

"What time is it, Lieutenant?"

"Nineteen hundred hours, sir."

"Send my supper to the bridge Lieutenant. Also bring me some of my usual hot blend with a touch of almond, please. It looks like we will be tied up here for a while and transmit the coordinates of the landing bay, Liuetenant Jacob."

"Yes, sir. Right away, sir."

***

"*Freedom* ship, *Freedom* ship, come in!"

"Joe, we are receiving a transmission from *America*. Their information on the new cruiser is somewhat limited so they are going to send a transmission to earth and try to find out more about this

Cruiser. We should hear from them shortly and the coordinates for the landing bay are coming through."

"Great, decode and log them into the computer, Chuck."

"Yes, Joe, I'm on it. Transmission received, Joe. The landing bay is armed with batteries on either side of the entrance. The forward bays are tied up with fighters and construction, but there will be seven bays available. They will be sending out a signal frequency on 46812H. Our overhead and forward computer scanners will be able to read their position and relay it to us when we are in range. The scanners and overheads have been programmed and, Joe, we are ready to embark. All systems are working properly and shields are at 100 percent."

"Good work, Chuck. Report on the aggressors, Derek?"

"Joe, seven ships are dead astern and making their move and, Joe, they are closing fast. We have about a thirty-five seconds."

"Round number one. Let's get it done."

Joe veered to port, set the engines on maximum speed, and hit the upper blasters sending the ship fifteen hundred feet down toward the bottom of the Starship. As our fighter approached *Station America* we cut our speed to three-fourths maximum speed and flew close by it. We ascended along the Starship and were right at the landing bays before we could cut speed enough to land.

"There they are!" shouted Dawn.

"I know, but our approach is too fast, and I can't cut the speed enough to make a safe landing."

We flew right by narrowly missing the exhaust vents, turned to port, and soon we were out into space. It wasn't long before several laser blasts struck our defense shields and not just from one area, we took hits on every side. We flew back under *America* trying to stay as close to her as possible and since the Air Force Cruiser would not provoke a war we were almost assured there would be no neutron bombs or torpedoes coming at us. We knew we would still be taking on massive laser blasts but personally I felt staying close was in our best interest. I was confident that our shields would hold up to multiple laser infractions without taking on severe damage.

"Derek, how are the rear shields holding up? You seem to be taking the brunt of our hits."

"They are on us like fleas on a dog but our shield is holding fine. I scored on two ships and damaged a third. I've been able to punch a hole in their shields and hit them with torpedoes. The laser is really not that crippling. I can't seem to concentrate my beam to be real effective," replied Derek."

The Starship was enormous compared to our fighter and their gunnery emplacements were every forty to fifty meters. There must have been two to three hundred thousand of them. With their help, we could easily land, but it didn't look like we were going to get any, at least not very soon. We flew along diving into large passageways constructed by the uneven contour of the ship. If you were to describe the outside appearance, it would look like a city street with many different shaped buildings throughout. They would protrude all along the surface in many sizes and shapes producing a mazelike appearance. As scanners detailed the surface of the ship, you could see distinct shapes and sizes. Windows and antennas were present. It was pretty clear that these quarters were added on to the ship. Just as we learned on earth, it was very evident that the main ship used to be exceedingly smaller and that these quarters were added on as the community grew. As more laser blasts bounced off our shield we noticed *Station America* starting to activate their defense shield and prepare for battle. There were huge metal doors closing everywhere there were windows. Even though the deflected laser shots were basically harmless, they activated their defense system and soon the ship glowed of a deflector shield, which gave the appearance of a smooth gray ball surrounding the ship. Just amid ship were thousands of lights illuminating every landing bay on the ship. The bays extended in a complete circle around the ship taking up a vast majority of its midsection. There were three rows of landing bays. Now it was easy to see where they housed seven thousand ships. It appeared omnipotent. Soon we approached the enormous engines and as our temperature rose exponentially. We banked hard to port trying to stay clear of the intense heat coming from the engine exhaust.

"Derek, how many on our tail?"

"Three, and they don't seem to be very aggressive."

"Where are the rest, Dawn? Something is up and I think that cruiser is about to make its play."

"Joe, our scanners pick up the rest of their force dead ahead five thousand meters. We banked hard to starboard and set a course for a convenient landing bay. The three Air Force fighters were now in hot pursuit."

"Joe, they just scattered four to port, three to starboard, and five below rising to meet us. Five torpedoes launched from the ships below, but they are aimed dead ahead of us."

"What's going on, Dawn?"

We veered to port and heard five distinct explosions. The ship shook violently for ten seconds then we headed back on course for the landing bay.

"Cut speed, Chuck, to one-half. We are going to try to land this vessel.

"*America*, three thousand meters and closing."

"Joe, we have four more torpedoes launched and once again aimed ahead of us."

"Well, they can't do that all day. The next time, I'll just blow the torpedos up."

I banked to starboard avoiding a confrontation with the torpedoes, and its debris as well as the three Air Force ships that fired them.

"I got another one, Joe," Derek bellowed through the communicator.

"There is only one on our stern!" shouted Pamela.

But before Pamela finished her last word, that large cruiser lay dead ahead about twenty-five kilometers.

"Listen up! That cruiser is coming up fast! It's time to face reality, Dawn. I don't know what they have up their sleeve, and I am not going to waste time finding out. Dawn, lock three torpedoes on that cruiser."

"Three locked on the cruiser, Joe!"

"Fire, Dawn, all three torpedoes."

"Right away, Joe… Joe, they won't engage."

"It's got to be the tractor beam. We need to get out of here and in a hurry."

I pulled back hard on the steering mechanism, and soon we were facing away from the cruiser but heading no where.

"Chuck, what's going on? Dawn, give me the distance to the cruiser."

"Joe, it's stronger than I thought. We are at three-fourths power on all three engines, and we are losing distance. They're pulling us in."

"Four thousand meters, Joe. We are losing this battle and soon."

"That's what I thought. Chuck, give me full power on all engines."

"You got it, Joe, but in fifteen seconds, we will begin to move backward again. It's just too strong. I'm overriding the computer and still we don't have enough power."

"Distance to that cruiser," Dawn.

"Thirty-seven hundred meters and starting to close in pretty fast."

"Joe, three bogies at ten o'clock and closing for the kill. They are just going to hold us here until the fighters arrive. We will be a sitting duck and they will just destroy us. They will be in rocket range in fifteen seconds."

"Joe, we'll burn up the engines if we keep this up. We're not going anywhere fast," exclaimed Chuck.

"We are losing distance more rapidly now, Joe," screamed Dawn.

"Okay if that's the way they want to play, we'll just have to play it their way. Here we go down and dirty. Let's see how you like this one!"

"What are you going to do?" asked Dawn, who was now very excited.

"Chuck, log in the coordinates for the source of that tractor beam. Give me half power, Chuck, and hold those engines steady. I'll need full power soon. Dawn, lock torpedos 8, 9, and 10 on those coordinates."

As the orders rang through the ship, Joe did a 180-degree turn, righted the ship and headed straight for the Cruiser.

"Full power now, Chuck!"

"Are you crazy?" screamed Chuck.

"Give it to me, Chuck, and no questions. That's an order, *now*! Dawn, engage the fire mechanism on the torpedos as soon as it's locked in on its coordinates. Then, hold it down manually. Do not—I repeat, do not—let go no matter what happens."

"But, Joe, the firing mechanism is short-circuited. They won't fire."

"Just do as I say. Let me worry about the torpedos. Just follow orders!"

"Yes, Joe, straight away, sir!"

"Position of that cruiser?" Dawn.

"Cruiser three thousand meters and closing fast… twenty-seven hundred meters… twenty-one hundred… two thousand…"

"Joe, we are really getting close to that cruiser. I'm starting to see people on the bridge. You are going to have to move us vertical, or we are going to tear up their defense sensors. Joe, we are starting to get some flak from the batteries under the landing bays. Our starboard defense shield is loosing power fast."

"I'm aware of that, Dawn, just keep those torpedos on fire, and if we get out of this situation prepare for the worse because I'm not sure how this ship will respond. It will take me a while to get her under control."

***

Inside the starship, the crew starts to get concerned about the outcome.

The commander said, "They have him flanked on both sides. It's amazing they are still in the battle. They should have been obliterated, or that tractor beam should have had them on board by now. That cruiser is dead on, and they are no match for that size ship. I think they just about had it, Leutenant. There's not much we can do for them now, and soon they will be back with their own kind. They gave it a good try with overwhelming odds. If we interfere, we start an intergalactic war. What do you think, Leutenant. Do we risk war for such a small crew that aren't even our own people? Then, what do we believe, Lieutenant, liberty, the pursuit of happiness, the right to choose for yourself. They have a dream to become free, to live a life together, to bear and raise their offspring. No drugs to control their lives, minds, or souls. They see, just as we did, a life full of emotion, laughter, kindness, comfort, truth, honesty, and love. Why, then, should we not help them? We can help them, obliterate the opposing fleet, and welcome them into our society."

"That surely would mean war, sir," said the lieutenant.

"War, a horrible thought, but what do we think the *Freedom* ship is involved in right this moment."

"Can we risk the lives of our Air Force, the lives of our commonwealth, maybe the lives of our friends on earth… over four people… one ship? A condemned ship at that, exclaimed the Lieutenant. Sir, the decision is yours, and we all stand with you."

"The decision is mine, yes, Lieutenant. The decision is mine."

"Lieutenant, make ready all fighter pilots, condition red alert. Arm all weaponry, battle station red, and be prepared to defend the *Freedom* ship."

"Yes, sir, we will be engaged and ready for battle in twelve seconds.

***

"Dawn, are you still manually holding that fire button?"

"Chuck, full power. Are we at full power?"

"Yes, Joe, you have full power!"

"Nineteen hundred meters, Joe!"

"It's time to make them decide their own destiny," I replied.

"Joe, we will have contact in fifteen seconds and let me tell you it will be a heck of an explosion."

"Joe!" cried Derek. "What are you doing now? You are going to kill me yet! I'm not ready to—"

"Eighteen hundred meters and closing fast!"

"We're still at full power, Joe."

"Fifteen hundred meters!"

***

At the Starship, the crew gets the military ready to engage the enemy, hospital staff is preparing for casualties, the pilots are inside their fighters with artillery loading their weaponry and arming their batteries.

"Commander! Commander, look!" cried the Lieutenant.

"He has turned the ship around and is headed straight for the cruiser and at top speed. Looks like he means business. I'll tell you one thing, this guy is either really brave and has some unique plan up his sleeve, or he is a lunatic!"

"It appears that he knew he was in this mess all by himself, and I bet he feels like they finally backed him into a corner. His options are all used up. The question is will the enemy sacrifice a brand new multi-trillion-dollar exclusive cruiser for a small fighter being flown by a crew who doesn't want any part of them? He's pretty smart, and he has guts too. He may not need our help after all. Come on, break off that tractor beam.

Back inside the fighter *Freedom* Ship.

***

"Come on… Come on, shut that beam down."

"Joe! Joe, we are going to crash!"

"Hold steady… Hold steady…"

"One thousand meters."

"Joe, they are moving away. The tractor beam is down!"

"Yes, now, Dawn, launch!"

"Torpedoes launched, Joe."

At that moment, I banked hard to port and flew just off the starboard bow of the cruiser.

Then there was an explosion.

The ship started to shake violently, and as I pulled hard once again to port trying to elude the debris flying off the cruiser, we started to spin uncontrollably.

"Dawn, hit the lower blasters."

"Joe, I can't… I'm too disoriented. Help me, Joe!"

Dawn had to close her eyes to keep from passing out, and I was feeling pretty sick myself.

I knew I had to hit those blasters to slow us down in order to get back control of the ship so I closed my eyes and focused on where the blaster button should be and in a desperate moment lunged forward to engage the blasters.

As I hit the button, the ship started to slow down, and I could hear everyone dispose of their lunch rather violently.

"Sorry, everyone, but I'll have control here in just a moment."

"Joe, the tractor beam is out, and it looks like there was some major damage on the cruiser," bellowed Dawn.

Cheers rang through the headphones.

"You did it! You did it!"

"We sure did, and if it's a war they want, we'll just have to give them one!"

"Are you crazy? We've been doing it for weeks now."

"It's our turn now, Derek. I need a position on all their fighters and a status report on the cruiser, Dawn."

"The cruiser is at half speed and headed for space, Joe, and we have a squadron behind us. That makes seven ships astern and three positioned on the other side of *America*."

I turned the ship around and headed straight for the squadron. "Chuck, how's our fuel?"

"Just under half our reserve."

As I flew at the squadron they scattered, and we flew down below *America* and up the backside trying to surprise, the three loners on the other side of *America*. As I came around starship, I caught a glimpse of one fighter veering off my port bow. I shot a torpedo manually and headed up toward the top of the starship, and the other swerved off my starboard bow with me right on his tail. As he banked to starboard he launched a torpedo and his tail gunner started a rapid-fire laser round to our bow deflector shields. The torpedo flew close under us and out into space. We returned several laser blasts to the stern of the Air Force ship. I increased speed and fired a continuous laser blast opening a hole in his defense shield. I gained firing lock, skewed to my port, and shot a torpedo from my stern as I headed back to the Starship. Momentarily, we heard a devastating explosion. It seemed unimportant to cheer, and soon it looked like we could make another attempt at landing.

"Joe, that squadron has regrouped and they are waiting for us at the starship."

"Yes, I figured that. Dawn, contact the starship."

"Commander," she said, "this is *Freedom* ship. Come in."

"Transmit. This is the Commander. How can we assist?"

"Sir, our radar shows three of the ten ships in that squadron are real close to your engines. If you could fire them up all of a sudden, move the starship two thousand kilometers forward and eliminate those three ships, it might just even out the odds."

"Done, Captain. We will engage the engines in ten seconds."

"Thank you, sir."

Within seconds, the engine fired up. The light produced by the engines was brilliant, and the noise from the engines obliterated the explosion of the three ships. Soon they disappeared from the radar.

The Air Force ships had scattered in all directions surprised by the move made by the starship. Our radar showed two closing fast on our stern, so I dropped a timed neutron bomb, and they veered off starboard and port. The blast did minimal damage to their shield.

"Joe, a torpedo off our port side, coming fast!"

I banked to starboard hit the bottom blasters and heard the torpedo pass by us and move on into space. As our heads and stomachs returned to normal, the scanner showed two Air Force ships dead ahead, and before I could aim and fire, Dawn had two torpedoes engaged and launched.

"Thanks, babe! You got them."

"Positions, Dawn?"

"Four dead astern and firing lasers."

"It's getting pretty hot back here, Joe! I need some help!"

I hit the blasters from below, which threw us toward the Starship, but two Air Force fighters were just waiting for us. They poured on laser blasts to our starboard shield. I pulled the ship to port and scooted around the top of the starship coming up fast on two more Air Force ships. Dawn got a computer lock on one, and I hit the other with continuous laser blasts weakening its starboard shield. The second ship was destroyed. Derek had a direct hit to the underside of a ship banking port, and it was time to make another run as I dropped the power to half and hit the upper blasters. The ship dropped to the base of the starship, and once again, there were three on my tail.

"Joe, help us back here!"

"Commander, I am going to make a pass behind the engines. Maybe we can trap them again. On my command, engage the engines."

"Affirmative, Captain."

We took several hits on our stern shields, hoping to give them a sense of accomplishment and trying to bait the chase. I veered to port then to starboard, cut speed, opened her up, hit the lower blasters, and then ran for the starship engines.

"Still on our tail, Joe, and closing."

"Now, Commander."

The engines of the Starship roared behind us, and the radar showed two ships banking hard to port the other to starboard. The two ships to port avoided any damage, but the other ship lay dead in space.

"Well, we got rid of another one."

"There are more ships coming from that Cruiser, Joe?"

"How many do we have to deal with now?"

"It's hard to tell, Joe. They just keep reappearing on the radar. They are definitely sending reinforcements from that Air Force Cruiser."

"Damage reports, Chuck."

"Well, Joe, our starboard shield is heavily damaged. The port shield has 30 percent damage, the bow is approximately 85 percent functional, but we lost about 70 percent on our stern."

"Joe, we have two on our starboard side and one coming in fast on our port trying to acquire a missile lock."

"Joe, they'll have computer lock on us in three seconds!"

I hit full power along with upper blasts that threw us into space weaving from side to side just about to throw us into an uncontrolled spin once again. I cut out forward speed and threw her into neutral. The Air Force ships passed by us, moving too fast for the computer to hold a lock. As the ship settled down we started to advance again.

"Joe, we have two on our port bow closing fast and one coming from our starboard stern."

"Okay, Dawn, let's try something. Let them get computer lock and leave the rest tome!"

"You are really crazy?" exclaimed Dawn.

"Yes, I am. Now do it."

Soon, we were once again in computer lock all the way around and within second's torpedoes were launched. As soon as they were launched, I hit the lower blasters and threw the ship once again into neutral.

We rose exceedingly fast. Blood came pouring out of Dawn's nose, and Pam was vomiting in the back of the ship. Chuck got lightheaded and started vomiting as well. Derek and I became very nauseated but were able to maintain composure. Shortly afterward, several explosions rang throughout the ship.

"Joe! Joe!"

"I know, Dawn. Is everyone okay now?"

"Yes, Joe, fine. But I don't know if our bodies can take another one like that."

"Yes, I know," I replied.

"Well, just as we moved out of the area the starboard bogie's computer obtained a missle lock on the port bogie and vice versa. Consequently, an explosion sent debris from the ships on our starboard side right into the bogie on our port side and along with a heat seeking missile. Both were destroyed."

"Full power, Chuck."

"Joe, those maneuvers really messed up some of the circuitry on our middle engine. I can't get her to fire."

"Bogy, two o'clock on our port side."

"Chuck, dispose of it."

He then launched the engine off into space and rerouted the gas flow, and within seconds, we were back to full power.

"Laser blasts to our starboard shield. It's weakening, Joe," cried Dawn.

"Okay, I've got one more maneuver up my sleeve so hold on because you are not going to like what I'm about to do."

No sooner did these words come out, Joe flipped the ship upside down, facing the port shield to the enemy and giving the starboard shield a rest.

"Close your eyes if you start to feel sick."

"Okay, Joe, but I don't like this one bit!"

We took some heavy fire, which would have destroyed the starboard shield, but with that maneuver, we retained power on all our shields. Within thirty seconds after that exercise on our heads, Derek obtained a computer lock on the Air Force ship and destroyed it.

***

Conversation on the bridge of *Station America*.

"Commander, Commander, I just can't believe this guy playing cross computer-lock, flying upside down and all that intense maneuvering. How many fighters has he destroyed or disabled? This is incredible."

Cheers rose throughout the bridge every time another kill was made or pursuer eluded.

Commander of *Station America*'s thought process.

It reminds me of some of the stunts I used to pull. It also reminds me of a good friend I left on Altaur many years ago. In fact, only he knew how to use these maneuvers. Could it be him... or someone who learned from him?

"Commander?"

"Oh yes, Lieutenant. He's an amazing young flyer, or maybe he's not so young. I've seen these maneuvers many years ago. In fact I used to..."

"What sir?"

"Oh, nothing, Lieutenant. Carry on."

***

I turned the ship around and headed once again for the Starship. "Dawn, give me a position on the remaining Air Force ships."

"Right now, there are three entering the back side of the starship."

"Maybe, we could just blend in with the Starship, assess our damage, and wait for them to come and look for us. We might be able to surprise some of them and take out a couple more before landing. Their scanner shouldn't pick up our ships electrical activity with so much interference. We will be shielded by the starship. With all that electrical activity, it will take them hours to find us and by that time we can regenerate some of our shield power."

"Joe, that's not true," Pam's soft voice came quietly over the headset.

"Why, Pam?"

"The Starship runs on neutron E45S tort power, and we run on electron E65F mode power. The scanner will be able to pick us up, and we will stick out like a sore thumb."

"Can we cut all power after we lock into the starship?"

"We sure can!" exclaimed Chuck, "and it will only take seconds to achieve power to all systems, but if they see us on a visual, we are sitting ducks, Joe."

"If we stay out here we'll never get enough rest to assess damage, check weaponry, and make our final plan for approaching the landing bay."

We flew in low and fast and sat the ship up under its artillery emplacement just below the bridge of *America*. Air Force fighters flew by us constantly never noticing. Our camouflage seemed to work perfectly. We sat there unseen on the underside of that battery for ten minutes working out a plan for our final approach. The only problem is the shields couldn't regenerate cutting off the power.

We all met just behind the cockpit, except for Dawn who was to stand watch. If they found us, she would have to power up and disengage our ship to get us back in space, and believe me, sooner or later, they would find us."

"I've been thinking about an approach and let me tell you it's not going to be easy. They keep sending more and more Air Force ships at us."

"You think they would give up by now," Chuck said.

"You don't know them," Derek said.

"Joe, these Air Force pilots are alot better than those Guardian pilots."

"Yes, the Air Force squadrons are selected from the best of the Guardian pilots, and they are flying the new A-45 Airships. Let me say they are not very happy with us destroying so many of their new ships. These pilots will not give up either until we are destroyed. They live by a strong code of ethics and are sworn to success or die trying."

"Crazy society. I just don't know what drives them," Chuck said.

"Let's start with the damage report, Chuck. Then, I will give you my plan."

"Starboard shield is 25 percent intact. Stern 45 percent intact, port 75 percent intact, bow 50 percent intact. We lost our middle engine and our fuel reserve is down to one-fourth tank. Computer is intact, weaponry system is intact, navigational system intact."

"Derek, how about our rear weaponry?"

"Pam's out of laser loads, and I have one load left, three torpedoes, no neutron bombs, but we have four laser loads available in the front."

"Not much is it? Take the front loads I'm going to be to busy to use them."

"Thanks, Joe. This will definitely be our final approach whether we make it or not."

"Well, here's how our approach will take place. Dawn, your earphones on?"

"Yes, Joe, you're coming in loud and clear."

"This will be our last attempt to land the ship. Fuel is a real problem, so this is it. We'll drop from our position, head west, and come around to the bay on course 136. Our starboard side will be protected by the Starship on this course. It should take us about thirty-five seconds to get to the bay and another minute to make our approach and land. That is, if the engines hold out with all the hits we are going to take. We will have a short period of time where our starboard shield will be vulnerable just before our approach. We have to make sure it will be protected especially from torpedo hits so, Derek, save your ammunition and try to eliminate every torpedo fired at our starboard side. We can only take one torpedo hit on that shield. Once we get into the bay, I am not sure what will happen so I guess we'll have to depend on *America* at that point. The best thing to do is to get out as soon as we can. Our weaponry will be low, but the fuel tanks will go up like a ball of fire so it is imperative we move fast. It's a good thing those bays can be jettisoned. Our approach will protect our starboard side and once we are in they can jettison it quickly or if it's undamaged, once we get out, retract it back to the space station."

"Okay, that does it. Let's get it done, 'cause it's now or never!"

"Joe, the scanner is picking up alot of activity. I don't think we will get a clear drop no matter how long we wait here."

"Okay, Dawn. Get us out of here!"

We dropped from the protection of the Starship and headed out into space circling around to get our starboard shield facing the Starship. We took several laser blasts, but there was minimal damage.

"Joe, they are laying it on us now."

"Just keep those torpedoes away, Derek."

The ship began to take heavy fire, and our shields were weakening more and more. I kept hitting our top and bottom blasters trying to make it hard for their computer to get a lock on us, but they kept hitting us harder and harder. Several burst of energy on our main engine eluded several torpedoes, but it took its toll on our starboard engine.

"Chuck, we are losing power."

"Our starboard engine is gone."

"Jettison it."

"Yes, sir."

"Joe, two Air Force ships dead ahead."

"They probably think we are out of ammunition! Lock in and fire, Dawn."

"Lock, firing!"

"Joe, we are taking hits one right after another. Our shields are weakening back here!" said Derek.

"Chuck, give me full power."

We banked to starboard and headed for the Starship lining up our approach.

"*America*, we are coming in."

"*Freedom* ship, we are taking on heavy fire so we are launching our support group now. Steady her up and come on in."

"*America*, we only have one engine, and it's at full power. Our others have been jettisoned. Our shields are practically gone especially on our starboard side. Navigation is out, and we are smoking at our port and stern sides. They are killing us, sir. Can we have some assistance? Our fuel is low, our fire power is almost depleted, and I have no alternate options to take."

"Joe, we are one thousand yards and closing. We will contact the bay in thirty seconds."

"Well, we will need some help from above if we are going to make it."

"Joe, our stern shield is gone, port has 25 percent, and starboard shield is gone."

"Come on baby, hold on! Just a little longer."

"Joe, we have two torpedoes coming from our port side."

"Joe, you're going to have to break off our approach, or we will be destroyed."

"Pam, Derek, and Chuck put your emergency belts on and get prepared for a crash landing. Its going to be a pretty rough landing."

***

"Commander! Commander! They are getting murdered out there. We have to help them. The bay is only five hundred yards away."

"We can't interfere with their affairs, but in my opinion the torpedoes pose a security threat to our ship. Right, Lieutenant?" replied the commander.

"Indeed, Commander!"

"I have had about all I can take and it's about time we joined this party. Attention, support group. This is the commander-in-chief. I want you to concentrate on destroying the torpedoes launched by the Air Force ships. I repeat only the torpedoes. They cause a threat to our ship and our nation. The rest is up to them. This way we are not breaking our end of the treaty."

"Affirmative, Commander."

***

"Joe, the two torpedoes are gone and the support group from the Starship is taking out all the torpedoes that threaten our ship."

"We can thank them for this one, and it came at the right time because another ten seconds there would have been nothing left of us!"

"Oh no, Joe. There's a fighter poised at the entrance of the bay, and he's not moving. We are on a collision course with him."

"*America! America*, listen up! There's an Air Force ship at the bay entrance. I have one torpedo left. I am going to shoot it at the fighter, and when he breaks off, you better destroy that torpedo and fast. We are losing power, and I cannot—I repeat *cannot*—maneuver."

"Dawn, firing-lock."

"Ready, Joe."

"Fire."

As the torpedo headed toward the Air Force fighter, it took off into space, and the support group exploded the torpedo extremely close to the entrance of the landing bay.

"Watch out for that shrapnel!"

"*America*, how's the bay?"

"Mostly external damage, keep your approach."

As we drew closer and closer to the bay, shrapnel from the explosion ripped through our tiny ship. Laser blasts kept gnawing at our craft. Smoke was coming out of everywhere; damage could be seen all over the ship. Chuck and Derek were continuously putting out fires with the computer's damage repair unit. The craft was extremely hard to control. Dawn and I were both struggling to keep her on course. The Air Force fighters weren't about to give up, and we were bound and determined to enter that landing bay in one piece. Torpedoes were exploding all around the ship. Shrapnel from the torpedo explosions destroyed our visual scanners, our main computer system and blocked our direct vision.

"Chuck, is our navigational computer operational?"

"No, sir. It's been destroyed."

"Give me a break. A blind landing on a moving target with one engine. Cut power to one-third and prepare for the worst."

***

"*America*, we have lost all visuals and computer navigation. This will be a blind landing and I will appreciate any assistance I can get from command."

"Captain Ferrous, we have a blind approach coming in with coordinates that have been previously been locked into your bay. You'll have to talk them in."

"Sir, that has never been done!"

"Confidence, Michael. We have no other choice. Do your best."

"Yes, sir. I'll give it a try!"

***

"*Freedom* ship, this is Captain Ferrous. I will be guiding you in, sir."

"Joe, call me Joe. And I need the help now. Talk to me."

"Hold steady, Joe. You are about two hundred meters away from the bay entrance. Bring your nose up thirty degrees and move her to port. We have raised the net and evacuated all personnel except for the fire teams so just get her into the bay and we will do the rest. Come on, Joe, bring her nose up fast and move to port, or you'll leave half your wing in space."

"Sir, I cannot maneuver her very well, and port seems to be the hardest."

"Have you cut your speed?"

"Yes, sir, to one-third."

"Then increase it back to one-half that might help your entry."

"Yes, sir."

"Chuck, back up to one-half speed."

"Joe, that's too fast for entry!" cried Dawn.

"I know, I know, but it's his ballgame, Dawn. We'll just have to trust him."

"Joe, I will tell you when to cut your speed, but I will also want you to jam her into reverse on my command. That might slow you down enough once you are in the bay."

"Sir, I can hardly hold her steady."

"Come on, Joe. Hang in there. More to port, more to port, Joe."

"I'm trying, sir."

"Your wing is clear now, Joe. Just keep her on course. Joe, you are drifting to starboard again. Okay, try this. Cut your engines, and give one intermittent engine thrust to keep that wing inside the parameter of the landing bay. Your momentum should carry you in now… One hundred meters."

"Now, Joe! Thrust!"

We were losing speed, even though the engine thrusts kept us on course for several seconds, but we kept on drifting onto a course adjacent to the side of the bay.

***

The bridge of the starship *America* were experiencing their own troubles trying to defend the *Freedom* ship and secure their safety.

As they made their final approach the conflict between the support group and the Air Force fighters became heated.

"Commander, the Air Force ships are firing directly at us, now forcing us to contend not only with their torpedos but also with their aggression. One ship has launched a torpedo while the others are trying to distract us with direct fire."

"Captain, you are to protect our mothership along with your fighters even at the cost of damage or annihilation of the Air Force ships, and that's a direct order. We have been fired on first, and it has been recorded. You have my permission to protect our interests."

"Thank you, sir!"

As the support group from *America* turned its fire on the Air Force ships the confrontation became very destructive. Several of their fighters were destroyed along with several extremely damaged.

As *Freedom* ship came to within a few hundred meters of the bay, the Air Force ships backed off and flew out into space.

"Keep her steady, Joe."

"It's awfully quiet out there, sir. What's happened?"

"*America*'s support group has just attacked the Air Force squadron, and they hightailed it back home."

"Sir, we are losing power rapidly."

"Chuck, what's going on?"

"That intermittent energy surge has overheated the engine, Joe. We just lost all power."

"That's okay. I think your momentum will bring you in, but get ready for a crash landing because your starboard wing is not going to make it. Brace yourself. You are really smoking now, Joe. Try to keep her nose up a little higher. Joe, your nose has cleared the bay, the wing has torn away from the ship, and you're moving into the net too fast."

What was left of the ship tore through the nose of net, but the reinforced body of it held steadfast. The ship touched down on to the bay floor with a large crash and fires started all over the ship. After a moment of being stunned, we all unbuckled our emergency straps and headed for the exit located just below the cockpit.

"Let's go! She's going to blow!"

The hatch opened up and smoke came rushing in from outside of the ship. Flames surrounded the forward hatch.

"We'll never get out of here this way, Joe. She's burning up too fast!"

As the words came rushing out of Derek's mouth, a stream of white foam covered the front hatch spraying down into the cockpit.

"Now, Pam! Go! You next. Dawn, Chuck, Derek! Crawl as fast as you can!

As we all exited the ship, we could see flames everywhere. We jumped down to the floor of the bay and ran toward a group of firefighters amidst six feet of flames and burning hot steel. Large doors slammed shut closing off the single landing bay from space. The flames shot high in the air as the heavily damaged engine blew up toward the doors.

"Sir, is the whole crew out?"

"Yes, sir!"

"Then follow me."

As we followed the firefighter, a new set of doors were closing in front of the main entrance to the Starship."

Large fire doors were closing in several areas around the bay. Just as we entered the landing bay, the outside doors slammed shut. We ran following the firefighter as he rushed over to a small switch on the wall. It was illuminated by a red light. In fact, there were several switches located about every three feet with a trap door after every switch. As soon as the firefighter pulled the switch, a trap door opened just to the right of the switch.

"Come on. This way. It's a slide. Just sit down and go."

In succession, all of the crew slid down the opening in the trap door. All except me.

"Sir, I have got to go back."

"What? Are you crazy?"

"If I don't shut the reactor down, the whole ship will blow."

"Sir, it's taken care of by the emergency systems in the bay. The extra large doors conceal the fire and prevent it from spreading to the Starship," he continued. "It also isolates any and all explosions from the main body of the Starship. All personnel have left through the trap doors, and soon a fire resistant chemical will flood the bay.

Smoke will be vented through those huge vents in the ceiling. Look, sir, up there!"

"But the reactor is more than a regular reactor. We had to modify it to give us the power we needed to achieve stronger defense shields."

"Sir, don't worry. As soon as you go down this shoot upon my command, the whole bay will be jettisoned out into space."

"I understand, but if that explosion is violent enough, it could send the whole bay back toward the starship. We have to go back!"

"No, no, sir!"

At that moment, I ran back to the ship with the firefighter following close behind. As we entered the ship, the whole bay started to be sprayed with the fire-fighting chemical.

"There's the computer."

"Hurry, sir, hurry! We will jettison in thirty seconds!"

"Logging in. It will only take a few seconds, sir."

I keyed in 773-471-77.

"Now the switch!"

As I pulled the switch, the firefighter was halfway out of the hatch. All the power shut down, and I was right behind him. He was halfway across the bay when I jumped down to the floor. As I hit the landing, the chemical produced a slick surface on the floor, and down I slipped injuring my ankle and not being able to get up.

"Fifteen seconds until the bay is jettisoned!" alarmed a computerized voice over the loud speaker

"Oh no! My ankle!"

"Sir! Sir!" said the firefighter.

"That's a heck of a way to get out of here, sir! Can you walk?"

"I think my ankle is broken."

At that instant, the firefighter picked me up and slung me over his back. "Ten seconds until the bay is jettisoned," repeated the voice.

***

Derek, Pam, and Dawn entered the ships command center.

"Derek, where's Joe?" cried Dawn.

"I don't know. He was right behind me. At least I thought he was."

"Commander, we are missing someone. Can you check the monitor."

As he turned on the monitor, smoke and chemical fumes blocked any view of the bay. He proceeded to put on an infrared, selective heat analyzer that visualized any human body heat through the chemical produced inside the bay. Soon, they saw a man carrying another man quickly across the bay floor.

"Use your belt! Use your belt now!" shouted the commander.

At that moment, the firefighter reached down at his belt and pressed a button. Within seconds, the firefighter jumped into an opened trap door located on the floor in front of him. Shortly after clearing the portal, it slammed shut, controlled by electronic eyes fixed at the entrance to the passage. The bay jettisoned, and within seconds, an explosion rocked the ships command center. Within seconds, the vibration and shock wave stopped and sighs of relief was felt throughout the command center.

The commander turned from the monitor and thanked everyone for a job well done. I'm very proud of all of you. Your work was extraordinary.

"The firefighting team of bay 1102 will receive the highest medal for bravery given to our people. Their job was done with precision, organization, and without a flaw! Excellent job, my friends. I commend you. And for Captain Michael Ferrous, he will receive the medal of honor and be given the rank of Major First Class for his heroic effort in the rescue of our new and welcomed friends. Now let's welcome them!"

"Are they safe?" Dawn asked.

"Yes, ma'am! No doubt about it! If the emergency hatch closed before the bay jettisoned they will most definitely survive, that is, if they can swim."

"What? Swim?" Dawn looked puzzled.

***

As the trap door closed above us, I let out the most deafening scream of my life. We dropped some twenty feet into a wonderfully refreshing pool of water. As we hit the water, a small amount of steam rose to the ceiling. As we surfaced, I forgot all about my ankle and lay there floating with my face looking straight up at the ceiling. Within a few seconds, I heard an explosion as the landing bay was jettisoned into space.

"Captain, are you all right?"

"I sure am. Thanks for saving my life. I owe you one, Captain."

"Captain Michael Ferrous, sir. How's the ankle?"

"What ankle, Michael?"

Michael pulled me over to the steps and helped lift me up to some medical technicians. Derek, Pam, Dawn, and Chuck were waiting as they put me on a stretcher.

"Man, Joe! That was way to close! You're crazy. What was so important—oh, the reactor! It would have been a real mess if that would have blown."

"Joe," Dawn said, "this is the commander. He's responsible for saving our lives."

"Sorry about your landing bay, sir."

"Don't worry about it, son. You did great job. I am very proud of all of you."

"Sir, this boot has to come off. The swelling is getting worse. We will have to cut it off," said Tony one of the technicians.

"These are very special boots given to me by a very special person, and I will want them repaired as soon as possible."

"Did Eric give you those boots, Joe?" asked the commander.

"Yes, sir."

"He is a very special friend of mine."

"Mine too, Commander."

"I heard how you rescued him from Balem. We are all grateful to you for returning to us a well respected citizen who has contributed extensively to our cause."

"Sir, Chuck is his son, and without his ingenuity, we would not have made it to your starship."

"Yes, I know Chuck, but the last time I saw him, he was running around looking for bugs. He has turned out to be a remarkable man just like his father." As the boot was gently cut at the seam, the pressure released from my foot was tremendous. They cut the bottom of my trousers exposing my leg enough for them to set and inflate an ankle stabilizer. As they were attaching the air support, the commander noticed the mark on my ankle.

"What's that, Joe, on your ankle?"

"Oh, the mark. I have had it ever since I could remember. I thought my protector put it there for some type of identification, but I'm not really sure why it is there. He never told me where I got it or why it was put there."

"Release that air support from his ankle, Tony, just for a minute," requested the commander. "Joe, look at my wrist." The commander pulled up his sleeve and exposed and identical mark on his wrist.

"Joe, did Eric see that mark?"

"Yes, sir, when he put my boots on just before we left on our mission. He said it was some sort of tradition, and when he saw the mark, he sure did look startled and had this funny look on his face."

"He never said anything to me. Probably so our judgement would not be impaired by the emotion of knowing that you are my one and only son. He is a very wise man... a very wise man. You are my boy, my only son! I placed that mark on you at birth."

We held each other affectionately for what seemed like several minutes. My heart and my soul were filled with joy. In my wildest dreams, I never thought I would be able to meet, know, or love my father. I started to weep with joy and happiness. His body trembled as his emotions poured out with jubilance. We started to talk, simultaneously several times, but just stopped and held each other close. Soon, we were separated, and the medics picked me up and put me in a small emergency commuter shuttle. They said I was to go straight to the hospital facility to get my ankle fixed.

"Sir? Commander?" I said.

"Yes, Joe?"

"You are a grandfather to a beautiful strong baby boy, and his mother is standing next to you. Commander, knowing he was being taken from us, I placed the same mark on the inside of my boy's upper arm close to his axilla thinking maybe someday I might be able to—"

"Rest now, my son. We have plenty of time to talk. Proceed to the closest hospital, Tony. Dawn, you shall stay with us at our quarters. My wife will be happy to meet you. Derek, Chuck, and Pam, your quarters will be close by until you can become familiar with our ship and our nation. Chuck, the next shuttle with supplies from earth will be here soon. I know you are anxious to contact your father and mother. Make yourself at home, and feel free to contact them. Just use a coded message. We will use the video communicator after things settle down."

I was hurried along to the medical facility, and before long, with the newest technology in orthopedic surgery, my ankle was repaired, temporarily immobilized, and almost as good as new. Also, the pain was totally eliminated by the latest advancements in anesthesia. I fell asleep very fast that evening and rested peacefully feeling wonderful at achieving my goal and receiving a tremendous bonus at the end of my journey, my father. Something I never would have envisioned. My own flesh and blood to greet my arrival. What a magnificent experience I was granted by my all-powerful, merciful, and all loving Lord and Savior Jesus Christ. I was so very thankful.

CHAPTER 14

The New Beginning

I slept for a very long time, and when I awoke, my stomach felt like it had shriveled to nothing. The noise it made was embarrassing. The nurse taking care of me reassured me that the food was excellent, and it would be here soon. I found out from the staff that the commander was planning a feast to commemorate my arrival, and from how they talked, it was going to be bigger than our own Independence Day feast. There, I would meet my father's friends and start a whole new life together with Dawn. I was sure ready to get out of the hospital and begin my new life. Just as I tried to move to the chair next to my bed, Derek came rolling in with the most tantalizing cup of coffee I had ever smelled.

"How are you doing, Joe? I didn't think you would ever wake up."

"How long have you been here?" I asked.

"Well, we all took turns, each of us hoping you would wake up on their shift, so it looks like I was the lucky one. Here, try this!"

"This coffee is good, Derek. This place has potential."

"Yes, sir. You should see this place… The design and the engineering is just brilliant. No wonder the Star Cities leave it alone. They are no match for *America*'s technology. Eric, your father, and a group of scientists developed it, and rumor has it that same group of scientists are working on plans for another starship even better than this one. These people are amazing!"

"No, Derek, our people… Remember, we made it. And this is our society now! Hey, man, get my clothes. I've got to get out of here!"

"And where are you going, sir? I've received no orders to release you. Now get back in bed," commanded the nurse.

"Sorry, Joe. Oh, by the way, have you heard about the celebration?"

"Yes, I heard a little."

"It's going to be big! I can't wait!"

"Hey, are we assigned yet?"

"Well, Joe, I have been, but you are on sick leave for six weeks. I am already working on developing a scanner intensifier and computerized aiming device for the Starship fighters. Joe, those American fighters are beautiful and guess what? I have some really great news. Everyone knows now. You and Dawn are going… Oh, I can't tell you."

"Come on, Derek, don't play this game. Have Dawn and I been assigned together?"

"No, no."

Dawn knocked on the door and entered at the request of Joe.

"Oh, hi, Dawn! How are you doing?"

"Just fine, Joe. How about you?"

"Just great!"

"Well, did you tell him, Derek?"

"No, ma'am. I was about to, but I didn't really get a chance to. I'll see you later, Joe. Dawn can finish for me."

"Derek, wait! Dawn, what is going on?"

"Joe," Dawn began, as tears welled up in her eyes. "I have some special news for you. I am carrying your baby."

"What? Dawn, how long have you known?"

"Since before we left earth, but I didn't want to jeopardize your decision making or cloud your judgment. We will deliver in seven and a half months. Give or take a few weeks."

"That's wonderful, Dawn! So that's why you got nauseated! I should have known!"

"I love you, Joe."

"I love you too, Dawn. By the way, you and Eric should get together. You two are thinking on the same frequency."

"We did sort of get together. I transmitted a message to him asking his opinion when you were sleeping aboard the ship. He advised me to keep silent and then told me about your father."

"You are really something, Dawn. I love you very much, and I respect your decision not to tell me. Eric's too. I do believe I would have had second thoughts of aiming our ship toward that cruiser at full speed, if I had known you were pregnant. Dawn, would you get my clothes? I have to move fast or that nurse will come back and put them away again. I am ready to get out of here and celebrate all the great news I have been hearing. Hey, Dawn, do you know? Do you know if it is a boy or a girl?"

"Yes, I know Joe, but I thought I'd keep it a surprise. Actually, I told your father. We are the only ones who know."

"What! You're not going to tell me? Come on, Dawn. I will find out some way or another. Come on, tell me!"

We left the hospital passing the nurse's station when my nurse was on break, and we went to prepare for the celebration. As I entered our room, I saw my clothes hanging on the back of a chair. There laid out was a beautiful blue leather jacket trimmed in gold. On the pocket were medals for bravery and a commander's medal for leadership. There were several others mounted on the chest along with one, which was called the Purple Heart. I was unfamiliar with its significance. As I glanced over toward the closet, I caught site of my boots neatly repaired and shining brilliantly from the reflection off the lamp next to the bed.

Dawn's dress was a stunning white, satin, gown with brightly shining diamond cut stones around the neckline. It was truly magnificent. We all met at the celebration and sat as the guests of honor with the commander-in-chief. The celebration in all its glory stirred many emotions. It was wonderful to achieve such a high goal and be blessed with the opportunity to be reunited with family you never knew. The feeling of warmth and security, joy and happiness, love and gratefulness filled my heart and soul.

The beginning of a new life, with family and friends, was so overwhelming and gratifying, plus the announcement of our new baby so exciting that I couldn't be more happier. The people, the journey, and the experience was so thrilling, but the greatest feeling of all comes when you have gained genuine freedom for yourself and your closest friends, those you love. Yet deep inside there is one feeling that supersedes all others, and that is the feeling of being so grateful for the relationship you develop together with the Holy One, Jesus Christ, who created you and died for everyone's transgression past, present, and future to ensure salvation for all who trust and believe in Him as their Savior. The whole experience would be impossible without his divine intervention powered by the unconditional love He has for His creation.

ABOUT THE AUTHOR

Gary Mollica is a Physician Assistant in Anesthesia and works at Northside Hospital in Atlanta, Georgia. He went to the University of Cincinnati for two years and completed his anesthesia training at Case Western Reserve University. He has been in anesthesia for forty years now, spending most of his time in obstetrical anesthesia. He has six children and four grandchildren and been married to his beautiful wife for thirty-four years.

He wrote the book thirty-five years ago as a secular book, but when he started getting serious about publishing the manuscript, the Lord led him to transform it into a science fiction novel with a Christian theme of spreading the Gospel. His main goal was to make it into a Christian romance adventure that would stir the hearts of both men and women and show them how it patterns after the unconditional love the Lord has for His followers. His main goal is to give his Lord and Savior Jesus Christ praise, honor, and glory because of the love He shows His followers every day.

CPSIA information can be obtained
at www.ICGtesting.com
Printed in the USA
BVHW071153200519
548789BV00002B/94/P